MW01626363

Sutton Tales

ISBN: 978-1-954517-83-7

Designed and produced by:
Indie Author Books
12 High Street, Thomaston, Maine
www.indieauthorbooks.com

For more information visit sites.google.com/view/larrydyhrbergauthor
Printed in the United States of America

SUTTON TALES

Larry Dyhrberg

For Michelle, Caroline, and Annika, who listened to the endless telling of the stories and lore that became the foundation for *Sutton Tales*. *Ma chère famille, je vous aime.*

Jenifer,
Don't need no
fences to make good
neighbors in this
neighbor-hood.
Thanks for all,
Larry

Acknowledgments

MANY MOONS AGO, MONICA WOOD, a wonderful colleague and role model, told a gathering, "There are two kinds of people: writers and people who want to be writers. The difference is that writers write, all the time." I've tried to follow that wisdom ever since. I've been honored to have been supported over the past decade by the Fiction Writers Workshop at the Osher Lifelong Learning Institute at the University of Southern Maine. Kim and Tana, Denny, Joan and Sidney, JaneAnn, Lindy, Nancy, Barbara, and Fernando: Thank you for your insights and encouragement. Special thanks to Ellen Santora who, with great patience, guided me into the world of electronic editing. And finally, to Mme. la Reine, Michelle J. Fournier, merci beaucoup for your expertise, patience, and loving encouragement.

Je m'appelle Hélène Honoré

JE M'APPELLE HÉLÈNE HONORÉ LÉVESQUE. I'm Hélène Honoré Lévesque. If I were speaking, you would probably hear just a hint of my heritage in my voice. It's been many years since I spoke French as my mother tongue, but the intonations are always there in my ears. "Eh-Len, On-oer-ey, Leh-veck." But to many of my childhood friends, I'm "Heck" or "Heckie." My first name, shortened, was the land of the damned. My middle name, on the tongues of elementary classmates, conjured up pictures that none of us were ready to acknowledge. Thus, "Heck." And I have to admit that it's been a heck of a journey.

My story, *mon histoire*, begins, like so many of my generation, with a trip from the hard farms of Québec to the mill towns of New England. My grandfather, Clément DuBois, had banged around Canada for a decade. At age twenty-five, he returned to his village outside Montréal and within weeks laid claim to a sixteen-year-old girl, Caroline Trémont. Married by the local priest, the new couple departed by train for Massachusetts in March of 1900. Family lore has it that when they crossed the border, Clément said to his francophone bride, "Americans speak English. From now on you will speak English as well." Somehow, through long silences, the young woman managed to learn enough of the strange, chaotic language to survive, but never enough to pass. Québecois French, however, was always on her tongue in the home, her domain.

After three bitter years working the docks of Boston Harbor, Clément came home one day and announced they were leaving the next morning for Sutton, Maine. Word had come through the Franco pipeline that there were jobs to be had in a spinning mill but especially in the Nine Falls Paper Company. A cousin, Marcel DuBois, after tending the flow of pulp into the processing machines for five years, had been elevated to foreman on the number two machine, especially to serve as the connector between Anglo management and newly arrived francophone labor. A colleague, Hartwig Olsen, likewise tended to the recently arrived Danish laborers who served the demands of the number one machine.

Along with their meager possessions, Pépere and Mémère carried their first child, Céleste, who in time would be my *chère bonne maman*, onto the Boston and Maine railroad north to Portland where they were met by Uncle Marcel, who guided them by streetcars to Sutton, their new home. There they stayed with *la famille DuBois*, sleeping on a mattress in the living room on the second floor of a three-story that looked out across a playground, past the spire of St. Hyacinth Church toward the mills that marked the upper and lower falls of the Nine Falls River. Over the next few days, Pépère Clément was hired as a laborer in a wholly francophone crew at the paper mill. Caroline and *Tante Jacqueline* searched the neighborhood and found an apartment there in Frenchtown. That evening the men moved the mattress, along with a small table and two chairs that neighbors had shared. Three settings of tableware, two plates, three bowls, a fry pan, two small pans, and a tea kettle set the newly arrived DuBois family into the new chapter of their saga.

The years flowed on in the rhythms of the mill and the family. Pépère worked through "the towers," the rotating eight-hour shifts (get-up, sit up, and days). Mémère adjusted mealtimes to match and, in time, managed piece by piece to furnish the apartment. And the next decade was marked by the annual addition of another infant and another, five of whom survived into childhood and beyond. "*Une machine à bébé*," her husband bragged to the neighbors and to the family back in Québec. And when Caroline and her friends allowed that the flood of newborns was daunting, they would recall the advice given by Monseigneur Fortin that all that was needed was that "they should live like brother and sister."

Céleste passed her childhood exemplifying the second stage of the immigrant experience in America. While Clément and Caroline always saw themselves as French Canadians in a new world, their children, largely unconsciously, became Franco-Americans, native-born citizens but always with the ethnic qualification. Her neighborhood, Frenchtown, backed up to Scotch Hill and two generations of textile workers who had fled Great Britain. And across the river valley rose Irish Hill, mirroring her world. Less clear to her sense of places was the neighborhood of Oxford Mills, across the river and away from the shops of downtown. On the rare occasions when Caroline took her eldest child by bus into Portland, Céleste stared, gape-mouthed, at the ample Victorian homes of mill management and the town's professional class.

Through her childhood, Céleste thrived in her classes at St. Hyacinth's School. The nuns, *les soeurs* to her parents, drilled their charges in English grammar, numbers, and the importance of their loving, if stern, God, his beloved son, the Blessed Virgin Mother, and a seemingly endless litany of saints. Rules were strictly enforced, punishment for transgressions swift with the slap of a hairbrush on the hand or a swat to the rear with the yardstick by the slate blackboards. Two of her classmates, Peter and Teddy, were the most common miscreants. After school one day, Céleste, almost breathlessly, recounted to Mémère that Sister Mary Thérèse had smacked Peter's palm five times for whispering to Teddy. And then, when Teddy laughed, Sister gave his hand six blows.

Maman Céleste loved school and was always near the top of her class. At the end of her eighth-grade year, she was chosen by the nuns to read a scripture passage at the ceremony marking the end of her class at St. Hyacinth. The mother superior spoke to her flock. Their graduation was not an end but rather a commencement. Their education, earned by hard work, the guidance of the holy sisters, and the love of their Lord and Savior, Jesus Christ, would guide them in whatever paths they would follow. Céleste floated on Mother Mary Margaret's words; high school and, perhaps even worlds beyond seemed like a dream that could become real. It was not to be.

As August flowed toward September, Céleste began her preparations for entering Sutton High School. She was thrilled with the prospect of new and challenging classes and of making connections with students from all the neighborhoods of the town. And then one day, Clément DuBois came home from his day shift and called his wife and eldest daughter into the living room. There he laid down the law. He could not accept the wasteful foolishness of high school. He had found her a paying job, doing housework and caring for the children of Mr. and Mrs. Clark. Mr. Clark, the factory manager at the Stevens Textile Mill, had assured him that if she worked hard there would be a position for her in the mill as soon as she turned sixteen. A good job with the promise of a better one. She could help pay her way in the world and could save a few dollars here and there. "And besides," her father said, closing the conversation, "you're only going to get married, like all good young girls."

And, of course, Pépère was right; there was only one path for a dutiful girl like his Céleste. But she hated the jobs laid out for her. The Clarks' grand home, their beautiful furniture on thick carpets that sucked up any untoward noises. The kindly way that Mrs. Clark laid out her chores, while never for a moment suggesting anything but command. And then the move to the mill halfway through her fifteenth year, the foreman, Mr. Sullivan, conveniently unaware that she was not yet sixteen.

Céleste despised the mill, hated the clacking of the machinery, the dust and fiber in the air. And she especially detested the sapping of her mind by the constant need to concentrate on the spindles to protect both the endless, unchanging thread and her fingers. For ten hours a day, six days a week, her world was nothing but spinning and whirling. When the Saturday whistle blew, ending another week, she and her friends Estelle, Josephine, and Rose walked up the hill toward home, trying to summon the energy to meet for the weekly dance at the American Legion Hall. Then Sunday: ten o'clock mass, followed by household chores and dinner, after which Pépere would collect his portion of her pay. And then time to read her latest book from the library and then to bed to gather strength for the seven o'clock whistle marking the next week of her life.

And Pépere Clément's prediction of marriage came true as well. At one of the Legion dances, Céleste noticed a new young man standing across the hall with the other stags. And it was clear that she had captured his eye as well. When she smiled, he walked across the floor, dodging the dancers, smiled, and said, "Hi, I'm François. Wanna dance?" And that was the beginning. Years later Maman would tell me that he'd swept her off her feet, but it was also so clear that he'd swept her out of the mill too. They were married in August 1918. My mother had just turned seventeen. As a little girl, I used to stare at the photograph in our living room of Maman in her white bridal dress, her direct gaze young and hopeful.

I, Hélène Honoré, joined *la famille Lévesque* on August 31, 1923, at last fulfilling Maman Céleste's longing for a daughter, a girl following three sons: Paul, Eugène (whom we all called Geno), and Erland. Through my early childhood, my brothers and I whirled and danced and sang as if we were somehow parts of a single creature. But then, one by one, *mes frères* moved on and away from our second-floor home on North Street, hide-and-seek with their friends Dicky, Michel, and Armand, pickup baseball on the playground behind St. Hyacinth, and long days at the big, brick Green Street School. Maman explained to me that "boys will be boys" and that my girl's life brought different rules and different expectations.

And as my childhood passed, I learned how those differences played out in real time. Our lives were shaped by the ever-flowing paper on the machines by the ever-flowing river. Papa's world was determined by the rotating shifts, the towers—get up, sit up, and nights. We learned to be quiet on the afternoons and evenings when he had to wake at eleven to start his night shift, the get-up. Maman planned meals to match his shifts—breakfast at eleven, a.m. or p.m. The Sunday between each tower shift was our only sure time together. We would all go to mass. Then I would help Maman in the kitchen while my brothers were freed for two hours of outside play. Papa sat by the radio in the living room, smoking his Camels, a quart each of local home brew and bootleg Canadian whiskey next to his chair, and the *Sunday Telegram* sports page bringing updates on the Red Sox and how the Sutton High boys had done in the rotating seasons' contests.

We three generations of les familles DuBois et Lévesque rode on the rhythms of the mills and the church. Pépère Clément helped his new son-in-law to integrate into the rules and the culture of the Nine Falls. Along with a living wage, the mill offered informal perks. As long as the pulp flowed into the paper machines, and the gleaming Nine Falls Standard paper curled onto the massive white rolls, destined for publishers and businesses across the nation, management turned a blind eye to how the crews functioned, long breaks in the men's rooms, or a laborer whose lunchbox contained only tobacco and half-pints of cheap whiskey. When I was about five years old, Pépère and Papa combined resources and bought a shorefront lot on Broad Lake, a beautiful clear treasure a half hour's drive from Sutton, which had drawn in other Franco workers at Nine Falls. As if by magic, pickup trucks drove to the lake, loaded with lumber from the mill's yards. There the men crafted small cottages, all with porches facing eastward. At night I would fall asleep, cradled by the lapping of waves and the long, whistling calls of the loons.

Looking back now, my childhood years spanned a golden, if brief, moment in the world of Sutton. My friends, Alice, Thérèse, Sophie, and I played on the playground and in the park by the Nine Falls. Maman was kept busy with the household and another daughter whom we all called Petite Bénédicte. Paul, Geno, and Erland played the American sports of the seasons and embarked on adventures unknown to their parents and sister. And, as always, our family life, as that of all our neighbors, flowed on with the glossy paper of the Nine Falls, the ever-changing towers, and Papa's regular payment slips to be redeemed at the local bank each Thursday. The promises given to my Québecois grandparents seemed to have been fulfilled, especially when they and my parents, les familles DuBois et Lévesque, purchased a two-family house on the edge of Frenchtown. The monthly payments shifted from the landlord to Sutton Bank and Trust. And I had my own second-floor bedroom with a pink, fluffy comforter on the little bed and my dolls and books and my very own crucifix on the wall. Of course, in time Bénédicte was moved from her crib in my parents' room into mine. But no matter, I lived in the heart of God's good gifts.

But even to me, la petite Hélène, there were times in which our golden life seemed to lose its glow, if only for a moment. If I asked Maman what those moments meant, she would give me the softest answer she could conceive. It was only later, much later, that I would come to understand the violence and tragedy and grief that hid behind her deflective responses.

Over time, I came to recognize a man who walked around the edges of our neighborhood and our awareness. Seemingly beyond age, he was gray and grizzled, bedecked in a strapped undershirt (what we called a "pépère shirt.") and filthy, tan pants, talking to himself or to others unseen. He was so peripheral that none of the kids of the neighborhood even remarked on his disappearance when the last leaves on the tall elms fell and the first flakes of winter rode the wind off the ocean or his sudden return, seemingly on April winds. When, I was probably five or six, I asked about the man.

"Maman, who is that old man who walks around all day?"

She paused for a moment as if to find the right words. "Oh, *ma chère*, he is not that old. Before you were born, he went off to fight in the Great War, to save *la belle France* and the world from *les Boches*, the Germans. And when he came home, all his youth and future had been spent. He is sad and strange, but we must respect him and help him as best we can."

It was only years later, after my childhood and innocence had fled, when I learned of the machine guns, the exploding shells, and the gas that flowed across the fields of Belgium and France, that I understood where that strange, unnamed man, a specter of World War I, had lost his innocence. It was only after the next great war, to save the world from Hitler, the Nazis, and Japan, that I came to understand the nature of loss, from the gas of Auschwitz, the "necessary" clouds over Hiroshima and Nagasaki, and the arithmetic death of soldiers, one by one by one.

But for little Hélène those rare questioning moments came as a dark bird lighting on a branch and then flitting away. Today, I think of those points of awareness as like children's books and what's-wrong-with-this-picture? drawings. To understand that something, anything, was wrong with my life as a little girl in Frenchtown, Sutton, Maine, the USA, the world, threatened the innocence that promised me a life that my very being gave to me. And that innocence, on all my levels of awareness, floated me through the 1920s, like a leaf floating down the Nine Falls, unaware of the sudden, roaring current over the dam and down the rapids under the mill.

When I was five, I entered St. Hyacinth's elementary school. On the hill above Frenchtown, the Nine Falls, the mill, Sutton, and beyond, the sisters welcomed us to the arms of God's great gifts: knowledge, learning, and following Our Savior's grace. Sister Mary Thérèse was my sub-primary teacher. Her round face, framed by her black-and-white wimple, the folds of her black habit, alternated warmth and sternness, depending on the behavior of her flock. The day started with a prayer, then math, then reading, a break for milk and animal crackers, and finally religion. After running home for lunch and a faster dash back to pass beneath the gaze of one of the sisters, we had spelling, a review of the morning's math, and penmanship.

Each day finished with another period of religion. I remember one time that Sister Mary Thérèse led us in prayer. Then she made the sign of the cross. "Children," she said, "we must all be clear of our need to live in the arms of Our Savior and His Church. Especially, we must learn to avoid the others in the world, all to be damned, who would try to draw the weak among us from His Love."

My classmates and I sat silently, trying to understand the lesson that Sister wished us to receive. Who were those "others?" What did it mean to be damned? Afterward, one of my classmates, André, said that he thought she meant that the bad people would be thrown into the deep water behind the mill's dam on the Nine Falls. Somehow that didn't seem right, but as I had no better explanation I let the moment and my bewilderment pass.

As the years flowed, there were moments where the world and Sister's lessons seemed to take on clarity, if not real understanding. One summer evening when I was seven or eight, Paul and Geno came home late for dinner, both so upset that Maman's admonitions didn't make a dent. When they had calmed down a bit, they explained that they had been attacked, first with words and then with fists by a few boys from another part of Sutton. "We were just trying to be friends," Paul said. "They were playing touch football and let us join in the game."

"Everything was going great," Geno added. "And then Paul made a super block. He knocked the guy head over teacups. And the guy got up all angry."

"He ran up at me, shoved me in the chest and called me a "fucking Frog," Paul said. "Shouted that we should 'get back across the river where we belonged.' I tried to tell him it was just part of the game, but that made him even madder. And he and his buddies started pushing and punching us. We tried to hold our own, but there were too many of them, so we had to run."

"The last thing I remember," said Geno, "as we headed toward the footbridge, was them clucking and crowing like we were a couple of chickens… from the wrong roost."

We sat at the table, speechless, dinner on pause. Finally, Maman broke the silence.

"*Mes fils*, there are always going to be people who will hate you, even though they don't know you. Our world is full of anger and fear. But Our Savior teaches us to turn the other cheek, to love those who love us not. Only by doing so can we hope for God's peace on Earth."

"But," Papa said, "you must always stand up for yourselves and against those who wish to make you and your people less than you are. I'm proud that you attempted to stand your ground if only for a moment."

Years later I discovered that my brothers' confrontation was an aftermath of a time of fear and anger in Sutton and across the nation. In the years following that first World War, there was a reemergence of the Ku Klux Klan and a spread of its hatred and fear throughout America. And this time, the hatred, the lies, and the violence of hooded mobs in white sheets was directed, not only at negroes in the South, but in the cities of New England toward new "others": Jews, Catholics, and, too often, the families of the newly arrived peoples, the Slavs, the Italians, and, in Sutton as elsewhere, the families of those who had made their journey from Québec, we Franco-Americans. In my early teens, Dorcas, a friend from across the Nine Falls whom I met in high school, told me that her parents had told her of one night, looking across the river toward Frenchtown and seeing a tall cross burning in front of the spire of St. Hyacinth. We marveled that only a decade later we could have our friendship, that the hatred of others had waned.

The kitchen table was one of the centers of my life on the second floor of *la maison DuBois et Lévesque*. Often I would sit there on a stool, helping Maman with supper preparations or just drifting on the rich smells of her bread or pies in our new electric oven. She would tell stories about her childhood and the lessons Mémère had passed on about what it meant to be a young Québecois Catholic girl. God our Father gave His great gifts to the faithful, the Holy Rules for the good life. And His Son, the Holy Jesus Christ, whose glowing soul lit the path to heaven through the Church.

"Ah yes, ma petite, but for us, God's daughters, Our Holy Virgin Mother, Blessed Mary the Mother of God, shows us our special path." She walked over to the table, took a sip of tea, and drew me into her gaze. "God's men, our fathers and husbands, live with the daily torments of life in the world, of work, and the demands outside the home. And from those torments, and from the stain of Adam, are too often tempted to stray. We women are blessed with home and family. We must be loving partners, always understanding and forgiving their trespasses." Then, as if an inner clock had sounded its alarm, she walked over to the stove and removed three golden loaves.

"Maman," I said, "can I go out and find my friends?"

"Mais oui, ma petite chérie. Let's wake and change Béné. You can take her in *la poussette*, good practice for a young mother-to-be."

The other center of our home was the radio. An RCA console, taller than my five-year-old self, sat in the living room between Papa's chair and the divan. If the oven was Maman's, the radio was Papa's fiefdom. Whether returning from a shift at the mill or preparing for eight hours in the steam and din, he controlled the dials as she did the thermostat. Often we could listen to a half hour of music from the stars of American culture: Paul Whiteman, George Gershwin. And the family revered the singing of Rudy Vallee, a boy from a mill town in Maine, much like our own Sutton. "My time is your time," seemed like a lyric promise that I could find my niche in this new America.

On the evenings when Papa was home, sports gave time together for father and sons. Friday night boxing matches—Jack Dempsy (The Manassa Mauler), Gentleman Gene Tunney, Luis Firpo (The Wild Bull of the Pampas), baseball—Babe Ruth, Lou Gehrig, Tris Speaker, or football—The Galloping Ghost Red Grange. Although no one minded if I, petite Hélène, sat in a corner listening to the shouts of the announcers and the roar of the crowds, it was clear that I sat outside the inner circle of the men of the house.

The Mutual Radio Network brought the news of the nation into Frenchtown, Sutton, Maine. Turmoil around the world, revolution in Russia, the rise of Hitler in Germany, big business and labor turmoil in the USA. Papa would sit with his quarts of ale and whiskey, raising his glass in a toast to President Coolidge or New York Governor Al Smith ("a good Irish Catholic friend of the working man"). I especially remember one evening in the fall of 1929 when the news was about nothing but the crash of the stock market. Although I had no real understanding of what that meant, clearly Papa saw it as a huge problem, even to the point that when Maman came into the living room from tucking Bénédicte in for the night, he tried to explain this moment to his "little woman." "But, praise Jesus," he said, "it will hurt the rich, the bankers. But for us, ah well, the paper will continue to roll off number two machine, and each Thursday will be payday." He lit a Camel, exhaled a contented cloud, and poured two fingers more of the Golden Wedding into his glass.

And Papa was right about the mill, until he wasn't. As 1930 slunk into '31, the downturn of the big money world of stocks and corporations spread across the country and whacked the little people while the bankers and stock mavens eased their pain with rich, green bandages. In the Midwest, the farmers fled drought and sinking markets for wheat and beef. Maman told me about the "Okies," the bankers who took their farms, and their long, sad trail westward in search of a future. "It's so different, ma chère, from when Pépère and Mémère left Québec for their life in America. They were told, and they believed, that hard work and family would be the path toward a house, a home. And here we are, living the promise."

But the American hunger for paper shrank, slowly at first and then faster and faster. The trainloads of Nine Falls's rich, glossy paper sat in the yards as the New York world of publishing, finance, and greed throttled down. And as the trains remained motionless, the paper machines slowed; the vats of wood pulp rotted, unstirred; the mountains of pulp logs ceased to shrink; and the lumbermen in Maine's vast forests took their saws and axes and followed the rivers home.

For a time, the management of the mill did their best to keep all their laborers—the "Canucks," the "Paddies," and the "Squareheads"—working, if on shortened hours. But, almost as part of a Depression script, in time the men began to come home with empty lunch boxes, final checks for the bank, and no shift for the next week. So Pépère continued on the job with the others with seniority. But Papa slunk up the stairs into our apartment, grabbed the Balentine and Golden Wedding quarts from the kitchen, and collapsed into his chair. He sat there for almost a week, too befuddled to even turn on the radio, and, many nights, too frozen in place to walk across the apartment to his bed.

But for me, petite Hélène Honoré, life didn't seem that different, that sad. My seven- and then eight-year-old self played with my friends, gave proper attention to the Sisters at St. Hyacinth's School, and in the dark of my bedroom, whispered to my favorite doll so that I would not disturb sister Bénédicte in her crib and Papa in his chair. Through an open window, I would listen to the night, praying that soon the roar of the mill and the grinding of freight train wheels would mark a return to days past, the only future I could imagine.

Later, Maman would tell me that their lives jolted between hopes for a better future and the crushing weight of reality. For a time it seemed as though organized labor, a union of paper workers, might stand up for the needs and rights of the men who tended the machines. In decades past, the Nine Falls Mill had negated any worker organization by paying well and providing benefits both directly to "the Family" and to the town of Sutton: a park with a swimming pool and athletic field next to the river, a gymnasium to teach clean, American sports to the children of the town, recreation leagues for the laborers of the mills, a library were all gifts, although with the barely spoken understanding that all at NFP were family. Even as the Depression loomed, Memorial Day, The Fourth of July, and Armistice Day were all marked by parades, ceremonies in the park, and bean suppers put on by the Lions Club and the American Legion post.

And so, when the American Federation of Labor began a campaign to organize the mill the response of management was immediate and brutally effective. Some workers loyal to the company (or terrified for their jobs), quietly passed on information of union plans and the local workers who were involved. "Scabs," Pépère called them. "Unemployed" was their swift reality.

But all was not dark in Sutton. In 1931 the high school basketball team went on a great run to the state championship. The Blue Flames were like a group photo of the ethnicities that made up the town. Ludger Fortin and Toots Morin, and *mon frère* Paul from Frenchtown; Paddy Driscoll, Stevie Dwyer, and Marty Walsh from Irish Hill; Walter Wilson and Francis Forsythe from the large homes of the management side of the river; and, the rock around which the whirl of hoopsters flowed, Hartwig Jensen, a six-four, square-chinned manchild of the Danish enclave near St. Olaf's Church. When "our boys" returned victorious on a dark February afternoon, the whole town turned out for a parade down Main Street to Crosby Square. Geno and Erland took me in tow for the celebration and boosted me up onto the top of a phone booth where I bathed in the glow of the streetlights and a moment of community pride.

When we returned home, my brothers left me with Maman in the kitchen and fled for further celebration with their friends. I told *ma mère* all about the parade and how Paul was up on the trailer truck parked at the square that elevated the Blue Flames above the throng. She smiled and continued kneading the dough for the week's bread. I dropped onto the floor and tickled Petite Bénédicte, celebrating my French. "*Coucou, petite. Je t'aime beaucoup.*"

After a bit, I got up and walked out of the bright warmth of the kitchen to the dark of the living room. As my eyes adjusted, I saw Papa in his chair, glass in hand. I walked over to him, but it was as if he couldn't see me, although his eyes were wide open.

"Papa," I said. "There was a great parade for the Blue Flames. Everybody was so happy!"

I stood there for what seemed forever. Finally, Papa turned just a bit and looked at me. It seemed like his eyes were returning from somewhere far, far away.

"Paul was up there with the rest of the team," I said. "He had the great biggest smile!"

Papa grunted from somewhere way deep inside. Slowly, the glass with Golden Wedding found his lips. "Glad he had the…chance." His eyes sank back to wherever that far-off place was. "I could have had… I could play pretty good. Had to work…so you all can play." And then, *mon père avait disparu*, gone back into the depths of his glass.

Yet another role for the big mill on the Nine Falls was that of weather forecaster. Very early on, I learned to look out my window to the soaring chimney. If the smoke was blowing downstream, toward the ocean, we could expect a good day, borne on west winds. However, if the smoke surged upstream, the east winds promised rain or snow. I learned how to prepare to meet the ever-changing whims of the weather, along with the flow of the joys of childhood, buffeted by gales of adult conflicts and pain.

Three days after my thirteenth birthday, I awoke to a Sutton bathed in gold and green with wisps of western breeze. September 3, 1938, promised to be special. I put on my new blue dress, purchased the week before with my savings from babysitting for the Forsythes in their big house across the river. I bounced into the bathroom and fluffed my brown hair, hoping it might hold at least a hint of curls. I looked directly into my mirrored eyes. "Today," I whispered. "Today you are a high school girl."

I floated into the kitchen. *"Bonjour,* Maman," I said.

"*Ah, bonjour, ma belle fille*," mother Céleste said. "You are ready for your big day? A high school girl!" She took the pan off the stove, walked to the table, and dropped a glop of oatmeal into my very own, green bowl. "Eat up. You should not be late on your first day!"

Geno and Erland barely looked up from their bowls. Clearly, high school was not as exciting to them as to their little sister. Other than the sport of each season, the only other thing that Sutton High School promised them was that Friday at 2:15 would always arrive, one week closer to graduation and their grown-up life with Nine Falls Paper. And Paul, my eldest brother, had fled school and hometown two years earlier, signing on with FDR's Civilian Conservation Corps. Along with other boys from the mill towns and seaports of Maine and points south, he had been stationed down east on Mt. Desert Island, where manual labor constructing the roads, bridges, and trails of Acadia National Park, turned them into men. He sent us a little black-and-white photo of himself and two other CCC-ers taken on top of Cadillac Mountain. Young, healthy, and hopeful, they waved cigarettes and smiled for the home folks.

My first days at Sutton High passed in a blur. Moving from class to class, crowds of girls and boys in the halls, teachers who neither looked nor taught like the Sisters of Mercy at St. Hyacinth's grammar. I began to believe that I could grow up.

At the end of the school day, the first Thursday, at my locker, a girl who I'd noticed in my English and math classes walked over to me. "Hi, I'm Dorcas," she said. "And you're Helen, right?"Her smile and tone helped me to believe that she wasn't putting me down.

"Actually," I said, "It's Hélène—Eeh-len."

"Well, I guess I'll learn how to say it right. But…just for now let's change the Hell to Heck—Heckie. The other girls will get that easier. I mean, what the heck, Heckie."

I gave an inner shrug. What the heck. Heckie it was until, every school day when I crossed the bridge over the Nine Falls, I would revert to Hélène and review my day as the francophone Frenchtown fille I knew, down deep, that I was. I would sit at our kitchen table with a slice of Maman's bread and we would talk about the day and my classes in French. All in French except for introduction to algebra. For that, neither of us had French words, or for that matter, English ones. Maman took great joy in my high school days, days that had been denied her by Pépere DuBois's dictate that high school was not for girls.

Very quickly, Sutton High School gave lessons, not just from books, but from the expectations of the outside world. There were a seemingly endless number of groups: classes, courses of study, different sides of the river. The teachers and guidance counselors made it clear that, for most of the girls, especially those of us from Frenchtown, either business or home economics, were the more fruitful paths. For the boys, one of the trades from the vocational department—electrical, metal working, carpentry—would promise a smooth transition from school to the mill. For the clump of boys for whom school was like a four-year sentence, the general course. And at the top of the ladder, boys and girls who, either by defining intelligence or family status, were accepted into college prep.

Even though I was never fully clear why, I always hated this stacking, the sorting of young men and women onto the different shelves of what society deemed "useful" and "natural."

The boys sports teams ruled Sutton's attention. The Blue Flames basketeers could fill the stands while the girls were consigned to a Thursday afternoon game in the gym, six players split on offense and defense, the mid-court line segregating, denying the fullness of the boys game. And the cheerleaders, swirling, posing, offering their practiced adoration to the boys who would be, someday, their men. None of our teen queen schoolmates swirled for the girl hoopsters.

But there were golden moments as well. Freshman Reception was a long-term tradition at Sutton High. Each fall, after the first month of classes, on a Friday evening, faculty and upperclassmen gathered in the gymnasium to formally welcome the most recent batch of newcomers. At the given hour, the freshmen would march the length of the gym between rows of folding chairs occupied by the veterans of the Blue Flames world. When it was our turn, the Class of '42, dressed in our best, entered and took our seats in chairs facing those already initiated. Mr. Sampson, the principal, welcomed all and asked Miss Arnold, the senior English teacher, to offer a prayer. God's blessings invoked, Mr. Sampson spoke to his newest charges. Bits and pieces still remain in my memory. The importance of community, especially in troubled times. Individual responsibility for good behavior. And then, one by one he called our names and we stood, for a moment of recognition.

The formalities complete, we vacated the gym to the second-floor study hall where the home economics department had provided snacks and drinks. At the same time the Gold Star Club members cleared the gym floor in preparation for the dance that would complete our welcome into "dear old Sutton High School."

Students and chaperones flowed back to the dance. Two of the senior boys from the Electrical Department had set up a sound system. Another pair took on the roles of disk jockeys, spinning records that attempted the dual challenge of energizing the dancers and satisfying the standards of the adults.

After a few dances with Sophie and Thérèse, I stood off to the side, trying to make sense of the evening and where I fit in. Suddenly, a young man stepped into my line of sight. "Hi," he said. "My name is Jim. May I have this dance?" For a second I felt as if everything—the music, the dancers, the world outside, my breath—had frozen. I nodded and followed James Stuart Fredericks onto the floor.

After that sad, scary week, Pépère came upstairs after his tower and told Papa that his slot on the number two machine was open and waiting. Perhaps because of the union scare, perhaps out of community solidarity, management returned the mill to almost full employment with shortened hours and pay. And, almost as if another part of the deal, it became clear that supervision of the departments would be given over to the first men on the machines. As long as the paper rolled, men came and went as they wished. Perhaps a father who worked on the digesters would skip away to watch his son in a Blue Flames practice in the gym, another might walk up to the corner for a haircut and a half hour of conversation. Or, as became the case with Papa, a "quick" trip to Owney's Tavern for a couple of mugs of Narragansett, the official beer of the Red Sox.

For me, the days at Sutton High were full of excitement and promise. After eight years with the Sisters at St. Hyacinth's, my teachers seemed to offer a world of open ideas and rewards for personal growth. In our civics class, Mr. DiRenzo talked of the importance of citizenship, using our collective family experiences to celebrate the American Dream. Miss Franks in ninth-grade English assigned poetry that spoke of the experiences of real people and encouraged us to try our hand at verse. She gave me an A and some very kind comments on a poem I wrote about the Nine Falls after a storm. Algebra, well, it was algebra. As Dorcas told me one day, she could find no way that algebra existed in the real world.

Friendships appeared and grew. To the girls in my classes I was established as "Heckie." No matter, we were friends and they had their own nicknames. During our lunch breaks we sat in the gym and talked about rumors of the older kids, the fashions in the windows of the two women's shops on Main Street that we could only hope to wear, and boys—this one and that one, who liked whom, and what it all might mean. "Jim," Sophie said. "He's such a hunk." And she looked at me, hoping for a clue of how I would react to the mention of James Stuart Fredericks.

And it seemed that Jim's paths and mine crossed as if there were a plan. We danced at the teen center on Friday evenings, and he never questioned when I told him that I had to be home for Maman's ten o'clock curfew. One Saturday in October, in the glow of a Blue Flames football win, we sat on the bleachers and talked about…well about what I can't recall, just that we did. Another time he told me that at long last his parents had given him the okay to get his driver's license. "Maybe some afternoon we can take a spin together," he said. I could only nod. And then I waited for that afternoon to arrive.

One afternoon in April I was home, watching Petite Bénédicte while Maman and Mémère made their trip to the IGA market. After they returned, I helped stow the week's provisions away. There was a knock at our door. I opened it and there, with a smile that shook my heart, was James Stuart Fredericks. Maman walked in from the kitchen and stared at this unfamiliar young man.

"Maman," I said. "This is Jim. He's a friend from school."

"Ah," she replied. "Won't you please come in…Jim." We sat down in the living room, almost as if there were a script: Maman and I on the couch, Jim in Papa's chair. There was just a moment's pause. It seemed like forever.

"Madame Lévesque," he said. "Hélène and I have become friends during this school year. And I would like your permission to ask her out to a movie tomorrow night."

Maman gave him a long look. "And your parents, they know of this?"

"Yes, ma'am. I've told them how lucky I am to have made her friendship."

"Well, then…" She paused as if confirming her evaluation. "Yes, that would be fine."

And that was the beginning of a part of my world that flowed as gently as the Nine Falls on warm summer days. And summer finally arrived to mark the end of my freshman year. Maman helped me to line up a number of babysitting jobs for Frenchtown women who were returning to the mill in the sorting department. I kept my earnings in a little box on my dresser, planning on being able to buy a back-to-school outfit from one of the women's stores on Main Street.

Jim was increasingly a part of my life, and thus of the Lévesque family. He had a job working for a farmer in the town next to Sutton, helping with the cattle and harvesting the hay and corn crops. When our schedules allowed us, we took rides in his family's Model A Ford, went to a movie at one of the many theaters in greater Portland, or just hung out with our friends in the park by the Nine Falls. One sunny Saturday, we drove over to Old Orchard Beach. We walked through the crowds of tourists, listening to the accents of vacationers "from away"—Massachusetts, New York, and especially les Québécois—speaking the tongue of my heritage. After sharing pier fries and sodas, we returned to the Ford, gathered a blanket and towels, and walked to the beach. Finding our special place in the throng, Jim spread the blanket, and we shucked our clothing down to our bathing suits. We ran, hand-in-hand, down to the water and dove into a wave. Then I stood and stared at his—my Jim's—young body, tanned from the summer sun and firming into manhood from endless pitchforks of hay.

When our time together stretched into the evening, we understood that my curfew was ten o'clock and that we would arrive home following our outings. Not for us the dark corners of the park or the isolation of gravel country roads. In time, we kissed and hugged. But I always kept in mind Maman's *leçons des hommes*. Boys would be men, and God had made them as they were. It was for us, *les femmes de Dieu*, God's women, to set boundaries, for our own good as well as theirs. And so, as we came together on the front seat of the Model A, my left arm was always planted firmly on my chest. And Jim, cher Jim, never tried to move it.

And then, on the last day of August, 1939, my sixteenth birthday, the joys of that summer crashed to an end. Jim drove me home well before our curfew as we both had to work the next morning. As we approached my house, my home, I was shocked to see some of our neighbors standing outside, next to the Sutton police car. Jim pulled up and, wide-eyed, asked me if I wanted him to come in. I shook my head. He reached over and stroked my face. "It will be okay," he said. After a parting hug, I climbed down and watched him drive off to "his side" of the river. Then I took a deep breath, walked past the little crowd, and entered into whatever life's twists held for me.

In the first-floor hall, I looked into my grandparents' living room. Mémère, Aunt Jacqueline, and Cousin Eugénie were clustered around the couch. Bénédicte sat off to the side on the floor, looking off into space. My grandmother turned to me as I entered.

"Mémère," I said. "What is...what is the problem?

Her eyes were flooded. "*Ah, ma chérie....*" She turned back to the couch.

I walked over to them and thought I would faint. There, curled up like a rag doll, was my mother. Her face was red and swollen, and one eye was closed, lost in a purple mass. "Oh, Maman, Maman!," I cried. But it was as if her hearing were as smashed as her face.

Aunt Jacqueline motioned for me to follow her out into the hall. "Oh, Hélène," she moaned. "It was your father! The bottle took him and threw him against your mother. *C'est horrible, horrible*! Pépère is upstairs with him, with the police."

I had to see, had to try to understand. I ran up the stairs and into our living room. There in his chair, flanked by two Sutton patrolmen, was *mon papa*, hunched over, seemingly unaware of me or the world he had smashed along with his wife's face. Pépère came over to me. "Hélène," he whispered. "I need you to go downstairs. Right now this is a place just for men."

I turned and walked downstairs in the only home I had ever known to my grandparents' apartment. We women gathered in the living room. No one spoke, but from time to time a moan or a whimper testified to our being. After what seemed an endless time, the police came down the stairs. One looked into the room. "We'll be going now," he said. "Mr. DuBois will fill you in on our recommendations." We waited, six women and my baby sister.

Finally, Pépere came down the stairs and joined us. "Here's how we will proceed. François understands how wrong he has been." He looked down at Maman. "Céleste, he begs your forgiveness and promises to mend his ways. For tonight, I will join him upstairs. Hélène, you and Bénédicte will go and stay with your aunt and uncle until your mother and father can safely come back together. Your brothers, Geno and Erland, young men, can stay with François until all can be united. Tomorrow I will ask Monseigneur to come and minister to your parents. Now, come with me and we will gather clothing for you and your sister. Then we can all get some rest."

It would be three months before my little sister and I returned to our home. For the first few weeks, Uncle Robert would return from his tower at the Nine Falls and fill us in on Papa's progress—he had returned to work; he seemed better, he was not sneaking out for beers at the tavern. Aunt Jacqueline often went to our home to help Mémère while Maman was mending. Her face looked "much better." Monseigneur Desjardins was visiting with his messages of hope and forgiveness. After a month, Bénédicte and I began to make visits to our home, a few minutes to pick out new outfits from our room, after school with cake and tea, an hour with both our parents after Papa's shift at the mill. And finally it was decided that things had "returned to normal," and we moved back to the only home I had ever known.

But things were never "normal." The laughter, the hugs, the sense that *les familles DuBois et Lévesque* were bonded in love had slipped away. Papa had mostly put his old friends Balentine and Golden Wedding aside. He worked, slept, and turned his weekly pay over to Maman. Geno graduated in June and followed the traditional path of Sutton young men from high school to beginner's slot at the Nine Falls. He and three of his friends rented an apartment in Frenchtown. Maman made it clear to me that his place was off-limits. No matter.

That summer, I was immersed in Jim. He had graduated third in his class and had been named in the Blue Flames yearbook as most handsome, most popular, and most likely to succeed. There were moments when I had to look in the mirror and convince myself that, yes, James Stuart Fredericks loved me, Hélène Honoré. As our summer jobs allowed, me babysitting for women who had returned to the mill, Jim in the rotating towers as a bottom layer paper laborer, we flowed together like the Nine Falls to the sea. The seashore, the beaches at Big and Little Loon Lakes, a dance, a party at a friend's house, hamburgers and French fries at Watson's Grill—all moments in what had become love.

We knew, of course, that the flow of summer would lead to the rapids of September. Jim would depart for his freshman year at Dartmouth College, a full day's drive from Sutton. Even as my love prepared for his next chapter, doing his assigned summer reading, buying the wardrobe that would establish him as a true Ivy League man, we rarely spoke of our separation. I took it as a token of our love that he would tell me of our future when the time came, and that I would trust him with all my heart.

One Saturday evening in mid-August, we sat in his Model A outside la maison Lévesque. As I started to exit after a final long hug and kiss, my love stopped me with a hand on my thigh.

"*Ma chère*," he said. "My parents would like it very much if you could join us for Sunday dinner tomorrow."

It was the first time I had been invited to his home. I had met his parents at the Sutton High graduation. His mother had been kind and had acknowledged that her only son and I had connected in a powerful and acceptable way. "Yes," I said. "Yes! It will be great to see the inside of your home. I'm sure that Maman will be glad as well."

"Great! I'll pick you up after church, say about noon?"

"Oh yes! I'll go to ten o'clock mass. That will give me plenty of time."

The next day, I sat in the living room window and watched as my love drove up the hill through Frenchtown. As he parked out front, I walked over to the mirror and took a quick peek at my best dress and made sure my hair was fluffed just right. Papa looked up from his papers and gave me a nod. I walked over to the kitchen door and called in, "Maman, I'm off with Jim."

"Enjoy, *ma chère*. Say hello to his parents."

I hurried down the stairs and out to the car. Jim had jumped out and come around to the passenger side. "My dear Miss Lévesque," he said. "May I have the pleasure of your company at dinner in my humble abode?"

"*Bien sûr*," I replied. And as my love bowed and opened the door, I climbed up to depart on my next adventure.

We drove down the hill, across the Nine Falls, through downtown Sutton, and into the Oxford Mills neighborhood of large houses, green lawns, and towering elm trees, the homes of managers, doctors, and bankers. Jim pulled into a three-lane, paved driveway and parked next to a large, black Buick sedan. He dashed around the Ford, opened the door, and gave me his hand as I climbed down. Then, hand-in-hand, we walked up to the front door of the dark green shingled house, his home, larger than any dwelling that I had ever visited.

We walked into a front hall and past a grandfather clock that soared to the ceiling. Then we entered the living room where, on either side of a large brick fireplace, sat his parents. Mr. Fredericks rose and extended his hand. "Please excuse my poor French," he said with a smile. "*Alors, bienvenue chez nous,* Mademoiselle Lévesque." For a moment I was caught by the thought that I should curtsy. I made do with a handshake and a whispery "*Merci, monsieur.*" Mrs. Fredericks smiled and, with a sweep of her hand, seated her son and me on the Victorian sofa with swirling dark wood carvings on its arms and rich figured brocade upholstery. After a few minutes of chatter about the rapid passing of the summer, the need for rain, and Mrs. Fredericks' upcoming trip to Paris in the fall, a young woman came to the doorway.

"Excuse me," she said. "Dinner is ready, whenever you are."

"Thank you, Diane," said Mrs. Fredericks, as she stood and, with another sweep of her hand, ushered us toward the dining room. There, a massive golden oak table was set for four. Jim's father moved to one end and pulled back the chair for his wife. James did the same for me on one side and then walked around to the other. Mr. Fredericks took his seat at what clearly was the head of the table. Mrs. Fredericks picked up a little brass bell and shook it gently. The door to the kitchen opened, and the young woman entered carrying a tray that she set on the buffet behind the lady of the house. Then, one at a time, she placed bowls of clear soup before each of us.

I followed James's lead as he bowed his head over the first course. Mr. Fredericks said a brief grace, looked up and said, "Soup's on!"

"I hope you like the consommé," Mrs. Fredericks said. "It's from a recipe I picked up one summer in Normandy."

I took a sip of the dark, shimmering soup. For all the world it tasted like the beef stock that Mémère made from butcher's bones and handfuls of herbs from our little garden. I took another sip and looked up into the gaze of the three Fredericks.

"*C'est bon?*" James' mother asked.

"*Magnifique,*" I replied. And we all returned to our soup.

And so our dinner continued: roast lamb with a thin, herbed sauce, scalloped potatoes, and green beans. Diane was in and out of the kitchen, clearing dishes, presenting the lamb to Mr. Fredericks for carving and serving, filling water glasses that had hardly been touched. Mother, father, and son chatted, always remembering to draw me in to the topic of the moment.

As we finished the main course, Mr. Fredericks leaned back in his chair, sighed contentedly, and looked over at me. "I hope you've saved room for dessert."

"Oh, yes," I replied. "It was all wonderful."

Mrs. Fredericks said, "I'm afraid the lamb was a bit overdone. And, of course, if we'd been transported to Provence, there would have been wine, perhaps a subtle Burgundy. So hard to find a good wine in Maine. No matter. We're pleased you could join us, Hélène." As if on cue, *la serveuse* entered and began to clear the table. "Diane," the matron said. "I think we'll take dessert in the living room. Perhaps give us ten or twelve minutes to settle in."

"Of course. Just give your bell a jingle."

With that, we four diners rose and walked back into the living room. Mr. and Mrs. Fredericks claimed their chairs by the fireplace. James and I sat on the sofa, close but not quite touching. The grandfather clock in the front hall ticked and then chimed twice.

"Is everyone ready for dessert?" Mr. Fredericks asked. James and I nodded. Mrs. Fredericks picked up her bell and shook it several times. As if she'd been hiding in the hall, Diane swept in and served us from a tray of four golden cream puffs with chocolate drizzled on their caps. "Will we all have coffee?" the matriarch asked. Silence and nods confirmed the order. "Thank you, Diane. We'll take our coffees anytime now." Diane left, and I thrust my spoon through the pastry, finding a flowing, golden custard dotted with a few ripe blueberries. For a moment all was quiet, save for the occasional clink of spoon on China.

"My dear," Mr. Fredericks said. "I do adore your *crème pâtissiere*." His wife nodded.

Diane returned with a tray carrying a silver coffee pitcher, four tiny cups, a sugar bowl, and a small pitcher of cream. "Do you take anything in your coffee, Hélène?" asked Mrs. Fredericks.

"A little cream, please," I said.

"No sugar?"

"Thank you, no."

She served me and then, with no questions, Mr. Fredericks and James. "Charles," she said to her husband. "Perhaps a bit of sherry would be in order?" It was really not a question.

"Of course," the lord of the manor replied. He rose, walked over to a dry sink, and filled four tiny goblets with a golden liquid. He handed one to each of us, sat, and raised his glass. "A toast to James as he prepares to depart for the next chapter of his life." We raised our glasses in reply, and James and I clinked glasses. In unison we sipped the sherry, the first taste of an alcoholic beverage I had ever taken. Mr. Fredericks gave a long, contented sigh. "Nice," he said. "About the best to be found out here in the provinces." Another silence as we finished our dessert.

"Dartmouth!" Mr. Fredericks said at length. "Still hard to believe you opted for Dartmouth when Yale beckoned. Family legacy and all."

"It just felt right," James said. "I really didn't want a city."

"Think of it as Yale with mountains," added his mother. "Although, it would have been convenient if we could have shared transportation to and from New Haven with the Bushes." We sipped our sherry. "And you, Hélène, are you thinking about schools after Sutton High?"

Her question jolted me a bit. "Well, not really," I replied.

"Remember, mother," James said. "She's just going to be starting her junior year."

"Well, it's never too soon to think of one's future." She drew me in with her gaze. "By the time I was your age, I knew that Wellesley was going to be the place for me. A beautiful campus, nearby Boston. One of the Seven Sisters, not as far out in the provinces as Smith and Holyoke. If you happened to like it, I could put in a good word.…No hurry, of course."

"Thank you, I replied. "You're very kind to…."

"Ah, Wellesley," she continued. "The hallowed halls, the pathways beneath the ancient trees. Young women there from far and wide but all of a kind."

"What was your major, Mother?" James broke in.

"English literature, especially the Brontes," she replied. "*Mais j'ai adoré mes cours de langue française aussi.*" A nod to me. "And we learned life lessons, that we, who were blessed with higher education, had the responsibility to give back to those less fortunate. That has informed my life in Sutton, the library committee, the Women's Club." Another nod to me, like an abbess to her postulate. "More coffee, my dear? Charles? James?"

Finding no takers, she tinkled her bell, and Diane materialized to clear dessert. After a few minutes, it became clear that it was time to depart. "Mr. and Mrs. Fredericks," I said. "It was a wonderful meal. Thank you for your hospitality."

"It was our pleasure," the lady of the manor replied. She rose and gestured toward the hall. "James has painted such a portrait of you for us. Clearly a work of romantic realism."

"Best luck for your junior year," his father said. Then I followed their son, my love, out past the grandfather clock and into the bright Sunday afternoon of Sutton, Maine.

James pulled the Model A up outside my home. We sat for a moment. "I'm glad to have met your parents," I said.

"And they really enjoyed meeting you." A pause. "Sometimes they can seem a bit stuffy; it's the tone of the world they grew up in. But underneath they're really warm and loving."

The afternoon slid by.

"Jim," I said. "I can't believe that in three weeks you'll be leaving, disappearing from my world."

He reached out, and I slid across the seat into his embrace. "No, Hélène. I won't be gone. Just that we'll be together in a different way, thinking and remembering each other. Letters will be our way of loving across the miles. We can share our thoughts and feelings, like long hugs." A long pause. "Hélène. I love you so much. That won't ever change."

We kissed, and his strong arms held me in that truth. Then I slid out of his car and returned to another world, *le monde* de la famille Lévesque. Three weeks later, when I was in my eleventh grade English class, James Stuart drove off to Dartmouth College.

I loved Sutton High School. Now that Erland, my youngest brother, had graduated, the halls of the old brick building were free of fraternal competition or observation. Dorcas, Alice, Thérèse, Sophie, and I coalesced into a sisterhood that overrode issues of course of study, family history, or on which side of the Nine Falls we lived. As juniors we could glide down the halls, radiating our feminine arrival over the sophomores and freshmen. "Bing vs. Frankie, J. Dorsey or T. Dorsey?"

Holding firm against Papa's preference, I continued in the college prep track. I really felt that I was learning—how to read, how to write, and how to think on my own. American history seemed more than just some pages in a text book. Mr. DiRenzo explained the twisted story of European conflicts. "Don't kid yourself," he said. The 'Phony War' will explode at Hitler's whim. Just catching his breath after Poland." And the German army confirmed his prediction in October with the Blitzkrieg chaos and death that tore across Holland, Belgium, and into Paris. Suddenly, our country was standing with Britain, sending arms, ships, and planes to back up Churchill's promise of resistance and survival.

And as Churchill stood for British courage, President Roosevelt led our country in its surge toward strength and commitment. Factories switched from cars and refrigerators to tanks and planes. Swarms of men and women spread out across the country to do the work that the times demanded. Boys and girls in Scout uniforms collected scrap metal for the cause. There was hardly a town, a family not drawn into the work of war.

And the war, the war that followed by only two decades "the war to end war," reached into Sutton, Maine, and to la famille Lévesque. In April of 1939, my eldest brother, Paul, left his job with the CCC on Mount Desert Island, took a train across the border to McAdam, New Brunswick, and enlisted in the Canadian army. In a letter to Papa and Maman, he explained that he felt he must stand against the Nazis, to reclaim the green of Normandy, the captive source of our family. Then, in late October 1940, President Roosevelt, presiding over the first "peacetime" draft in our history, read the birthdates of young men who were being called to the cause. And the fifth number, September 19, called Geno to serve in our army. Two weeks later, Erland, just eighteen, enlisted in the navy. And as les frères Lévesque answered the call, President and Mrs. Roosevelt's four sons entered the services as well.

In spite of the dark anger and fear, there was much in my life that offered sunshine and hope. At home, Papa, for the most part, held firm in his battle with "Father Whiskey" and "Uncle Ale." In November, he, Pépère, and Uncle Marcel took their vacation to hunt deer in the North Woods, as if to celebrate President Roosevelt's election to a third term. Maman and Mémère went to mass at St. Hyacinth almost every day, praying for peace in the world and lighting candles for Paul, Geno, and Erland. No longer petite, my little sister, Bénédicte moved from our shared bedroom to the one that had housed our brothers. In what felt like a wisp of wind, she transformed it from a barracks into a pink grotto of girlhood, but also a reminder each night that nos frères were no longer at home. Together, each Saturday night, as if a religious calling, we listened to *Your Lucky Strike Hit Parade*, absorbing the songs to be debated and discussed as American scripture in the halls of Sutton High.

At school, I found a growing sense of connection with Miss Franks and the world of literature that she opened for me. One day at the end of my college prep junior English class, she asked me to wait a moment. "Hélène," she said. If you have time, I'd like you to come back after school."

It took me a moment to collect my thoughts. "Yes, of course, Miss Franks. Is there a…problem with my Longfellow essay?

"No. Not at all. I just think you and I should have a chat. Now hurry or you'll miss lunch."

I nodded my acceptance, walked out of her classroom and up the flight of stairs to the large study hall that doubled as the lunch room. Dorcas, Alice, Thérèse, and Sophie watched me walk over.

"We thought you were going to miss lunch," Alice said.

"No, no. Miss Franks wanted to talk to me."

"Finally figured out you've been using Jim's old essays?" Dorcas asked, with a grin.

"Or his *loooove* letters," Thérèse crooned.

"I doubt that," Dorcas said.

The school day crept toward 2:15. As we left the chemistry lab, I told Dorcas that I'd meet her and the others at Vachon's Drugstore for our weekly soda fountain session. Then I turned and walked through a throng of Freshmen, wondering what my summons foretold. Outside room 203, I took a deep breath and then walked in.

Miss Franks looked up from a pile of white lined papers. "Oh, hello, Hélène. Thank you for coming. Have a seat. I'll be just a moment." While she shuffled the essays, I chose a desk in the front row. Miss F looked over at me across a row of books on her desk. "Hélène," she started. "I wanted to take a moment to tell you how pleased I am with the progress you're making in our English class."

I felt a bit flustered. "Thank you. That's really…nice to hear."

"It seems like ages since our paths first crossed in your freshman year." She chuckled. "Do you remember Joyce Kilmer's 'Trees'?"

"Oh, yes. It was the first poem I ever wrote about." I waited.

"And a worthy choice. It's a wonderful gift, God-given I think, the writer's offering of a part of herself to a reader. Words, rhythms, pauses, rhymes." We sat for a moment, as if in the slender space between verses. "Hélène, in my years of teaching, I've had only a handful of students who I felt had the gift of truly learning and the potential, the courage, to make that learning a path through life. My dear, I believe that you can be on the first steps toward that world."

"Thank you," I said. "You're very kind."

"If you are willing," she said. "I can work with you, show you the universe of thought. Would you like that?"

"Yes, please. Oh, yes, I would love that."

She reached out to the rank of books on her desk, selected one, and riffled through the pages. "Here's a good start, I think." She rose, walked around her desk, pulled up a chair and sat next to me. Leaning forward she spread the book on the student's desk. "Emily Dickenson, 'The Belle of Amherst.' Just listen: 'This Is My Letter to the World,'" A pause. "'This is my letter to the world/ That never wrote to me.'" She finished the two verses. "What do you think?"

"Well," I said, "it's hard to say, just from listening."

Miss F smiled. "And there's a lesson. Poems, more than any other form of writing, combine the gifts of reading, speaking, and listening. When you find a verse that seems to have merit, read it quietly, read it aloud softly, and let the printed word and the poet's voice come together in meaning." She took a slip of paper from inside the cover and placed it as a marker. "Take this," she said. "Read this and another of Miss D's works, 'The Soul Selects Her Own Society.' Read silently and then aloud. Hear and see her words. Then contemplate the message." She stood and walked around her desk. "That's more than enough for today, my dear. I look forward to our next meeting."

"Thank you, Miss Franks," I said. Standing I looked across the teacher's desk, the established boundary in the school that I felt had opened a bit. "Thank you so much."

Then I took her book, turned, and walked out of her room. And then out into the world. I walked down Main Street toward downtown Sutton, past Dorcas's stately red brick home, the Methodist and Congregational churches, The Men's Shop, Fortin's Women's Shoppe, the five and ten, the A&P market, and finally Vachon's Drugstore. I went in and over to the soda fountain. My four friends were just finishing their regular treats: a scoop of chocolate with nuts for Dorcas, a black-and-white frappe for Alice, custard pie and strawberry ice cream for Thérèse, and Sophie's choice: a vanilla ice cream soda. The juke box was playing "This Can't Be Love," as it seemed to every time we five gathered there.

"Did Miss F read you the riot act," Thérèse asked? "Finally figured out you've been copying my essays?"

I rolled my eyes in full drama mode. "Oh, yeah. As if. She just wanted to point out a couple of things about my essay. No big deal."

Dorcas looked at me for a moment. "Nice when someone cares enough."

We walked out onto Crosby Square. Dorcas and Alice turned left up Main Street. Thérèse, Sophie, and I walked across the bridge over the Nine Falls, past St. Hyacinth's golden spire, to home.

On the evening of January 6, 1941, la famille Lévesque gathered around the old Philco console radio in Pépere and Mémère's living room to listen to

President Roosevelt's speech to Congress and to Americans far and wide on the state of our nation. His voice, now familiar as that of a beloved uncle, called on all to play our parts in increasing our nation's strength and security, to support the British in their hour of need, to make the sacrifices of labor and financial support necessary for the cause. And then our president explained that, in the end, all this was necessary to protect the four essential freedoms that defined and protected us: freedom of religion and of speech, freedom from want and from fear. As his speech finished, we heard the swelling applause of our congressmen, Supreme Court justices, cabinet secretaries, and those citizens fortunate enough to be in the balconies above.

As I sat on the old sofa between Mémère and Maman, I felt for a moment as if I could hear the applause from the homes in Frenchtown, in Sutton, Maine, and like a surging tide, across the nation. Then, suddenly, I felt that the president had forgotten one true freedom that affected us all in some way: the freedom from loneliness. How deeply my dear mother missed her sons: Paul with the Canadian forces in England, Geno in the last weeks of his basic training in South Carolina, and Erland, having just turned nineteen, on his way to the great naval fortress of Pearl Harbor in Hawaii.

And, in the core of my being, how deeply I missed James Stuart Fredericks, my Jim. As his sophomore year at Dartmouth unfolded, his letters arrived a bit less frequently. As always he tried to share his college life with me: life in his fraternity—beer and brotherhood; his classes—the engaging and the deadly boring professors; his economics course—that the math classes he had suffered through at Sutton High suddenly seemed to have actual, interesting use. And in each and every letter *mon cher* reassured me across the miles between our two worlds that I was always in his heart. His second semester would end soon, and he would hurry home and into my arms.

We all felt the war, each in our own way. Pépère, Papa, and all the laborers at the Nine Falls Mill found their work hours added overtime to meet the demand for paper for myriad military uses. No one who wanted a job was turned away. In the sorting and packaging departments, women even took on the role of foreman. Paychecks were ample to the point that my parents purchased war bonds with the hope that those savings would help finance whatever peacetime world would follow war.

I continued to love high school. The pleasures, intellectual and social, that I had always known took on a feeling that all was a part of preparation for whatever roles war and, hopefully, peace would present. Each day began with teachers and students alike standing and reciting our "Pledge of Allegiance" followed by a prayer for those in need or danger, near and far. While all courses were infused with a sense of the war as a common patriotic sheen, if one listened carefully and read the newspapers and magazines with an open mind, there were questions about the nature of the conflict and what ends could be imagined. Mr. DiRenzo pointed out the flash points on the wall map of Europe: the bulge of Nazi territory, the strange line drawn between that world and Stalin's USSR, seemingly mortal enemies now as allies.

Miss Franks's English class continued as the core of my studies. There we marched along the path of American literature: Longfellow, Melville, Poe. Walt Whitman's "Oh Captain, My Captain" called up the grief of loss. And, like an antidote to despair: "I celebrate myself, and sing myself." Often, at the end of a school day, I would return to her classroom where, seated on either side of her desk, we would discuss one of the poems in greater depth than a class period offered.

On one such afternoon, my teacher reached into her briefcase and took out a small, plain covered book. "Hélène," she said. "I've been thinking of a novel that could be useful to your path." She handed it over to me. "*All Quiet On The Western Front* follows a young soldier's journey through the chaos and fear of the First World War as he considers lessons he has been taught by his culture and the deep truth of the lessons he is learning in the trenches. When I first read it, only a few years older than you are now, in my second year at Smith, it shook me as nothing I've ever experienced." A pause. "As you will see, Erich Maria Remarque is looking at war through the eyes of a German soldier, thrown into a tragedy that befell the youth on both sides of the battle lines. As are German youth today, he is The Other, and yet as the shells explode and harsh gas creeps across the fields of France, he is no different than The Other sworn to his death."

We sat silently as I opened to the first page. *We are at rest, five miles behind the front.* "Thank you," I said. "It sounds like a powerful book."

"Read it slowly. Let each few pages settle into your sense of that one boy." Another pause. "And, Hélène, let's have this reading be just between us. I'm afraid that the powers that be would not be able to see beyond the politics and the fear of the moment."

I nodded. "I understand. Thank you for sharing it with me." She nodded, and I added the small volume to my school books and left. My footsteps echoed as I walked down the hall and out onto Main Street toward home.

Winter grudgingly gave way to spring in Sutton, Maine. The gray piles of snow along the city streets melted, the liberated waters trickling into the

Nine Falls. The remaining sand and trash was swept up and carted away by the city road crews. When the skunk cabbage leaves along the river burst open, Papa, Bénédicte, and I tramped down a path to the river above the mills. There, a tradition of Maine, we picked the tight green whorls of fiddlehead greens. "*Le goût du printemps*, the taste of spring," Pépère would always say.

April gave way to May. Each morning as I dressed for school, I would close my eyes and mentally check another day off the calendar, another day closer to Jim's return from college. As if in a waking dream I thought of warm days, sharing rides to secret spots, his arms drawing me near. And one day a letter arrived confirming my reveries. My love would arrive in Sutton on May 17, a Friday. After unpacking and dinner with his parents, he would drive across the river and into my arms. "*Mon amour.*"

At last, as I sat on the porch, Jim's Model A Ford drove up the hill, past St. Hyacinth's playground, and up to the home of la famille Lévesque. As he jumped out of the car, I floated down the stairs. We held each other in an embrace that was at once powerful and as light as a spring breeze. He stepped back and then reached out with both hands to my cheeks. He kissed my forehead. "Oh, my love!" he said. Then he turned, opened the passenger door, waited while I climbed in, then walked around and took his place behind the wheel. As he started the engine, he looked over and said, "I thought we could go in to the Western Prom and watch the sunset." He put the car in gear, and we drove off through Sutton, toward the big city and the next chapter.

In the green park on a high bluff looking west, we could see the tall chimney of the Nine Falls Mill, the pivot point of our hometown, and beyond that the far-off foothills of the White Mountains. We got out of the car and walked over to a gazebo. Jim drew me into his arms and we just sat in the cascade of our love.

As the sun began its descent, Jim sat back and moved away just a bit so that our eyes could continue our embrace. "My sweet," he said. "I have something new to tell you." A pause. "I won't be going back to Dartmouth in the fall." Another pause. "I've enlisted in the Army Air Corps to be a pilot....I will leave for my training next Tuesday."

I sat, shocked beyond any reply. It was as if a part of my future were melting and running away to the river and into the ocean.

"I just felt I had no choice," he said. "I owe our country no less than your brothers are giving to the cause of freedom."

"But...." I tried to control my breathing, to still my surging brain, to hold back tears. "It seems so sudden....I mean...next Tuesday!"

"It was sudden for me as well. As the spring came to the mountains, I read of our country's mobilization. Watched fraternity brothers withdraw from the college and enlist. I knew that I couldn't hide behind history and economics classes. So when an enlistment officer came on campus, I made my decision. He agreed that I could finish my semester, take my exams. But that meant that I would only have these few days to move my belongings home…and to hold you in my arms."

After another long hug he touched my cheeks and wiped away the tears I had hardly known I'd wept.

"We will win this war, whenever it begins. Your brothers on land and sea. Me in one of the slashing, silver fighters that are rolling off our assembly lines. America will carry the day. And I will return to you, ma chère Hélène, to our future, of home, children…you and me, together forever."

Just for a moment it seemed to me that I could hear the tone of a recruitment message on the radio, the sense of destiny in a FDR fireside chat. But that strange clarity melted into a whirlpool of love and fear. I had no words.

"My parents, of course, I had to let them know my plans from the beginning. They are going to have a gathering of a few friends at our camp at the lake this Sunday. They want you to be there with us. I'll pick you up around one o'clock…if that's okay."

I just nodded. "But Tuesday?" I said.

"The sooner the better, I guess," said my love. Then we walked back to the Ford and drove back to Sutton, past his grand house, the mill, across the river, and up the hill to my home.

"The next couple of days are going to be crazy," Jim said. "Packing, paper work. But I'll see you Sunday."

There was nothing left of the moment except for a hug and a kiss. And as I walked up the steps of home, the purr of the Ford as it drove away.

Thus, a Sunday unlike any I had known arrived. After Mass, our family returned to our home, and Mémère and Maman dove into finishing dinner. Pépère and Papa sat with the Sunday papers in the company of "Father Whiskey" and "Uncle Ale." I walked into my bedroom and began changing into an outfit—tan slacks and a white blouse with a red and blue scarf—that I felt would be right for the Fredericks's lakeside cottage. Bénédicte walked in. My sister who was no longer my "little sister."

"How are you doing?" she asked. "This must be a tough day for you and Jim's family."

"I guess I'm okay. I can't really get my head around it all. Especially how fast everything is happening." I took a deep breath and let it flow out at its own pace. "Do you think this outfit will pass Mrs. Fredericks' inspection?" I asked with a little grin.

"For sure," Béné said. "You'll be *la belle du lac*." We both laughed. Then we heard the tooting of a Model A's horn. I gave Béné a hug, walked past Papa on his chair, blew a kiss to Maman in her kitchen. Then walked out to whatever the day and the future held. I climbed into the Ford and gave my love a kiss. As he drove off, he reached over and turned on the radio. Our Sunday was filled with Duke Ellington and his band calling on all to "Take the A Train." I thought of all the twists and turns life would take.

Sunday afternoon had arrived on a wisp of warm spring air. We rode silently up the curves and hills of River Road, tracing the path of the Nine Falls. After a half hour, he turned onto a narrow side road and then into a gravel path that skirted a farm yard. He stopped at an old wooden gate, got out, and swung it open. After driving through, he shut the gate, and then we continued down a long hill. Glimpses of Little Loon Lake flashed through the trees. After a half mile, my wonderful chauffeur slowed as we passed a dozen or so cars parked on the edge of the path. Finally he pulled into a parking space in front of a large, dark-stained log camp. Over the door a sign proclaimed CAMP CONTENT. Jim came around and opened the door for me. "My sweet Hélène," he said. "Welcome to my favorite spot on Earth." Through the screened windows I could hear the social murmurings of the gathering. I took a deep breath and, as I entered, Jim reached out and gave my shoulder a reassuring squeeze.

We passed through the kitchen into a broad living room that faced the lake. Guests were arrayed in groups, chatting, laughing, as if this afternoon was somehow a joyous occasion, a graduation, a commencement of some sort. In one corner, a dark wooden table offered a profusion of liquor bottles, mixers, and a bucket of ice. Clinking glasses seemed like percussion to the upbeat jazz of conversations. As I scanned the room, the only faces I recognized were Diane, the Fredericks' maid, and Mr. and Mrs. Warde, my friend Dorcas's parents. Jim got me a glass of ginger ale, and a highball for himself. Then I followed him out onto the broad porch. A scattering of guests stood around the lawn atop a bluff that looked out over the lake to the splashes of greens of the hills beyond. From down by the beach, other voices wafted upward.

Jim's parents stood at one end of the porch, greeting their guests, as one might have imagined the Lord and Lady of a manor receiving lesser nobility. I followed their only son over to them.

"Ah, here he is, at last!" his father announced. "Sutton's Eddie Rickenbacker in training!"

"And Miss Lévesque," Mrs. Fredericks added. "My dear Hélène. So glad that you could join us."

I followed Jim around the porch and back into the living room. He introduced me to a sampling of Sutton's finest. Diane and I made eye contact, as if we understood our status as valued "others." I followed my love to the bar where he refilled our glasses, offering me an upgrade, which I politely refused. Then we walked back out onto the porch and over to his parents.

Mrs. Fredericks nodded to her husband, reached over to a hook attached to the log wall, and took down a small brass triangle and rod. In a seemingly practiced sequence, she tinkled it. As people looked up, she announced, "Everyone—please join us in the living room." Then she and her husband led their son, their neighbors, and me, Hélène Honoré, inside.

The guests settled themselves into an arc surrounding their hosts and Jim, who held my hand. A few of the men returned to the drinks buffet. Diane wended her way around the room, collecting empty glasses, small plates, and rumpled napkins. Mr. and Mrs. Fredericks stood with stately patience as the gathered settled into the moment.

"My friends," Mr. Fredericks intoned. "We've invited you here to recognize, to celebrate, the next brave step of James Stuart Fredericks, our dear son, into his manhood. As you know, Jim has chosen, freely chosen, to enter the service of the Army Air Corps. In two short days he will join the young generation of true Americans, to defend our freedoms from the myriad dangers we face." There was a smattering of polite applause.

His wife continued, "And I know you will all hold him, and all the sons of Sutton and afar, in your hearts and minds." She paused. "And I would be remiss if I did not introduce James's new, dear friend." She turned toward me. "Mademoiselle Lévesque." Her tongue drew out the syllables. "Hey-lenn. We are glad to have you with us today and in the difficult days to come." She reached over to a little table, picked up a small, gift-wrapped package, and handed it to me. "From us to you, a small token of our connection, your connection to one we love so dearly. Please, ma chérie, open it."I tore off the paper and found a box of writing paper and envelopes. "Thank you," I said to his parents. "You're very kind."

"*Et merci à vous*. I'm sure that your letters will be yet another tie of James to home." She nodded to her husband.

"And now, friends and neighbors," he said, "we thank you for joining us today. I know that James will cherish your kindness, support, and love of our country." The gathered Suttoners took their cue and, calling to those on the beach, began to walk to their cars. I stood next to Jim as he shook hands with the men and endured the glancing hugs of the ladies.

And suddenly, my friend Dorcas stepped up to me. We embraced, and then she stepped back and took my shoulders in her hands. "Chère, chère Hélène," she said. "I had to be here for you as well as Jim." We hugged again and then she turned to follow her parents. The cars coughed and roared toward the hill and away to Sutton, Maine, on the Nine Falls River.

Soon there were only Jim, his parents, and me, standing in the sudden silence. Only the splash of the waves on the shore of Little Loon Lake and the clink of glasses and small China plates as Diane cleaned up after the gathering.

The rest of the day, a warm Sunday in Maine spring, was like a blur. The ride up and away from the lake, the sudden glimpse of the tall chimney of the mill as we crested a hill on the edge of Sutton, crossing the Nine Falls into Frenchtown, parking by my home—all like snapshots of a world that I would have to fight to hold near. And then my love held me close. "There comes a time," he said. He reached over into the glove compartment of his Ford and took out a square, tan envelope. "From me to you, the address on the outside is my APO address," he said. "Open it if you wish, but why don't you wait until later to read the letter." I opened the envelope as carefully as possible. Inside I found two pages of the handwriting I had come to recognize as his. The folded sheets held an eight by ten inch copy of his Sutton High graduation photograph. "This old me will have to do for now," he said with a bit of a laugh. "In a couple of months I'll update it with the new me with my lieutenant's bars, a fighter-bomber pilot at last."

Then we shared a long, silent hug. "There comes a time," Jim said again. And I climbed down from the car and walked up the stairs of my home, hearing the roar of the departing Model A over the background sighs of the Nine Falls Mill.

I walked into our apartment, the only home I'd ever known. And for a moment all seemed normal. Papa was in his chair, listening to the end of the Red Sox game with his companions, "Father" and "Uncle," rooting against the enemy, the Yankees, a nation detested only a little less than the Nazis.

He looked up and gave me a wave. Bénédicte came out of her room and walked over to me.

"How was the party at the lake?" she asked.

"It was fine," I said. "Let's go into the kitchen with Maman. No need to tell the story twice." Béné nodded, and we walked away from the roar of the Fenway Park crowd. Ted Williams, Papa informed us, had just hit a home run.

Maman was at the counter, arms deep into her deep, yellow mixing bowl, kneading the dough for our weekly bread. "Ah, ma chérie," she said. "*Tu as passé une bonne fête*? She lifted a floured hand and waved Béné and me into chairs at the table. "Maybe some tea," she said. "The dough is almost finished." Scripted, knowing our parts, we sisters rose to her command: cups and saucers onto the table, water heating on the stove, teapot prepped with four bags of Tetley Tea leaves. The mixing bowl enshrouded with a damp dish towel, the three of us, les femmes Lévesque, watched the steam sneaking out of the teapot spout. Béné and our mother sat quietly, waiting for tea and my story. Maman poured. I took a deep sip.

"Well, it was not awful. The guests were all very proud of Jim, gave him their best wishes." We all took sips. Maman broke the pause, getting up for a plate of cookies. She returned, and they waited. "It was kind of strange, in a way. When Jim and I arrived, the party had been going on for a couple of hours. Then his parents made their little speeches and then hustled the guests out. He and I hadn't been there for more than fifteen or twenty minutes." I let that roll around in my mind. "It seemed like the party was more for his father and mother, to make sure everyone in Sutton society knew what a great job they'd done raising their son."

"Maybe they didn't want Jim to have to be in the spotlight too long," Béné said.

"Maybe," I replied. "But it never felt like the spotlight was off them. And his mother introduced me to the guests, making a point of showing off her French. And she gave me this fancy stationery, as if to remind me that I have a duty to write to Jim…as if I wouldn't."

"I'm sure it is *très difficile*, very hard, for his parents." Maman said. "I know I can never find a moment of rest from my fears for *tes frères*. It feels like the war is very, very close, even if the country is not fighting. *Mon Dieu, les avions des Boches*, they are dropping bombs on England, on the land where Paul has chosen to fight." She got up and walked over to check her dough.

"It's going to work out okay," Béné said.

"I guess that's all we can hope for," I replied. "I need a nap." I finished my tea, got up, and walked over to the sink with my cup and saucer. I looked first at Maman and then at Béné. "Merci, merci beaucoup." I picked up the stationary gifted by Mrs. Fredericks and the envelope from her son and walked out through the living room. It seemed the Red Sox had lost another. Papa spread out his hands in a gesture of "what can you do about fate and luck?" "*C'est la vie*," he said.

"*Mais oui, Papa*," I replied. "*La vie est étrange*."

I walked into my bedroom, dropped the Fredericks' papers onto my nightstand, and flopped onto my bed, my forearm over my eyes. One breath. Another breath. And then I dropped off to sleep.

I am riding in Jim's Model A. It is dark, a dark, dark countryside, away from the glow of the Nine Falls Mill. The car runs up and down the hills on a narrow black tarred road. The radio is playing Frank Sinatra singing "I'll Be Seeing You," with Tommy Dorsey's band playing backup in what sounds like a dirge. "I'll be looking at the moon/ but I'll be seeing you." Rain begins to slash at the windshield; gusts of wind buffet the car. Headlights probe the darkness, the curves. And then I look over at the driver's seat and there is no one there. My Jim is not there. I am alone in the storm.

Then Béné is stroking my forearm, whispering that it's time for dinner.

May became June. Each evening I wrote a page or so to Jim on the creamy stationary I'd been gifted as part of his departure. I mailed them off to him, almost as a checking-off of the weeks of his service. But I never got any reply from my love. After civics class one day, Mr. DiRenzo explained that probably the officer training rules kept him from writing; I had to believe he was correct. I had put Jim's picture in a frame I bought at the local McClellan's department store. It sat on my bedside table, the last thing I saw at night and the first thing as another morning arrived. Somehow I couldn't bring myself to read his farewell letter. It remained in its envelope in the bedside table drawer. Many times I took it out and even removed the two small pages, but it never felt as if the time were right.

Junior year at Sutton High drew to its close. I gave my final report in civics class: "The Constitution and War." In the discussion afterward, we argued over whether President Roosevelt had gone beyond his granted powers by expanding the military and giving aid to Britain in his Lend-Lease Act. I survived trigonometry, although once again I agreed with Dorcas that, as with algebra, there was no existence of trig in the real world. In college prep English, we discussed *The Red Badge of Courage* and how we humans react to fear and duty in a violent world.

Later, in what had become a weekly meeting, Miss Franks and I contrasted Stephen Crane's view of soldiers in the Civil War to that of Erich Maria Remarque's German soldier's disillusionment with his childhood lessons of honor, duty, and respect for authority, especially his teachers.

"And that is just why they let us down so badly. The idea of authority, which they represented, was associated in our minds with a greater insight and manlier wisdom. But the first death we saw shattered this belief.... And we saw that there was nothing of their world left. We were all at once terribly alone; and alone we must see it through."

On the last day of school I stopped by her classroom to say goodbye to one who had become much more than just a teacher of English. She looked up and smiled.

"I want to thank you for all your help this year," I said.

"Oh, Hélène," she replied. "It has been a great learning experience for me, as well. It's rare that a teacher will have a student with whom to share great works and great discoveries."

"I'm really looking forward to senior English. And again, many thanks."

For a moment, it seemed as if my mentor were going to stand. Rather, she reached out across her desk, and we shared a clasp of hands. "We'll talk about life after high school. I feel I can hear the women at Smith calling. Until then, be well, my dear."

We shared a smile, and then I walked out into my last summer as a high school girl.

As June drew toward its close, the convulsions of a world at war took an explosive twist. On the 22nd, Hitler and his Wehrmacht smashed his cynical pact with Stalin and invaded the USSR. While still, in theory, neutral, the US ramped up preparedness and began supplying Russia with military aid. A growing debate raged between those who supported FDR's call for standing strong against dictatorship and others, both in and outside of government, who advocated for "fortress America" and isolation.

La famille Lévesque was drawn along by the tides of war. Erland, in Hawaii, wrote to tell us that he had been assigned to duty on a heavy cruiser, the *New Orleans*, part of the Pacific Fleet. More and more it seemed that our navy was gearing up for conflict with the Japanese, probably in the South Pacific in support of the British and French colonies threatened by "the Nips." Geno had finished his basic and advanced infantry training and had been assigned as a fire direction tactician with an artillery battalion, for the time being in Texas. And at long last, Paul, the eldest, sent a letter from England.

His Canadian division had been assigned to a training base in the Midlands and had, at least for now, not faced the onslaught of Nazi bombers.

But as the conflict roiled, in the news and our living room, I had no word from Jim. I continued to write, as much to reassure my fears as to share news of the home front with my dear. One afternoon, Dorcas and I met in the park on the banks of the Nine Falls. She told me that her parents had had dinner at the Fredericks's home the week before.

"Mr. Fredericks told my folks that they had heard from Jim and that his flight training was going well. It looked as if he was going to be selected for fighter-bomber training."

"Well," I said. "That's what he was hoping to get. I guess that's good news. Did they say anything about how he was doing?"

My friend paused for a moment. "My mother said that Mrs. Fredericks said Jim was so busy, so deeply committed to his training, that he'd hardly had time to even drop them a note. I guess that makes sense...."

As the summer unfolded, I filled my time with taking care of my cousin Eugénie's two little children. Only a year older than I, she had left Sutton High after her sophomore year and four months later married Frankie Gouzie, an older guy from our neighborhood. That had been followed in quick succession by two children, a boy and then a girl. I mentioned to Maman that it seemed that was a bit quick. She sighed and replied, "*Ah, mais oui, ma fille*. But as Monseigneur says, 'To temper God's blessings with children, the man and wife must live like brother and sister.'"

Now, Eugénie and her mother, Tante Jacqueline, had both taken advantage of the surge of demand for paper at the Nine Falls Mill and had jobs in the sorting department. Along with Uncle Robert, their finances were booming, although at the cost, as Aunt Jacqueline said, of so little time with *les petits enfants*. Throughout Frenchtown, families were showing the results of the return of good times: summer dresses, new Fords, re-shingled roofs, a week's vacation at the lake, children who could plan to complete high school. Of course we were all aware of the looming threats across both the shrinking moats of Fortress America. But for now we could hope, could pray for peace.

But for me, Hélène Honoré, there were times when, as the sun began its summer descent behind the western hills, that I would stand alone at the crest of the Frenchtown hill, gazing to the east. Nearest, I could see St. Hyacinth with its golden spire gleaming in the day's last light. Next, in the valley of the Nine Falls, was the mill giving off a less exalted glow. And then the eastern slope of Sutton, Maine. And to me it was as if the Fredericks's neighborhood, mon cher James' home, was swallowed in a dark cloud that my eyes could not penetrate.

Then, on August 30, 1941, the day before my eighteenth birthday, Mr. O'Connor, our postman, brought me the gift I had been wishing for since May. In our mailbox, along with the telephone bill and pages of ads for the local markets, there was a slim, white envelope, addressed to me, Hélène Honoré Lévesque. And in the upper left corner I read: James S. Fredericks/ APO 370/ United States Army Air Corps. Shaking like a reed on the riverbank, I hurried up the stairs, into our apartment, and into my bedroom. I sat on my bed, turned on the bedside table lamp, and moved my love's photograph so that his eyes met mine. Then I carefully opened the envelope and, somewhat afraid of what would follow, took out a single sheet of white, lined paper. And there, in handwriting that I recognized and dreamed of, my Jim's voice spoke out to me.

Dear, chère, chère Hélène,

I am so sorry that I have not written since I left Sutton and your arms. I have no excuse, only an explanation that our training has been so intense, so totally consuming that by each day's end, all I could do was collapse on my cot, after polishing my boots and making sure that my aviator's outfit was neat for the next day. And then I would lie back, hands under my head, and drift off to hard-earned sleep, always thinking and then dreaming only of you.

And now this first part of my new life is drawing to a close. On September 9, my air corps company will be given our first lieutenant's bars and will be sworn in as part of the armed forces that will keep our country free and beat back the evil forces that threaten all God's people. Then my fellow fliers, who have become like brothers (I know it sounds corny, but it's true) and I will be sent to Maxwell Air Base in Alabama to begin advanced training as fighter-bomber pilots. You probably remember that when I last held you in my arms, I told you that that was my dream. And here's the best news!!! Before our transport to Maxwell we are being given two weeks of leave. Fourteen days!!

Of course, travel up to Sutton from McGuire Air Base here in New Jersey and back will take two or three of those days each way, but still, for a week I'll be as much a civilian as I'll be for the next three years. I've spoken to my parents by phone (they accepted my collect call!) and they want to meet me at my Uncle Ted and Aunt Gertrude's place in Marblehead, Mass. After a couple of days we'll drive to Maine. And then there will be their friends giving best wishes, and church. But I've told them that I MUST have at least a whole day to spend with you. And they understand. So I'll let you know when I'm in town. And then my Model A (God it seems like ages since I've driven—you don't drive planes!) will crest the hill and you will be mine forever.

À bientôt, ma chère, chère Hélène.

I read my darling's letter three times and then slipped it into the little drawer on top of the one, still unread, from the day of his departure. Two weeks, two weeks and he would return, as he had promised, if only for a ripple in the flow of our lives. Two weeks. I stood up, took a deep breath, and walked out into the living room, as if to ride the current toward my love.

Béné looked up from her book. "Are you okay?" she asked.

It took a moment to focus. "Yes," I replied. "Yes. Why?"

"When you came home you just went right to your room, hardly noticed that Papa and I were here."

"Sorry. I'd just gotten a letter from Jim! After all these days! Opening it was the only thing in my mind. Yes, I'm okay."

"And how's he doing?"

I looked around the room and noticed that Papa had put his *Sutton Democrat* down and was listening while looking off toward the kitchen. "He's coming home," I said. "His basic training will be over in about a week, and then he will have about a week before heading off to fighter-bomber school."

"Oh, Hélène, I'm so glad for you," Béné said. Then she got up and came over for a long hug. "Let's tell Maman." As we headed for the kitchen I looked back and saw that Papa was watching his two nearly grown daughters. I thought I could see the hint of a smile on his unshaven face.

Maman was sitting at the kitchen table with a cup of tea. Her cheeks were reddened from the oven. "Ah, mes filles," she said. "Hélène, your birthday cake, just like you asked, *un gâteau au chocolat*, is almost finished. Strawberry jam filling and chocolate icing, correct?"

"*Oui, Maman. C'est parfait.*" Béné and I sat down. "I have some news," I continued. "Jim is coming home! He'll be here in the middle of next month for a couple of days before he leaves for more training."

"Oh, that is wonderful news," Maman replied. "Tante Jacqueline, Oncle Robert, et Cousine Eugénie , they will be so happy for you when they come for your birthday party tomorrow. But such a short visit!"

"I know. But I guess I have to be grateful."

"It's been so long since nos frères have been away," Béné added.

Maman just looked at her tea. Then she sighed, stood, and walked over to the oven. She took out the two baking pans and tested one with a toothpick. "*C'est fini*," she said. Now I can start fixing dinner. Remember, ton père, he's doing the night tower tonight."

The next day les trois femmes Lévesque returned from eleven o'clock mass to find Papa at the kitchen table with a coffee. After we changed out of our church outfits, Maman beat up the frosting for the cake while Béné and I set out the dishes, cups, and silverware for my party. Then we puffed up the living room and moved in the kitchen chairs. Béné disappeared into her bedroom and returned with a small package wrapped in birthday paper. "Here, dear sister," she said. "A little birthday gift. Why don't you open it now? Just us two."

I tore off the wrapping. It was a small notebook, bound in dark green. "Oh, Béné, it's lovely. Thank you so much."

"I thought it would be really nice for a journal," she said. "Someday you and Jim can share it…maybe with your children." She gave a happy little giggle.

Later that afternoon, my birthday party, my eighteenth, seemed to acknowledge that Hélène Honoré was no longer a little girl. I shared the news of Jim's homecoming with the relatives. It was clear that Cousine Eugénie and Béné were excited by the story, like a tale in a *True Romance* magazine. Uncle Robert and Papa expounded on patriotism and all that we on the home front were doing to support FDR and the troops. Andy and Beverly, Eugénie's kids, played with the little wooden cars and trucks that les enfants Lévesque had pushed around when we were younger and so much more innocent. And after the cake and hugs and best wishes, la famille DuBois took their leave.

Then, on Monday, September 1, 1941, it was back to school. Mr. Sampson welcomed us, "the proud Sutton High School Class of 1942," to the culmination of our high school years, leading to the commencement of whichever paths would open to our young lives. Then we all stood, recited the Pledge of Allegiance, and sang "God Bless America."

I tried to settle into what was supposed to be the crowning year in Sutton schools for me and my classmates. But whether senior math, French IV, current events and civics, or even English IV, my concentration ebbed and flowed, always toward my Jim's arrival. One day in French, Mr. Charrette snapped me back to our discussion of *Tartuffe*. "*Alors, Mademoiselle Lévesque! Tu es endormie*?" Most of my classmates giggled, but in my moment of confusion, I saw Dorcas looking at me with real concern. Later, we met in the hall.

"Heck," she asked, "are you okay? You seem kind of somewhere else."

"I'm okay, I guess. It's just that Jim's homecoming keeps creeping into my mind."

"I'm sure," my best friend said. "You always know where you can find me."

"Thanks. Thanks so much," I replied. "I just wish I could speed up the days."

And as I checked off each September day, my family understood my distance at the dinner table, my disappearance, earlier and earlier, into my room for homework and bed. "*Dors bien, ma chère*," Maman would say. Often Béné would meet me as I crossed the living room and gift me with a hug. "Six more days," she'd say, continuing the countdown. And Papa, with his papers, would turn down the radio as he waited to depart for his get-up tower at the mill.

And then, Saturday, September 14, just before I fled to my room and Miss Franks's English assignment, *The Sun Also Rises*, the telephone rang. I picked it up and said, "Hello?" with a bit of a whisper in my voice.

"I have a person-to-person call to 'Hay-Leen Laveck,'" said the operator.

"Speaking."

"Go ahead, please."

And then it was him, or at least his voice. "Hello, my love. It's me, and I'm almost home, almost home to you."

"Oh, Jim…Jim! It's been so long! It feels like…."

"I know!" he said. "Me too." Then his voice dropped into a more instructive tone. "We're driving up from Marblehead this evening. We should get there around midnight."

"And tomorrow!?"

"Mother insists that we all get up for church at eleven. And then starting around two o'clock she's set up a gathering of family and friends. If it works for you can you join us a bit later, to let the first wave ebb, maybe about four?"

"Oh, yes. Oh, yes! And what about Monday and Tuesday?"

There was just a moment's pause. "I'm still not sure what the parents have mapped out." And then as if he could sense the pause in my breath, "But they know, I've been very firm, that one whole day is just for you and me."

I exhaled. "Well, I'll cut my classes on either day." I giggled. "That will be a first for me."

"I promise it will be worth it!" he laughed. "Okay, my uncle's phone bill is climbing. Oh, ma chère, I can't wait for our first hug."

The phone clicked. And just as I set it into its cradle, Papa walked in from the kitchen, carrying a fresh quart of Balentine. Maman and Béné followed. They sat down, not as inquisitors but as ma chère famille. "That was Jim," I said, as if an explanation was necessary. "He'll be home late tonight. He'll be here for three days."

Papa sipped and then said, "Better than nothing."

Béné and Maman both stood and shared hugs. Seemingly there was nothing left to be said, at least for the moment.

Sunday morning arrived warm in the glow of early autumn. Maman and Béné bustled around the kitchen, prepping for the family meal of the week. They toned down the volume of their chatting so as not to wake Papa, asleep after finishing his night on the "get-up" shift. I dressed for Mass and then laid out another outfit, one I hoped would be just right for the moment that I walked back into Jim's world.

And then it was time for church. Les trois femmes Lévesque walked down the hill and into the gray stone sanctuary of St. Hyacinth. As at every Mass, as I entered I dipped my fingers in the font of Holy Water and traced the sign of the cross. We slipped into a pew, Maman nodding to neighbors, and knelt down as Monseigneur Desjardins began the liturgy.

My mind wandered away from the ritual and came to rest on the stained glass window above the altar. The morning sun shone across the Nine Falls River, illuminating God's servant and Our Savior's Holy Mother. Mary the Virgin, dressed in blue, glowing on a morning one thousand, nine hundred and forty-one years after the miracle of her Son's birth. Her face radiated acceptance and compassion, her eyes fixed on the promise of paradise she and all the faithful were given. And then I was called back to the now of church and family and Jim. I followed Maman and Béné out of the pew, and up to the altar to receive holy communion, the body and blood of Our Savior. And as I looked up toward the altar this time, my gaze was drawn to Jesus in agony on the cross, His gaze away from Earth and into the eternal heavens.

Back home, we walked in to find Papa enthroned in his chair, a cup of café au lait laying the base for later visits from "Papa G and Uncle B." The headlines of the *Sunday Telegram* told of grinding battles between the German and Soviet armies and the seemingly unstoppable flood of the Japanese across the face of Asia. Béné and I set the table while Maman removed the pot roast from the oven and began to whisk her legendary gravy, enriched with just a splash of red wine. Then as we gathered *à table*, Maman offered a prayer, beseeching Our Savior to protect Paul, Geno, and Erland, les fils, nos frères, as they served our nation's call to arms.

The afternoon ticked by so slowly. The Red Sox trailed. Dick Tracy and Superman each saved the day. The kitchen cleaned, Maman plopped down at the table with a cup of tea. I was washed over with a sense that, while nothing so far of this day was different from all our Sundays, my young life was flowing, like the Nine Falls toward the final cataract and then the sea. At long last, the old clock on the wall read three o'clock. I went into the bathroom, freshened up my face and fluffed my hair. Then in my bedroom I changed into my best outfit, one I hoped would help present me as a young woman rather than a love-smitten girl.

I walked into the living room to find my family gathered, each trying to make the moment seem normal. I picked up the car keys. Papa looked up and I blew him a kiss. Béné gave me a long hug. Maman walked to me, stroked my cheek, and drew me close. "*Tu es une bonne jeune femme, ma chère*" she whispered. A good young woman.

Feeling borne on their love, I turned, walked down the stairs and over to the Chevy. For a moment, I was struck by the realization that when Jim first came into my life, I was too young to drive. I climbed in and drove off, down the hill, over the river, following the path that love or fate had laid before me.

As I drove up to Jim's house, cars lined both sides of the streets. People were walking down from the high front porch where Mr. Fredericks stood, as if offering benediction. I pulled into a space a half block down the side street and walked back to the house. People nodded to me as they passed. As I reached the front steps, Mr. Fredericks recognized me. "Ah, Hélène, at last. Please go right in. James is waiting for you." Then he turned to another couple and bid them farewell.

I walked down the front hall, past the stately grandfather clock. At the living room entrance, I met Diane, the Fredericks' serveuse. Rather unexpectedly, she gifted me with a hug, whispering that Mrs. Fredericks was in top form. I walked in and there, to his mother's left and a half step behind, was

Jim. He stepped out to me, opened his arms, and drew me in, into his heart. "Oh Hélène, my Hélène! It's been so very long!"

I melted into his embrace. "*Jim, je t'adore.*"

Suddenly, as if from very far away, I heard the clearing of a throat. Jim stepped back, recalled to proper decorum by his mother's presence. "Ah, Hélène," she said. "Welcome to our home. It seems like forever since we dined together. I hope that all is well with your family."

"Yes, thank you. We are well and it seems like my brothers are all safe in their units."

"We can only pray for the safety of all our brave men who serve our country." Then she reached out and placed her hand on her son's arm. "If you'll excuse us now, my dear. The gathering is coming to a close and there are many of our friends who wish to bid Jim their best wishes." Then she guided her only son toward the front hall.

Feeling rather abandoned, I walked around the room, past the rich, red brick fireplace, looking at the gently used volumes of English and nineteenth century American literature. Then I noticed a side table with a plate of hors d'oeuvres and a short cut glass vessel filled to near the top with a light brown liquid. I tried a stuffed mushroom cap and then nibbled a thin slice of dark bread with a golden yellow, oozing cheese. I picked up the glass and sniffed. Clearly it was a variety of liquor, although it smelled much less harsh than that of Papa's Golden Wedding that had so informed my childhood nose. I sipped. There was a bit of a burn, but then it settled into my stomach with a feeling of release. I sipped again and again. Then, hearing footsteps, I took a short swallow, pushed the glass off to the side of the table, and stepped away.

It was Jim. Alone! He walked over to me with open arms. As he bent for a kiss, he paused and sniffed. "Thirsty?" he asked. I shrugged. Then my love drew me into a kiss, the kiss that I'd been dreaming of for months. "Tomorrow. Tomorrow is our day. I'll pick you up at nine."

"What are the plans?"

"To be together. A late breakfast? A ride out to the ocean? And let's top it off with a swim and a picnic for two at Camp Content. The water ought to be just perfect for an evening swim. And then, the sunset over Little Loon Lake, like a warm blanket. Sound okay?"

My thoughts swirled, whether from the drink or the kiss.

"It's all that I've been dreaming of."

"Don't forget your swimsuit. There are plenty of towels at camp."

There were footsteps in the front hall; then someone cleared their throat.

Jim stepped aside a bit as his parents walked in, his father relaxed and hearty, his mother a bit drawn yet with a hint of fire in her eyes.

"Well, my boy," his father said. "It's clear that Sutton wishes you their very best as the next step of your grand adventure unfolds." He reached over and gave Jim's shoulder a hearty smack.

"Thank you, Father," Jim replied. "It's much appreciated."

"Your mother and I have a few items, documents and family plans, that we wish to go over with you this evening. Better to see to it tonight before the clock winds all the way down." He made a half turn away from us, facing the living room door. Mrs. Fredericks stood stark still, her gaze never leaving her son and me.

I took my cue. "I really need to be going, too," I said. "My parents will be pleased to know what a great reception Sutton gave your son." Jim and I started to leave. Then I turned back to where his mother stood. "Mrs. Fredericks, I appreciate being able to share moments with you and your son."

For a moment, her face was a blank. "Well, my dear," she said, with a chill like a December wind off the ocean. "As I'm sure that your parents would agree, family is not easily shared."

Jim took my arm and guided me out into the evening. "I'm sorry for that," he said. "Please understand that Mother is distraught about my leaving for training. She's proud of my service but…well, I've been the center of her world forever. I guess it's a little hard for her to share." He took a deep breath. "And tomorrow is ours." We walked down the curved granite stairs from the porch and down the street to the Lévesque Chevy. "Drive safely and sleep well," said my love. "I'll see you at nine sharp tomorrow."

Monday, September 15, 1941, bloomed like a gift from God. The leaves on the old maple just outside my bedroom window shone brightly, untouched, as yet, by frost. I chose my light green slacks and white blouse, packed my swimsuit into a small shoulder bag, and walked out to meet the day.

Papa and Maman were at the kitchen table, sharing a coffee after his late night shift at the mill. Mon père looked at me, startled that I hadn't left for school.

Maman stepped into the breach. "François, Hélène is staying home from school. She and Jim are going to have a day to share together."

Papa looked at me and then nodded. "*Je comprends*," he said.

"Thank you. Thanks for understanding, merci," I said. Then I stood and walked out of the kitchen.

Maman's voice followed me. "Be safe, ma chère."

Outside in the morning, I stood and looked around the neighborhood that for years had been the anchor of my young girl's life: the row of two-family mill town houses facing the playground, St. Hyacinth's School next to the red brick convent, the spire of God's gray church. For a moment I tried to envision how my life would flow out and away from the moment: graduation, a job, marriage to James Stuart Fredericks, children, a different town or state? Would this house, this home, become a place to visit on holidays, for funerals? My eighteen-year-old reverie ended as Jim drove up in his Model A, windows down, radio playing Glen Miller's "In the Mood."

He climbed out of the car, walked around, and gave me a deep, playful bow. "*Ma chère mademoiselle, bienvenue à notre jour*!" I curtsied and spun a pirouette to my side of our so-American coach. My chauffeur, my love, climbed in behind the wheel, reached down to the starter key, and then gave my thigh a quick pat. "We're off," he said and we drove down the hill, across the Nine Falls toward breakfast.

The rest of the morning seemed a combination of snapshot moments and a flow of scenes from a script that was ours alone. The Marcel's Diner was a collage of voices, clanking of dishes, and the smell of real Maine maple syrup on my stack of pancakes. Our special spot, the green park on the Western Promenade, where four months earlier Jim had told me of his enlistment. He asked me how school was going, how it felt to be a grown-up senior? Beyond "okay," I really didn't have much to say. Then we drove off, out of Portland, and back to Sutton. He pulled in next to DiMatteo's Variety Store and ran in for Italian sandwiches, chips, and sodas. Then we followed the winding road out of town, along the Nine Falls and finally back to the long dirt drive down the long hill to Little Loon Lake and the Fredericks' cabin, Camp Content.

Our supper stowed away, we went into the separate bedrooms and changed into our swimsuits. On the porch, Jim handed me two large fluffy towels: "One for drying, one for lying." We walked down to the beach, the sand warmed by the September sun. We spread out our towels and then Second Lieutenant Fredericks sprinted onto the dock and made a long, shallow dive. It seemed the sunlight on Little Loon created a halo around the splash. He surfaced, dove, and emerged like a porpoise. "C'mon in," he shouted. "The water's fine."

And the water was fine, still holding its summer warmth, feeling smooth and embracing. We swam and dove, and came together, splashing, disappearing, and floating into each other's arms. Then onto the beach and our towels. Lying on the warm sand, our hands met. And the afternoon passed in those cycles of wet and dry, energy and rest, separate and reunited.

"Hélène," Jim said. "This is such a gift." We both lay on our backs, looking skyward, through the limbs and leaves of a maple tree on the shore. "You are such a gift." I reached over and found his hand. "No matter what the war brings, I'll have you with me." He rolled over on his side and stroked my cheek. "This is what we will be fighting for: to be free and safe and with the one we love."

Then he stood, ran across the dock, and, once again, dove deep into the lake. I sat up and watched the trail of bubbles that marked his passage. He surfaced, waved back to me, and dove down again, and then standing waist-deep in the cove, blew me a kiss. "Time for sandwiches," he said.

We retraced our path up to the camp. He shook the sand off the lying towels and spread them over the deck railing. Then we took our drying towels into our separate changing rooms. By the time I came out, Jim was spreading our supper on the table on the deck. He attacked his Italian sandwich as if it were a stand-in for Mussolini. I nibbled mine, aware that our supper was another scene in the unfolding of our lives together. His Italian reduced to a rubble of diced onions and green peppers, Jim walked into the camp and returned with a whoopie pie. "A perfect end to a perfect meal…on a perfect day…with my perfect person," he said. Then we clinked bottles—his Coke, mine orange soda. He sliced the round of chocolate cake layered with white frosting. "Choose your half," he said.

We cleaned up after supper and washed our dishes. Back on the deck, we sat in the two wooden chairs, our hands clasped over the slight gap between the armrests. The sun began its descent behind the hills across the lake, an earlier evening marking the passage of the seasons. We marked time by chatting: my school year, his fellow trainees with whom he was forging a bond, Mr. Direnzo's sermons about the evils of fascism and Hitler, Jim's training officers' paeans to the strategic importance of air power. Darkness spread across the lake. The coming night was filled with the washing of little waves on the beach, the haunting calls of loons, birds chirping in the trees.

"How about one last swim," Jim asked.

"I'd love that," I replied.

We walked into the living room. On a little table between the two bedroom doors, sat two more large, fluffy towels. Jim picked one up and offered it to me. "I'm thinking there's no need to get into our wet suits," he said. "Just wrap yourself up in this."

I paused, just for a moment, and looked out into the night. Then I took the towel and went into Mr. and Mrs. Fredericks's bedroom. Very slowly, almost cautiously, I undressed. Looking into the oval mirror over Jim's mother's chest of drawers, I checked to make sure I was fully enrobing myself in the towel. Then I walked out where Jim awaited me, his towel securely wrapped around his waist. "All ready?" he asked. I nodded, and we walked out onto the deck, down to the beach, to the end of the dock. Jim smiled and turned me so that I was pointing into the cove. Then he moved his back up against mine. "On the count of three," he said.

"One…two…three!" I heard the splash from his dive. A deep breath and I dropped my towel and slipped into the lake. Jim approached with a gliding breast stroke. He stood, facing me, his shoulders above the water. Then he reached out and placed his hands around my head and pulled me gently into a kiss. Then another. "Oh, my sweet, sweet Hélène," he said. And his arms drew me to him, into a long, quiet embrace. And it felt wonderful; it felt right.

We swam and splashed, separated and came back together. Blew mouthfuls of water at one another. Laughed and shared the moments of silence. Finally, Jim asked, "Had enough?" I nodded, and we floated over to the dock. With a final splash, Jim hoisted himself up and wrapped his towel around his waist. He picked up my towel and, turning away, said, "Here. I'll hold this up for you."

I slid up onto the rough pine boards, took the towel and wrapped myself in it.

"I'm good," I said and turned to walk off the dock. Jim followed me up the hill, onto the deck, and into the living room. As I started toward the parents' bedroom, my love stepped up behind me and gently reached out onto my shoulders. He moved his head next to mine and said, so softly, "Let me help you." Then he took off the towel and began to dry my shoulders, my neck, my back, my front. Then, dropping the towel, he took my hand and led me into his bedroom.

The night passed softly. Loons called, crickets chirped. And I, Hélène Honoré Lévesque, became a woman. Under the comforter on Jim's bed, we whispered words and phrases that surrounded the reality of our love. I felt as though I were in a dream, a dream that had no words, no beginning, no end. Just the warmth of our love, the so soft touch of his hand. Then Jim said, "There comes a time." And I walked away, into the other bedroom, and dressed. When I walked out, he was there. He opened his arms, and I walked into his embrace. "I want you to know this is real," he whispered. "It is you and me, for now and forever. I love you, Hélène. You must believe me."

"Oh, yes, Jim," I replied. "I know. I know."

We gathered up our swimsuits and the various towels. Then we walked out of Camp Content and climbed into the Model A. Jim looked at his wristwatch. "Two thirty a.m.," he said. "I hope your parents aren't worried." All I could do was shrug.

The road back to Sutton was at once familiar and now totally different. Jim drove into Frenchtown and up the hill to la maison Lévesque. The glow to the east of the mill presaged the coming of dawn. The only night sounds were the groans of the digesters. Jim drew me over to him.

"I'll call you later today. After we've both gotten some sleep."

"When are you leaving?" I asked, trying to relax into his hug.

"It won't be until late afternoon. I have to catch the train to Boston; I think there's one at four thirty. I wish we could have some more time together, but I don't think that will fit in with my mother's schedule. For sure I'll call." Another hug, and I climbed down from the car, my wet bathing suit a memento of the night that had changed my life. As I walked up the stairs to the front porch, I heard Jim drive away.

I tiptoed into our living room. The lamp next to Papa's chair was on, both for me and his return from the night shift at the mill. I went into my room, undressed, and flopped down on my bed. I tried to sleep but the sounds of the evening kept whispering in my mind's ear: the splash of waves, the cries of loons, my love's breathing, my cries of discovery. I dozed off but then heard Papa come in from the front hall and walk into the kitchen. When his footsteps returned to his chair I knew, from the years of our lives, that there would be just two fingers of Papa Whiskey and a short glass of Uncle Ale to help him gear down to get some rest before the next shift.

I awoke with a start. My alarm clock read eleven thirty. I walked out through the living room and into the kitchen. Maman was sitting at the table. The scent of baking rolls filled the room.

"*Bonjour, ma chère,* Maman said. "You had a good time?"

"Oh yes, Maman," I replied. "Jim and I talked and swam and talked and talked."

"*C'est bon,*" she said. It seemed as if she wanted to ask for more but somehow couldn't.

"Have I had a phone call this morning?" I asked. "Jim said he would call."

"No. No one has called."

"I think I'll take a quick bath."

"Bon. The rolls should be done by the time you're through."

I bathed with the bathroom door ajar in case the phone rang. Then I dressed in an outfit that I thought would be casual but not too much so for Mrs. Fredericks. When I walked out into the living room, Papa was in his chair with coffee and a fresh, golden roll. He turned down the volume of the twelve o'clock news on the radio.

"*Bonjour, Papa,*" I said.

"*Salut, ma fille,*" he replied, looking at me as if I were a messenger of the past night's news. I felt I had nothing I could share, at least at that moment. He turned the radio back up. There was little news from Europe; the "phony war" in Western Europe continued. At home President Roosevelt had returned to the White House from his weekend at Hyde Park. Mrs. Roosevelt was in California overseeing the USO facility for troops gathering for deployment in Hawaii. I sat as silent as the phone.

After a while, Béné returned from school. "Did you have a wonderful time?" she asked.

"Yes." I glanced over at Papa, who seemed about ready for a nap before his shift. "Yes, it was fine."

"I looked in on you when I was ready to leave for school. You seemed to be fast asleep. Miss Franks asked if you were sick. I didn't give her any details."

"Thanks for that."

As the clock ticked onward through the afternoon, I became more and more anxious. Where was Jim? Why wasn't the phone ringing? Was everything just a dream? Finally, I couldn't stand what wanted to be my normal life in my home. "I'm going for a walk," I called out to anyone who was listening. Béné walked in from the kitchen. "Okay if I join you?" She glanced over at Papa and his smoldering Camel. "I could use some fresh air. If it's okay…"

"Of course. Let's go."

We walked downstairs, out into the yard and onto the playground of St. Hyacinth's school. After a couple of laps around the field we sat down on a pair of swings.

"Are you okay, Hélène?" she asked? "I don't want to butt in, but it's clear that you're not yourself."

"I'll be all right," I said. "Jim and I had a wonderful time, just the two of us. But…he was going to call me today, after we'd gotten some sleep. And he was supposed to catch a train to Boston around four thirty, just about now. And…well, the phone hasn't rung all day."

"I'm sure he'll call. It must be crazy at his house right now."

"Oh, God, Béné. Oh, God, I hope so."

We climbed down from the swings and walked another loop around the playground.

After supper, I retreated to my room, leaving the door ajar for Jim's call. Maman and Béné went to bed; Papa was in his chair, dressed for work, ready to head out for his midnight-to-eight shift at the mill. Finally, a bit after eleven, the phone finally rang. I hurried to answer it before Papa could get out of his chair. I picked up the receiver.

"Hello!" I tried to keep the anxiety out of my voice. "Hello?"

The voice, his voice, crackled over the miles between us. "Hélène…Oh God, I'm so glad it's you!"

"Oh, Jim…!" As I spoke, Papa stood, walked across into the kitchen, and, lunchbox in hand, walked past me and out the door, a full half hour before his usual departure time for his get-up shift at the Nine Falls.

"Jim…what…?"

"Listen my sweet. I only have a couple of minutes on this call. Let me tell you what's happened. I'm back at Maguire, in New Jersey. When I got home this morning, after I dropped you off, my parents were up, waiting for me. My mother…Oh my God, she was having a complete emotional collapse. Screaming and crying of how I was abandoning her, breaking up our family. It was crazy."

"Oh, Jim…I'm so—"

He cut me off. "This has to be quick. The only thing that could calm her down was for us to leave immediately, to get me to Boston and back to Maguire. She and Father had already started gathering together what I'd be taking back into service. Then, sometime around nine thirty, we climbed in Father's car and set off directly for Boston. I kept saying that it wasn't necessary, that I could take the train that afternoon. But it didn't matter. Mother insisted, and I could tell that Father was more concerned for her than for the end of my stay at home. So it's been crazy; catching trains, switching stations, catching a late bus from Penn Station down to Maguire."

There was a moment's pause, and I tried to honor his silence.

"So tomorrow," he continued, "my training company will be sent off to Alabama, to Maxwell Air Force base. I'll send you a letter with info when I get there. Hélène! I've got to go! But I need you to know, need you to believe, that everything we shared last night was good and right. You are mine; I am yours. And I will carry your sweet face with me through this war to the very end. *Hélène, je t'aime beaucoup…beaucoup*!"

My voice caught. I took a deep breath. "*Et moi, je t'adore, mon cher* Jim."

The phone connection clicked off. I replaced the receiver gently. Walking into the bathroom, I brushed my teeth. Then I returned to my bedroom, changed into my nightgown, and tried for a few hours of sleep before the next school day.

As September trudged toward October, I tried to establish some sort of "normal" to my life that had soared and then plunged like a fighter plane in battle. I managed to concentrate on my classes, more as a way of passing the day than from engagement. In the halls of Sutton High, I walked with my friends and listened to their chatting while knowing that, for me, gossip about boys and football Saturday nights had lost all importance on a Monday night at Camp Content on Little Loon Lake.

At home it seemed that my days were ordered by checking the mail each afternoon for a letter that never came and waiting in the evening for the phone to ring. I tried to understand, to grasp, that my beloved Jim was so caught up in his flight training that there was no time to put pen to paper or to stand in line for the pay phone in his company's PX. But I knew, had to believe, that as my beloved so often had said, "There comes a time."

And then, in the first week of October, there was another huge bump in the path that my life was following. My cousin, *ma cousine*, didn't make her visit. I had first met her just before I turned thirteen. Maman explained to me that this monthly visit was one of the tests that God laid before all women. *La cousine* was a coded term in our family, based on some French or Québecois fable that she couldn't recall. Now, I tried to explain her absence to myself: "I'm young." "There's too much going on." "*C'est la vie.*" And I managed to push away any anxiety and to keep her absence to myself. There was school; there was family; there was the view past St. Hyacinth and out across the Nine Falls valley to the horizon, to the "wild blue yonder," that had called my love away from me.

Besides, there were the great dramas brought to our lives by the daily papers and, especially, radio broadcasts. Tragedies of every description jolted la famille Lévesque. On October second, the Nazis blew up six synagogues in Paris. Three days later, when Dodgers catcher Mickey Owen dropped a third strike, the Yankees rallied in the ninth inning to win the World Series four games to one. In Paris, a tragedy beyond comprehension.

In New York, a tragedy only if one was a Dodgers rooter, or in Sutton, Maine, a Red Sox fan.

In time, as the war progressed, it felt as if the battle fronts, the horrors, the ebbs and flows of destruction blurred and took on a sense of normal. The Germans approached Moscow and Stalingrad while the British tried to stem the Japanese tide in Malaya. Valiant New Zealand troops attacked Italians in Tunisia. Toward the end of October, Walt Disney's "Dumbo" offered release: a flying elephant with a mouse as his navigator appearing moments after the newsreel film clips of diving Luftwaffe bombers and piles of smoking rubble in London and Birmingham. On November 7, Papa reported that the gallant RAF had made a counterattack on Berlin and other German cities. "*Voilà, les Boches.*" "Take that, you Germans!"

But for me, Hélène Honoré, his "good news" hardly registered. For three weeks by then I had been awaiting the arrival of *ma cousine*. This time I couldn't find pathways of easy answers. The next day, at the end of a school day that had hardly registered, I caught up with Dorcas in the hall by our lockers and asked her if she had time to chat. Then we walked outside and sat down on one of the benches in the school yard. She waited, a friend who was always there.

"My cousin hasn't come," I started. "It's been two times in a row that she hasn't shown up."

There was a long pause. "Oh," she said. "You mean…Aunt Flo?"

I nodded, our Franco and Anglo cultures meeting in understanding.

"And…there's a reason?" she continued.

All I could do was nod.

"Well what do you think you…we should do? How can I help?"

I took a long deep breath, trying to contain the tears welling up. "I've got to tell my family…Béné and Maman."

Another long pause and then Dorcas, my dearest friend, asked gently, "And Jim…?"

Now the tears flowed. "I don't know. I just don't know! I haven't heard from him since he arrived in Alabama." I wiped my eyes and tried to breathe. "And I don't know what I can tell him, what I should tell him, while his whole existence is in the cockpit of a fighter plane!"

Dorcas nodded. "You're right. Start with the Lévesque women who love you. And know that I'm right here for you. Just let me know any way I can help." We stood up and shared a long hug. My friend reached up and wiped my cheek. We walked away from Sutton High, down Main Street. At the entrance to her big brick house we embraced again, and I continued downtown, across the bridge into Frenchtown. Past the gray stone church, I walked up the hill and across the playground to home.

As I walked up onto the porch, I checked the mailbox. It was empty. I took a deep breath, then another, and started up the stairs, thanking God and the mill management that Papa was working the day shift. I climbed up the stairs and went into our living room. Bénédicte was sitting on the couch, reading her English textbook. *Ma belle soeur* looked up and smiled. I sat down next to her and with only a couple of sobs told her that my cousin had abandoned me. Béné's eyes grew wide. Then she reached out and stroked my cheek. "Let's get Maman," she said.

We walked into the kitchen and, as if it were a normal school day afternoon, sat down while Maman made tea and served cookies. Then after a silence and some sips, I told Maman that *ma cousine* had gone missing. Her face reflected concern and understanding, but not shock or surprise. Then she sent Béné downstairs to get Mémère so that three generations of Lévesque women could face this moment together.

When the four of us sat down at the table and after I had told of my situation for the fourth time in one afternoon, Maman and Mémère concluded that there was only one answer to what path should follow: we must sit down with Monseigneur Desjardins and ask for his—for God's—directions. It was decided that until then it would be best if I stayed at home. Tomorrow my mother and grandmother would go to early morning mass and there ask him for an appointment later in the day. And until then, it was decided, the men in the family had no need to know. "Our Lord and the Holy Mother willing, all will be well." And for me, Hélène Honoré, it seemed like there was nothing I could say in reply. I fled to my bedroom and Jim's smiling face behind the glass of the picture frame.

The next afternoon, Mémère, Maman, and I walked down the hill and around St. Hyacinth and entered the church offices next to the rectory. Father Girard, a young priest who had just joined the Sutton clergy, greeted us and then, knocking on Monseigneur's office door, announced our arrival. As if ordered by age, or depth of faith, les femmes Lévesque followed him in.

What followed has been blurred by time and regret. Mémère took the lead, explaining to Monseigneur the situation in which our family had found itself. Brief questions followed: was my pregnancy confirmed? Was the father a practicing Catholic? "Yes" and then "no." At no time was Jim's name mentioned, only that he was in the military. Having digested the answers, he pronounced his conclusions.

"Because you, my child, have conceived this child outside the bonds of holy matrimony and because it is not possible that the father, both because he is not of the true faith and is not in the area because of service to the nation…it is not possible for you to raise the child within the arms of the Church." He paused. "The sisters of our community have sister convents to the north, in Québec. I will direct Mother Mary Joséphine to contact one of them and request that they take you into their care for the duration of your confinement. Then your child will be given over into the arms of a family recommended by the local church." Another pause, this one a bit longer. "And my prayers and those of your loving family will beseech our Lord and Savior to offer forgiveness for the moment of transgression which has brought you here." He stood behind his desk. "Mother Mary Joséphine will contact you when the arrangements have been made." He made the sign of the cross. "Now go with God and Our Holy Mother's blessings."

I followed Mémère and Maman out of the office and down the hall, our footsteps marking our passing away from the judgment. Then we retraced our path up the hill, past the convent, across the playground to home. Maman called upstairs to Béné and then we four, *les femmes Lévesque*, sat down together. Mémère explained the monseigneur's solution and that there was nothing to follow, except God's will be done.

That evening, after Papa and Pépère returned from their day at the mill and after a dinner of which I could barely take a bite, the three generations of la famille Lévesque gathered in our living room. Mémère took the initiative and described my condition, our situation. Pépère and Papa agreed that there was nothing to be done but to follow the path, however sad, that Monseigneur had laid out for us. It was decided that Mémère would reach out to a relative, Emanuelle Trémont, who lived in Magog, an hour outside of Montreal. When the time came for me to depart, Mémère and I would take the Mountain Division train across northern New England into Québec. We would meet with Emanuelle, and she would take on the task of guiding me into the arms of God's sisters. Tomorrow we would send a telegram to the Trémont family, alerting them that a letter of request for assistance was on its way.

In the meantime, it was agreed that I should return to school, to keep as normal a pose in the community as possible. Of course, once I disappeared from Sutton, the word would spread. However, we would tell only Tante Jacqueline et Cousine Eugénie. They were family and deserved to know the sad truth. It seemed that there was nothing left to say. Mémère asked us to bow our heads. Then she said a little prayer for forgiveness and for a birth in faith for one to be born, not in a manger, but in the dwelling of His holy sisters. The family meeting finished, I retreated into my room.

The next day was the longest Friday of my young life. In my classes, in the halls of Sutton High, I tried to pass for "normal," to answer questions in class, to smile at my friends' jokes and bits of gossip that now seemed pointless. About a dozen times, Dorcas asked if I was okay and I nodded yes, although okay seemed blurred beyond any clear meaning. But I had to keep telling myself that in the end I would be okay, a Québecois family with a new baby would be okay, and Airman Lieutenant Fredericks would be okay. Jim and I would be okay.

When the last buzzer of the day freed students into the weekend, I walked down the second floor hall to Miss Franks's classroom. I knocked on the door and stepped in. My favorite teacher looked up. "Ah, Hélène. Do come in." I walked over and sat down in the front row across from her desk and waited while my mentor shuffled papers. Finally, she looked up. As quickly and directly as possible, I told her of my situation, withholding only the father's, Jim's, name. Then, in the quiet of a Friday afternoon classroom, we sat for a moment, silent.

"Well, my dear," Miss Franks said. "I'm very sorry that this huge detour in your path has arisen." We sat for another, seemingly longer, moment. "I must say that your situation speaks volumes on the uneven burden that pregnancy places on the mother-to-be. Fathers continue their lives in the outside world; women retreat into seclusion, be it in a convent in a foreign land or in their wifely kitchens. However, I have every confidence that you have the strength and intelligence to rise to this challenge and continue your path toward a truly emancipated female."

"Thank you," was all I could manage.

"And now, let us discuss how Sutton High School can help to ensure that path. I will check with Mr. Peters in Guidance to see which courses you must complete to graduate with your class next June. My guess is that you have earned extra class credits in your first three years so that perhaps you need only a few more, specific courses. English Four, certainly. When I get that information, I will ask for a meeting with Principal Sampson and, perhaps, Mr. Direnzo and we can strategize how to set up a correspondence course for you." Another pause. "Hélène," she continued. "If I may be so bold as to ask, when are you due to give birth?"

"Sometime in the first weeks of June," I replied.

"Ah, probably too late for you to take part in the Class of '42 graduation ceremonies. Just as well, I suppose. The diploma is what is crucial. And now, my dear, I must gather up this mountain of essays that await me. I will try to catch up with Mr. Peters. Once I have your credits information, I will ask Mr. Sampson for a meeting, perhaps next Tuesday."

"Thank you so much, Miss Franks," I said. Then I stood and walked out of her room, down the hall past my locker. It seemed that my weekend homework assignments were of little importance. At the head of the stairwell leading down to the exit, I stopped and took a deep breath. Then I turned, walked back to my locker and took out my math, American history, and English notebooks. Homework would help fill the void in my life and, I sensed, provide some foundation for whatever path would unfold in the months to come.

A week later, Father Girard called Mémère and told her that Mother Mary Joséphine had heard back from her Ursuline sisters in Québec. She would await Mémère at the convent to share the news and set the path for my young life. The following Monday, I tried to steady myself through another school day while overwhelmed by uncertainty of what my future held.

That afternoon, the three generations of Trémont–Lévesques gathered around Mémère's kitchen table. Then, over tea and coffee cake, she laid out the structure of my confinement. I was to be taken in at Le Pensionnat et Monastère des Ursulines, in Stansted, Québec. Both a convent and a boarding school for girls, the sisters would be able to provide me support throughout my pregnancy while also offering some courses that would help guarantee my graduation with the Sutton High Class of '42. The sisters also had close contacts with the diocesan officials who organized adoptions of babies born in circumstances like my own. I would be allowed to receive one mailing from the outside world every two weeks and to return each of the postings. The plan was that Bénédicte would be in charge of the mailings. She would keep me up to date with the goings on in the family and send assignments from my teachers. The clergy of St. Hyacinth's would cover the cost of the postage and la famille Lévesque could send American dollars north with me to pay Canadian postal charges. Finally, the Stansted sisterhood would welcome me into their community on December 10, a little more than three weeks off into my chaotic, young future. "C'est la vie," Mémère said.

"*Oui*," replied Maman. "It is all sad but so much less so than the lives of the young women, outside the arms of the Church, our Loving God, Our

Savior, and the Blessed Virgin. Babes themselves, wandering the streets of cities, prey to the world of men and sin." She rose, walked around the table and, standing behind me, drew me back into her embrace. "*Je t'aime beaucoup, ma chère*," she said. "*Toujours*."

"And I love you, Maman," I replied. "Forever."

The next three weeks were a blur. A suitcase retrieved from the attic. My clothing sorted and replacements purchased at Fortin's Women's Shoppe in downtown Sutton. Pens, pencils, notebooks to allow my education to continue. A few books that could fill the long hours on my own in a community that I only dimly understood. Envelopes and stationary to keep my family and friends up to date. And, of course, Jim's photograph.

Thanksgiving Day came and went in a flash. Luckily, Pépere and Papa had the night shift at the mill and so were both home for our family feast. Pépère offered a prayer at the table asking God to give his protection to our sons in the nation's service and, not quite as an afterthought, asking the Holy Mother to grant her grace to *notre belle fille Hélène*.

On Sunday, December 7, the Lévesque women went to Mass at St. Hyacinth. As I sat in the pew between Mémère and Maman, I fought off tears as Monseigneur's homily spoke of Our Savior's love and the Father's forgiveness. While I knew of my family's bonds, it was hard to believe that I could receive the same from others: Church, Frenchtown, Sutton. The words of prayer bound my mind and stilled my lips. As the parishioners followed the procession out of the echoing sanctuary, I ducked my head away from Father DesJardin's farewell. It was as if I needed all my strength to walk with my family up the steep hill, past *le couvent*, for the last Sunday that I could imagine.

I managed Sunday dinner, pushing shards of chicken in Maman's gravy. The talk at the table ebbed and flowed as one after another tried to find something to call up "normal." I begged off dessert and fled into my room where I checked the list for my suitcase and my exile. As the walls of my sanctuary seemed to press inward, I went to the phone in the living room and called Dorcas. We made plans to meet in the park on the bank of the Nine Falls around four o'clock. Left unsaid was that we would be saying our farewells.

When I walked into the park, my dear friend was sitting on one of the swings. I took the one closest to her, and for a bit we just swung back and forth, our feet rising above the banks of the river, toward Frenchtown and the dim glow of the remains of the Sunday December sun. After a bit we dragged our feet on the hard gravel and came to a halt.

"How are you, Heck?" Dorcas asked.

"Oh, I don't know," I replied. "It's like there's too much happening for feeling."

She stepped closer and drew me into an embrace. For a long time we two, friends for years, from the two sides of the river, held each other close. It seemed that there were no further words, at least for now.

Finally she stepped back. "It's chilly. Why don't we take a walk down along the river? If you've got time."

We both knew that these were the last moments that we would have together for any span we could imagine. I just nodded, and we set off on the path that wound toward the mill, its glow in the eastern darkness. At the final bend of the river before the eighth of the Nine Falls, we skirted a baseball diamond. Dorcas walked to the edge of the river and over to a small, dark sculpture set on a granite base, a boy, sitting naked on a rock. A dog, his dog, lay curled around his master's feet.

"I've always loved this," she said. "Do you know its story?"

"I've seen it," I replied. "But no; I don't know any story."

"Well, there's the real story and a legend. The real story is nice but not too exciting. Miss Stevens, Cornelia, the daughter of Charles Willis Stevens, the owner of the Nine Falls, dedicated the statue to the memory of her uncle who was the longtime manager of the mill."

"That's nice," I replied. "Family is so important."

"Of course, it helped that she had tons of money. She never married and so I suppose didn't have to think too much about all the acts of charity she could give to Sutton: the library, parks, gymnasium."

"What about the legend?

"For years the kids in Sutton believed that the statue was a memorial to the manager's son who had drowned in the river. And that his loyal dog drowned too, trying to save his master. I mentioned the story to my grandfather, and he set me straight—no boy, no dog, no drownings."

"Well, I guess that's for the best," I replied. "Truth should be better than fiction."

"Nowhere near as good a story though. And, you know, the last few times I've looked at it I've wondered about what it says about our world."

"What do you mean?"

Dorcas looked at me for what seemed a long time. "I've just thought about why the sculptor chose a boy, not a girl?" Another long pause. "It's like it's all right for there to be a naked little boy, with his twisty little thing for all the world to see. But somehow it wouldn't be okay for his little sister to be naked on a riverbank, with her little dog…or…. No matter. It's getting late. I'd better get home; civics homework is waiting."

We shared another hug and walked up the hill to Main Street. At Dorcas's red brick house, we bid farewell and, as so many times before, I retraced my steps across the bridge into Frenchtown and up the hill to my home.

I walked in and found the door into my grandparents' apartment open and the family gathered around Pépère's radio.

"What is it? What's happened?" I asked.

Papa looked over at me. "The Japs!" he said. "The goddamn Japs have bombed Pearl Harbor. They've started a war with us."

Maman looked as if she was on the edge of shock. "Erland," she moaned. "Oh, Erland. Oh, God, please make him safe!"

The next afternoon the Trémont–Lévesque women—Maman, Béné, and I—gathered in Mémère's living room. Again, their radio was the pivot point around which our lives as Americans seemed to revolve. Suddenly, the room was filled with the famous booming cadences of President Roosevelt. Today, FDR spoke slowly, pausing around his phrases: "Sunday, December Seventh, Nineteen Forty-one…a day which will live in infamy…." And by the time he finished and a swell of applause passed through the House of Representatives, our nation, at last, was on the final road to war.

Maman was still on the edge of shock. There was no word from Erland, and given the chaos in Hawaii, we had no idea of when we might hear if he had survived Japan's attack on our Pacific Fleet. The speech ended, Maman, Béné, and I returned upstairs. No one had suggested that, even in the face of war, my banishment into Canada and the world of the Urseline Sisters should be postponed. Mémère and I would depart as planned tomorrow at nine in the morning. I checked my meager belongings, lay down on my bed, and fought off my tears.

Around five o'clock, Pépère and Papa burst into our apartment, home from a shift at the mill that had been like no other. In every department, men had brought in radios so that, over the grind and swirl of the machines, they too could listen to FDR's speech to the Congress, the nation, and the world. Papa shook open the day's edition of the *Portland Evening Express*.

"*Mon Dieu*," he shouted. "Thank God! Erland's ship, the heavy cruiser *New Orleans*, is not one of those smashed by the Japs."

I thought Maman might faint. "Oh, the Blessed Mother, thank you. Thanks to you for protecting our dear son."

"And our prayers for Paul and Geno," added Mémère. "Wherever their service has taken them."

And deep in my being I tried to pray, to believe. "And Jim, oh please, Jim."

After dinner, it was confirmed that, despite the shocks that we, the country, and the world were experiencing, Mémère and I should embark on our trip toward my exile.

"It's too soon to tell if the war will shut down our borders," Papa said. "And anyway, Hélène, you may be safer there than here on the coast. Who knows what the U-boats may have in store."

And so it was. The next morning, after Béné and I shared a long hug, Mémère and I climbed into the family Chevy, and Maman drove us into Portland to the great stone train station. As I got out of the back seat and grabbed my luggage, I looked to the east at the high bluffs of the Western Promenade, crowned with leafless trees in the December morning. It seemed to testify to the changes in my life since Jim and I took our last ride in his Model A, parked on the Promenade and looked westward into what we believed was our future.

Maman and I embraced. "Go with God, my child," she said. "The Blessed Mother and the holy sisters will help you through this tough time."

I could only nod, wiping a tear with the rough sleeve of my winter coat. Then Mémère and I turned and walked into the station. I fought off the urge to turn back, fearful that if I did, I wouldn't have the strength to continue on my journey.

Mme Trémont DuBois and her *petite-fille* climbed aboard the St. Lawrence and Atlantic train and took our seats in a passenger car. After what seemed a long wait, the steam locomotive began to chuff, and slowly the train pulled out and headed north. After forty-five minutes, it pulled to a stop in Danville Junction. Passengers disembarked, replaced by others. Mémère explained that this was the station that served the twin cities of Auburn and Lewiston, two other Maine mill towns. In the past we had visited relatives on both sides of the Androscoggin River, French Canadians who worked in the textile mills.

"Do you remember the beautiful church, Saint-Pierre-et-Saint-Paul, that sits on the hill in Lewiston?" Mémère asked. I nodded. "I think it is the most beautiful of all the Catholic churches I have seen in Maine," she continued. "You will see many other examples of holy architecture in Québec."

The train continued its way northward, and my grandmother continued her travelogue. This town, that set of waterfalls. We stopped in the pretty village of Bethel and then crossed the Maine–New Hampshire border.

After another hour, we entered Berlin, New Hampshire. A paper mill sat on the riverbank. Mémère said it was the Brown Paper Company. From my perspective, it was hardly distinguishable from the gray stone and dark brick buildings of the Nine Falls Mill in my hometown. We left the not yet White Mountains of New Hampshire and skirted the still somewhat Green Mountains of Vermont. Then, four hours into our journey, we reached the border with Québec. The train stopped and a Canadian border official boarded and began walking down the aisles checking out the passengers. Finally he approached Mémère and me.

"*Bonjour.* Good day, mesdames," he began. "*Préférez-vous anglais ou français?*"

Mémère deferred to me. "Uh…I guess…anglais…English, please."

He smiled. "Bon. And may I ask where you are from?"

"We live in Sutton, Maine. It's next to Portland."

"Ah, Sutton. I have distant relatives there. Do you know any of the Vaillancourt family?"

"*Certainement,*" said Mémère with a smile. "Mme Rachael is a very good friend. She and her family live just…."

"Small world," the officer interjected. "Now where are you going in Québec?"

Again, my grandmother deferred to me.

"We're going to Stansted, to the Ursuline Convent."

"Ah. And you will be going to the boarding school? I've been told it is a very good place for young women" I nodded. "Now, are you bringing any products, any items that should be declared?

"No. Nothing to declare," I said. "Just me, I guess."

"And how will you be getting to Stansted from the train? Our route doesn't come near.""Mémère stepped in. "We will be getting off in Coaticook. My cousin who lives in Magog will drive over, meet us, and take Hélène down to Stansted. I'll just wait at the station there and take the return train down to Portland."

"*Ben oui. Une longue journée pour vous, madame.*"

"*Pour toute notre famille,*" she said.

The officer gave a slight bow and moved on down the aisle to the final pair of travelers. He climbed down from the car, and we heard the conductor's whistle blow. Then there was the huff and puff of the steam locomotive, and the St. Lawrence and Atlantic headed toward Montréal on its great river and away from the Nine Falls, tumbling through Sutton to the ocean and away from this new chapter of my young life. Mémère and I rode in silence for most of an hour, and then the train began its approach into Coaticook. As it hissed to a stop, we stood, retrieved my bags and, alone, walked down to the exit and out onto the platform. Again, the conductor's whistle blew, and as the train pulled away, we turned and walked into the little station house.

A woman of Mémère's generation stood and walked over to us. "Ah voilà," she said. "*Caroline, c'est toi? Vraiment?*"

"*Mais oui, Michelle,*" my grandmother responded. "*Vraiment. Et aussi, ma petite-fille Hélène Honoré.*"

The Trémont cousins chattered as we gathered up my bags and walked out of the station. After we put the luggage into the trunk of my great-aunt's Pontiac, she suggested *un petit café* before she and I departed on the two-hour drive to Stansted. We walked across the main street of Coaticook and into a coffee shop. The cousins ordered coffees and I a hot chocolate and, at my great-aunt's suggestion, a beignet, a pretty good jelly doughnut. Pastry eaten, drinks finished, we walked out into the fading sunlight, over to the car.

"Well, ma chère Hélène," Mémère said. "I'm afraid it's time to part." She drew me into a long hug. "But only for your time with the holy sisters. And you will be in our hearts and prayers."

"Merci, Mémère," I said, holding back what felt like a river of tears. "I love you all, la famille Lévesque, so very much."

"God be with you, my child," she said. She reached into her purse and took out an envelope. "Here, my dear, a few extra dollars to help with postage." Then she turned to her cousin. "*Encore, merci, Michelle.*" Then she turned and walked away and into the station, destined to return to our world by the Nine Falls—or whatever would remain of it.

Tante Michelle and I drove out of Coaticook and down along a rural highway through the Québec countryside. Darkness fell, and then as the moon rose, the December snow gleamed on the long, rectangular fields that ran away from the highway. The lights of farmhouses and occasional villages with two cross streets and, always, a church, white wood or gray stone, with a rectangular, peaked steeple marked our passage. We rode in silence, me with my sense of the unknown in my second tongue; my chauffeur—well I could only guess.

After two long hours, we drove into Stansted and up to *le couvent,* three brick buildings that towered over the other buildings of the town—the gray stone church excepted. Tante Michelle parked, and we walked up to the door of the lefthand building. She rang the bell and we waited in the cold for what seemed another hour. Finally, a slit in the dark wooden door slid open and a pair of eyes under the white edge of a wimple looked out at two strangers at the gate.

"*Bonsoir*," a disconnected voice said. "*Puis-je vous aider?*"

Tante Michelle explained that, as had been planned, she had brought Hélène Honoré Lévesque up from America to enter the care of the Urseline Sisters.

"*Bien sûr*," the voice replied and then told us to collect my baggage, and she would welcome us in.

We walked to the Pontiac and then back to the door. It opened, and we stepped into a dimly lit hall. There, an imposing woman stood, robed in black with a white wimple enclosing all but the center of her face. "*Alors*," she said. "*Je m'appelle Soeur Frédérique*." Her gray eyes drew me in. "*Et toi, tu es Hélène Honoré?*" I only nodded. There were no further words of welcome. A brief conversation in rapid Québecois ensued, and then Tante Michelle turned to me.

"I must go now, my dear," she said in English. "The drive to Magog is an hour, and it is late—for all of us." She opened her arms for a farewell hug. "*Bonne chance, ma chère. Tout va bien se passer*." Then she turned and walked off into the night.

Sister Frédérique picked up one of my bags and motioned for me to follow her. We walked down the hall, the hard soles of her shoes clicking echoes off the walls. After climbing three flights of stairs, we walked down another hall, stopping before a brown wooden door. The sister opened it, stepped in, and turned on a ceiling light that barely lit a small room with a narrow bed, a chair, a little table, and a small chest of drawers.

"*Voilà*," she said. "*Voici ta chambre*."

"*Merci, Sœur Frédérique*, I replied. There was a long silence.

"*Le matin on commence à six heures. Tu vas entendre les cloches*." She turned and walked out the door, closing it. Her muffled steps left me in an isolation beyond my young ability to comprehend.

Les cloches, the bells, wrenched me out of mercifully dreamless sleep into the reality of my small room. Hurriedly, I pulled on the same outfit that I'd worn on my trip into holy exile. Soeur Frédérique rapped on the door, and I followed her down the hall, down the stairs, and into a small chapel where twenty other Ursuline sisters gathered for morning prayers. I sat; I knelt; I tried to say the prayers in my second tongue; I tried to believe.

And so the rest of December flowed toward 1942: prayers, breakfast, alone in my room with my books, my journal, and secreted in the desk drawer, away from the eyes of the sisters, my photograph of Jim, gifted in the last days of our innocence.

On Monday, January 5, following a New Year's Day that passed with no sense of celebration beyond the usual mass, the students returned from their holidays. As I marked the fifth month of my pregnancy, it was determined by *la mère supérieure* that my "condition" was too visible for me to participate directly with these sixteen girls in their final high school year. My holy minders determined that I would stay behind a screen at the rear of the classroom with Soeur Frédérique or another sister. And thus I sat through classes in trigonometry, French and Canadian literature, and medieval history.

Once a week, the students gave reports on current events, the only contact I had with the outer world as I waited for Béné's biweekly letter from Sutton along with clippings from the Portland newspapers. I learned that American troops were battling the Japanese for control of the Philippine Islands and that United States troops had landed in Great Britain where they began training for the defense against the Germans. My brothers, mes chers frères, Paul and Geno wrote home from their bases in England that all was well. And from Hawaii came news that Erland had shipped out on the *New Orleans* toward distant battles across the broad Pacific.

Over the ensuing weeks, I was able to glean some sense of the makeup of the class from furtive glimpses around the screen. About half the girls seemed to be North American Indians, an observation that Soeur Frédérique confirmed. She explained that one of the foundation goals of Ursuline schools was to take in girls from the various Canadian tribes and integrate them into Québecois culture. So, in a sense, I had a connection to those girls: we were outsiders being offered spiritual and cultural keys to unlock the doors into acceptance.

For the most part, Béné's letters were full of chatter about goings on at Sutton High School: basketball scores, the annual talent show, which boy–girl couples were current. All of that seemed as removed from my world as the reports on the war and the changes to American society that was gearing up for the battles to come. Wholly outside my outcast ability to comprehend was the news that Japanese American citizens on the West Coast, *citizens*, had been driven from their homes and into internment camps. I thought of my civics classes at Sutton and Mr. DiRenzo's impassioned sermons on equality as a base value of the American soul. A worthy perspective, as long as one was not "the other."

Closer to home, the major development was the construction of a shipyard across the harbor in South Portland. The yard would build the freighters needed for supplying our troops and allies across the Atlantic and create good paying jobs for men and women alike, as the Depression continued to ebb through the costs and profits of war. My memory took me back to that morning on the Western Prom when Jim and I gazed east to the ocean and west over Sutton to the White Mountains and what seemed to be our endless future together.

In early March, Béné's packet contained a small envelope addressed to me in handwriting that seemed familiar. I tore it open and found a letter from Miss Franks.

My dear Hélène,

I hope this brief note finds you well in what must be trying circumstances. However, I am sure that the same strengths that made you such a stellar student will serve you well in these hard times.

Bénédicte tells me that you continue to pursue your studies and has passed on the essays that I sent. I have told Mr. Sampson that I am confident that, come June, you will have earned your Sutton High School diploma.

I hope that you are able to consider directions open to you on your return. There are academic paths which talented young women such as yourself can pursue. I will be only too happy to help you consider your options on your return.

Until then, my dear, be well and safe.

Sincerely,

Selah Franks

I reread her note and lay back on my narrow bed. I tried to envision what those options could be. College? Jim? A family? In Sutton or away? None of those seemed any more clear than the misty view out of my window of the church steeple and, beyond, a hill with bare trees awaiting the call of spring. I looked across my little room at the crucifix on the wall above my little bureau. The miniature rendition of the Lord Jesus hung twisted and, it seemed, aloof to anything other than his cruel end at the hands of mankind and its rules. In that sense, at least, the Son of God and I could empathize. But other than this brief personal connection, the whole Catholic edifice seemed increasingly separate from whatever the future held for Hélène Honoré. A line from the rosary twisted through my head: "Hail, Mary, full of grace, help me hold onto my Jim's face."

On the second Thursday in March, a class on Molière was interrupted as one of the sisters tiptoed in and whispered something to Sister Frédérique. My minder gestured to me, and I followed her away from *Le Bourgeois Gentilhomme*. With no explanation, she led me down the hallway and then across the yard to le couvent. I was ushered into the office of Sister Marie Dominique. *L'Abbesse* gestured for me to sit before her desk. Then she informed me that she had received a telephone call from my family back in Sutton. Sadly, they informed her that my grandfather had passed into the arms of the Loving God Our Father and His Beloved Son. "*Ton grand-père, Clément DuBois, est mort. Je suis navrée.*" I sat, frozen in my sense of isolation from those I loved. The sister continued, explaining that his passing had been sudden and free of pain. At noon, after his night shift at the mill, Mémère went into the bedroom and found that he had died in his sleep. She paused, allowing me time to digest the news. Then she explained: of course it was tragic, but now his good life on Earth was to be rewarded in heaven; of course it would be impossible for me to return to Sutton for his services. And they, les soeurs Ursuline de Stansted, would offer special prayers in his memory for the following week. A nod to Soeur Frédérique and I was led away to my tiny room and left alone with my memories.

But, of course, I was not alone. As the days flowed into months, I was always aware of my tiny, unseen companion. Especially following meals, there were flutters deep inside my belly as I shared nourishment with…him?…her? I could not tell. And so I called it *Bébé*, just baby. Often I walked around my confinement room, humming the lullaby of my childhood: "*Petit escargot/ Porte sur son dos/ sa maisonnette.*" The little snail carrying its home on its back. "*Aussitôt qu'il pleut, il est tout heureux.*" When it rains, he is happy. And somehow Bébé would understand, from my measured pacing, from the tones of my voice, and in its own time would relax and lie quiet in its darkness. As I filled with this blooming life, my young body changed, my belly expanded until I could hardly see my feet as I circled my room or followed Soeur Frédérique down the bare halls and into my exile behind the classroom screen.

Here and there, my exile was tempered by momentary connections with Soeur Geneviève, the youngest of the Stanstead sisters, a novice. During daily prayers or in the dining room, she sometimes shared her shy smile.

As our paths crossed, we managed to exchange a few words, always aware of the looming presence of Soeur Frédérique and the other, older Ursuline sisters. One evening, as we shuffled away from dinner, the back of her hand brushed against mine and then she passed a small, paper-wrapped package into my palm. "*Un petit cadeau de ma famille,*" she whispered. When I arrived in my room, I saw that the packet, a shared gift from her family, was half a chocolate bar. I secreted the contraband in the small drawer of my bedside table and for the next few nights I allowed myself a nibble when I took out Jim's photo to say goodnight.

Toward the middle of April, Béné's letter brought big news. *Grand-mère Caroline et mes parents* had made the decision to sell our two-family home on top of the Frenchtown hill and to buy a single-family house in a new development out on the edge of Sutton. The house should be finished by the end of August. A new home, they believed, would reduce the upkeep chores and the sad memories of Pépère's passing. And, Maman thought, a new home would reinforce my fresh start when I returned. I sat at my table, stunned. Yet another twist in the life of Hélène Honoré leading away from all that my young years had known.

Béné's mailing also contained clips from the *Portland Press Herald*. One told of the Doolittle Raid on Tokyo. On April 18, a flight of bombers had flown from our aircraft carriers seven hundred miles to Japan, carrying out a very successful raid on oil depots and other military targets. She thought perhaps that good news would cheer me up as I thought of Jim passing through his flight training, edging ever closer to going to war. Then, from a different region of my young mind, I remembered a poem that Miss Franks had assigned: Henry Wadsworth Longfellow's "The Midnight Ride of Paul Revere."

> Listen my children and you shall hear
> Of the midnight ride of Paul Revere,
> 'Twas the eighteenth of April of '75
> And hardly a man is now alive
> That remembers that famous day and year.

It felt as if in the stories of war, only the names and weapons changed. A country needed its heroes.

Then one day as I returned from the classroom, Soeur Frédérique handed me an envelope. She explained that though it was not from Bénédicte, they would give it over to me, a single departure from the rules. I looked at the return address and realized it was from Dorcas. I thanked the sister and entered the sanctuary of my bedroom. I sat at my little table and carefully opened the envelope. It contained a single sheet of note paper, folded over another, smaller envelope. I opened the note and read in my best friend's handwriting:

Dear Heckie April 30, 1942

I got this from Jim. He said that he's sent several letters to you but hadn't heard back. He thought that maybe I could pass his note on to you. Here it is.

I hope you're doing as well as can be. Your friends here in Sutton send you best wishes and love. We can't wait for your return.

Much love,

Dorcas

I got up and crossed my little room. I took Jim's picture out and returned with it to my table. I propped the photo up so that my love's face, in black and white, watched me as I tore open the envelope. I took out a letter in his scrawly handwriting, took a deep breath, and began to read.

Chère, chère Hélène, 4/18/42

Oh God, I hope this finds you! Oh God, I hope this finds you! I've sent letters to your Sutton address but have never gotten a reply. How are you? Where are you? I am just about finished with my advanced flight training. To be a pilot has been my dream, along with my dreams of you and our life together when this crazy world gets sane.

Security means I'm not able to tell you where I will be stationed. I can only say that soon I will look down on the green fields where Lévesque, Trémont, and DuBois families had their origins.

My fellow airmen and I will do our very best to help those towns and fields to be free once again.

Someday the war will end, and I'll return to your arms. I miss you every day, every moment.

All my love,

Jim

I read the note a second time, took a deep breath, and, opening the drawer in the table, took out two envelopes and sheets of note paper. First I jotted a note to Dorcas: thanks for reaching out and, especially, for forwarding the letter from my dear one, doing as well as can be expected, probably won't make it home for graduation but soon afterward and we can catch up, sending thanks again and much love. Then, more slowly, dabbing the occasional tear trickling on my cheek, I wrote to my love, my Jim.

Mon cher Jim, May 7, 1942

Merci, merci, merci mille fois pour ta lettre. Thank you a thousand times. I don't know why the earlier ones you sent didn't arrive. I can only guess.

I hope that you are well and safe as your deployment nears.

"Green fields" and "little villages." You'll have a view of the land of my ancestors that they could never have had, except maybe as angels. If during your flight you see them, please tell them that Hélène Honoré says, "Bon matin avec amour." Good morning with love.

The truth to you, my love: I am spending my days in holy exile in a convent in Québec A tiny life, notre bébé, is exploring my belly, moving ever closer to the light—at least as much light as awaits in this dark world. Sometimes I wonder if it feels, as it floats up against my body? Support and love like I did that night in your strong arms, our night, in the warm waters of Little Loon Lake?

Sadly, when notre bébé comes into the light it will be taken to be passed on to others who are judged more proper, more deserving of a child. There is nothing I can do. All power lies in the hands of others who can judge me, judge us, to fulfill God's will. I'm trying so hard not to be bitter. I know that judgment cannot take away who I really am, and who we, you and I together, really are.

I will return to Sutton with my head held high. And I will await your return into my arms. Please, please be safe, my love.

Je t'aime toujours toujours.

Hélène

As I prepared to fold the letter, for the first time since my arrival at le couvent I wished that I had some lipstick so that I could plant a kiss over my scribbled name, a kiss that Jim could see. *C'est la vie.*

I addressed the envelope and inserted my love and the truth that Jim and I shared. I carefully pushed the envelope into the one I'd addressed to Dorcas, my dearest friend. I only needed to add it to my monthly packet to be sent to la famille Lévesque. On the top of the pile, I added a note to Béné asking if letters to me from Jim had somehow never arrived at my—our—home. Also, I enclosed the final essays that Mr. DiRenzo and Miss Franks had assigned: Civics: "Citizenship and the War Effort"; English IV: "A Descriptive Essay on Something Important in Your Life." For Civics: "Equality And Respect in Time of War." For English IV: "A Late Summer Evening On A Lake In Maine." I lay back on my little bed and, closing my eyes, tried to send messages to my dear: How I was. Where he was. What the fates would bring until we would be reunited. "Hail Mary, full of grace. Send my love over time and space."

More and more, Bébé reminded me that I was not alone. My belly began to have contractions, briefly, as if this tiny life were giving me fair warning. I gathered my courage and told Soeur Frédérique. For the first time in the half year she had been my minder, she reached over and patted my arm. "Praise God and the Blessed Mother," she said. Later, she returned and told me that soon I would have a visit with Madame Frésnel, the midwife for the Québecois community around Stansted. She would assist me when it came time for my delivery. Until then, it had been decided that it would be better for all if I stopped attending classes, as final exams were approaching, and little new material would be covered.

And then, on June 2, 1942, Bébé announced that its time had arrived. I awoke early in the morning to find my bedclothes soaked. And my belly, my entire being, was racked with contractions, ever more regular and intense. Soeur Frédérique came to lead me to prayers and then left to have Madame Frésnel summoned. Then she led me down to the basement of the convent to a room that was used for the medical needs of the sisterhood.

The hours passed: morning, afternoon, evening, pushing, relaxing, pushing, pushing. Then, as the clock on the wall approached nine, Madame Frésnel cried, "*Pousse, ma chère. Encore, encore!*" And, in an instant, my body felt the passing of that tiny life that had shared my space. A slap and then a cry. "*Une jeune fille, une jeune fille parfaite,*" she said. There was a momentary pause as I heard the shuffle of footsteps and then the voice of Soeur Frédérique thanking God and the Holy Mother as she took Bébé, my little, perfect baby girl, out of the room and off to whatever future others had planned for her. I could only lie still on the table of her delivery and try to fight off tears, trying to send my love to Jim across whatever chasms the world had to separate us.

Two weeks later, when it was judged my young, unshared breasts had ceased lactation, I packed my belongings, carefully layering Jim's photo in the changes of clothes I had scarcely needed over the past half year. Soeur Frédérique led me to the office of *Soeur Marie Dominique. L'abbesse* told me that preparations had been made for my return home. Praise God, the baby had been placed with a couple who had been denied a birth of their own. They were thrilled with parenthood and were deeply committed to raising their little girl with love and in faith. And arrangements had been made for my return home: in an hour, a bus over to Coaticook, and then the St. Lawrence and Atlantic down to Portland. The tickets had already been purchased. "Go with God, my child. We will pray that your journey, your life, will be blessed with the forgiveness promised by the Lord Jesus Christ." And with that, Soeur Frédérique led me out of the convent. There, we were met by a gentleman from the congregation who drove me down to the bus station, confirmed that my tickets were in order, wished me well, and departed. I was alone.

I watched as the southbound St. Lawrence and Atlantic chugged into the station. I rose, lifted my small bags, and walked out onto the platform and into the passenger car. For some reason, I took a seat facing to the rear. The train's whistle blew, and my homeward journey began. I watched as the green fields and woods and golden spires of village churches of Québec passed out of sight, away from the sad chapter of my young life. Was one of these towns where *Bébé* was beginning her life? Safe in her little crib, did she have memories, dreams of the dark, warm universe of my belly?

The train chugged to a stop as it reached the border. An American border agent stepped into the car and walked over to me, the only passenger. He smiled as I handed him my identification papers.

"Good day, miss. *Bonjour, mademoiselle*. Do you prefer English or French?"

"English is fine," I replied.

"I see you're returning from the Ursuline school in Stanstead. Did you have a good year?"

"It was interesting. I think I learned a lot."

He handed back my papers. "I'm sure your family down in Sutton will be happy to have you home. Enjoy your journey." He nodded, walked to the rear of the car, and climbed down onto the platform.

The rewind continued as the train headed south. Berlin with paper mill chimneys, Bethel settled down in the midst of hills and mountains, Danville Junction. Each stop carried me farther from the brick buildings of the Stanstead convent and school. Away from Soeurs Frédérique et Geneviève, the classroom with its shunning screen, Indian girls taken from their roots. As the train pulled away from Danville, I switched seats, now facing forward past Gray, North Yarmouth, Cumberland and Falmouth. And then into Portland and up to a stop at the gray monolith of Union Station.

I gathered my bags and walked out onto the platform.

"Hélène! Hélène!" I heard my mother's voice for the first time in 1942. I hurried over to where she, Grand-mère Caroline, and Béné were waiting.

"*Oh, ma chère, ma chère*! You're home, home at last!" I was enveloped in the love of les femmes Lévesque. I followed them out of the station and over to the gray family Chevrolet. My bags stowed, Mémère and I climbed in the back seat, where I sat behind Maman, as Béné started the engine, my little sister who could now drive. Then she drove out, westward, into Sutton and home, and whatever twists and turns awaited me.

We passed the dark green Victorian home of my beloved. A light glowed in the living room where I had first made my acquaintance with Mr. and Mrs. Fredericks. Then we passed off to the right the looming buildings of the Nine Falls Mill. My best friend Dorcas's red brick house marked the arrival in downtown Sutton and we crossed the river, turned right and then left into Frenchtown. We passed St. Hyacinth, that cold, gray stone church where the terms of my exile had been decided upon, and then turned up the hill past the le couvent. And finally, a light glowing on the porch, the brown double-decker that was the only home I had ever known.

As we four Lévesque women entered the front hall, Mémère opened her door and walked into her darkened living room. "I'll bring the bread for supper," she said.

Maman, Béné, and I mounted the stairs and entered our living room. Papa was sitting in his chair with his Golden Wedding and Ballantine Ale on the table next to him. He took a sip of the whiskey. "Oh Hélène! Ma chère. I'm so glad you've come back to us. I've, we've missed you." Another sip. "If only your Pépère could have been here as well." A swallow of ale. "*C'est la vie.*"

I walked over, bent down and kissed his forehead. "*Je t'aime beaucoup, Papa.*"

"I'll put the soup on to heat," said Maman.

Béné and I took my luggage into my bedroom, mine again after almost a year of exile.

As I started to unpack, my little sister, no longer so little, went into her room and returned with a small package of envelopes. She handed them over to me. "These are your letters from Jim," she said. A tear moistened her cheek. "I'm so sorry. It was decided that it wouldn't be good for you to get them while you were…away." She didn't say, and I didn't ask, who had made that decision, just one of the many choices that had been made for me. I put the packet on the bedside table. I had no words. Rather, I opened my arms and drew her into an embrace…unspoken forgiveness.

The next morning I woke up in my own bed—for the first time in 1942. I walked out to the kitchen. Maman et Mémère were sitting at the table with cups of tea, waiting for the bread dough to rise.

"*Tu as bien dormi, Hélène*?" my grandmother asked.

"*Pas mal,* Mémère," I replied.

"There are a few doughnuts in the breadbox," Maman said. "They're a day old but probably still pretty good." It felt strange to be conversing in both French and English.

"They have to be better than any I've had since…since I went off to Québec." I walked over to the counter, selected a doughnut, and poured myself a cup of tea.

"Do you have plans for today?" she asked.

"Well, I think I'd like to go over to Dorcas's and have her bring me up to date on Sutton news. And then I'll go to the high school. They have my diploma. Miss Franks will probably be there. I'd like to see her. She's been so kind."

"I'd drive you across the river, but your father has the car. He's on the get-up shift this week."

"That's fine. Where's Béné?"

"She has a babysitting job at the Wilson's; they're a young couple across the river with a new baby. They both have jobs at the mill lab. Such complicated lives."

There was a momentary drop of energy in the room. "Well, I'm sure she'll take good care of a little one," I managed. I finished my breakfast, washed my dishes, and walked down the stairs and into the morning.

As a younger, more innocent me had done so many times before, I walked down the hill, past St. Hyacinth, and across the Nine Falls into downtown Sutton. The Men's Shop and Fortin's Women's Shoppe were featuring summer in their windows: bathing suits; light, pastel dresses; plaid shirts. Vachon's Drugstore where Dorcas, Sophie, Thérèse, and I had shared high school gossip over pie à la mode and soda fountain drinks. Main Street rose smoothly up to Dorcas's red brick, stately home. I walked up onto the porch and rang the doorbell. After a moment, my best friend's mother opened the door.

"Ah, Hélène! It's so nice to see you. Won't you step in?"

I followed her into the vestibule. "Hi, Mrs. Warde. Is Dorcas home?

"Oh, I'm afraid not, my dear. She and her father have made a trip down to Massachusetts. He had business of some sort in Boston. And then they'll drive out to Wellesley. We thought it would be useful for Dorcas to get a feel for the campus and her dormitory before the fall semester begins." She paused. "You did know that she has been accepted at Wellesley?" A smile. "Her first choice. It's all quite exciting."

I tried to ease the moment with a small fib. "Yes. She told me all about it, back in the spring. She sounds very happy."

"Well, we're very pleased. A wonderful place for a young woman."

"I think that Mrs. Fredericks, Jim's mother, said she was an alumnus."

"Alumna," Mrs. Warde gently corrected. "Well, Dorcas should be home late tomorrow. I'll tell her you called."

"Thank you very much." I walked down to the sidewalk, turned, and continued my path to another, even larger and more imposing brick edifice: Sutton High School.

I walked into the school and up the stairs to the main office. I took a deep breath and pulled my shoulders back, the better to present a mature Hélène Honoré. Principal Sampson was standing behind the counter.

"Oh, good morning, Hélène. Welcome back. You're looking very well."

"Thank you, sir," I replied. "It's very nice to be home."

"Well, if you'll wait just a moment, I'll get your diploma. I've had it on my desk ever since the graduation ceremonies." He turned and disappeared into his inner office. After a moment he returned and with a flourish handed me a blue, imitation leather booklet. "Go right ahead and open it," he said. "A prize that you've justly earned." I opened it and saw the proof that another part of the challenge of my exile had been met.

"Thank you sir," I replied. "I very much appreciate all the support that I received from you, Mr. DiRenzo, and Miss Franks."

"I think I saw that she is in the building, finishing up the school year's odds and ends. I'm sure she would be very happy to see you." He nodded toward the door. "And again, all our congratulations."

I walked out of the office and up the foot-worn wooden stairs to the second floor. A right took me into the corridor in which much of my abbreviated senior year had taken place. The third classroom door on the left was slightly ajar. I knocked and stepped in. Miss Franks looked up from her desk.

"Oh, Hélène," she said. "Welcome back, my dear. It's so wonderful to see you. It seems like forever."

"Thank you, Miss Franks. It's great to be home."

She gestured to a desk in the front row, the same seat where we had had our parting conversations eight months before. I walked down and took my seat. "You are looking very well, Hélène. I'm sure your family is thrilled to have you home again." We sat for a moment. I was unsure of how the conversation should continue. She broke the silence. "I want to tell you what a wonderful job you did with your assignments. It was as if each essay marked a further step into academic maturity."

"Thank you. I think I learned a lot."

"I was especially drawn to your final essay, 'A Late Summer Evening,' if I remember correctly."

"Thank you. I loved that we were allowed to choose to write from our own experience."

"And you did it very well. It seemed you had taken up Hemingway's sense of simple, direct expression to suggest the unspoken." We sat for a moment, both reflecting on the essay. "And now, Hélène, if you don't mind my asking, what are you envisioning for your next step?"

I gathered myself to answer a question for which there were so many components: family, money, school, job, Jim. "Well, for now I think I need to get a job. I've been told that the shipyard in South Portland is hiring, including women for actual construction jobs. It may be a good way to earn some money and to help the war effort." The last seemed a bit more directly patriotic than I felt but, I hoped, would help my entrance into the world of adults.

Miss Franks nodded. "Indeed, my dear. But I'm thinking more about your continued education. Certainly, you're more than ready for college."

Again, I gathered my young self. "Well, I would love to think that college is possible. But I'm not sure, costs and all."

"Well, as you may remember, I am a proud alumna of Smith College. My four years in Northampton were the making of me, both academically and as a woman. And I've kept my connections to the college. They have started a program intended to attract young women from many different parts of our rich American tapestry. And, for deserving working-class young women, there are now specific scholarships based on need as well as academic potential. When I heard of the program, I thought at once of you."

"Oh! Oh, that is so kind of you. I don't know if…."

My mentor gently held up a hand. "There is no need to decide immediately. Talk things over with your parents. And if it seems as if Smith would be right for you, please let me know, and I can facilitate your admission. Let me give you my address and telephone number, in case I'm not in school when you decide. Feel free to call me." She reached into her desk, took out a notepad, jotted her information and handed it to me. We sat for a moment. "And now, my dear Hélène, I simply must do battle with my desk. So much to be purged at the end of another school year." She paused. "And, if it all comes together and your first year unfolds like I'm sure it will, perhaps I might make the trip to Northampton the spring for Illumination Night, a tradition during commencement weekend when alumnae gather for a reunion with classmates."

I stood and said, "Once again, many thanks, Miss Franks. I will talk with my parents when I get home. Thank you." I turned, walked out of my English IV world, down the stairs and out into the June morning in Sutton, Maine.

As I retraced my steps downtown, I tried to create some picture, some timeline, of where my journey might lead: two months—a job? College? Three years: Jim's return from his service? The marriage of my dreams, *un bébé* of my own? The late morning sun warmed my back as my hopes, my dreams warmed my heart.

As I approached the bridge across the Nine Falls, I looked up and saw a pair of women approaching from the Frenchtown side of the river. I recognized Thérèse and her mother. Glad to see one of my closest school friends, I smiled and waved my hand. In response, Mrs. St. Clair took hold of her daughter's arm, guided her across the bridge, and passed with no acknowledgment of my greeting. Shocked, I watched them walk away. For a moment I felt like a ghost: mostly invisible, a source of fear to those whose paths might cross mine. A deep breath and I continued on my journey.

The family's Chevrolet was parked outside. I entered and saw that the door to Mémère's apartment was open. I walked in and found one side of the living room filled with cardboard cartons. Maman came in from the kitchen.

"*Ah, ma chère*," she said. "*Bienvenue*. You had a good visit at school?

"*Oui, Maman*." I held out my diploma.

Smiling, she drew me into her arms. "We are so very proud of you. And so happy you have returned." She gestured at the brown boxes. "Mémère and I are starting to pack. There are only a few weeks until we move to our new home. When you go upstairs, why don't you put the water on for tea. We thought that we would take a ride out to the cemetery. The flowers by Pépere's stone can use some water."

Upstairs, in my room, I laid my diploma on my desk, next to Jim's photograph. It felt as if the two currents of my life, my love and my mind, were somehow seeking some form of connection, sense of balance. A deep breath and I walked through the living room and into the kitchen. I filled the tea kettle and took out three cups and a plate for cookies from the jar on the counter. Then I sat and waited as the kettle started its whistling air, a lament or a prelude?

When Maman et Mémère returned, we sat over our tea, the cookies untouched for the moment. I braced myself and told them the strange story of the St. Clair women passing me by on the bridge. A long moment passed. Then my grandmother reached across the table and took my hand. "*Ah, Hélène, je suis désolée.*" Haltingly, she explained that Monseigneur had made a pronouncement to his flock. The Holy Church, God, His Son, and the Holy Mother required that women who had fallen from grace outside of wedlock were to be denied acceptance by the congregation. In a word, I was to be shunned. "Of course, we, your family, will continue to give you all our love and support.

And," Maman continued, "as time passes, the love of God will offer forgiveness, as we have already done. You are always a part of us."

There seemed nothing left to say. Then Maman rose and returned the untouched cookies to the tin. I cleared the cups and teapot. Then we, the three Lévesque women, returned to Mémère's apartment to continue boxing up shards of our Frenchtown lives.

Later, after Béné's return from babysitting, Mémère, Maman, my little sister, and I piled in the car and drove over to the St. Hyacinth cemetery, located just across a side street from the Sutton Acres community cemetery. The separation spoke to the boundary between the Catholic and Protestant communities in our town. We made our way through rows of memorials, often topped by a cross or spire, to an area of clearly more recent stones. And there was the modest monument of my grandfather: Clément DuBois: b. 1873; d. 1942. Below, awaiting her reunion with husband and God was carved: Caroline Trémont, b. 1884; d. Les quatre femmes Trémont–DuBois–Levesque hugged through our tears. "*Un homme formidable,*" said his widow. "*Mais oui, Mémère,*" I replied. "*Impeccable.*" The sun began its descent beyond the maple and spruce trees at the cemetery edge. Then, all that remained was to retrace our path to home and supper.

The next morning, I traveled by bus from Sutton, across Portland, to South Portland and the booming shipyard. There, I searched out the employment office. The gentleman who interviewed me asked what my plans for the future held. Holding back specific details of my young story, I explained that I was a recent Sutton High graduate and was looking forward to joining the war effort while helping my family's finances, especially as they were purchasing a new home. He did not ask, and I did not volunteer, whether any longer term options were awaiting me. He offered an entry level job in production and suggested that steps up the employment ladder could be there for a bright, young woman such as I seemed to be. I could begin my job starting next Monday. I thanked him, walked out past the looming skeletons of US naval freighters, and retraced my steps back to Frenchtown.

At dinner, I told my family about my new job. Papa finished his glass of Balentine and nodded approvingly. Then I took a deep breath and told them of Miss Franks's offer of help with my admission to Smith. There was a moment of silence. Maman stepped into the breach: "A kind and generous offer." Papa countered: "Why college when you have a good-paying job?" Mémère: "A real chance for chère Hélène to take the next step up on our family's ladder." Bénédicte: "You've earned the chance, overcome challenges." In the end, Papa shrugged and gave his blessing. I would reach out to Miss Franks to see if Smith would judge me worthy.

Back in my room, I took out the last of my stationary I had been gifted to take into my exile. On a spare sheet of Nine Falls paper I drafted a note to Miss Franks, set it aside, and then gave it a careful proofread. Then, on the stationary, I copied my request that she reach out to Smith's admissions office. My family was in full support of my decision. I would set aside as much of my shipyard wages as possible to help defray college costs. And, as always, many thanks for her support. I addressed the envelope, folded the letter and sealed it in. Then, I looked into James Stuart Fredericks's eyes in the black-and-white photo that had been with me throughout my journey. "There comes a time," I whispered. "Until our time." Then, as I did each evening, I took another of my love's letters, cached in Sutton, Maine, during my exile in Stansted, Québec, and read of another day of flight training, of the camaraderie of his platoon, and of his undying love of "*chère, chère Hélène.*"

July unfolded as I entered the adult world of employment. I was placed on the afternoon shift at the shipyard, a third-tier helper on a welding team. It felt as if there were an entire, so-complex world inside the huge gray freighter. Voices echoing, steel plates crashing into place, cascades of sparks from the welders. I discovered that the work was rewarding, although never easy. I was proving myself and helping in some small way to provide support for our American troops, my brothers, Jim. Two other helpers were women of about my age, a bit of a buffer against the man games of the rest of the crew. Often, when overtime took us into early morning, there would be no bus to Sutton, and I would stay at the Portland apartment that Mary and Sophia shared with two other young workforce women. As the world of Southern Maine turned toward the morning, we would gossip about the evolving stories of men and women at work together. "It would make a good soap opera," Sophia suggested.

* * *

Then, the first week of August brought another avenue on the map of Hélène Honoré's life. When I returned home after my shift, there was a thick envelope on the kitchen table, addressed to me, the return address printed on the upper left corner: Office of Admissions, Smith College, Northampton, Massachusetts. Alone at midnight, I tore open the envelope and unfolded the contents. It offered congratulations for having been selected as a member of the Smith College Class of 1946. A second page informed me that I had been awarded a scholarship that would cover all costs of tuition, fees, room, and board beyond whatever level of payment I could afford. A third page described the Smith mission of providing an open, caring, and challenging environment for talented and motivated young women.

Alone in the early morning, I let my mind take in the flipping pages of Hélène Honoré's life: September 1942: my first days on the Smith campus; summers at the shipyard; May 1946: graduation. But where? Where and when was Jim in this future? When would his service be ended? How would we balance his final two years at Dartmouth? My Smith days? Our lives together? For now I would try to focus only on the near term. Bringing my family on board, reaching out to Miss Franks and Smith, bringing Jim up to date, preparing to be a college student. I gathered up the contents of the life-changing envelope and switched off the kitchen and living room lights. In my bedroom I undressed, pulled on my nightgown, and sitting on the edge of my bed, looked over to my Jim's photo on my desk. "*Je t'aime, mon coeur,*" I whispered.

More and more it felt like my young life, la vie d'Hélène Honoré, was like the rushing Nine Falls River after a summer downpour. I tried to prepare myself for my next life step, to Northampton, to Smith. Dorcas and I shared strategies about what we needed for life in college dormitories: clothing, toiletries, mementos to keep our homes and families in our hearts, pens, a dictionary, a thesaurus. And my job at the shipyard brought a real sense of purpose and a solid paycheck each Friday. On the nights that my shift ended so that I arrived home before Papa departed for his night shift, we two, father and daughter chatted about the world of work, really the first time that our conversations went beyond the norms that had directed my childhood.

When I arrived at work on Thursday, the 20th of August, my fellow workers were abuzz with news from the war. Radios had reported an attempted invasion of occupied France by the armed forces of the British Commonwealth. In spite of a coordinated assault from sea, land, and air, the attack on the coastal city of Dieppe had been lashed by the entrenched German forces. A brigade of Royal Canadian infantry had fought bravely, but in the end had been beaten back into the Channel. Over one hundred planes of the Royal Air Force had been lost to German fighters and antiaircraft fire. At that moment, the war, which I had always known as a flow of stories from newspapers and radio, became real. Paul, my eldest brother who had volunteered to fight with Canadian forces…was Paul among the thousands of missing and dead soldiers on the shores of France? And oh, my God, *mon Dieu*, if the RAF had suffered such losses, what horrors awaited American airmen like my love, my Jim?

I thought back to when Miss Franks had guided my reading to *All Quiet on the Western Front*, seemingly a lifetime in the past. Remarque's portrayal of the two facets of war—the broad, strategic, heroic and the singular—one lonely death among the multitudes. I remembered the sad power of, "And that is just why they let us down so badly…." And here I was, Hélène Honoré, doing my part in the war effort, helping America to prepare to win, to triumph, rising above the piles of dead, lonely individuals, the cost of power, of nations.

That Sunday I awoke in my room, into the silence of a weekend. Papa was doing his get-up shift at the mill. Maman and Mémère were at mass at St. Hyacinth. Béné was sleeping in after the Saturday night dance at the Legion Hall. I sat up, stretched, and walked out to the kitchen. While I waited for the tea kettle to whistle, I sat and tried to run through my mind how the next two weeks would unfold. My last day at the shipyard would be next Friday. The following week would be taken up with sorting and packing for my departure to Smith. We had checked the train schedules and found I could travel from Portland to Northampton with only two transfers in just under ten hours. Monday, August 31, 1942, would be my nineteenth birthday. My journey into the next chapter would begin almost one year since Jim and I had spent our parting night together at Camp Content. I could hear the call of the loons across the warm September night. A knock on the door jolted me back into my present. I walked into the living room and opened the door. There stood Dorcas, my very best friend.

"Hi, Heck," she said. "Can I come in for a moment? I nodded of course and then she followed me into the kitchen.

"Can I get you some tea?"

"No, no thanks," she replied. "I can't stay long." We sat in a pause. "Hélène, I'm so…I'm so sorry, but I've got some bad—sad—news that I need to share with you." Another pause. I tried to take a breath and just waited. "Well, last night Mrs. Fredericks called my mom. She told her…Heck, it's Jim. An Army Air Corps chaplain called…Jim's been killed in a plane crash. There weren't many details, some kind of an accident near a base in England." Tears streamed down her face. It seemed she could hardly breathe.

Somewhere deep inside, I'd known the moment I saw my friend's face, unexpected at my door on a quiet Sunday morning. "Oh, my God, Dorcas!" I managed. "Oh, Jim! Oh, my Jim!" We stood, and she walked over and drew me into her strong arms. We stayed locked together for what seemed to be… time seemed frozen. Finally I managed to ask, "Do you know anything more?"

"I'm so sorry; that's all. My mother thought that Mrs. Fredericks had called, because they were long time friends but also because she hoped that I could bring the news of their loss, their tragedy to you. I'm sure…they must be in shock. Heck, I know you know how much Jim loved you. That afternoon at Jim's farewell party at Little Loon, when he looked at you, it was just so clear to everyone there." Again, we embraced. Then we heard the downstairs doors open and close as Mémère and Maman returned from mass. We waited in the kitchen for my mother to enter. Somehow I managed to tell her that in an instant Hélène Honoré's life had changed.

"*Oh, ma chère, ma chère*!" she cried. "*Je suis très, très désolée*!" She turned to Dorcas. "Thank you for being such a good friend to Hélène. She is so very lucky to have you."

"And to have such a wonderful family," Dorcas replied. "I'm sure that you'll all get through this somehow, together." We stood for a moment. We heard Béné come out of her bedroom. "I really have to go now," she continued. "You know where I am, Heckie, anytime at all." A final hug and she walked out into the hall and down the stairs.

Béné came in, and Maman told her the sad news. Then my dear sister walked down and brought Mémère back upstairs. *Les quatres femmes Lévesque*, as so many times before, sat at the kitchen table sharing strength and love.

The next day the *Portland Press Herald* ran a short article on its front page about the tragic loss of one of Sutton's most promising young men, James Stuart Fredericks, in the crash of a B-24 Army Air Corps bomber near the coast in England. Details were limited, but it seemed that the plane had suffered an engine malfunction while on a training flight over County Surry, south of London. There were no survivors among the crew of six airmen.

The obituary pages of the paper, headed by a photo of Jim in his airmen's garb, related a barebones biography: his young years in Sutton sports, academic achievement, his decision to leave Dartmouth for defense of his country. There would be a two o'clock memorial service the following Sunday, August 30, at the Oxford Street Congregational Church. There would be no visiting hours.

That evening, following dinner, our family gathered in the living room to come to grips with the paths, the decisions that faced me. Maman and Mémère made it very clear that whatever choices I, Hélène Honoré, made would have their unwavering support. Did I think it was possible that I could cope with moving to a new world at Smith, two states away from my home? Papa stressed that my job at the shipyard could provide a solid, regular foundation as I moved through these hard times. Béné, my dear sister, suggested that perhaps, if I felt ready, Smith would give me direction and support, a safe place to continue. I could only listen, to feel their love through all the paths they suggested. The decision would be mine alone. I told them how much that love, and their trust, would give me the strength to move onward. Then I retreated to my bedroom and, in black and white, Jim's smiling face. Somehow, I managed to drift off to sleep. Then, in the darkness, I awoke from a dream, remembering only the call of loons across a summer lake…and my love's voice reminding me, "There comes a time."

Somehow I made it through the week. I decided that I wasn't up for another week at the shipyard. I called the employment office and spoke with one of the women on the staff. She was very kind in response, thanked me for the part, however brief, I had played in their war effort, and wished me well in the next steps of my young life. I divided my days between continuing preparations for my departure, walks around Sutton, retracing moments, and looking at Jim's photo when I first awoke and as I was trying to slip into sleep, unsure of what dreams might inform my waking life. On one of my walks I stopped in at

Dorcas's home. My dearest friend gently asked how I was doing, where I was going. We agreed to meet on Sunday and go to the memorial service together.

On that Sunday, the last day of my eighteen-year-old self, I dressed in my best outfit and walked over to meet Dorcas. We walked down Main Street where the tall, gray-spired Congregational Church sat on the corner of Oxford Street, near the brick and concrete mass of the Nine Falls Mill. We entered the church and found two seats in a pew halfway back in the rapidly filling sanctuary. At two o'clock, the bell in the steeple began a long series of tolls. Then the organist began playing a somber prelude, and Mr. and Mrs. Fredericks, clad in black, walked down the aisle and took their places in the front pew.

The service unfolded with hymns unfamiliar to my once-Catholic ear. The minister spoke movingly of service and family and loss, all standing on the rock of God's love and His promise of a holy life after the trials of death. And above all, he offered the condolences of the people of Oxford Street and the Sutton community at large to the Fredericks family, whose dear son had made the ultimate sacrifice to the nation and a world caught in the flames of war. A prayer, a final hymn, and then, as the organist played a recessional, the parents of my Jim walked down the aisle, Mr. Fredericks nodding left and right to familiar faces and Mrs. Fredericks locked in an iron gaze above the mourners, up toward the round, stained glass window. And then, row after row, the gathering followed them toward the sunlight and warmth of a late August Sunday.As Dorcas and I reached the exit, we saw that Mr. and Mrs. Fredericks were standing by the doorway, listening and responding to the sympathies of the mourners. As we approached them, Dorcas shook Mr. Fredericks's hand. Mrs. Fredericks acknowledged her and then asked if her preparations to depart for Wellesley were going well. Then my friend stepped ahead, and I was face-to-face with Jim's parents.

I reached out my hand to the father. "Mr. Fredericks," I managed. "I am so…I am so very…." My voice caught in my throat.

He enveloped my small hand in both of his. "Thank you, Hélène," he said. "We know how dearly Jim held you. His letters to us were filled with his hopes and dreams of a life with you at the center."

"Thank you, sir. I can only imagine…your loss." I turned to the mother. "Mrs. Fredericks…."

She stilled my voice with a gaze that seemed to be locked in some sort of overriding strength. "We must all be strong, my dear. Life is often not fair. And so we must be strong." A pause. "And will you be leaving soon for Smith?"

I was frozen for a moment, surprised that she knew of my plans. "Yes," I managed. "Miss Franks has been wonderful in helping me toward this opportunity."

"Well, I'm sure that you would agree that this past year has been like no other for each of us." Again that iron-willed gaze. "We offer you our best wishes." Then she turned to the couple who were following us down the aisle.

Dorcas and I walked down along the river and up to the sculpture of the boy and dog, where we had parted nearly a year ago. "I've been thinking about this," she said. "It's like a portrayal of a world that strips us naked, all those boys, all the dead boys scattered. But somehow it's not totally awful… the loyalty and love of the dog on the banks of a river on a summer day, innocence trying to win over fear and grief."

I had no answer. But in my mind I called up the memory of James Stuart Fredericks and his love, Hélène Honoré Lévesque, together in the warm water of Little Loon Lake. And my love saying to me, "There comes a time." I reached out and took my friend's hand in mine. Then we walked along the Nine Falls, upstream.

When I got home, Papa was in his chair, the Red Sox facing the Senators. Surprisingly, he got up and followed me into the kitchen. Maman turned from the counter where Sunday supper was being prepared. "Oh, Hélène," she cried. "On the table…there is a telegram. For a moment I froze, unsure if I could bear another piece of bad news. "It's from Paul, from England. Read it."

I picked up the yellow sheet of paper and unfolded it. The black lettering said, "Dear family. I am safe and well. My battalion had only twenty losses. We will win this war. With love, Paul."

The next evening, la famille Lévesque celebrated my nineteenth birthday. Uncle Marcel DuBois, Aunt Jacqueline, and Cousin Eugénie with her two little ones came to share the cake. Later, after the men had retired to the living room, my cousin and aunt apologized for the shunning they knew I had faced on the streets of Frenchtown. It was terrible, the punishment that Monseigneur and the Church had forced on its congregation. But, please, I was to believe that in their hearts they loved me and had faith that I would follow my path as a strong young woman.

As the day for my departure for Northampton neared, I reviewed my train connections, checked and rechecked my packing, and tried to envision the next step into the unknown. I wrote a thank-you note to Miss Franks. Dorcas and I met at Vachon's Drug for pie and ice cream, sharing our excitement and just a bit of trepidation for our entrance into the world of the Seven Sisters, the world of women's education.

Sunday, September 7, my last full day as a Sutton, Maine girl, unfolded as normally as my departure allowed. Mass, dinner, Red Sox on the radio. Clattering in the kitchen. Mémère and Maman once again going over plans for the family move to the new home on the edge of Sutton. Then, unexpectedly, there was a knock on our apartment door. I walked over, opened it, and there stood Diane, the Fredericks's domestic helper, whom I had not seen since the farewell gathering at Little Loon Lake a year before."Diane," I managed. "It's so nice…to see you. Won't you come in?"

"Hélène," she said. "Mr. and Mrs. Fredericks are outside. We came over together. They don't wish to intrude on your family's Sunday but, if you would, they would very much like to see you for a moment."

"Of course," I replied. And then I followed her down the stairs and out into the yard. Jim's parents were standing together next to their dark blue Buick. And next to them was Jim's Model A, the car in which many paths of our so-short life together had unfolded. I walked over to them, followed by Diane.

"Mr. and Mrs. Fredericks," I said. "This is such a nice surprise."

For once, Mrs. Fredericks opened the conversation. "Hélène, we understand that you are about to embark on your college life at Smith."

"Yes, ma'am," I replied. "I'm leaving by train tomorrow morning."

"Yes. Mrs. Warde told us so. I had called them to wish Dorcas well as she prepared for her entrance into Wellesley."

"I'm very happy for her," I said.

Mr. Fredericks continued. "James's mother and I were talking about you two young women, such great examples of the path education provides for those who have earned their place." A pause. "Well, we felt that we might be able to ease the journey for you a bit. And so, we wish you to have our dear boy's auto, to offer the ease of the open road between Sutton and Northampton."

"I…I don't know what to say," I stammered. "You are so kind…I…."

"No need, We wish you all the best. In the glove box you will find the new certificate of title in your name and the registration form for the new license plates." Another pause. "And, oh yes, we have continued the auto insurance and the AAA roadside assistance plan in your name. You will be covered until August of next year. Oh, and here are the keys."

"And now, my dear," Mrs. Fredericks said, "we simply must be on our way. Diane…" she nodded in her direction, "Diane was kind enough to drive the Ford over. We will drop her off on our way home."

I tried with all my young strength to fight back tears. "I'm so very grateful, Mr. and Mrs. Fredericks, that you thought of me in this way. Thank you so very much."

"And we are forever grateful to you, my dear," Mr. Fredericks said. "You brought great happiness to the life of our son." With that, he took his wife's arm, turned and walked to the Buick, Diane following two steps behind in their wake.

I rushed upstairs and told my family about this great surprise. Maman and Béné wrapped me in their arms. Papa seemed truly moved in a way I had never really seen before. It was as if the car, Jim's car, freely given to me, solidified in his mind the depth of the love that his daughter had shared with James Stuart Fredericks, a love that spanned the Nine Falls River from our Frenchtown apartment to that tall, green Victorian home. I, Hélène Honoré, two generations following the arrival of *les Québequois* into America, testified to the strength of their hopes and hard work.

The next morning my family helped carry my worldly goods down the stairs to be stowed in the rumble seat trunk of the Model A. I placed my purse on the front passenger seat, next to a roadmap the Frederickses had left for me. And on the floor, safe from sudden stops or bends in the road, I placed a small cardboard box carefully filled with stationary, Miss Franks's address, and letters from my late love, securing his black-and-white photograph that had followed me in a year that I had managed to see through.

I drove out of Sutton, across Portland, below the bluffs of the Western Promenade where Jim and I had looked toward the western horizon. Then I connected with US Route One and headed southward to the next chapter of Hélène Honoré Lévesque.

Growing Up Gilbert

The Russians Are Coming

GILBERT, STEWIE, AND VINCE WALKED OUT of the woods and up Warren Place. Vince carried his father's pickax, and the Jenkins brothers each carried a spade. They were covered with dirt after an afternoon digging foxholes in the Tall Pines. They had chosen their site carefully on the side of a hill that ran down to the brook. Then they set up their mortars facing toward the hill beyond the pine grove, the location of the Russian troops. Off to the side of their fortress was an old, hollowed out oak tree, providing an elevated, secure platform where, in turn, each boy could stand watch and call down instructions to the gunners during their battles. Now, having once again saved Sutton, Maine, from the Red Scourge, they were heading home for supper. As they reached the corner of Woods and Warren, they saw that Tommy and his friend Junior were sitting on his front steps. The brown Victorian had a porch that wrapped around the turret-like expansion.

Gil remembered with a momentary shiver that last year when Tommy's father died suddenly, he had crept up on the porch and peeked into the living room. There he saw Tommy stretched out on a couch, seemingly neither asleep nor really awake. At home, Gil told his mother what he had seen. She replied that the boy probably was tired out, both from the shock of his loss and the strain of dealing with adults and their approaches to death. Now Gil and his best friend, Vince, both eleven, and nine-year-old Stewie veered off course and walked over to where the older boys, both eighth graders, watched their approach.

"Wow, you guys are grubby," Tommy said. "You been digging the Panama Canal or something?"

"No way," Vince replied. "We've dug a whole bunch of foxholes for when we're fighting the Russians. No matter how many we splatter, they just keep coming."

Stewie jumped in, "Yeah, but we drove them back today. All the way to the top of Oak Hill."

"Hold your ground," Junior said. "Sooner or later, headquarters will send you reinforcements."

"And air power," Tommy added. "That's the key in modern wars. Sabre Jets and B-47s."

The whistle at the Nine Falls Paper Mill blew. "Supper time," Gil said. "Come on, Stewie. Mom doesn't like us to be late."

* * *

Katherine Jenkins bustled around, checking the meatloaf and baked potatoes. She called out to her friend Eva who was sitting at the round kitchen table. "Just a second. Supper's just about ready."

"Take your time, Katie." Eva replied. "It all smells chust luffley."

Katherine wiped her hands and sat down with her friend. Petie, her five-year-old third son, was banging around his toy earth mover in the corner of the dining area. Two-year-old Allie bounced in his swing chair. Their mother took a sip of her tea, a deep breath followed by a long exhalation.

"It's been a long day," she said. "I'm glad you could stop by, Eva. It's nice to have an adult to chat with."

"Well, I can't stay long," her friend said. "Franz will be waiting for me and supper. Sometimes I wonder how you manage with the four boys and Dr. John avay. How long has it been now?"

"Over a month," Katherine replied. "Sometimes it feels twice that long. Even though his practice hours were crazy long, he was still here."

"Und how much longer will his training be?

"A little more than three months, down at Fort Sam Houston. And then he'll find out about where he's going to be sent. God, I hope they don't send him to Korea! Two years in the army is bad enough, but if he has to go to the war…well, I just pray that he gets a posting at some medical facility here in the States."

"Well, it's chust awful that this world can't figure how not to go to war. You would think that the two great wars would have been enough.

"And you of all people must know that, Eva. After what happened to your Germany, all the destruction, no matter how bad Hitler and the Nazis were. It's always the little people who suffer."

Eva took a long sip of tea and tipped her head back, eyes closed. "Sometimes I still see the city after the bombers had finished and the American soldiers arrived. My people were lucky; the Russians were getting closer all the time when the surrender came."

Katherine smiled and reached over to pat her friend's hand. "And so you met Franz and came to us here in Sutton. Maine must have seemed like another planet."

The back door banged open, and Gilbert and Stewie came into the kitchen.

"Hi, Mom," her eldest said. "Hi, Mrs. Jensen. I hope I'm not too late. Smells like a good supper." He walked over and gave his mother a hug.

"Go get cleaned up, Gil," Katherine said. You can help get the table set."

"I must go now, Katie," Eva said. "And Gil, my name is chust Eva." She stood.

"Thanks for dropping in," Katherine said. "It's nice to have a friend who can listen and understand."

"Well, you're a strong woman. And it all will work out. And, whatever, we have to believe that our government is doing what is necessary. When I think of how close the Russian army came to changing my life…well, I hate the wars, but I love our freedom."

The two women walked to the back door.

"Thanks again, for coming," Katherine said. "Will I see you at the Women of the Church meeting Saturday?

"With God's blessing," Eva replied. "Auf Wiedersehen."

Gil was washing his hands in the kitchen sink as Mrs. Jensen said her goodbyes. His head whirled around the complexities of the grown-up world that he overheard about peace and freedom, but the adults talked only of enemies, dangers, and war. Mrs. Jensen was a kind woman, but she was a German and only a few years ago, an enemy. She had fled the Russian army to the safety of the American zone, but the Russians had been our allies. Now they were the enemies. And Korea: we were at war again. The South Koreans were our friends; the North Koreans the enemies, even though they had lived in the same place for centuries. But somehow the South was free, like us, and the North had become communists out to take away that freedom. And across the Yalu river was Communist China and beyond that the Soviet Union. In social studies class, it was easy to see that there was a red swath that ran from Germany to the Pacific Ocean. And squeezed between China and Korea was Japan, once our enemy but now our friend, as if Hiroshima and Nagasaki could be put aside. But there were still atom bombs, more and bigger. And on top of it all, his father was now in the army, doing his duty to his country, while at home his family lived in fear, unspoken, of what might come after his training came to an end.

The day before Dr. Jenkins left for Texas, he called his eldest into the living room. "Gil," he said, "These next months are going to be hard for all of us. I'm going to miss you every moment of every day. But it's going to be especially hard for your mother. She's a wonderful, strong woman, but she's going to be on her own, without a man around the house. And so, I need you to be strong and help her in every way you can. It's a lot to ask of an eleven-year-old. but I know you're up to the task. And know I love you all."

"I'll do my best, Dad," Gilbert replied. "Honey and I can keep tabs on Petie and Allie."

"Ah yes, a boy and his dog. There's no stronger bond in all the world."

* * *

Friday morning, Gil and Vince approached the Woods Street Elementary School just as the Nine Falls Paper Mill eight-o-clock whistle blew. The solid, two-story brick building was fronted with thick granite slab stairs, leading up to a broad porch flanked with white columns. Two eighth-grade boys wearing the white straps with the badge of school patrol boys stood at the top of the steps, monitoring the arriving hordes. "No skipping steps," one of them intoned.

The friends mounted the stairs one at a time and entered the central hall of the school. To their left was the stairway that led upstairs, where dwelled seventh, and eighth graders, along with the office of Mr. Cleveland, the principal and upper-level math teacher. The boys continued past the stairs and to the right to Mrs. Franklin's sixth-grade room. Slipping into their seats, they continued their discussion of the upcoming game of the Sutton High football team.

"Who would have guessed," Vince said, "that we'd be 5 and 0 with a chance to lock up the league title tomorrow."

"Yeah," Gil replied. "If they can just get past the Patriots…they could end up undefeated."

"And a home game, too. Let's make sure to get there early."

"I hope the game doesn't go too long. I have to be home to take care of Petie and Allie by four thirty. My mom has a church meeting to go to."

"Shouldn't be a problem," Vince said. "The Blue Flames should have it wrapped up by then. I mean Bunny Beale at quarterback will…."

"Good morning, class," Mrs. Franklin interrupted. "Let's get settled in. Please rise and join in the Pledge of Allegiance."

The twenty-three sixth graders stood and faced the American flag on its slanted pole next to the blackboard.

"I pledge allegiance to the flag of the United States of America. And to the republic for which it stands: one nation, indivisible, with liberty and justice for all."

The students sat. "Thank you, class. And now Martha will read the daily devotion."

Martha Miller stood and walked to the front of the room, carrying a white-covered Bible. "Today's reading is from Psalm thirty-seven:

"Fret not thyself because of evildoers, neither be thou envious against the workers of iniquity. For they shall soon be cut down like the grass, and wither as the green herb. Trust in the Lord, and do good; so shalt thou dwell in the land, and verily thou shalt be fed. Delight thyself also in the Lord: and he shall give thee the desires of thine heart. Commit thy way unto the Lord; trust also in him; and he shall bring it to pass.'"

She smiled a leader's smile and sat down.

"Thank you, Martha," Mrs. Franklin said. "That was a very well-chosen passage, especially in these difficult times. Now, please take out your math notebooks. We'll review the lesson on fractions from yesterday."

Following fractions and a lesson on sentence diagrams came the morning break.

Some departed for "the basement" as the boys and girls toilet rooms were called at Woods Street. Mrs. Franklin sent Vince and Terry to get the white and chocolate milks and the packets of Nabs crackers for recess.

As the class returned, the refreshments were doled out according to their personal accounts. Gil took his chocolate milk, shaking the bottle as he returned to his seat. He would have liked some of the peanut butter Nabs, but his mother felt that they were unnecessary with lunch only two hours away. Milk was another story, although she strongly advocated that he choose white at least half the time. Gil complied, as much as his fuzzy memory would allow.

Recess concluded, Mrs. Franklin called her charges back to order. "Now, class, it's time for our weekly current events reports. Who would like to share a new item about what's going on around the world?" Young hands waved in hopes of being chosen to report. "Danny. What do you have for us about our world today?"

Danny Poitras stood and looked at a sheet of paper. "In Korea this past week, our army has been supporting the South Koreans in the Battle of White Horse Hill. There have been lots of casualties, but our big guns and planes have pushed back nine regiments of communists. Over five hundred South Korean troops were killed in action."

Mrs. Franklin offered a grim smile. "Thank you, Danny. We must remember our brave soldiers in our prayers as they fight to protect South Korea and to keep our American way of life safe. And now, a bit on the presidential election. Elaine, can you bring us up to date."

Elaine stood and faced the class. "There's under three weeks until the election. Most reports in the newspapers and on the radio think that Eisenhower is pretty far ahead of Stevenson."

Mrs. F and the others went back and forth on the candidates. Gil strayed into thinking about his dad's strong views on the potential presidents and their parties. He was a strong supporter of General Eisenhower, a man, he said, "of real leadership ability and strong American values." Even more, Dr. Jenkins hated President Truman, "who wanted to destroy the freedom and independence of doctors with his plans for socialized medicine." Gibert was unclear on what his dad meant but understood that the president and the Democrats who supported him were "almost as bad as the communists in Russia."

Gilbert had discovered that there were "rats" hidden in "Democrats." When he pointed that code out to his father, the doctor complimented him on his vision and promised to point out that odd coincidence to his friends.

* * *

Gilbert and Stewie returned home after an hour of "off the wall" baseball with their friends. The kitchen was rich with the smell of tomato sauce. It was Gil's firm belief that his mother's spaghetti and meatballs were the best in the world. The fact that Vince and Johnny both claimed the same for their mothers only reinforced his sense that everybody else had the right to be wrong.

"Hi, Mom," he said. "When do we eat?"

"In about a half hour, sweetie," she replied. "Remember I've got a Women of the Church meeting that starts at seven. I'll need your help getting Petie and Allie ready for bed. Mrs. Nolan is picking me up at about six thirty. Ardis will be here to stay with you while I'm gone. How about you give Honey her supper?"

Dinner confirmed Gil's reverence for his mom's pasta —"skaggettey," as Petie called it. Then the two eldest sons cleared the table while their mother scrubbed the remains of dinner off Petie and Allie and took them upstairs. When she came down, she looked out the kitchen window. "My ride's here, boys," she said. Ardis should be here any minute. You can listen to *The Lone Ranger*, but then it's off to bed. I shouldn't be too late." She grabbed her coat and rushed out the door.

Esther Nolan smiled as Katherine climbed into her Pontiac. "Good evening, Kate. Glad you can make the meeting tonight."

Katherine leaned back against the vinyl seat and took a deep breath. "It feels good to be out for a bit. And thanks for the lift, Esther. It's a big help."

Esther backed her two-toned sedan out onto Glen and turned right onto Main Street. St. Olaf's Lutheran Church sat on the flats by the Nine Falls, the first of seven churches in the mile leading into downtown Sutton. The car parked in the local Ford dealership lot, the two friends crossed the street, entered the church, and walked down into the meeting room on the lower level. A dozen members of the Women of the Church group had gathered. Eva Jensen spied her friend and walked across to greet her.

"Good evening, Katie," she said. "I'm so glad you could make it."

"It's nice to be out," Katherine replied. "Ardis must have been running late, and I had to leave Gil in charge. I hope she got there soon."

"Well, I'm sure he can hold the fort until she does. He's getting more grown up every day."

"Too fast, I think sometimes. Well, here's Pastor. Time to get started."

Pastor Peter Andreason was in the second month of his leadership at St. Olaf's, replacing Pastor Hartvig Sorenson, who had retired after a quarter of a century of service. In contrast with his predecessor, Reverend Andreason was thin, intense, and decisive. One of a new generation of Lutheran ministers, American born and tempered by the Great Depression and World War II, he was committed to leading his congregation toward living the gospel in the new challenges of the Cold War. The Women of the Church took their seats as he walked to the front of the room.

"The Peace of God be with you," he said.

"And with your spirit," replied his flock.

The Pastor slowly and smoothly made eye contact with each woman. "Peace," he continued. "Peace is the great gift of the Father to those of us fortunate enough to live in this good nation. And it is through His Son that each of us is reminded that our great gifts are won by following the true path to the sanctified life, now and in the life to come as promised to those who believe."

"Amen," murmured a single voice.

"And it is you, the women of this congregation, this church, this faith, who are especially called to testify to those around you—your family, your neighbors, your fellow parishioners—who perhaps are less firm in their faith." He paused. "I'm sure that all of you know the great challenges that face those of us who truly believe. Our world today is faced with powers that are bent on our destruction. Every day further demonstrates the godless, dictatorial reach of the Soviet Union. Some of you may have relatives who have disappeared behind the Iron Curtain. We can only pray for them and support our freely elected leaders, who are committed to containing the spread of that evil, atheistic empire." Again, he paused. His little congregation sat silently, unsure if the homily was at its end. Pastor Andreason took a deep breath, exhaled, and continued. "We can only hope that our leaders in Washington and our brave leaders in uniform can make wise choices as the enemy twists and probes to find weaknesses in our security. We must keep in our prayers those from our community who serve. Especially tonight, we pray for Dr. Jenkins who answered his nation's call, leaving his dear family behind." He nodded to Katherine, who held his gaze. "As for us, here in the peaceful community that is Sutton, each must be on the alert for those in the shadows who would plant seeds of discontent and weaken our resolve. Fellow travelers, "progressives," these true believers invite disunion in the name of equality and what they call justice. You strong women must be God's foot soldiers, through your loyal support of your husbands, good teaching of your children, and good works through the Women of the Church and the other worthy organizations you support. God be with you and good night." He gave a strong smile to the group, turned, and walked to the stairway leading to his study.

After a brief business meeting, the women were served coffee and cake by the refreshments committee. Katherine, Eva, Esther, and Dorothy Skillins, members of the outreach committee, sat together to discuss plans for an ecumenical service inviting the other Sutton churches to welcome Pastor Andreason.

Dotty Skillins, the chairwoman of the committee, summed up their plans to date. "So it's agreed that we will send invitations to each of the other churches in town. Kate, many thanks for volunteering to draft the letter."

Katherine looked at her notes. "Are we sure we want to address invitations to the different church councils, rather than the ministers and Monsignor Desjardins?"

"I think it's better that way," Esther said. "That way it seems less official than if Pastor Andreason were contacting the other clergy."

"I can't help but wonder if St. Hyacinth's congregation will join us," said Dotty. "At times there seems to be a divide wider than the Nine Falls between us Protestants and the Catholics. I can hardly imagine how our oldest members will react if the priests really do walk into our sanctuary. I'm sure some of them still believe the convent is a place for priests to hide their women. And so it's really important that we make sure that we welcome all who come. We are all Christians of course," Dotty continued. "And Kate, I'm sure you'll find just the right words."

Eva, who seemed to be returning from some far-off place, looked around the parish room as if for any strange faces. She took a deep breath and said, "I must say I was bothered by the words of the pastor, by his message this evening."

Esther turned to her and said, "What do you mean, Eva? I thought he was both warning us about our frightening world and complimenting us for being God's faithful servants."

"I couldn't help myself. As I listened, all I could hear was the words of people in my city, my beautiful Dresden, before the war; those we trusted and obeyed: the mayor, the other National Socialist leaders, my pastor in our old, good church. They also were warning us about our enemies, near and far, who only wanted to destroy the Fatherland."

Dotty responded, "But you can't mean that his message was anything like the hate and violence that the Nazis preached."

"No, no, of course not. But I remember how the eyes of the people in my neighborhood switched from welcoming to suspicion. Of the Social Democrats who stood for election against the party, the other countries, and, of course, the Jews. Rachael Cohen lived down the street and was in my class in school. And then one day her family packed up and left for England. The paint of the swastika on their front door was hardly dry. And we always needed protection against The Others"

Katherine leaned forward and took Eva's hand. "I think I can understand your concerns. John and I are friends with a couple, Charlie and Evelyn Rush, who live in Portland. They're both doctors and are very involved in the free clinic that cares for people less fortunate than we all are." She paused as if considering the path of her words. "They're very concerned with social justice and the inequalities that they see around them."

"Heaven helps those who help themselves," Ester said.

"And calls on us to reach out to the least among us. Anyway, back in 1948, they were very active in the local Progressive Party trying to get Henry Wallace elected instead of Truman or Dewey. I went to one of the rallies with them. It felt like a good place, but with three little kids and John's growing practice, there just wasn't time. And I have to admit that my husband wasn't as open to their platform. He felt that even Truman was too liberal, especially because of the idea of national health insurance. He used to joke about 'Truman coffee…You know…White House Drip.'"

Sylvia, the group chairwoman interrupted, "Well, ladies, I'm sure your plans will set up a great community gathering. But now it's time to turn off the lights. God bless."

* * *

Saturday gifted a perfect mid-October morning, clear and cool but with a whisper of summer's warmth on the breeze. Gil and his gang gathered on Dr. White's lawn for football and divided up, five against six. Timmy O'Hara, two years younger than the others and skinny, was the extra on his brother Terry's team. Mostly he stayed out of harm's way, although once before he had tagged Jane just before she broke away for a TD run.

Jane Millard was the only girl in the neighborhood sports gang. She was in Gilbert's grade, although she went to Saint Anne's Catholic School. While not as big as Steve or as fast as Vince, she was at least the equal of any of the boys in overall sports ability and second to none in competitive zeal. "She's real tough," Gil had explained to his dad over a post-baseball dinner. "And she doesn't even throw like a girl."

The game raged back and forth. Gilbert made a nice run for a score after Timmy jumped out of his path and fell over backward. Jane threw two TD passes in a row to Vince. Finally, it came to the last possession before lunch break. Gil took a snap from center and pitched the ball to Steve, who lumbered toward the goal line and the winning score. But Jane flashed up behind him and dove for a game-saving, two-handed tag. Her fingers got caught in the beltless waistband of Steve's dungarees, and as the two players tripped and fell short of the tulip bed that served as goal line, their momentum pulled the ball carrier's jeans down to his knees. Steve jumped up and, pulling his pants up over his tri-colored briefs, ran out of the yard and down Monroe Place toward home. Jane stood, straightened her T-shirt, and said, "We win." And with that, the players dispersed for lunch.

As Gil walked out of the Whites's lawn, he saw Tommy sitting on his front porch. The older boy waved to him, and he walked over.

"No war in the woods, today?" Tommy said.

"No way, it's football season," Gil replied. "Like a warm-up for the Blue Flames big game this afternoon."

"Well, I guess your commies will stay put up on Oak Hill. You said you bombed 'em pretty good the other day. Just like our guys in Korea. Say, how is your dad doing in the army?"

"Mom got a letter the other day," Gil said. He's doing okay, about done his basic officer's training, and then he'll go over into the hospital. He'll finish up in three months."

"And then what?" Tommy asked. "Is he going to Korea?"

"We don't know. I hope not. But Dad says we gotta win this war. To keep us all safe."

"Maybe it won't matter anyway," Tommy said.

"What do you mean? Why wouldn't beating the commies matter?"

"Because of the H-bomb. I heard that the Russians are building this bomb that's so powerful that when it goes off, it could blow up the whole world."

"But that would be stupid," Gil said. "It wouldn't make sense to blow themselves up too."

"But if they could," Tommy explained, "then everyone would just have to surrender to save the world. And the commies would rather have the world be destroyed than not have everyone under their control. Kind of like better red than dead."

"Dumb," Gil said. "And if that's gonna happen, why should we, my dad, go to Korea?"

"Cause the free world has to hold the line," the older boy explained. "And that's why our scientists have to get the H-bomb first. If we've got it, then they can't use it."

"Why not? "

"I guess because ours would only blow up Russia—or maybe Red China and Korea too. Anyway, it would be cool to be first, just to show 'em."

It all seemed too much for Gilbert "Well, I gotta get home for lunch. Did you see Stevie run out of the yard?"

"It's never good to get caught with your pants down," Tommy replied.

* * *

After a long week, Saturday evening came like a sigh. Stewie and Gilbert had cleaned up after the traditional supper of baked beans and red hot dogs. Petie and Allie had been scrubbed and deposited in their beds. The three youngest brothers shared a bedroom on the second floor across from their parents. Gil, in an unspoken rite of passage, had been moved to a bedroom on the third floor, part of a two-room suite that had been the maids' quarters during the 1920s when the gray Victorian had been owned by one of Sutton's scions, the chief financial officer of the Nine Falls Mill. Now Gil sat in the living room listening to a high school football game on the radio.

Katherine poured herself a cup of tea and sat down at the kitchen table with a box of stationery and a pen. She took out a sheet of paper, crafted in the mill that was the cornerstone of the city's economy, and started to compose her weekly letter to her husband:

Dear John,

Hello, Sweetheart. It's been a long week on the home front. The kids are fine but it's always like three of the four balls are in the air at once, all going in different directions. Gil is a big help. I worry a little that I expect him to be more grown-up than he's really ready for. But he's really a great kid, and when I can take the time to look at him, I can see the Jenkins genes in his face.Of course, home is where you aren't. We miss you awfully and are just counting the days (God! I hope it's just a few months and days.) until we'll all be together, wherever that may be. And I'm sure it's a whole lot harder for you, alone in the officers' quarters down there in Texas. I loved the snapshot you sent of you and your three comrades in arms. Pretty handsome in that uniform, Captain Doctor Jenkins!I'm holding my breath, waiting for the big news of where you'll be assigned. I try not to pay too much attention to the news from Korea and pray that the war won't spread, needing more doctors. I won't mind if I'm a captain's wife somewhere in the States; four kids: that's got to be enough to keep you here and us together.

Along with the home front, I'm involved in a Women of the Church committee that's trying to set up a service to welcome Pastor Andreason with people from all the other churches in town. It's going pretty well but....

* * *

The doorbell rang. Katherine put down her pen, walked through the front hall, and opened the door. There stood Bill Sawyer, their next-door neighbor. She was a little taken aback. The Jenkinses and the Sawyers observed good neighborly relations, whether across the fence in the backyard or crossing paths while shopping in downtown Sutton. But this was the first time that he had appeared at her door, at least since John had been off for training.

Nevertheless, she gave him a smile and said, "Well, good evening, Bill. Won't you come in?"

Her neighbor, seemingly in his late fifties, stocky with a ruddy complexion, stepped over the threshold, then paused as if unsure of whether to continue. "I hope this isn't a bad time for you, Katie," he said. "I don't want to impose, but I want to ask your opinion, as a neighbor, about an important issue."

She thought there was just a hint of a slur in his diction, but couldn't be sure, given the suddenness of his appearance and the infrequency of their conversations. "No problem, Bill, the kitchen is all cleaned up, and the little kids are off to bed." She turned and moved down the hall toward the living room. "Here, let's sit down. Can I get you a cup of coffee?

He followed her into the living room and nodded at Gilbert. "No, thank you very much. I never drink in the evening…coffee, that is." He gave her a little smile and plunked himself into Dr. John's green leather easy chair. "I don't want to overstay my welcome, but I do have a kind of adult topic to share." He looked over at the boy again.

"Gil," his mother said, "please go up and check on the boys. Tell Stewie that he needs to wash up and not to forget to brush his teeth. And then why don't you listen to the game up in your bedroom where you won't be bothered by grown-up talk."

"Okay, Mom." He stood up and walked to the door, then turned and looked back at this unexpected visitor. "It's nice to see you, Major Sawyer." He walked out of the room and up the staircase that led to the second floor.

He paused and then walked over to a landing at the top of a second set of stairs, narrow and unlit, which led back down to the first floor between the hall and the kitchen. His mother had explained that the original design of the house had included that stairway so the maids wouldn't have to walk through a gathering of guests when the previous owners entertained. He sat down on the fourth stair from the bottom and leaned back against the wall, listening for the voices in the living room. He wasn't sure why he had detoured from his mother's request. Somehow it just seemed he should be nearby.

Bill Sawyer broke the silence. "So what do you hear from John? He's way down at Fort Sam Houston, right?" Katherine nodded, and he continued, "I did a stint there, back in thirty-nine, if I remember correctly. I'd just gotten promoted to master sergeant, was the number one noncom for a brigade commander."

Katherine replied, "Oh, I didn't realize you had been a sergeant; I guess I've only heard you called Major Sawyer and just thought you'd always been an officer."

"No ma'am; those were different times. I enlisted in the regular army in thirty-five as a buck private. The service seemed a lot better than signing on for one of the civilian make-work crews that Roosevelt and his left-wing advisers were setting up: PWA, WPA, CCC. I never could have kept all those letters straight. The army was straightforward."

"But how did you end up as an officer, as a major?"

"Got to thank Hitler and the Japs for that. When we came ashore at Anzio, damn near every junior officer in our battalion got killed or wounded. I got my first battlefield commission on day three, and by the time Mussolini met his Maker, I'd jumped three more grades up the ladder. It was my noncom experience that did it. Those new "cherry boy" lieutenants never had a chance against real soldiering. Pardon my French."

"Well, you've earned your retirement. You must be very happy not to be caught up in Korea."

"Yep. Enough was enough. And my pension check shows up regular as rain. Besides, there's plenty for patriotic Americans to do right here on the home front. And that's what I wanted to talk with you about."

"I'm afraid I don't follow."

"God, I wish that Dr. John was here. This is really man-to-man stuff." He paused and looked around the room as if he were searching for ghosts. "Well anyway, here's the deal: you surely must know that Senator McCarthy has been shaking the branches and watching commies fall out of their nests."

Katherine took a deep breath. "Yes," she said. "Anyone over the age of ten must be aware of the upheaval his revelations are creating."

Sawyer pushed on without remarking on her tone. "And it's not just down in Washington and in the big cities. Places you'd never think would shelter reds are being infiltrated. Even right here in Sutton, there is an active cell of subversives planning to spread their ideas and weaken the foundations of our hometown."

"But…who do you mean? How do you know?"

"You just got to know what to listen for. The communists and their liberal brothers try to hide their real goals behind big words like 'liberty' and 'equality.' But what they're really working for is to take those things away from all of us, bit by bit. Why do you think that the lefty Papermakers Union keeps a full-time office right here in Sutton when the mill has never, ever been organized and, please God, never will? We need to get the word out and let everyone know. Germany caved in to the Nazis because no one was brave enough to stand up and speak out. That's why I've come to you."

"Me?"

"Well, like I said, it would be better if the man of the house was home, but he's not, and so I'm hoping you'll help me to break this threat to our town."

"What do you want me to do?"

The Major rose from his chair and walked over and sat down on the sofa, next to his hostess. "I know for sure that there are Soviet agents right here, right now. My plan is to get them to expose themselves…." He paused for just a moment and looked into Katherine's eyes, searching for a reaction. "…that is, to come out and admit who they are."

Katherine pulled back a few inches farther toward her side of the couch. "But even if you are right, what has it got to do with me?"

Sawyer stood up and began to pace across the room as if on stage to his one person audience. "You're a well-respected woman in Sutton. Someone who may even be seen as a liberal. We can get the word out through the grapevine that you would be open to joining The Cause. We could lure the local leaders into coming here to make their sales pitch. And we could wire the room so that FBI agents and I could be in the cellar with a tape recorder. Once they spill the beans on themselves, we—the G-men that is—can make the arrests and remove one more threat to our nation and our freedoms."

"But why me?" she asked. "If you're so sure, why can't you set the trap in your own home?"

"Those reds would never fall for it if it was me," he replied. "I'm too well-known around town. And also, Eunice, the little woman, could never stand the excitement. Her nerves, you know."

"Bill, I'm sorry, but I can't agree to that, to your plan." She stood up and took three steps toward the living room door. "The people you seem to fear are representatives of American workers, believers in social justice and the New Deal. They're citizens just like you and me, living their lives as their beliefs tell them they should. I have friends who fit into that dark picture you've created. They're good people who care about this community and want our country to live up to its promises. I'm afraid you have gotten too caught up in McCarthy's fear and slander." She took another step toward the hall and turned. "I need to check up on the boys, so goodnight."

Gil sat on the stairs, wondering what the ensuing moment of silence meant, what he could do. There was a shuffling of feet from the living room into the front hall. He heard the front door open.

Then Sawyer said in a voice both louder and higher pitched than before, "I'm sorry that you can't see the crisis that's all around us. We know who the enemies are, maybe even including your friends."

The door slammed shut.

Gil sat frozen in the dark stairwell. His mother walked past him. He heard the faucet run briefly. Taking a deep breath, he walked into the kitchen. His mother was sitting at the table, staring off into space.

"Hey, Mom," he said. "Major Sawyer left, huh?"

"Yes," she replied. "He's gone."

"What did he want? I mean he looked kind of serious when he came in."

"Grown-up stuff, Gil. Like a lot of people in today's world, he's afraid."

"Of what?"

Katherine sat still, looking at her eleven-year-old, trying to decide how to reply. "Oh, Gil, it's sad that you kids have to be a part of this dangerous time, to be thinking of dangers so early in your lives."

"You mean Korea and the Russians and the A-bomb?"

"It's so different than when I was a girl in the twenties. All we were thinking about was when the new movie would start playing and whether Bing Crosby was more popular than Rudy Vallee"

"Rudy Vallee? Who was he?"

"He was the first popular singer that I remember. Came from a mill town not much different than Sutton. He went off to college and then somehow became the singer that all the girls wanted to date and all the boys tried to copy."

"Kind of like Eddie Fisher now?"

"I guess so. Anyway, I want you and your brothers to feel safe and happy. People get so caught up with ideas of danger that fear takes over."

"Were you afraid, just now I mean, with Major Sawyer?"

"No, not afraid. I think he's a good man who gets carried away with how he sees the world. I just try hard not to get caught up in other people's fears."

Gilbert looked across the round table. His mother seemed very tired.

"I wish Dad could be here," he said softly.

"Oh, Gil, so do I," she replied. "More than anything I want us all to be together again." She took a sip of water and straightened up in her chair. "And it's going to happen soon. Another three months; all we can do is wait for that moment to come."

Gil tried to think of something that would cheer her up. "Hey Mom, did you hear that the Blue Flames beat the Patriots today? Twenty-eight to twelve. Sewed up the league title."

His mother seemed far away. "That's nice," she murmured. "Bedtime, big boy. Don't forget your prayers."

"I won't." He paused. "Mom, do you think God really has time for a kid's prayers…with the world so messed up? With the A-bomb and all?"

"We have to believe that He's with us all the time. Even when it's hard to see His work. That's what faith is about."

"Okay. Sleep tight."

His mother managed a little laugh. "Don't let the bedbugs bite."

Katherine listened to her eldest's footsteps mounting the maids' stairway. She sat for a moment and then walked across the kitchen. She took a jelly glass out of the cabinet, reached underneath the counter, and took out a half gallon bottle of cream sherry. It took some effort to unscrew the cap, unopened since her husband's departure. She poured the glass half full, recapped the squat bottle and returned it to its hiding place. Then she walked back into the living room, sat in the cream-colored easy chair, and took a tentative sip. John always kidded her about being a cheap date: "After one, she's done." The old wall clock ticked. She took a longer swallow and sat back, listening to the quiet of her home and the muffled roar of the Nine Falls Mill. Another long draft, and she leaned back and rested her head against the chair's back. Gradually her world slipped into a swirling mix of the wine, her agitation from the evening's visit, and her memories.

* * *

She is sitting in the shade of the old cottonwood tree beside her home in Nebraska. Her mother is hanging laundry nearby. Suddenly, two men appear from the dirt road which leads out of town and off across the bluff at the end of the river valley. They seem as dusty as their surroundings. Her mother leaves the clothesline and walks over to meet them at the closed gate of the picket fence.

"Good morning, gentlemen," she says. "Can I help you?"

"'Mornin', ma'am," the older of the pair replies. "We was wonderin' if maybe you had some chores we could do? We been on the road a bit. Or maybe you could spare us a bite to eat?"

"No work here right now. But if you want, you can go on down to the cattle tank and clean up a bit. I'll see what I can find for a lunch." She turns to Katherine. "Daughter, you stay right here with your brothers and make sure they don't get into any trouble." She nods directions to the strangers and walks into the house.

* * *

September of 1945. Katherine, five months pregnant with her second child, stands at the little kitchen sink in the small apartment on the hospital grounds. John takes a swallow of his Narragansett beer and swings two-year-old Gilbert up and around the room. He sets the boy down and laughs as Gil sinks dizzily down to the floor. Then he walks over, gives his wife a hug, and pats her expanding belly. "Five months down, four to go," he says. "And what a change, he'll be born into a world of peace. And we'll be on to the next step...a place of our own, my new practice, and you keeping the home fires burning."

"Maybe he'll be a she," Katherine replies.

* * *

September, 1948. She is in a packed and energized crowd in the Exposition Building in Portland. Charlie and Evelyn Rush stand with her as they await the arrival of Henry Wallace, presidential candidate of the Progressive Party.

"It's great that you're here, Kate," Charlie says. "Down the road, you'll be able to say you were part of the path to a greater America."

"Liberty...and justice," Evelyn adds. "Right now, right here is what it means to be a free person."

* * *

Katherine took a deep breath, followed by a long sigh. She picked up the glass, crossed the kitchen, poured the last sip of wine down the drain, rinsed the glass, and set it on the sideboard. She slowly turned and surveyed her domain. Then she walked through the door and up the stairs toward her rest.

In their room, Stewie and Petie were sound asleep in their iron-framed beds. Allie was curled up in the corner of his crib. His mother reached in, softly moved him into the center of the mattress, and pulled up the light blue blanket. She stood for a moment, listening for sounds of movement from overhead in Gilbert's room. Hearing none, she crossed the hall, changed into her flannel nightgown, and slid into her empty bed.

* * *

Gilbert woke to his mother's call up the stairs. Lying in his bed, he could hear the rush of the wind past the dormer window that looked out over Glen Street. Without looking, he knew that the smoke from the Nine Falls Mill's tall chimney would be blowing upstream; there would be a storm in the air. Wednesday, halfway through the school week. The next weekend, touch games with his buddies and the Blue Flame's high school playoff game against the Rams seemed an awful long way off. He rolled out of bed and began to throw on his personal uniform: white T-shirt, sweatshirt with the Blue Flames logo, and his least favorite pair of dungarees that hadn't gone through enough wash cycles to lose their brand-new look. As he started down the stairs to the second floor, he suddenly remembered that this wasn't just any Wednesday. He sped down the stairway and into the kitchen.

Katherine Jenkins was flying around the kitchen, giving little Allie another spoon of Pablum, wiping milk off Petie's chin, and admonishing Stewie to finish his orange juice, no matter that he didn't like it. "It's good for you; you won't get a cold." As she turned to go into the pantry, she spotted her eldest son.

"Gil, good morning, sweetie. Go over to the stove and help yourself to oatmeal. And hurry it up; you and your brother need to leave for school pretty soon."

Gilbert grabbed a bowl and scooped out a glop of oatmeal, not his favorite but better than the gritty Maltex that his mother tried to sneak past them every so often.

"Hey Mom, okay if I have brown sugar today?"

"I guess so. But please pick up the pace. I don't want to get another call from Mrs. Franklin wondering if you're home sick." She sat down at the table next to Allie's high chair, steered another spoon of cereal into his waiting mouth, picked up her coffee cup, sipped, and leaned back against the chair.

Gil sat down across the round table. "So, Mom," he said. "How did it come out? Did Ike win?"

"He sure did," she replied. "The radio is saying it's one of the biggest landslides in this century."

"Well then, Dad must be really happy. The general slaughtered all those 'damned old RATS!'"

His mother leaned forward and drew him in with her eyes. "That's not right, Gil. It's okay to be glad your favorite won. But people in the other party are good Americans too. Governor Stevenson is a thoughtful, patriotic man And the people who were for him want the best for our country, even if their ideas are different from the Republicans."

"Okay, Mom. I was just kidding." He turned to his next younger brother. "C'mon, Stewie. Wipe your puss, and let's head to school. That's something that even General Ike can't change."

* * *

Gilbert leaned back from his desk and let his gaze swing around the room. Most of the other twenty-two sixth graders in Woods Street Elementary were still finishing their vocabulary quiz. He was sure that he'd nailed nineteen of the twenty words they had been assigned. He was a little shaky on "altruism" but hoped his definition was generalized enough to at least get some credit. Vocab and reading were never problems; spelling and arithmetic were another story.

Mrs. Franklin brought him back into the moment. "All right now, class," she said. Please put your pencils down and pass your quizzes up to the front. Before you do, make sure that your name is on the paper." She paused and looked around the class; her eyes seemed to focus on prior offenders. "I can usually figure out the owner of a single unsigned quiz. Two or more makes it more of a task than I want when I'm correcting in the evening." The yellow-striped pages rustled as they made their way toward judgment day. "And now," the teacher continued. "It's time for Friday current events. Who would like to start us off?" She scanned the waving hands. "Ronnie, we haven't heard from you for a long time. What about our world do you think we should know?"

Ronnie stood and looked at his newspaper clipping. "Our government just announced that we've exploded the first hydrogen bomb in history. They say that the test took place somewhere on an island in the Pacific Ocean and that it was a big success." He stood and waited for release from the spotlight.

"Thank you, Ronnie. That is a very important piece of news for all of us. Does anyone have further information that would be useful? Yes, Martha?"

Martha Miller stood up, picked up a sheet of paper, patted her hair into place, and replied, "The explosion took place November first on Eniwetok Atoll in the Marshall Island chain. It had an explosive force of ten-point-four megatons."

Gil felt his concentration begin to slip. He turned at his desk and stared out the tall windows that faced to the north. Nearby he could see two maple trees which had shed most of their leaves. Only a few yellow and brown holdouts twisted in the breeze. Farther beyond was a tall elm, leafless; behind that, the gray concrete chimney of the Nine Falls Mill pierced the sky, a thin stream of smoke flowing toward the east. And above all was the gray November sky, a solid blanket of low slate clouds, swirling. Then, suddenly, the wind ripped a gap in the cloud sheet, a slash of blue and then a red and yellow explosion of color on a single round cloud roiling in the passing November day. He thought back to his conversation with Tommy. Well, it seemed that the whole world hadn't blown up, no matter American or Russia. The gap in the clouds closed, and the gray sheet flowed on.

"Gil…GilBERT!" Mrs. Franklin intruded into his maelstrom.

"Yes, ma'am? I'm, I'm sorry."

"Do you have anything to add to the class discussion?" Her voice seemed supportive rather than angry.

"No. I mean, no, ma'am. But…."

"Yes, Gil?" The tone had softened.

"Well, I wonder why we just learned about the test?"

The teacher paused for a second and replied, "What do you mean?"

"Well, like Martha said, the explosion took place over two weeks ago, and we're only now getting the story."

"An interesting question; any ideas, class?"

"Maybe cause it's so far away?"

"Their radios got knocked out?"

"They didn't want the Russians to know?"

Mrs. Franklin held up her hand and the room settled back into order. "And you, Gil? Do you have any thoughts as to why?"

He felt as if he was on the edge of some understanding but that knowledge was just over the horizon. "The bomb was set off on the first day of the month, three days before the election. Maybe they didn't want us to know before people voted."

"You may be right," the teacher replied. "And if that were the case, I'm sure that our government had good reasons for doing so. In this new world, we citizens have to trust that our leaders are leading us well." She took a deep breath and exhaled back into her usual classroom persona. "And now, class, it's time for decimals. Please take out your notebooks."

* * *

Gilbert thought that Christmas vacation ended much too quickly. There had been one really good snowstorm that had piled drifts around Sutton. They reminded him of photos of Saharan dunes that he'd seen in a *National Geographic* in the library. One drift piled up to the top of the Jenkins's garage door. Gil and Stewie hacked away at the pile with such little success that Katherine phoned Tommy and hired him and Junior to come and liberate the family car. Afterward, Gil, Stewie, and Vince plowed through the tall pines toward the Nine Falls Mill. On the railroad tracks they found a line of half-buried freight cars. They climbed up the steel ladders to the top of the cars and cannonballed off into the snow. But now that was all past, and the first Friday of school in 1953 awaited. The brothers and Vince slipped and slid up the icy slope of Monroe Place toward Woods Street Elementary. They pitched a few halfhearted snowballs at the birch and spruce trees in Mr. Fredette's yard and then trudged up the granite steps into the arms of education.

Having survived five days of decimals, sentence diagrams, and current events, Gil rushed home and into the kitchen. His mother sat there, a cold cup of tea on the table next to a pile of mending. Petie and Allie were on the floor, each with his favorite stuffed animal. Honey jumped up off her mat and ran over to greet her friend. Katherine looked up and said, "Happy Friday, Gil. Glad to be done for the week?"

"Oh yeah," he replied. "I'm pretty tired of tenths and hundredths. Fractions are a lot easier."

"It's all part of your expanding world. There are some gingersnaps on the counter. Why don't you help yourself to *one*."

"Thanks, Mom!" He walked over, picked one up, and returned to the table. He stood for a moment, trying to sense the perfect pause before his request. "Say, Mom. Do you think I could go to the Blue Flames game tonight?"

"Well, I guess maybe. It's a home game?"

"No it's not. It's intown against the Bulldogs."

"And what's your plan for transportation? The Exposition Building is a pretty big place."

He hurried into his defense. "I'm going with Vince. His dad is going to drive us in. And first he's going to take us to Del's Hamburger Heaven for supper."

Katherine looked hard into his eyes. "I didn't know that Mr. MacAllen was a sports fan."

"Well, he's not going to the game. He'll drop us off and then come by to pick us up. I think he's got some errands to run or something."

"And how will he know when the game's over?"

Gil had that one covered. "He can check on the radio. WLRC is doing play-by-play."

"Okay. I'm sure that you and Vince will behave yourself. And there will be a lot of grown-ups from Sutton there who know who you are."

Her eldest son spun around in excitement. "Super! I know the Flames are going to be up for the game. It's a big one." He paused for a second, took a deep breath and said, "You know, Mom, last year right about this time, Dad and I went to the Flames–Dogs game. I kind of wish he was here for this one."

"I know, Gil. I'm sure that he does too. Why don't you write him a letter tomorrow telling him about the game?"

"Great idea, Mom! And I can clip the piece on the game out of the paper and send it to him too. I'm going upstairs and change. Vince and I want to dress up a little for the big game."

* * *

Katherine brought Allie downstairs from his nap and put him in the playpen in the den. She got herself a cup of tea, picked up the newly arrived *Saturday Evening Post*, and walked back into the den. Stewie was trying to explain to Petie how to play Chutes and Ladders. No matter that his instructions weren't working too well. The older brother played for both of them and kept up a running commentary of what was going on and why he was winning. Their mother sat down on the sofa and opened her magazine to an article about comic books and their impact on American youth. The front doorbell rang.

Katherine switched on the porch light, stepped into the entryway from the front hall, and opened the door. There in the late afternoon darkness stood two men dressed in three-piece suits and businessmen's hats. As she looked at them, she somehow knew instantly who they were.

"Yes, gentlemen," she said. "How may I help you?"

"Good afternoon, Mrs. Jenkins," said the shorter of the two. "I am Agent Marsters and my partner is Agent Springer. Agents of the Federal Bureau of Investigation." Each man produced a wallet and opened it to display official looking cards set off by small brass badges. "These are our identifications, ma'am. If you don't mind, we would appreciate the chance to talk with you for a few minutes."

"Why yes…of course. Won't you please come in out of the cold?" She turned and led them down the hall and into the living room. Her mind raced to her husband's last letter that had arrived two days after Christmas. John had seemed so frustrated by their separation. But he couldn't have deserted! She gestured toward the empire style couch. "Please sit down."

They sat on the edge of the sofa, placing their hats carefully to the side. Katherine took a seat on the cream-colored wingback chair next to John's old green leather chair. She gazed at each of the agents. In turn they fixed her with steady, noncommittal eyes. In the den next door, she could hear Stewie explaining the rules, that you couldn't go up the chutes, just the ladders. Finally she broke the silence. "So, gentlemen, what is it you want to talk about?"

Agent Springer leaned forward. "Well, Mrs. Jenkins, we would like to chat about rumors that have come to our attention—about possible issues of disloyal members of the Sutton community."

Agent Marsters broke in. "As we follow leads as to patterns of radical, perhaps pro-Soviet, activities that threaten us all, we also want to reach out to good citizens whose names have come up. And you, with your contributions to your school and the PTA, we're glad to say, certainly seem part of that group."

"That's very kind. And so…?"

Springer took the lead. "I'm sure that you are aware that within the free boundaries of our political system, there is clear evidence of groups that threaten those freedoms from within as surely as those who have dropped an Iron Curtain around half of the world's people. It is our duty to ferret out those who, whether by treason or misguided idealism, can only weaken our nation."

"I'm sure that you know the stories of people like the Rosenbergs," Marsters continued. "It was only through deep vigilance and the cooperation of good citizens that their treason came to light."

Katherine let their narrative slow. "I'm very aware of the Rosenbergs' story…and that there are some who question whether justice was done. But that was all about atomic secrets and spy rings. This is Sutton, Maine."

"But disloyalty seeps through the cracks throughout our society," Marsters replied. "Only by following traces of information can we be sure of those who are innocent and those who deserve suspicion."

"But what can I possibly do? Why have you come to me?"

Springer drew himself up on the sofa. "By answering, truthfully, a few questions we have regarding acquaintances of yours. It has been brought to our attention that a husband-and-wife team of local physicians, Drs. Rush, Charles and Evelyn, have been deeply involved in "progressive"—that is to say, leftist—activities in this area."

Marsters continued, "Community health care outreach and advocacy for President Truman's plan for nationalized, socialized medicine for two. And all under the umbrella of their deep involvement with the progressive movement and the Wallace third party candidacy four years ago."

"But do you have any proof of disloyalty or…?"

"Our role," Springer said, "is not to judge but to investigate. We always hope for the best of all our citizens. But the threats to this great country are too real to be passed over."

Katherine tried to steel herself, took a deep breath and said, "Gentlemen, I can only say with absolute certainty that the Rushes have never once given any evidence of being anything other than community spirited, patriotic American citizens." She could feel a wave of indignation rising. "In the five years that I've known them, they have always spoken to their faith in an America that can live up to its ideals and potential for everyone. And always as a part of their deep belief in citizenship." She paused. "For example, I went with them to a campaign rally for Secretary Wallace. And I have to say…."

Without raising his voice, Agent Marsters interrupted her. "Yes, we know that."

She felt her breath catch and chill flow through her body. "There is nothing else I can tell you," she managed to say. "And now I must see to my children. Goodnight."

The agents stood, nodded to her, and walked out of the living room and down the hall. As they reached the front door, it seemed for a moment as if Springer might turn back. But the moment flowed on and they departed with a gentle click of the latch.

* * *

Vince and Gilbert walked into the Exposition Building as the teams were finishing their warm-ups. The buddies veered to the left side of the court and down in front of bleachers awash with the dark blue of Sutton fans. They climbed up to a couple of seats in the next to the last row, not too far from some of their Woods Street friends.

To the left half of the court, the Blue Flames were weaving a figure eight layup drill. Gil marveled at the seeming ease and precision with which the high schoolers flowed toward the hoop, the ball hitting the floor only with an occasional bounce pass. Big Bob McIntyre was the star of the team, the center around whom the offense revolved. But Gil loved watching Buzzy Fournier and Bill Curley, the two starting guards, as they brought the ball up court flipping passes back and forth as they scoped out the cracks in the opponents' defenses.

He thought back to the previous season. He and his dad had come to as many Blue Flames games as Dr. Jenkins's practice allowed. It had been very special, just the father and eldest son, sharing time together. Bit by bit, Gil came to understand the rules of the game and some of the strategies. One time, a Blue Flames starter, Earl Epsom, picked up his fifth foul, and the game paused as he trudged to the bench past his replacement. Dr. John voiced his frustration, and Gil replied, "Don't worry, Dad, Coach Dolan will put him back in as soon as he can."

"You don't understand," his father replied, his voice raised just a bit. "That's his fifth foul, and he's out."

"You mean he can't ever play again?" Gil asked. "Not even next game?"

Back in the present, Gil looked up to the end zone balcony where he and his father had usually taken their seats. Dr. Jenkins had pointed out that it wasn't quite as crazy as down in the bleachers; they could concentrate on the game together. And the chances of someone coming over to ask a medical question were not as likely. Now he wondered where the family would be a year from now. Would his dad and he be able to go to games together when his dad was a soldier, not a doctor in his hometown? His eye was caught by a flash of blue and white, and he refocused on the Sutton cheerleaders doing their routine at the edge of the court. As these high school girls danced and swirled, their pleated skirts soared up and above their knees. Their heads were tilted back as if resting on their flowing hair. "Turn to the left/Turn to the right/Sutton Blue Flames/Win tonight!" And then the referee's whistle brought the two teams to the sidelines and around their coaches while the announcer introduced the lineups and then stood at attention while a scratchy recording of the "Star Spangled Banner" filled the hall.

The game was everything the sports writers had promised for weeks. The Flames were clearly the better team, but the Bulldogs earned their name with intown toughness and a couple of bad calls by the referees. At the start of the fourth quarter, the Suttoners were ahead by three. But Bob McIntyre had four fouls, and the opponents' zone defense was clogging the middle. The student section of the bleachers was awash with excitement and sound. Each time one of the Flames sank a shot or made a steal, Vince punched Gil on the shoulder, not even aware he was whacking his best buddy. And then, as the clock on the scoreboard ticked down toward two minutes left, Gil felt as if all the frenzy in the stands had faded away, and he was alone in the moment, watching a game as if for the first time. Fifty seconds left, and a pair of free throws by the Bulldogs' center, Carlo D'Avita, brought the underdogs within a point. Buzzy and Bill worked the ball around the outside. Thirty seconds, twenty-five. Then Buzzy lobbed a pass in to Big Bob who arched a short hook shot—off the back rim. For a split second it seemed like everyone—players, referees, the coaches, cheerleaders, and fans on both sides of the Expo—froze. And then Earl Epsom flashed to the ball and laid it in, only his second basket of the night. The Bulldogs hurried the ball up court, but a desperation heave with three seconds left fell way short, and the game was over.

Vince and Gil pushed their way out of the hall and found Mr. MacAllen waiting in the lobby. They followed him down the hill to the car and pulled out into the post-game traffic. All the way home, the boys took turns replaying the game. Their excitement more than matched their driver's lack of interest. The Chevy turned right off Main Street onto Glen and stopped in front of the Jenkins's home. Gil jumped out and then turned back to the car.

"Thanks so much for the ride, Mr. MacAllen," he said. "And dinner too. I love Del's loaded burgers. Catch you tomorrow, Vince."

"Great game," his best friend replied. "Maybe we can take our sleds up to Whitehouse Hill."

Gil shut the car door, and father and son headed down the block toward home.

Rather than walk around back to the kitchen door, Gilbert walked up the curving cement steps to the front porch, a bit surprised that his mother had thought to turn the overhead light on. He opened the heavy oak door and started down the hall toward the kitchen. But he noticed that a light was on in the living room and walked in. His mother looked like she was asleep but then could see that her eyes were open.

"Hey Mom," he said. "Getting a little rest?"

His mother turned toward him, seemingly returning from somewhere far away. "Hi, sweetie," she said. "Yes, I guess I have been. It's been a long day."

"And you didn't even have to go to school," he laughed. "Anyway, the Blue Flames won a close one. It was a killer game."

"I'm glad," she murmured. "It's always nice when the good guys win."

"You bet. Well, I'm going up to bed. Maybe you should turn in early too. Sleep tight. Love you."

"Don't let the bed bugs bite. Love you too."

* * *

Gilbert, Stewie, Vince, Stevie, and BJ dragged their sleds across the fields of Stanton's farm, up to the crest of Whitehouse Hill. To the east they could see the skyline of Portland. The sun glinted off the golden dome of the Catholic convent. Westward was the riverside mass of the Nine Falls Mill, its giant chimney bisecting the snow-covered pines on Rocky Hill.

The snow was perfect for sledding, packed solid by earlier visits with just a dusting of new powder. Whitehouse offered a steep, straight run with several natural bumps that served as sledding jumps. Stanton's Field was more gradual but much longer. Sledders could twist and turn toward the railroad spur that served the mill, contesting to see who could run farthest toward the Frog Pond and its brook next to the tracks. The buddies opted for speed.

After their fourth run, Gilbert and Vince trudged in the unpacked snow alongside the sledding track. Halfway up, they paused to watch Stewie flash by, over a hump with his feet pointing skyward, and on toward the farthest trail's end.

"Your brother's crazy fast," Vince observed.

"He's got no fear," Gil replied. "Or maybe no brains. He loves to win."

"Well, let's get moving. We need to do some more today. Weekend's almost over."

"Yeah, and it's only a week until tournament time. I think the Flames are ready to do business. Think your dad will take us intown again?"

"Oh yeah," said Vince. "I think he might even want to go himself."

"Wow! The town's really caught Blue Flames fever. Well, let's hit the slopes."

* * *

Gilbert and Stewie stood their sleds upright in the snowdrift next to the garage. They trudged up the stairs and into the entryway off the back porch. Honey met them and ran out into the yard and began to circle around, sniffing her own tracks from an earlier visit. The brothers shucked their outdoor layers. Stewie took their boots, filled them with crumpled newspapers, and lined them up next to the radiator in the kitchen. Gil gathered up snow pants, sweatshirts, winter coats, soggy mittens, and damp long gray socks with red and green rings at the top. He carried the snow-soaked mass down into the basement and spread it out over wooden drying racks near the furnace. Then he returned to the kitchen, drawn by the warmth and the aromas of supper.

Katherine was at the stove, removing the last two loaves of bread from the oven. She set the baking pans on the counter and turned to her eldest son. "Hey, sweetie," she said. "You and Stewie must have had a great afternoon on the slopes. I was starting to wonder if you were ever coming home."

"It was super, Mom," Gil replied. "And you have to take the good days when you can. It'll be spring pretty soon." He walked over to the cooling loaves. "Think I could have a slice now? It wouldn't spoil my supper."

"Better wait," his mother said. "Warm bread can upset your stomach. And we'll be eating pretty soon."

"Smells great. What's in the kettle?"

"We're having fish chowder tonight. Mr. Tripp had some really nice haddock yesterday, and I cooked it right then. Chowders and stews are always better if they get a chance to cool and sit overnight."

"Cool," Gil said. "It's kind of like we're eating on fishy Friday like the Catholics all do. Except that we don't have to."

"It's not that they have to, Gil," Katherine replied. "They choose to, as part of their religion. It's another way of showing connection to God."

"Good for us, though. Well, I'm going up and get into some fresh clothes."

"We'll eat in about a half hour. Check on Petie and Allie in the den. They're being a little quieter than I'm used to."

"Sure, Mom. It was great today on the hills. Stewie is really getting to be a dynamite sledder. He's better than some of the guys in my class."

He walked out of the kitchen, glanced into the den, and walked the two flights up to his bedroom. He shucked his shirt and red wool hunting pants and peeled off his T-shirt and long johns. Then he stretched out on his old, black, four-poster bed and pulled the quilt up to his neck. As the deep warmth drew him down toward sleep, he let his mind run over this world that swirled around him: basketball stars, math problems, swift downhill sledding runs, his mother's bread, Tommy and the H-bomb. He closed his eyes and tried to see his father's face, hear his voice. And then Stewie was at the door to the third-floor stairs, shouting up that it was time for supper and that Mom wanted him to get his butt downstairs right now.

The fish chowder was super as always: nice chunks of haddock, onions and potatoes cooked through but not mushy, a little skim of melted butter swirling on the warm milk. Gil sopped up the last of the liquid with a corner of his bread.

"Hey, Mom," he said. "Is there going to be dessert, or can I have another slice of bread?"

"Nothing special," Katherine replied. "Maybe later we can make some Indian pudding." The phone in the little corner by the chimney rang. "Gil, get that for me, will you?"

Gilbert walked over and picked up the phone. "Dr. Jenkins' home," he said, conditioned even in his father's absence.

"I have a collect call from John Jenkins," the operator said. "Will you accept the call?"

"Yes, you bet!" Gil replied. He held up the phone. "It's Dad!" he said.

Katherine took the phone. "Good evening, sweetheart," she said. "This is a nice surprise. Is everything okay?" She listened for a moment, put her hand over the phone's speaker and said, "Gil, I'm going to be talking with your father for a while. Will you get Petie and Allie down from the table and cleaned up? Stewie, it's your turn to clear the table." She returned to the phone. "All right, John. I can listen now."

Gil took care of the little ones while he listened to his mother's end of the conversation, trying to hear hints of what the future held for his family.

"Well, that's a relief," Katherine said. "I think stateside was the best we could hope for." She leaned toward Gil and motioned him toward Stewie and the sink. Long moments passed and then she said, "When will you know about housing? Should I start looking for tenants here?" Another pause. "Yes, I think it will be a lot easier if we fly down. Just a minute, I'll tear him away from the dishes. Gil, your dad wants to talk with you." She handed him the phone, picked Allie off the floor, and took a napkin to his face.

Gil felt as if he were on the edge of something very new. "Hi, Dad," he said. "How's everything down in Texas?"

"Everything's going fine," his father's sort of familiar voice replied. "But not for long. Next stop is Roanoke, Virginia. I'm going to be one of the doctors at the army induction center there."

"Where's that?" his son asked.

"It's a pretty good-sized city out in the western part of the state, near the Blue Ridge Mountains. Sounds like a good place to be. Sure better than Korea."

Gil could feel a weight he had hardly been aware of ebb away. "How long till we go down, Dad?"

"Can't say for sure. I'll drive up there when my training finishes in a couple of weeks. I'll scout out a house for rent, and then you guys can come down and meet me. I think for sure it shouldn't be more than a few weeks."

"Super, Dad. We all miss you lots."

"And me too, you," his father said. "And I know you'll continue to be a big help to your mom. The man around the house. Now, can you put her back on? We're running up a pretty good phone bill here."

"Okay, Dad," Gil said. "Thanks for the good news. Mom, Dad wants to talk with you again."

Gilbert walked through the front hall into the living room. On the bookshelf next to the fireplace was a bookcase, the lowest shelf of which held the red-and-blue-bound *World Book Encyclopedia.* He took out two volumes and walked over and plopped down in Dr. John's green leather easy chair. He opened to "Virginia" and studied the state map; Roanoke seemed a long way off, squeezed between North Carolina and Tennessee. Turning to the other volume he found two terse paragraphs: "The Star City of the South… western rail hub, named after the first English colony…." He sank down in the chair, closed his eyes, and tried to imagine a world away from Sutton, Maine…and his friends…the smoke from the mill's chimney streaming in the wind like a banner…the sports teams.

"Gil?" His mother's voice broke into his solitude. "Are you okay?"

He sat up. "Yeah, Mom. I'm okay. Just trying to get my head around all this new stuff."

Katherine sat down on the arm of the chair, reached over, and smoothed her eldest's hair. "I know, Gil. It's a lot for each of us to fathom. But we have to be thankful: your father is not going to be sent to the war, and soon we'll be a family together again. Virginia will be different. But together we'll make it all okay."

"I hope it won't be too long."

"All in its good time. And for sure, you'll still be here when the Blue Flames win the States." It seemed as if a real weight floated off his shoulders. "Oh yeah, Mom. I almost forgot. The Western Maines start next week. I wish Dad could be here. Maybe he'll call again, and I can fill him in."

"That will be great, Gil." She stood. "And now it's time to try to settle Allie down in his crib."

* * *

February gave way to March. Gilbert tried to focus on school, but somehow math problems and sentence diagrams seemed of limited importance when contrasted with his impending departure for Virginia. Mrs. Franklin seemed to be truly saddened to hear of her loss. She offered to write a note to his new teacher in Roanoke explaining what their class had covered. "And, if you don't mind, Gilbert, I can add a little testimony to the positive contributions you have made this year. We'll all miss you."

At home, his Mom was busy organizing for their departure. Happily, she had found renters: a young family whose parents went to St. Olaf's Lutheran. She told Gil that his dad was almost finished with his training and soon would drive up to Virginia and start the search for their new home. She worked with Gil and Stewie to decide which clothes they would take and which would be put in storage. There would be enough space in the moving van for their sports gear, but their bikes would have to be left in the garage at their real home.

On Friday afternoon, Gil and Vince left school and walked down Main Street for their weekly basketball game at the community gym.

"Boy, Gil," his best bud said. "I thought this week would never end. I'm really sick and tired of listening to Martha always know the answers. You'd think her arm would wear out from waving every time Mrs. F asks a question."

"Girls," Gilbert replied. "But I thought today that it's really great that today is Friday, March sixth."

"Why?" Vince asked. "What difference does the date make? Weekend is weekend."

"Because tonight's the State Finals and the Blue Flames have just got to zap the Rams!"

"So?"

"Well, if the game was going to be played next week, that would make it Friday the thirteenth. I mean, the Flames should really take it to those up-country guys, but it never hurts to keep bad luck off the court."

"I guess," Vince said, looking at his friend for a hint of whether he was serious or goofing around. "I just wish the finals were being played down here. The Expo would be rocking, for sure."

"The radio will just have to do," Gilbert said. "And I hear that if—I mean when—we win, there's going to be a huge turn-out of Sutton fans when the team's bus returns tomorrow morning. That's something we can't miss, for sure."

The boys walked up the stairs to the community gym. The boys from the Bridge Street team were already on the little court. "Let's hustle and warm up. Maybe every hoop we make can send good luck up to our team."

* * *

Katherine wiped Allie's face at the end of supper. "Let's get the dishes done, boys," she said to Gilbert and Stewie. "I've got to give your brothers baths tonight. They both look like they've been playing in a pigsty."

"Okay, Mom," Gil said. "Come on Stew; we've got to hurry up. It's almost time for the radio to start broadcasting the finals. Say, Mom, do you think we could build a fireplace fire in the living room? It would be great to listen to the game in there."

"Sorry, Gil," his mother replied. "In a little while Pastor Andreason is coming to talk over some church business. We'll be in the living room for quite a while. You can listen on your own radio up in your room. That way we won't interrupt."

"Okay, Mom. I'll keep you up to date with how the game's going."

"I'm sure that Pastor will be glad of that."

Dishes done, Gil trekked up the stairs to his bedroom. He switched on the radio and adjusted the tuning to WLRC, the local station carrying the game. He climbed onto his bed and adjusted his pillow as a backrest. A car dealership commercial finished, and the voice of Dex Franklin, the voice of greater Portland sports, flowed out into the room.

"And a good, good evening to sports fans across Maine, and especially to all you Suttoners along the banks of the Nine Falls. ABC Dry Cleaners, the spot to swat spots, is proud to bring you tonight's Class L State Basketball

Championship between the Blue Flames of Sutton and the Appleton Rams. The Downeast Convention Arena is jammed to the rafters with fans for what promises to be a game for the ages. We'll be back with the starting lineups after a few words as easy as ABC."

The game began, and from the outset it seemed like it was going to be the Sutton crew's night. Buzzy and Bill were working the ball around the edges so smoothly that the Rams' man-to-man defense was soon out of kilter. Five times in a row, one of the two Flames guards lobbed passes into the key where Bob MacIntyre had established himself as unmovable. Two right-handed hook shots, a fake and drive to the hoop, and a no-look pass to Earl Epsom and the "good guys" were up by eight. Gil's attention started to wane a bit as Dex relayed the "tidal wave of the boys from the Nine Falls."

The first quarter ended with the Flames up by nine. Big Bob tapped the center jump to Bobby, who whipped a long pass to a streaking Buzzy, who in turn threw up a one-handed shot from way outside the key. "And it's good, like an ABC dry cleaning job," marveled the announcer.

Gil tried to envision the scene at the game. Coach Dolan would be bouncing up and down off the bench, yelling instructions and working on the referees. The Sutton High cheerleaders would be spinning like tops, their skirts riding up and down in their enthusiasm. The fans would be roaring louder and louder with each of their team's scores. And the scoreboard clock would be ticking ever closer to half time.

And then suddenly, the roar of the game disappeared. A new and much more measured voice replaced that of Dex Franklin. "We interrupt our regularly scheduled program for this special news bulletin. The Moscow correspondent of the Mutual Broadcasting Network is reporting that the Soviet government has made public the death of Joseph Stalin. We will bring further details as they become available. We now return to our regularly scheduled programming."

Dex returned. "With three minutes left in the half, the Blue Flames are up by a dozen. The Appleton coach has called a timeout. We'll be back after these messages."

Gil jumped off his bed and ran down to the ground floor. Pastor Andreason and Katherine were sitting in the living room, each with a cup of tea. They looked up as Gil burst into the room.

"Mom, I just heard on the radio that...."

His mother held up a hand. "Gil, please say good evening to Pastor."

He felt choked up by the delay. "G'evening, Pastor. Anyway, I heard that Stalin is dead. The news just came from Moscow." He paused, unsure of his next step.

Andreason stepped in. "Well, the Lord teaches us to pray for forgiveness for all those who pass over, even the most sinful in his eyes."

Katherine said to her son, "Thank you for the update, Gil. Did the news interrupt the game?"

"Yes, Mom. It was almost halftime when they made the report. I'll go back up now and catch up. If there's any more news, I'll let you know." He left the room and trotted up the stairs.

Katherine turned to the pastor. "Such a heavy moment for a boy his age. It seems the news just floods with negativity."

"And it's so important that we who are blessed to live in a free land give thanks to our God. And that we remain vigilant and ready to stand for justice in a world in turmoil."

They paused as Gilbert rushed into the room again.

"Game over so soon, Gil?"

"No, Mom. Half time is just about over. But the news just came on that it doesn't look like Stalin died, after all."

"Thanks, sweetie. I'm sure it will all get straightened out sooner or later. Enjoy the second half." They watched him depart again.

"Well, Katherine," Pastor Andreason said. "No matter which report is true, we all will face our maker in the end. And we can rejoice in our certainty of God's judgment and blessings on those of us who believe and live out our lives in that faith. And now, I had best be on my way. Thanks for your hospitality. You and your family will be in all our prayers as you move on to your next adventure."

"Thank you, Pastor," she replied. "It's a blessing that we all await."

They rose, and she followed him to the door. As she closed the door behind him, she was awash with how the outside world seemed continually to demand entrance. She turned out the downstairs lights and climbed to the second floor. Stewie, Petie, and Allie were all deeply asleep. Her bed awaited her, another night alone. She climbed the stairs to Gilbert's room. The light was on by his bed and the roar of the state championship game filled the room. She walked in and sat down on the edge of the bed. Mother and son waited as the play-by-play continued. Finally, there was a time out and a break for a commercial.

"Gil, I'm sorry that the report about Stalin interrupted the game. But I really appreciate that you brought the news down to us. Any updates?"

"No, Mom," he replied. But we're almost through the fourth quarter, and I guess they'll let us know if anything's changed."

"And how's the game going?"

"The Flames have got it pretty much locked. Dex says that Coach Dolan is talking to the second string; he's probably going to give them a chance to play."

"That's nice. I'm going to turn in now. It's been a long day. Don't stay up too late after the game."

"I won't, Mom." He paused. "Say, Mom, is it a good thing that Stalin's dead? I mean, he was a pretty bad guy wasn't he?"

Katherine reached over and pulled the eldest close to her. "I don't think we should ever be happy about other people's ills. All we can do is try our very best not to let the world make us afraid or to get caught up in other people's misfortunes or mistakes."

"Makes sense to me, Mom. Have a good sleep. Love you."

"Me too, you, big guy." She turned and walked to the stairway.

Gilbert leaned back and turned up the volume on the radio a bit.

"And it's all over but the shouting," Dex was saying. "Coach Dolan has just called time out with seventy-three seconds left and the Sutton Blue Flames up by fifteen. The whole second string is reporting in and the soon-to-be State Champions are coming to the bench. One by one the coach is shaking their hands. Bob MacIntyre finishes his career with an all-time high of thirty-three points. Fournier and Curley, the slickest ball handlers this side of Bob Cousy, ran the offense to perfection. And all the others in the supporting cast played their parts; it was a real team effort."

The last seconds counted down, and the bedroom filled with the sounds of victory. Gilbert listened for a few more moments and then, as the announcer called for a return to the studio, he reached over and switched the radio off. The Blue Flames win felt too good to be smudged by any updates from Moscow.

Gil pulled on his pajamas and climbed into bed, turning off the light. His eyes adjusted to the darkness with just a glow at the window from the streetlight on the corner of Main and Glen. Off in the distance, the mill growled.

Gil tried to settle into sleep but his head wouldn't let go of a swirl of images and thoughts. Stalin's face with its angry mustache. The sound of a dribbling basketball. His dad's voice over the phone promising a reunion in the south. The photograph in the news magazine of the H-bomb test filling the sky in the South Pacific. Stevie's pants down around his knees after Jane's tag. His mother's hugs. It all kind of blended together.

And then it was morning, in his bed, in Sutton, Maine. Honey was lying on her pillow by the door, waiting for breakfast.

The Star City

THE TINNY VOICE OF THE STEWARDESS coming over the intercom snapped Gilbert's attention away from memories of the baseball field by the Nine Falls River into the Piedmont Airlines DC-3.

"Ladies and gentlemen, we are approaching Roanoke Airport. In preparation for landing, please make sure your seat belts are fastened and that loose personal possessions are secured. Also, please extinguish all smoking materials. Thank you for your cooperation."

Gil looked over to where his mother sat in the opposite aisle seat, holding Allie in her lap. Stewie was in the window seat, corkscrewed against the restraints of his seatbelt, looking out the oval window. Katherine motioned to Gil to make sure that Petie was strapped in. Then Gil turned in his seat and stared down at the clouds below the plane.

"Good afternoon, folks. This is your captain speaking. We are starting our final approach to Roanoke. There may be a bit of turbulence as we descend. Please make sure your seat belts are secured. For those of you in the seats to the right of the aisle, you should be able to see Mill Mountain with the towering white "M," the famous landmark of this great city. All of us at Piedmont Airlines thank you and wish you a good day."

The plane dipped to the right. Gil looked out the window. "I can see it, Mom," he said. "It's huge, as tall as a house."

Petie began to twist in his seat. "Wanna see. Wanna *SEE*!" he cried.

"You can't, Petie," Gilbert replied. "We're almost down now."

"Wanna see! ... *Wan NA SEE*!" The five-year-old squirmed against his seat belt.

Gil started to explain again. He looked over at his brother, who was clearly on the edge of a monster tantrum. He reached over and unsnapped the seatbelt. Then he grabbed Petie and pulled him over next to the window. "Okay," he said. "Okay, just sit real quiet and look out. I'll hold you." The plane's flight path steepened and then leveled out.

There was a bump, a second bump, and then the twin engines roared. Gil held Petie tight and then, as the plane began to slow, flipped him back into his aisle seat and snapped the seat belt. All secure, he looked over at his mother. Her gaze was surprised and questioning, but somehow he got the feeling that she wasn't too upset with his rule bending.

"Boys," Katherine Jenkins said. "Let's wait for the other passengers to get off first. Gil, you can help me with our carry-on bags. Stewie, you and Petie can go off together. Make sure you hold on tight to your brother." She stood, took a step backward in the aisle and let her sons follow the exiting passengers.

Gil paused at the top of the exit stairs and looked out at the Roanoke terminal. It was a whole lot smaller than the Washington National airport where they had changed flights on their way down from Maine. But somehow this place seemed to have a feeling of being "home," whatever that was going to mean. He led the way down the stairs trying hard to keep his balance with the two bags, one with extra clothing, the other with Allie's diapers.

Katherine planted both feet on the tarmac and set Allie down. "Gil," she said. "Reach in the clothes bag and get me Allie's leash. He needs to get some exercise." Her eldest reached into the yellow canvas bag and pulled out a ten-foot dog leash attached to a harness. He passed it over to his mother and watched as she pulled the straps over her almost-two-year-old son. Allie ran out to the end of his tether and then turned as if wondering what the hold-up was.

Gil watched and thought, *Well, I guess it's good to get some use out of the leash.* He swallowed hard and fell in behind the others moving toward the terminal.

Mother and sons passed through the gate and into the terminal. Katherine herded the boys onto the escalator. Stewie was first in line, and as he approached the top, he suddenly shouted, "Daddy! Mommy, it's Daddy." Gil looked up, and there stood his father, dressed in his tan summer officer's uniform, a huge smile on his face. Captain Jenkins stepped to the top of the escalator and was engulfed by his sons. Then he stood up and, reaching out, embraced his wife while Petie clung to one of his legs and Stewie jumped up and down like he was on a pogo stick.

Katherine took a deep breath and said, "Pretty handsome in that uniform, Captain Jenkins." And then the moment passed as Allie ran around and around his parents, binding them together with his leash.

Gil helped his father load the four gray Samsonite suitcases onto a push cart at the baggage claim. A negro man wearing a red cap approached the family.

"C'n ah help you with that luggage, Suh?"

Captain Jenkins smiled at him. Nodding toward Gil he said, "No thank you. This young man is the official family porter. Okay, boy. Let's get these bags moving. I'll meet you at the curb with the car." He headed for the exit, his family trailing behind.

After helping to load the luggage into the trunk of the green Mercury sedan, Gil climbed into the back seat with Petie and Stewie. His father eased out into the road and headed toward Roanoke. Off on the horizon Mill Mountain loomed, the huge white M seemingly carved into the trees near the peak.

"Wow, Dad! That big *M* is really cool," Gil said.

"Wait until you see it up close," Dr. Jenkins replied. There's a big park at the top of the mountain, hiking trails, and playgrounds for the kids. The local folks go up there to escape the heat down in the valley."

"Can we go up? Stewie shrilled. "Can we? I love good playgrounds."

"Once we get settled, sweetie," his mother said. "It's been a long trip, and we've got to get into our new house."

Gil looked out the window. "Are we going there right now?" he asked.

"Not yet," his father replied. "The movers brought in all the furniture and boxes, but it's going to take a couple of days to get settled. I've got duty at the center tomorrow but then we have the weekend. Should be ready to move in by the end of the day Sunday."

"Your father has us signed into a motel," Katherine continued. "It will be sort of like a vacation before the homework."

As if scripted, Dr. Jenkins turned left off the busy street and pulled into the parking lot of the Blue Ridge Motel, a string of green doors in a white one-story building. "And here we are," he said. "I've already signed in and have the key. Let's get you all unloaded and settled. Then we can have supper at that restaurant across the street. I've eaten there; it's pretty darn good. Afterward we can drive out and take a look at the house."

The motel room was sort of dull with a couple of pictures of mountains on the tan walls. Two double beds crowded into the room.

"Gil, you and Stewie get to choose which bed you want. Petie, Allie, and I will take the other one," his mother said.

"How about Dad?" Stewie chimed in. "Isn't he going to sleep with us?"

"That'll have to wait until we move into the house," his mother said.

"There's really not enough bed space," his father added. "I'll just have to wait until we're moved in. I've got my room that I've been renting. I'll just have sweet dreams of Sunday." He looked at Katherine with a big grin.

The family walked out of the room and across the Blue Ridge Motel's parking lot. After what seemed a very long wait, they hurried across the highway and up to the door of Josie's Home Restaurant. They paused outside the door to collect themselves. Gil's dad said, "Josie's was one of my very best discoveries in the month I was here alone. Nothing fancy, but it filled me up while I waited for my loving chef to come down and join me. Let's eat." He led the way into the restaurant.

A tall, thin, woman in a light blue uniform with white lace trim met them by the cash register. Gil's ears perked up at his first real chance to hear southern English. "Katherine and boys," his dad said. "This is Suzie, the best waitress south of Boston."

"Well Cap'n John, Ah'm glad to see you. An this here is your lovely family." She turned to Katherine. "I swear, ma'am, that you all are mostly his only topic of conversation. It feels almost like I already know y'all. But now, grab any booth and we'll get you some supper. I'll bring a high chair." She followed them to their booth and handed them menus. "It's all good tonight. Two specials: A fried catfish plate with fries and slaw and our own baked beans with twin hot dogs. Shall I give y'all a minute to think?" Captain Jenkins nodded, and Suzie retreated behind the counter.

"Boys," their father said. "You can't go wrong with anything on the menu. And you can order whatever you like; the only rule is you have to finish it. Gil, you and Stewie decide, and I'll help Petie. Kate, they have really good salads if you're thinking of a light supper after the long trip." The family perused the menu, and their dad signaled Suzie that they were ready. They gave their orders around the booth: a chef's salad for Katherine, mac and cheese for both Petie and Stewie, and the baked beans and hot dogs special for the captain.

Suzie turned to Gil. "And you, young sir, what's your pleasure?""

"I'd like the hamburger with french fries, please."

"A great choice. And what would you like on the burger?"

"Everything, please."

"Loaded, huh? Well I'm sure that you'll be happy with that. It'll be just a few minutes' wait. Thanks for your patience." She scurried off to the kitchen.

"It's going to be worth the wait," Dr. Jenkins said. One of our enlisted men at the center is a local, and he turned me on to Josie's. I've eaten here almost every night." He leaned across the table and took his wife's hand. "Kate, I'm just so…it's just so wonderful to have you all here. It's what's kept me going with this army life."

"And the same for us, John," she replied. The kids have really been pretty good, but some nights I've really missed grown-up talk."

"Two more nights, sweetheart."

Suzie returned pushing a cart loaded with meals. "Mac 'n cheese for the little guys; chef's salad for the missus; beans and dogs for the captain, and the loaded burger with fries for you, sir." She handed an oval dish to Gil. "Now y'all enjoy. If you need anything just give me a shout."

Gil picked up his burger and took a big first bite...and almost spit it out. "What the...this is not a loaded burger! It's got raw onions, pickles, tomato, lettuce and...mayonnaise." It felt like this was one more surprise than he could take.

His dad called the waitress over. "Suzie, there's a little confusion here: Gil ordered a loaded burger, but there's been some mistake."

"Oh, I'm so sorry," she replied. "What seems to be the problem, Gil?"

"Well, I wanted it loaded but there's no ketchup, mustard, or relish. And the onions are raw, not fried."

"Well, what we've got is a mix-up of South and North. Down here, a loaded burger is just like you got it. You mean you all really put all that stuff on a burger at once?"

"Yes, ma'am. That's what 'loaded' means in Maine."

"Well, I'm truly sorry. I'll just go back to the kitchen and ask Miz Josie to set things straight for you."

His father stepped in. "No, no, Suzie. It was an honest mistake and Gil can just try this new style out. Kind of a first step into learning Virginia. Okay, Gil?"

Gil felt trapped between "should" and "want to." "Sure, Dad. It'll be okay...and I'll know better next time." He picked up the burger and took a second bite. "It's actually pretty...interesting."

The five Jenkinses dug into their meals while Allie sat in the highchair, alternating between drinks from his sippy cup and French fries that Gil gave to him.

When they finished, Captain John leaned back in his seat and waved to Suzie for the check. "Great to share this with all of you," he said. "And I'm stuffed and happy. There's nothing in life much better than beans and a good dog."

Just for a moment, Gil felt a flood of loneliness. This was all so new, and there was so much from his real home that he missed.

* * *

The new house was going to be pretty good, Gilbert thought. It was covered with white clapboards with a different style of roof line that his dad called Dutch Cape. It was a whole lot smaller than their gray Victorian back in Sutton. The upstairs had two bedrooms and a bath. That meant that Gil would have to share space with Stewie and Petie. Allie would sleep in his parents' room. But, as his mother said, "It's smaller so we can be together."

They moved in on Sunday. Gil's brothers ran around like squirrels checking out their territory: up and down stairs, around the rooms on the first floor, and in and out the door that led to the backyard. Even Allie seemed to catch their exploration excitement, crawling around the living room and pulling himself up on the couch and easy chairs. Gil and his father finally rounded up the adventurers and herded them to the table on the enclosed porch just outside the kitchen. The promise of supper mellowed them down a bit.

Katherine stepped down from the kitchen, carrying a platter covered with a dish towel. "Here we go," she said. "Pancakes to welcome us all to our new home."

"I've been dreaming of this," Dr. John said. "Your great pancakes and my family come to me. The past four months felt like forever."

Talking was put on hold as the four males dove into the mound of pancakes.

"Mom," Stewie said, "don't we got any maple syrup?"

"None in the supermarket," his mother replied. "If you don't like the Karo, you can use sugar or jelly."

"I could eat a dozen just plain," her husband said and reached for his fourth. He paused and looked around the table. "So, guys, what's your favorite food right now? What could you have for dinner every day?"

Stewie jumped on the question like he had on his first pancake. "Tuna fish! I love it! Sandwiches! Noodle casserole with peas! Every day would be great!"

"Okay, Stew," his father said. "Try to get a little excited, why don't you. Gil, what's your pleasure?"

Gil felt a little moment of concern about how his father would respond. "Green beans, Dad. They're my very favorite vegetable. I love them fresh from Grandpa's garden, but the canned ones are great too."

"Hard to go wrong with that, Gil." He looked over at five-year-old Petie. "How about you, Petie? What do you love to eat?"

"Cheerios, Daddy. Me love 'em…with milk…an' sugar, too."

"So you love breakfast best?"

"Any time," Petie bubbled. "Always love Cheerios best."

"Well, guys," Dr. John said. "We'll have to see what we can do about your favorites." He turned to his wife. "So, Kate. What about you? Anything special now that you can relax and get back to being my private chef?"

Katherine paused a beat or two. "No, John. Nothing out of the ordinary. I'll make a list of staples before my next visit to Kroger's."

* * *

The next morning, the Jenkins family reconvened for breakfast. The sun shone in through the windows of the eat-in porch. To Gil it seemed higher in the sky and a whole lot warmer than the March Maine sun he had flown away from a week ago.

Doctor Jenkins, decked out in his tan summer army uniform with bright double-bar captain's insignia on his collar, pushed away from the table. "You haven't forgotten your toast technique, honey," he said to his wife. Standing, he looked at his sons. "Guys, make sure you help your mother clear the table." He turned back to Katherine. "Sorry that I have to have the car today. There are a bunch of brass coming from some headquarters, and I've got to make sure all the exam equipment is shiny. You've got the meeting at the boys' school at…what time?"

"Our appointment is at eleven," she replied. "The principal thought it would be good to give them a feel for the place and then have a few days to adjust to their new school before the Easter break and then they'll start up for real."

"Hope that the hike won't be too bad. It's under two miles, and you've got the morning to stroll down."

"We can go to the supermarket after the meeting. I won't be able to buy all our supplies without the car, but I can get supper stuff. I'll have to say it's not going to be quite as easy as walking the block to Graham's Market back home; probably not as personal either."

"Once things get settled, we can work out a schedule," Dr. John said. "I can take the bus into town once in a while, although I'll need a ride down to the bus stop." He stepped into the kitchen and picked up his car keys. "Wouldn't do to get my uniform all sweaty." He snapped off a salute to the boys. "Mind your mother, troopers." And then he turned and disappeared through the house.

Gilbert stood up from the table and picked up his cereal bowl. He walked into the kitchen and dumped the splash of milk left in the bottom into the sink. For a moment he felt as though he might break down into tears. Turning back to the porch he said, "Mom, is it okay if I go out for a while? Look around the neighborhood?"

Katherine paused for a moment and then said, "Sure, Gil. Your brothers can help with clean-up this time." But don't be gone too long; we have to leave for our school visit around ten. That gives you an hour or so. And make sure you pay attention so that you can find your way home."

Gil walked out of the house. He looked up and down Dyer Road. The houses were all done in different styles. Across the street, behind the single rank of dwellings was a huge open field. He turned to his right and began to walk up the incline, past a two-story red brick house and then an open lot that had a metal pole in the middle. A rope hung down from the top of the pole with what looked like a volleyball attached. He tried to envision what such a setup might be for. Then he walked up to the top of the street, turned right onto a second road, and went on to another corner where he turned right again. The details of the new neighborhood blurred as he trudged along the cement slabs of the sidewalk. In the distance, a dog barked. Gil suddenly felt more alone than ever before in his eleven years. He sat down on the curb and tried to think of what would be going on in Sutton on this Monday morning. What would they be doing in Mrs. Franklin's class? Would the people living in his house be settled in? How would Honey be doing in her new home? What was this new life going to be like? He leaned his head backward and looked at the blue sky through trees with leaves he didn't recognize. Then he stood and walked down to the next street corner and continued his journey.

His mother and brothers were waiting for him. Allie was strapped into his stroller and Petie was sitting in the red American Flier wagon.

"Okay, Gil," Katherine said. "We've got to leave right now. It's almost two miles down to your school. Why don't you pull Petie up the hill and then Stewie can have his turn when things level off."

Stewie latched onto the handle. "I can take him up the hill. It's not too big for me." He gave a grunt and yanked the wagon down the driveway and then up the grade of the concrete sidewalk. "C'mon, you all. Time's a-wastin."

Gil took hold of the stroller and said, "Hold on, Allie." Then he and his mother struck out after Stew and Petie who were approaching the first turn away from Dyer Road.

After about a mile, Stewie's head start was shrinking. "Wait up, Stewie," his mother said. "I need to check Petie's runny nose." The family reconvened and then continued on their way, past the rows of small brick and white clapboard houses, then the orange-red Methodist Church. In the distance, they could see the small shopping area and the looming presence of the R.E. Lee Elementary School. They paused, and Gil took over the wagon hauling duties.

"I wouldn't be surprised," Katherine said, "if people in this neighborhood might think we're a bunch of Okies."

"What are Okies, Mom?"

"Well, Gil, when I was a girl growing up in Nebraska, there were really bad years called the Great Depression. The economy of the whole country fell apart, and people went through hard times, especially the people who didn't have much to start with."

"And they were called Okies?"

His mother stopped and took a deep breath. Stewie grabbed the wagon handle. She took another deep breath and looked at Gil.

"See, lots of farmers lost their farms because of no rains and horrible dust storms. The worst off just packed up whatever they had and hit the road, looking for some way of surviving. Lots of them had old, beat-up trucks or cars but some of them ended up just walking along the country roads, trying to find someplace they might get a couple of days' work, or maybe a meal to keep them going. Oklahoma was really hard hit and so all those people came to be called 'Okies.'"

"But not you?" Gil asked.

"No, we were the fortunate ones. Dad, your grandfather, was able to keep his job as a brakeman on the Burlington. And our little farm was in a river valley, so we were able to grow most of what we needed. Mama used to take vegetables into town and get a little money going door to door."

"Wow! I guess we're pretty lucky."

"But now we'd better hit the road.

The Jenkins migrants arrived at the entrance to their new school. R.E. Lee Elementary School was carved into the lintel. They left the wagon and stroller on a patch of lawn next to the stairs. Katherine picked Allie up, Gil took Petie's hand, and the five Northerners mounted the steps.

They found themselves inside a dark hallway, unsure where to go. A man dressed in tan work clothes came up out of a stairwell and came over to them.

"Good mornin', ma'am. Can ah be of some help to you all?"

"Yes, thank you," Katherine replied. "We're here to get the boys enrolled. We've just moved here from Maine."

"Well, you'll be wanting to see Mr. King, our principal. His office is upstairs, directly across from the stairway."

Thanks very much for your help, Mr.…" She paused.

"I'm Jack Shorter. The kiddoes call me Mr. Jack." He turned toward the boys and scooched down until he was at eye level with Petie and Stewie. "Ah'm sure you boys are going to do just fine here at R.E. Lee. And if there's ever any problems you can just come down and find me in my office. Down in the basement between the boys' room and the boilers."

"That's very kind," Katherine said. "Say thanks to Mr. Shorter, boys."

"Thank you, sir," Gilbert and Stewie said. Petie retreated behind his mother and peeked out around at this stranger. Then the Jenkins climbed the stairs. They found the door marked PRINCIPAL'S OFFICE and followed their mother in. A woman was sitting behind a desk. She looked up as they entered and smiled.

"Good morning to you folks. Welcome to R.E. Lee. How can I help you?"

"I'm Katherine Jenkins. We've just moved here from Maine. My husband is in the army, at the local induction center. We need to get the boys enrolled for the rest of the school year, Gilbert in sixth grade, Stewart in fourth, and Peter in kindergarten. I sent a letter that we'd be arriving about now."

"Boys," the secretary said. "I'm Mrs. Martin. Welcome to Roanoke and R.E. Lee. I think you're going to find we've got a real good school here." She turned back to Katherine. "We did receive your letter. You'll want to see Mr. King. I think he's on the phone in his office right now. If you'll wait just a moment, I'll let him know you all are here." She gestured toward a row of chairs against the wall, turned, and walked through the door behind her desk.

"Well, boys, what do you think about your new school so far?" Katherine asked.

Stewie responded first. "It's bigger than home. I really liked Mr.…the janitor guy. He seemed very nice."

"His name is Mr. Shorter, Stew," she prompted. "Gil?"

"Well, it doesn't feel too much different than back home. It is a lot bigger than Woods Street. How about you, Petie?"

The five-year-old, pressed up against his mother, looked around with wide-open eyes. He said nothing, but his stare spoke volumes. Katherine reached around his shoulders and drew him even closer. "I think everything will be good, sweetie. Everyone here is going to be very nice to you."

Mrs. Martin emerged from the inner office. "Mr. King can see you now. Right this way, if you please."

Secretary, mother, and sons entered single file. Mr. King rose from behind his desk. He was a short man, a bit stout, dressed in a three-piece gray suit, white shirt, and regimental tie. He extended his hand to Katherine. "Welcome to Robert E. Lee. I'm George King. And you, young gentlemen, remind me what your names are."

"I'm Gilbert Jenkins, sir."

"And I'm Stewart Norman Jenkins but everybody calls me Stewie."

"Well, Stewie it will be," said the principal. He looked at Petie, scrunched along his mother's flank. "And you? What's your name?" Petie said nothing and pressed even closer to Katherine.

"He's kinda shy," Stewie explained. "It takes him a while to understand new people."

Katherine interjected, "Peter had just started kindergarten back home. It took him quite a while to be comfortable in the new setting. Our system in Sutton was really good about giving him special support."

"As can we," King replied. "We'll get him settled and then find out how we can be of help. Now, why don't you follow me and we'll introduce the boys to their new teachers."

Katherine said, "I need a few moments to get Allie straightened up. I'll take him to the bathroom while you take the boys. Tell me the room number of Petie's class and I'll meet you there." She turned to Gil. "Why don't you go into his classroom while Mr. King introduces him. Just stay there a minute so he won't feel too alone. Then Allie and I'll go in and stay with him."

"Okay, Mom," Gil said. "Petie, it's gonna be really nice." The family followed the principal out of the office and down the broad stairway to the first floor. They paused in the large, dim entryway. "Well," Mr. King said. "The classes for the little ones are on this level. If you need the boys' room, it is located…"

"Down in the basement," Stewie interjected. "Right at the bottom of the stairs, right next to the janitor's office."

"Right you are. I can see you're going to be part of our school in no time flat. And you can take the little one into the girls' room, down there and to the left," King said to Katherine. "Peter will be in Mrs. Lowell's classroom right over there, one-oh-seven."

Mother and child walked to the stairwell and disappeared downward. Gilbert took Petie's hand. "Come on, Stewie," he said. "We'll get Petie settled and then find our own classes." The boys followed the principal into the kindergarten classroom.

Eighteen pairs of five-year-old eyes locked onto the new arrivals. Principal King walked over to the teacher, a grandmotherly looking woman, and spoke quietly with her. Then they walked back to the brothers.

"Boys and girls, I'm happy to tell you that we have a new member of our class." She looked down at Petie. "His name is Peter Jenkins, and he comes to us all the way from the state of Maine. Peter, we're very glad to have you join us."

Gilbert looked over at Petie. It seemed that he was sinking down, getting smaller and at the same time sort of disappearing into himself. And his eyes! All Gil could think of was the photographs of lemurs that he'd discovered in a *National Geographic* back in Mrs. Franklin's class at Woods Street in Sutton.

"Petie," he said. "Stewie and I, we're going to go to our own classes now. Are you going to be okay? Mom and Allie will be here any minute."

Petie grabbed onto the leg of Gilbert's chino slacks. "No wanna," he said. "Don't go me!"

Gil felt like he was being pulled in several directions. Mr. King was edging toward the door, and Stewie seemed to be following in his wake. Mrs. Lowell sat down on a student's desk and leaned toward the five-year-old.

"Petie, can I call you Petie? We are really glad to have you here. It's almost story time. I'm going to be reading you and your new friends the story of 'Brer Rabbit and the Briar Patch.' Do you know that one?"

Petie shook his head and tried to disappear behind his big brother. The teacher looked up at Gil and very softly said, "I think it will be fine if you leave. I'll make sure to make him comfortable here." She nodded at Mr. King, and he and the two elder Jenkins boys backed out of the room and softly closed the door.

Things were sort of a blur for Gilbert after that. Stewie was deposited in his classroom. Then the principal led Gil upstairs. "Well, here we are, Gilbert. Mrs. Starr's room. We'll get you settled right off." He knocked on a classroom door, stepping through with his last charge in tow.

Now it was Gilbert who was the focus of a classroom full of staring eyes. Mr. King did the honors, and Mrs. Starr welcomed him and showed him to a desk near the high windows at the rear of the classroom. The class settled in as the teacher guided them back to their social studies class, something about Indians and the settlement of the Great Plains. Gil looked around at his new classmates, trying to create stories about these new faces.

And then he let his mind float back up to Sutton, to Mrs. F's classroom, to Martha whipping her hand up, always wanting to be called on first. Vince and the guys would be getting ready for early season baseball. The smoke out of the tall chimney of the Nine Falls Mill would be blowing downstream, toward the ocean, the local promise of a warm and sunny April day. Across the river, the steeple of St. Hyacinth's, the Catholic Church, would be shining in the noontime sun. And up the hill, Honey might be out in the Verrill's yard, waiting for school to be out for the day. Suddenly, he felt like he couldn't stand all this newness and the way his life at his real home had disappeared in the clouds underneath the airplane ride to Roanoke.

Then there was a knock on the door and Mr. Shorter came in. "Sorry to interrupt, Mrs. Starr, but Principal King asked me to come for Gilbert. His mother is waiting for him in the office."

"Of course," the teacher said. "Gilbert, it is nice to have you with us."

"Thank you, ma'am," he replied. He felt he should say something further, but it was like his head had drained out. He followed the janitor out and down the hall to the principal's office.

"I'll leave you here, young man," Mr. Shorter said. "You have a good day, you hear." He turned and headed down the stairwell.

Gilbert opened the door. In front of him a strange drama seemed to be unfolding. Stewie was sitting on the floor holding Allie with Mrs. Martin kneeling down next to them. His mother was holding Petie whose body seemed to have turned into a rigid arch, his head focused on the ceiling. An unending scream gave voice to the fear that had gripped him. Katherine was swaying, to and fro, whispering to her five-year-old. Gil thought that the principal was trying to take control but was in a situation in which there was little he could do or say.

Finally, Petie calmed down enough that his mother could deal with the rest of the situation. "I'm so sorry that things turned out this way. We'll try and reassure him that he doesn't have to be afraid here."

"And I just want to say," the principal responded, "that we're all sorry and concerned that he had such a bad time. You folks just take your time with him. We'll be here when he's ready to return."

"Thank you," Katherine said. She turned to Gil, Stewie and Allie. "Okay, guys. Let's head out. We've got a story to tell your dad when he gets home."

The family walked out of the office, down the stairs and out into the noontime sun. "Gil, please push Allie in the stroller. Stewie you can haul the wagon. I'll carry Petie, at least for a while." They headed down the first leg of their route back to Dyer Road and what, Gilbert thought, would have to pass for home, at least for the time being.

Back at the new house, Petie lay on the living room carpet and fell into a pattern of deep quiet followed by explosions of weeping. Several times, his mother, trying to collect herself through the routine of making dinner, left her counter and sat next to her son, stroking his head and whispering promises that everything would be all right.

Gil and Stewie went into the backyard and threw a baseball back and forth. At one point, Stew launched a throw that went way over Gil's head and into the shrubbery that marked the end of their lot. The brothers thrashed into the thick foliage, pushing branches aside. The younger Jenkins drove ever deeper.

"Stewie," Gilbert said. "You're going way too deep. It's gotta be closer to the edge."

"Nope," Stew replied. "I got it right here." He backed out of the thicket and tossed the ball to his brother. "Gave that a pretty good peg."

"No way I was gonna catch it. It was way over my head."

"See, that's the difference between how we throw. You are pretty ack… ac…you know, you hit the target, mostly.

"You mean accurate."

"Yeah. Ack…you…rate. Anyway, I can really heave the ball. I've got a strong arm."

"True, but it's no good if it isn't on the mark." The brothers walked back across the lawn.

"Hey," Stewie said "Dad's home!" They walked around the house where the family Mercury was just shutting down.

Captain Jenkins got out of the car. "Hey guys," he said. "Run in and get your mother and the other kids. I've got a surprise."

"Mom's kinda busy," Gil replied. "Petie is having one of his days."

"What I've got will perk 'em both up," said the captain. "Go on, Stewie. You be the pony express messenger."

Stew walked through the living room past Petie and looked through the open doorway into the kitchen. "Hey, Mom," he said. "Dad's home. He wants you and Petie to come out front."

Katherine turned from the sink. "It's not really a good time. You can all come in. Supper's almost ready."

"Okay, Mom." He retraced his steps, pausing to ruffle Petie's head, went out the front door, and down to the car.

"Mom says she's pretty busy right now. Maybe after supper would be better?"

"I guess it'll have to be," Captain Jenkins said. As he turned and walked away from the car, he gave a long sigh. Gilbert couldn't tell if his dad was tired or frustrated with the glitch in his plans, whatever they were. The boys followed into the house.

The family sat down to dinner. Petie stayed in the living room. "He's had a hard day," his mother said. "School was pretty strange."

"I'll go in and check on him," John said. "Maybe he just needs some encouragement. He and I haven't had a lot of time together over these past four months." He stood and walked through the open doorway into the living room.

The remaining Jenkinses turned to their meal.

"Hey, Mom," Stewie said. "This fried chicken is really good."

"Well, it's southern fried chicken; that's supposed to be special.'

"It's good," Stewie continued. "But I don't think it's any different than at home."

"But we're in Roanoke, Virginia," Katherine said with a very serious tone. "It's got to be southern."

Gilbert rolled his eyes and bit a hunk off his crispy coated breast. Stewie looked at him, then back to his mother, trying to figure out if he was being conned. "Oh, I get it."

"Yeah," Gilbert added. "I guess that means we can't have western omelets for breakfast anymore."

Their father came through the doorway carrying Petie. The five-year-old looked exhausted, drained of the energy to act on his fears. "Petie's going to be all right," Dr. Jenkins said. "We talked it over and I got him to see that he's got to have some of his mom's great food to feel better." He put his son down in the seat next to Katherine. "Okay. Now I'm starved and I can't wait to have some of my sweet chef's special fried chicken."

"It's different, Dad," Stewie said. "This is southern fried chicken but it's still really crispy and good." Captain Jenkins looked at his entourage, trying to figure out if he was being conned.

"Oh, I get it, he said." And with that, they all turned their attention to the meal. Petie seemed to brighten a bit with the comfort of food and family.

Dinner finished, Katherine told Gil and Stewie to clear the table and get started on the dishes. "No, boys," their father said. "I've got some surprises out in the car that dinner got in the way of. Let's go out and do that. The dishes can wait until after."

The family walked out the front door. Katherine helped Petie down the stone steps. Gil carried Allie on his shoulders. Captain Jenkins had Gil, Stew, and Petie stand in a file facing the car. Then he told them to cover their eyes until he gave the word. He reached into the back seat of the two-toned Mercury and removed three cardboard cartons. He laid each one out in front of one of the sons. "Okay, boys. You can look now."

Gil leaned down over the carton at his feet. "Hey, it's a carton of green beans. Canned ones. It says twenty-four cans. Cool!"

"Tuna fish," Stewie said. "A whole box of tuna fish."

"White tuna," his father said. "The very best."

Petie was standing in front of his carton, which was larger than those of his brothers. He just stood and stared at the box.

Dr. John knelt down next to him. "Okay, Petie. I'm going to open the box. You look carefully and see if you can guess what's inside." He pulled back the cover flaps of the carton and then very slowly pulled a yellow rectangular box up in front of his son's eyes.

"Cheerios!" Petie screamed. "It's Cheerios. Me luv 'em." He turned to his mother. "I have some now? For dessert?"

His mother replied, "Well, sweetie, we just had supper. Maybe we could wait…."

"Sure you can have some, Petie," his father interrupted. "Cheerios for dessert sounds like just the perfect end of a wonderful family meal." He looked at Gil and Stew. "You guys carry your cartons down in the basement. I'll help Pete in with his, and we'll all have Cheerios."

"Wow," Stew said. "The Lone Ranger would think this is great. Cheerios are his favorite breakfast. Says so on the radio." And the Jenkins platoon did an about-face and marched back into their barracks, laden with supplies for the family mess.

Dessert concluded and dishes done, Katherine herded her unruly flock upstairs. Stewie made a vain attempt to postpone bedtime, but his mother countered that school would start for real tomorrow, and he would want to be bright-eyed and bushy-tailed for his first day. As a compromise, she gave them an extra half hour before lights-out, a dispensation to be used for reading.

After Gil and Stew finished washing up and brushing their teeth, she took Peter into the bathroom. Ever since she had mentioned school, the excitement of "his Cheerios" for dessert had collapsed in on his fearful memories of their day at Robert E. Lee Elementary School. He sat on the toilet while his mother scrubbed his face and helped guide his hand with the toothbrush. By the time he rinsed his mouth he was trembling. Katherine ran her hand over his crew cut. Then she sat on the edge of the tub and drew her five-year-old close.

"It's going to be okay, Petie," she said. "You're a big boy now, and your teacher was very glad to see you today. She is a very kind lady."

Petie's eyes were wide with fear. "No want to…to go to school. Want stay here with you, Mommy."

His mother made a snap decision. "Okay, sweetie. We'll give you a couple of days to get used to being down here, in Virginia, in our new home. There will be time for just you and Allie, and me." She held him at arm's length and looked into his eyes. "That will be good. But then we've got to get used to school. And remember that Gil and Stew will be right there with you."

When she and Petie returned to the boys' bedroom, Gil and Stewie were spread out on their beds reading. She tucked her five-year-old into bed and sat with her hand on his brow."Guys," she said. "I think your brother needs to get to sleep. If you like, you can go down and read in the living room. But it's still a half hour until bedtime."

"Starting now?" Stew asked.

The boys trooped out of their room and down the stairs. Katherine stood and flipped the light switch. "Okay, little man," she said. "It's time for sleep. I'll leave the door open and the hall light on for you." She sat down on the edge of the bed again. "Would you like me to sing you a nighttime song?"

"Sing the Foxie song," Petie said.

"Now you lay back in your comfy bed and close your eyes." She began to stroke his head:

"Oh, the fox went out on a chilly night
And he prayed for the moon to give him light.
He had many a mile to go that night,
Before he reached the town-oh, town-oh, town-oh.
Many a mile to go that night,
Before he reached the town-oh."

By the fourth verse she could tell that, at long last, her son had relaxed and drifted off to sleep. She tucked the blanket around his shoulders and eased out of the bedroom.

Katherine walked into the kitchen and put on the tea kettle. John was sitting at the table on the porch with a cup of coffee. "I already perked some coffee, honey," he said.

"I think tea is better for me tonight," she replied. "I need something to ease me toward bedtime."

"Sorry it was such a rough day at the school. Any idea what it was that set him off?"

"I think it's just more of the same as back home. He's really afraid of anything or anybody new. I just feel so awful that he's having such a hard time."

"Well maybe we ought to consider keeping him at home, for the rest of the school year I mean."

"Really? John, we can't keep him home forever. He's got to learn to fit in with the outside world."

Her husband reached out across the table and took her hand. "Kate, I think we've got to face up to the fact that he's always going to have difficulties, issues with school, with other people…with anything new."

"I just can't accept that, can't believe that we would just give up on him because he's got issues different from his brothers."

"No, no. I don't mean that at all. In time I think we can figure out what his issues are, get some professional help in diagnosing his situation, and set up programs that will help him cope with the world."

"But we can't just hide him away. He's got to have the chance to experience new things, develop some confidence, be around people."

"Sure. But he's still a little kid. We shouldn't rush things. Maybe we should just wait on the end of the school year, it's only a couple more months. Then we'll have the summer to see how things work out." He could see the anguish in his wife's eyes. "We just need time to see how his language improves…to see if the anxiety becomes less of a problem. Sweetheart, we may have to accept the fact that he's more challenged than the other boys. Then we can make plans to help him as much as possible." He paused. "And I promise you with all my heart that we will."

"Maybe so," Katherine said. "I pray not; but it may be. But shouldn't we be exploring the school system here, to find out what special programs they may have?"

"We can, for sure. But, in the end it may not be necessary. After all, we know what a solid system Sutton has."

"What difference does that make now? You've got another year and a half of assignment here."

John took a deep breath. "Maybe not, sweetheart. It may not be that long until we're home."

"What do you mean, John?"

"Well, I wasn't going to say anything until I had more definite news, but there is a pretty good chance that we might be going home a lot sooner!"

"How? You've got your time to do."

"Well, you remember Fred Oliver?"

"The surgeon at Maine Eye and Ear?"

"Yes, and this year's president of the Maine Medical Association. Anyway, Fred has developed professional connections with the docs at Fort Williams over in Cape Elizabeth, and it seems like there's going to be a slot open there sometime not too far in the future."

Katherine took a deep sip of her tea and waited.

"Well, Fred put a good word in for me; pointed out that I'd have a good rapport with the inductees from Maine. And then he wrote a letter to Senator Smith and advocated for my transfer. Stressed the family issues and all."

"Do you really think there's a chance?"

John stood and took their cups to the kitchen sink. Then he returned to the porch. "Nothing's etched in stone, but I've got a pretty good feeling that we might all be headed back to the Pine Tree State sometime in the fall." He reached out, took both of her hands, and pulled her into a hug.

"Oh, John," she said. "Any place where we can be a family is okay with me. But it would be so wonderful if the boys could go back to their roots." She took a deep breath. "And I'll have to say I would love to be with my friends and neighbors."

"Time will tell; time will tell. And now Mrs. Jenkins, let's you and I head on up to bed."

* * *

Gilbert tried to settle into Robert E. Lee, with uneven results. The first day, Mrs. Starr reintroduced him to the class. "Ladies and gentlemen, you all will remember Gilbert Jenkins from his visit yesterday." She turned to Gil. "I hope that everything is okay, with your family, I mean."

Gil felt that he was in the spotlight, or the crosshairs, like Uncle Harry's telescope sight on his hunting rifle. "Yes ma'am," he said. "Everything's okay." He paused; the room seemed silent. "Thank you," he remembered to say.

"Well, we're glad to have you here. It isn't often we get a new student, especially one from so far away as Maine."

Now, Gilbert knew that he had been crowned as an outsider. He could sense a shifting in the seats of his new classmates. He hoped their guns weren't loaded.

"Now why don't you take that seat over between Barry and Fred. We're about to work on our world geography lesson." Mrs. Starr turned to a roll of maps over the blackboard as Gil walked to his seat, hoping above all else that he wouldn't trip. "We are learning about European nations right now. But for starters," she pulled down a map of the United States. "Can anybody tell me where Maine is, other than our native son, I mean?"

A plurality of hands were thrust into the air. The first student called correctly pointed out the Pine Tree State.

"And can anyone else tell us something about Maine that's different from all the other forty-seven states of our country?"

A longer pause. "Yes, Delores," the teacher said.

"I think it's the only state that has only one border on another state. I mean it looks that way on the map."

"Right on the button. Notice the other borders are with Québec and New Brunswick, Canadian provinces. And now, how about some things that Maine is famous for?"

There was yet a longer pause. Finally, Mrs. Starr turned to the newcomer. "Can you share some important facts about your home state with us, Gilbert?"

"Yes, ma'am," he replied. "Maine is really lucky; we have great natural resources. Almost all the state is covered with forests, and so lumber and paper are really big. And we have a long coast." He could feel himself being caught up in the excitement of being an "expert." "If you straightened out all the curves, the coves and bays of our coast the line would stretch all the way to the tip of Florida. So fishing is really important, especially lobster. I guess that's about it," he finished.

Off to his right and from a row or two behind he heard a male whisper, "And Yankees; it's full of damn Yankees." There was a momentary twitter before the teacher's iron gaze calmed the brass of the Confederates.

And then the class returned to the lesson of European geography: the different countries that were free and members of NATO and those so unfortunate as to be caught behind the Iron Curtain, the slaves of godless, communist dictatorship. Gil found that he knew most of the material covered. However, he fought off the urge to raise his hand with answers, in part because of his awareness of being the outsider and partly because he could visualize Martha, back in Mrs. Franklin's class in Woods Street, waving her hand, always knowing the right answer

Finally, school ended. Gilbert and Stew reunited in the hallway. They agreed that it hadn't been too bad. Stew said he'd already made three friends, one of whom wanted him to come home to play trucks someday soon.

They walked out of R.E. Lee and headed home, past Kroger's supermarket on their left and away from the Bijou Theater across the main street.

As the brothers turned the corner onto Dyer Road, they saw a truck pulling away from their new home. As it passed them, they saw painted on the side BERNSTEIN'S SELECT FURNITURE. They hurried up the sidewalk and into the front hall. From the kitchen their mother called, "Guys, come on out here through the dining room. Your father's working on a surprise for you in the living room." Only then did they notice that the entrance door to the living room was shut.

In the kitchen, Gil asked his mother, "What's going on, Mom?"

"Patience, boys. Your father's almost ready. Any ideas of what the surprise might be?"

"I got it," Stew shouted. "He's bought a whole store's worth of canned foods, enough to keep us supplied for the rest of our stay, too many to store in the basement!"

"Good guess, Stewie," Katherine laughed. "You sure do get your father. Good guess but wrong."

Gilbert felt as though a sudden bank of dark storm clouds had run over the moment. "Pretty sure it's not any kind of pet," he said, mostly to himself but loud enough that his mother glanced at him. She let the moment pass.

The living room door opened, and their father came into the kitchen. Gil thought that his dad's feet were hardly touching the floor. "Okay, boys and girl, it's time for the big welcome-to-Roanoke surprise." He turned and reentered the living room, drawing his family behind in the wake of his enthusiasm.

There up against the wall next to the fireplace and facing the sofa was a television set! Its cabinet was dark, reddish wood. On its top was a wire antenna. Gilbert rushed over to it and exclaimed, "Oh wow! It's an RCA, twenty-one inches."

"Sit down on the floor, guys," their father said. The three brothers plopped down on the oriental carpet. Katherine set Allie down between Stew's legs. "This is the big surprise that your mom and I have been planning ever since we learned that we were moving to Roanoke and that the city had two television stations, one each in VHF and UHF."

Katherine followed up. "Watching TV is going to be a reward for doing your chores and keeping up with your schoolwork. The way it works is that you can watch a half hour every school day, and on the weekends, each of you gets to choose a 'best program,' and all three of you can watch the others' favorites. But it's a privilege that you'll earn each week."

The rules and regulations barely grazed the boys' consciousness. "Can we try it out right now, Dad?" Stewie asked. "Is it all good to go?"

"Ready as it'll ever be," John replied. "The salespeople set it up and checked it out on delivery." He twisted a knob on the front of the set, and a clear black-and-white picture flooded their eyes.

"It's Howdy Doody!" Stew shouted. "Just like home at Aunt Eleanor and Uncle Harold's house! But without snow from the Boston station." He jumped up and began to dance and sing:

"It's Howdy Doody Time.
It's Howdy Doody Time.
Let's give a rousing cheer,
For Howdy Doody's here."

He reached down and pulled Petie up. Together, they danced around in a circle, singing along with the song.

* * *

School oozed into April. Gilbert liked his classes pretty well, although decimals hard on the heels of fractions were a bit tough.

Mrs. Starr was good at seeing when he was really open to answering a question, drawing him into the flow of the classroom. For the most part, his classmates ignored him, except for Delores and Margie. Sometimes when he looked up, one or both of them would be looking at him from across the room. As the days passed, he became less shy and would smile back at them as if he really knew what was going on.

It wasn't as easy on the playground. There, being ignored was more aggressive, letting him know that he was an outsider and a damned Yankee to boot. He played tetherball and softball with the boys but was always the last chosen and the last in the batting order. Sometimes, as recess was drawing to a close, Margie and Delores would walk up to him and chat about school gossip. Although they were speaking to him, they seemed to be having some kind of contest to out-do one another at seeming more grown-up and attractive. Gil liked the attention he was getting but at times felt like a badminton birdie, being whacked to and fro, pushed into the shifting winds of the morning.

Home had also settled into a routine that wasn't much different than back in Sutton. The biggest difference was that his father had a set schedule at the induction center, making mealtimes and evenings a regular pattern. And there was time for family outings on the weekends.

One morning, after the morning announcements, Mrs. Starr stood up from behind her desk. "Boys and girls," she said. "I'm happy to announce that the Roanoke school system has come up with an exciting new project." She paused and looked around the room, making sure that all her charges were with her. "This year will see the first citywide vocal festival for all elementary schools combined. Our class, along with Mrs. Peavey's group, are going to practice a musical presentation that will be done with all the other sixth-grade classes around the city, gathering in the municipal stadium in the river park downtown. Our first rehearsal will be held during our activity period tomorrow. I know this is very new but are there any questions?" A few hands shot up. "Yes, Caroline?"

"When is the festival going to take place, Mrs. Starr?"

"The plans are for the second Friday of May. Yes, Tommy?"

"What songs will we be doing?"

"I'm not really clear on that right now. When we have our first session tomorrow, Mrs. Skillings, the music supervisor, will be here to explain. She'll be working with Mrs. Naylor to introduce the pieces and, from time to time, will come in for rehearsals. And now it's time for some review on decimals. Remember, you've got a unit test coming up in about a week." With only a few groans from the boys' side of the room, desks opened and notebooks came out.

The next day, Gil's class and the other sixth graders went down to the auditorium at the other end of the school. The students took their seats and a tall, gray-haired woman stood up next to the piano.

"Good day to you, Robert E. Lee sixth graders. I am Mrs. Skillings, and it is my great pleasure to introduce the three pieces you'll be mastering for the festival. Our school committee members assisted us in the selection process. They felt that your songs should reflect pride in our rich heritage. We'll start with 'Dixie.' Next, a shortened version of our official state anthem, 'Carry

Me Back to Old Virginia.' And, finally, in honor of our great nation, we will conclude with 'America the Beautiful.' We have lyric sheets. Make sure you bring them to each rehearsal."

The mimeographed pages made their rounds of the forty-three sixth graders.

"Please listen and follow along as Mrs. Naylor plays the three tunes. On Wednesday we will have our first run-through." She nodded toward the piano. Gil sat back and let the melodies start to sink in. Each of the songs seemed familiar, but only 'America the Beautiful' was one that he had sung in school back in Sutton. When the bell rang, the students filed out toward their last class of the day, social studies.

After several sessions, the medley started to seem familiar. One day, after a rehearsal focused on the transition from "Dixie" to "Carry Me Back," school discharged its hordes. Gilbert and a group of other sixth graders headed out to the playground. Over the weeks since his arrival in Roanoke, his connections with other boys had improved. There were still awkward moments, but he felt less and less like a foreigner. Now he decided to establish himself further as one of the group.

"Hey," he said, in what he hoped was a steady tone. "When we were singing today, I remembered how we used to do 'Dixie' up in Maine." He paused; the others just stared at him. "Well, here goes:

Well, I wish I was in the land of cotton,
My farts stink, but yours are rotten.
Look away, look away,
Look away, Dixie Land."

He stopped and waited. There were no smiles.

Finally, Walton, the biggest of the group, stepped forward.

"Well, Jenkins, now I'm sure. For a while I thought you were okay. But now I know you're just another damn Yankee." He stepped toward Gilbert. He raised his hands, doubling his fists. "C'mon, Gillie. Let's see what you've got!"

Gil felt the panic swell up in his chest. He didn't think he could stand up to Walton, and even more, he really didn't think that fighting was right.

"No, Walt," he said. "I'm sorry if it was a bad joke, but it's not worth fighting over. I'm just going home."

Walton sneered at him and turned to his friends. "See, Yankees are all alike: chicken and snooty." He spit at Gilbert's feet. "See you tomorrow, cluck-cluck."

Stewie left his gang and walked over to his big brother. The two Jenkins boys headed for home. It took half the walk for Gil's pulse to slow. He was mad at Walton for showing him up and even madder at himself for trying to seem cool to the other boys. And he was confused by the three songs that had set the whole thing off. He knew that the Civil War had been between different parts of the country. But that had been way back in time. Why was there still such anger?

"Hi, boys," his mother said as they walked into the kitchen. "Have a good day at school?"

"Oh yeah, Mom," Stewie said. "Recess was great; after school the playground was even better. Oh, yeah, I got a hundred on my long division quiz."

"Super, big boy. And how about you, Gil? Learn anything?"

"I guess so," her eldest replied. "Excuse me. I've got to use the bathroom right away."

He sped out into the front hall and up the stairs. He went into the boys' bedroom and down on his bed. He put a forearm over his eyes and tried to slow his streaking mind. Then Stew was shaking his arm, telling him that their dad was home, and it was time to eat.

After supper, Katherine said, "Boys, please clear the table. And Stewie, you and Petie go upstairs and get changed for bed." As her sons left the dining area she said, "Gil, please come back in here. While your dad and I have coffee, we want to have a chat with you."

Gil was a bit startled but turned and sat down at the table.

Dr. Jenkins broke the silence. "Gil, your mother and I are a little concerned about how you're doing today. You seem to be a little out of focus. Are you feeling okay?"

His mother continued, "Did you have a bad day at school? It's not like you to come home and go right up to your room."

Gil's first impulse was to deny that anything was wrong. But the flare-up on the playground still seemed as unsettling as it had at the time. He opted for the truth, or at least most of it. "I had a kind of blow-up with some of the kids after school; one of the guys tried to pick a fight with me."

"What caused the problem, Gil?" his father asked. "Like they say, it takes two to tango."

"Well, I tried to be funny, did a takeoff on one of our chorus songs. It didn't work at all, and Walton got in my face. I told him I didn't mean anything by it, but he wasn't listening. Finally, I just had to walk away."

His mother stepped in. "What was the joke that went wrong?"

Gil took a deep breath and explained his version of "Dixie." "I wasn't trying to be a wise guy." He looked from one parent to the other, trying to gauge their reactions. His father seemed to be struggling to keep a serious face, but his mother appeared to be really upset. "I'm sorry. I really shouldn't have done it." The silence seemed to carry its own weight.

Finally, his mother said, "Gil, you need to know that people in different sections of the country have their own cultures that are very important to knowing who they are. And especially down here, memories of the Civil War run deep."

His father stepped in. "It's sort of like back home; Mainers really resent people 'from away' treating us like we're just a bunch of farmers and fishermen who talk funny. People deserve to have their way of life respected."

Gilbert could feel a lump expanding in his throat. "I get that. But why don't the kids down here give me the same kind of respect. I was born in Maine. That doesn't make me a damn Yankee!"

"Yes, for sure," Katherine said. "But it's also important not to give them any excuse to treat you badly. You're a great kid and you don't have to prove that, other than being yourself."

"Stand up for yourself," his father added. "But do it without stepping across lines."

"Okay, Mom. Okay, Dad. I'll do my best."

"Know that we're both proud of you," his father said. Were glad you're our number one son."

"And now," his mother added, "I've got to make sure your brothers are ready for bed. You must be ready, too. It's been a long day."

"Tell you what, Gil," his father said. "Why don't you and I watch a little TV together before you head up?"

The three stood and walked through the kitchen. His mother climbed the stairs. Dr. Jenkins and Gil went into the living room to settle in for the Wednesday Night Fights.

* * *

One Saturday, the family piled into the Mercury and drove north on the Skyline Drive to the Virginia Natural Bridge. Passing through the visitors' center, they walked down the path, along a stream, toward the bridge. Captain Jenkins led the way, Petie perched on his shoulders. Gil pushed Allie in his stroller, stopping with his mom to read the signs explaining the formation of one of the "seven wonders of the natural world." Stewie trailed behind, collecting rocks and throwing them across the rippled brook.

After a bit, Dad stopped and lowered Petite off his shoulders. "You're getting pretty big there, young man. I guess you can walk along with the rest of us for a while."

Petie looked around to his mother. "How long I got walk? It's too far?"

"No, sweetie," his mother said. "It's just a little farther. You can use the exercise. And your daddy's shoulders need a break." She scooched down and ruffled his hair. "You and Gil can walk along together. I'll push Allie right next to you."

Finally, they trooped around a bend, and there loomed the great rock arch of the bridge. After waiting for Stewie to catch up, they stood for a moment just taking in the monument.

"Well, boys," their father said. "There stands a great example of the power of nature. Amazing how that little brook could carve out that arch."

"Cool," Stewie said. "I wonder if anybody could climb up to the top on those smooth rocks?" His gaze moved up and down the stone face, as if he were planning a climb at any moment.

"Sure they could if they had the right training and special equipment." Dr. John paused. "I mean, one of these days someone is going to climb Mt. Everest; it's only a matter of time."

Katherine joined in. "I'm just struck by the power of God's nature. It's almost like a divine hand carved this out like a natural cathedral."

Gil stood a little to the side, gazing at the bridge. At once, he felt very small but sensed that he was growing along time's passage. He was pretty sure that he couldn't scale the rock wall yet but could imagine that pretty soon he'd be grown up enough to take on the challenge. And Everest, the world's highest peak, had always been one of his great dreams—to be the first, to do something no one else had ever done. And the North Pole. Admiral Peary had already been the first there, but the urge to go into a strange, white world still stirred his imagination.

Last summer, Auntie and Uncle Ted had taken him to Portland to visit Mrs. Peary, the admiral's widow. Her apartment had been like an arctic museum, with photos of Eskimo villages, shelves of knickknacks, and over the fireplace a twisted ivory narwhal tusk. He had left with a glowing desire for an arctic trek. He knew that Commander MacMillan sailed to Greenland each summer with a crew of students from Bowdoin College. He'd have to wait for that one for sure, just like Everest's summit could wait for his assault.

His dad's voice sliced into his reverie. "Okay, gang, let's head back to the visitors' center. There were some pretty great smells coming out of the restaurant."

"They got Cheerios?" Petie asked.

"Probably not, slugger," his dad said with a laugh. "But I bet we can get you a hot dog and some potato chips. Maybe a frappe? You like those milkshakes, don't you?"

Petie jumped up and down on the pathway. "Chocolate, chocolate, chocolate!" he chanted.

The family did an about-face and headed down the path, Stewie running ahead to pick up a rock and fire it at unseen bad guys across the stream.

* * *

Bit by bit, Gilbert felt as if he were entering a new world in Roanoke, a world which only he knew about. His regular life continued on as always: home, school, family. But on the edges, he began to step into new experiences that he kept to himself. His mother was always busy with Petie and Allie. Stewie had developed his own crew of friends and banged around the neighborhood playground or in the jungle of vines and bushes that grew at the edge of the field across from the Dutch Cape that passed for home. And his father wasn't in and out of the house as he had been back in Sutton. The induction center was a regular nine-to-five day, with dinner at six thirty. So Gil could slip away from parental attention, not every day, but when an opportunity presented itself. And it got easier to make up a cover story for his mom, one that would pass her inspection.

Once, Margie invited him to come home with her after school. On the chosen Friday, he helped clear the breakfast dishes off the table and followed his mother to the sink.

"Hey, Mom," she said. "Is it okay if I go home with a friend after school today?"

Katherine was bustling, getting Allie's cereal into a bowl. "Well, I guess it would be all right. Which friend?"

"Marty," Gil replied. "He's one of the guys that I play ball with."

"And his mother is going to be home?"

"Oh yeah. I mean, she's a housewife too."

"And you'll be home in time for dinner, right?"

"Sure."

His mother walked to the table and sat down with her youngest. "Well, have a good school day. And maybe sometime you'd like to invite Marty to come here."

"I'll make sure to ask him."

After school, Margie and Gil walked to the bus stop next to the Bijoux. The sign on the marquee offered up *The Creature From 20,000 Fathoms.*

"I love the movies," she said. "I go to a matinee almost every Saturday. How about you?"

Gilbert felt a tug of embarrassment. He opted for the truth. "Well, my mom has this thing about movies. I'm only allowed to go to one a month. And I can only go to the ones that she thinks are okay for kids."

The bus pulled up at the stop, and they climbed aboard, dropping a dime each into the fare box. Gil felt a little strange, like he should have paid for his friend's fare too. But the dime had wiped him out; he'd be broke until his quarter allowance on the weekend.

He followed Margie down the aisle and slid into a seat next to her. His hip brushed against her leg. As they rode along, he wondered if it would be cool to put his arm around her shoulders. It was hard to decide just how much of a friend she thought he was. So he just sat back and listened to her chatter about school. Then she reached up and pulled the stop cord. Gil followed her off the bus and down a side street to her home, a blue-gray ranch style house.

Margie's mom was in the kitchen as they walked through the house. She gifted the arrivals with a huge smile. "Well, hello," she said. "You 'all must be Gilbert. Margie's told me all about you."

"Hello," Gil replied. "I'm glad to meet you."

"And how are you adjusting to life down here in the South?"

"It's going really well." His mother's instructions guided him. "Thank you very much for asking. And thanks for having me here."

"It's a pleasure," she said. "Margie, why don't you and Gilbert take a few of these cookies and get started on that assignment you've got?"

Gil swung his attention to his friend. It was the first he'd heard of any school project. Margie didn't quite wink, but her eyes told him that they'd share this bit of fiction. She put four chocolate chip cookies on a plate and turned toward the door. "We'd better get going," she said.

He followed her down the front hall, past the living room, and into a bedroom floating with pastel colors. The bedspread on her high single bed was fluffy and pink. The curtains at the window were a light, gauzy yellow, barely dancing on the breeze. And there were dolls everywhere. They sat down on the soft blue carpet.

"I'm glad you could come today, Gil," Margie said. "It's hard to get to know somebody just in school."

Gilbert's mind raced around trying to think of a suitably cool follow-up. Nothing came and so he just smiled. The afternoon flowed as they talked of this and that.

Suddenly, Gil looked up at the alarm clock on the bedside table: 5:45. He jolted up. "Oh, wow, Margie. I didn't realize it was getting late. I've got to get home for dinner." He jumped up and started for the front door. Then he turned and hurried back to the kitchen. Margie's mother was sitting at the table, sipping a cup of tea.

"I've got to be going, Mrs. Coleman. Thanks for having me."

"You're always welcome, Gilbert," she said. "I hope you two made some good progress on that project." He thought there was a hint of amusement in her tone. No matter, he had to get back to Dyer Road. He followed Margie down the hall. She stood in the entry so that he had to squeeze past her. Their bodies brushed and he wished that he didn't have to push past so quickly. As he came to the end of her road, he looked back. The door was closed.

Gil half ran, half walked along the main road leading back to the north-west intersection near his house. The clock on the Methodist Church steeple showed 6:20. As he turned onto the last street leading to Dyer Road, he forced himself to slow down, to calm down, to prepare his script. The green Mercury was parked in the driveway. He took a deep breath, mounted the front steps, and stepped into the house. *Howdy Doody* was on the television, Stewie and Petie sprawled in front of the set. As he walked into the kitchen he saw his dad with his coffee mug at the table. His mother's back was toward him.

"Hi, Mom. Hi, Dad. Hope I'm not too late."

"No, slugger," his dad replied. "I was a little late myself. Your mom and I are just catching up on the day."

Katherine turned and drew her eldest into a hug. "Glad you're home, sweetie," she said. Did you and Marty have a good time?"

"Yeah, Mom. We mostly played catch in his yard. He let me use his dad's first baseman's mitt. He's a good guy."

After that, it got easier for Gil to go his own way. His allowance got him round trips on the bus to downtown Roanoke. There he wandered the streets, peeking into shops and reading the signs advertising all manner of things he didn't need. Once he went into a Woolworth's Five and Ten and just roamed the aisles. As he was heading toward the exit, almost without thinking, he reached over and picked up a tiny pink plastic doll baby. He walked on and slowly slid his hand into his pocket. In the safety of the street, he pulled out the contraband and stared at it. For all he was worth, he couldn't understand the theft. He walked quickly down the road and, at the first opportunity, tossed the doll into a trash container.

One Saturday, he told his mother that he wanted to go to the library down by his school to do some reading for social studies class.

"Sure thing, Gil," she said. "What's the topic you're working on?"

He hadn't thought that through but managed to pull "Egypt" out of his hat. "I'm going to study the gods and goddesses in the old tombs."

"Sounds like fun. When do you think you'll be home?"

"Oh, it shouldn't take more than an hour or so."

"Have fun, sweetie." She turned and lifted Allie out of his high chair. "Phew," she said. "Your brother stinks. Lucky you're leaving."

Gil walked up Dyer Road and struck out into his afternoon. He walked past his school and then the library. Crossing the main street, he joined the queue outside the Bijoux. As the doors opened, he walked into the lobby and, as the usher took tickets from other kids, slipped on by and down into the theater. He took a seat in the middle near a group where he hoped he'd blend in. The lights went down, and the newsreel began to report on Korea. Next came a Looney Tunes cartoon and finally the first film of the double feature, *Knights of the Round Table*. He tried to relax and get into the show but kept having to look around for the usher. And then he became aware that even one movie was going to last way longer than the hour he'd set up with his mother. Finally, his nervousness was too much. He got up and walked up the aisle, through the lobby, and out into the daylight.

When he got to the house, his dad was out in the yard. "Hey there, Gil. I'm about to start washing the car. Want to give me a hand?"

It seemed to the boy that fate had offered him a sure cover. "Sure Dad. I'll just yell in the door so that Mom will know I'm here. Be right back."

* * *

It seemed to Gilbert that Stewie had been awake before the June sunrise crept over the hills across the big field next to Dyer Road. His younger brother was up, dressed, and bouncing up and down across the bedroom.

"Stewie," Gil groaned. "It's way too early for us to get up."

"Yeah, Gil," Stew said. "But today's our big outing to Mill Mountain. It looks like a beautiful one, so we'd better get over there to make sure we get a good picnic table. I mean I think Dad said that the gates open at eight o'clock."

"Way too early. You gotta remember that Mom and Dad only get the weekends to sleep late. Tell you what: why don't you go down and watch the kids' shows on TV. And don't slam the door. We don't want to wake Petie, or it'll be over for all of us."

"Okay. But not too long. Don't want to waste the day."

Stu closed the door with only a little bang. Gilbert took a deep breath and rolled over in bed, facing the wall and away from the lure of morning sun. He closed his eyes and drifted off into dream world.

He was back in Sutton, walking up Glen Street toward Main and his gray Victorian home on the corner. He'd been playing down in the woods on the side of the hill between the tall pine trees and the little valley where the brook ran down toward the Nine Falls River. He'd climbed into the big oak tree to where it hollowed out into a secret compartment, an escape. But Stewie, Vince, and their other friends hadn't been there; he'd been alone. Now in the late afternoon dusk he could hear a dog barking up the hill. None of the houses had turned on any lights as yet. He walked across the three-lane cement driveway, past the sandbox, and up the back stairs. He pushed the door open and stepped through the coat closet entryway and into the kitchen. All was quiet and a little gloomy. No dinner on the stove, no brothers playing in the dining room, no Honey—even her dog bowls weren't by the brick chimney in the kitchen. He looked out the kitchen window and saw that the family Mercury wasn't there.

"Gillie, Gillie, Gillie! It morning. Time for get up, for breakfast!" Five-year-old Petie had climbed up on Gil's bed and was jouncing up and down.

"Huh? Oh, yeah. Okay, Petie." Gil rolled over from the wall and away from his home in Sutton, many states north and a world apart. He reached over and patted his brother's bristly crew cut. "Time to get up, huh? And today's our day to visit the big park. Are you ready?"

Petie's bouncing accelerated. "Yes! Yes! First Cheerios and then big swings. Lots of fun." And he jumped down off the bed and skittered through the door and down the stairs. Gil sat up, scratched his head, stretched, and followed his brothers down to meet the day.

In the sun-room dining area, Dr. Jenkins was sitting at the head of the table spooning Pablum into Allie's avid mouth. Stewie and Petie were already at work over their cereal. Their mom walked over from the stove with two cups of coffee and sat facing the windows onto the big backyard.

"Good morning, sweetie," she said to her eldest. "Get yourself a bowl and dig into breakfast. There's orange juice in the fridge, too. When you're set, we can talk over the day's plans."

"Okay, Mom," he replied. He walked over to the refrigerator, poured a glass of juice, grabbed his favorite green bowl, and returned to the table. He sat down at the end, facing his father, chose a box of cereal and poured out his breakfast.

His father smiled. "Wheaties, huh? Going for the 'Breakfast of Champions'? Who's on the box cover?"

Gil looked and replied, "Somebody named Preacher Roe. Do you know who he is?"

"Oh, yeah. He's a great pitcher for the Brooklyn Dodgers, a left-hander."

"He must be really good to be on the box, huh?"

"One of the best. And he's a real pitcher, not just someone who throws hard. He's one part of the puzzle that the Dodgers are hoping will finally get them to a World Series. Only top flight athletes make the Wheaties box."

"Like who?"

"I never got to have packaged cereal as a boy on the farm. But once I did an overnight with one of my classmates, Everett, and he had Wheaties for breakfast. If I remember right, the very first was Lou Gehrig, the Hall of Fame first baseman of the Yankees. A great player and one of the true gentlemen to ever play the game."

"Only baseball players?" Gil asked.

"Mostly, because it's our national pastime, the great American game. But I know that another one was a track athlete named Jesse Owen. He was famous for winning three gold medals in the 1936 Olympic Games—in the dashes and broad jump."

"Wow," Stewie jumped in. "He must have been really good."

"And even more so," Dr. John replied, "because he was a negro American competing against German athletes who had been told that they were a superior race. Americans felt really proud when we saw the newsreels of him in the movies."

"Anybody else?"

"I just read that Wheaties has also done a box with Roy Campanella, the all-star catcher for the Dodgers. A great player and another negro athlete."

Gil said, "Maybe next time we go to Kroger's we can get the box with his picture."

There was a long moment of silence as his parents looked at one another.

"I'm afraid that won't happen, Gil," his father finally replied.

"Why not?"

"Well down South there's a different way of looking at race. Negro athletes aren't popular down here."

Katherine stepped in, a half grim, half sad look spilling across her face. "Gil, you must have noticed that even though Roanoke has a lot of negroes, there's no real connection between them and the white citizens. It's a cultural thing that goes back way before the Civil War."

"But is that fair? I mean they're Americans, too."

"Well," his dad added, "that's what we'd like to think up in Maine. But here, what they call below the Mason Dixon Line, there's a real belief that the races are naturally born unequal. And because of that, there's an agreement called "separate but equal." Whites and negroes stay in their own groups and thus conflicts are damped down."

"Kind of like at school, huh?"

"Exactly," his mother said. "Everybody gets a chance, in their own neighborhoods." Her tone suggested that the discussion had reached a stopping point. "Now, guys, get upstairs, brush your teeth while your dad and I get Allie ready and pack the picnic basket. Mill Mountain calls."

With the picnic basket, diapers, and a change of shirt for each boy stowed in the trunk, the Jenkinses piled into the Mercury. Katherine and Stewie sat on either side of Petie in the back seat; Gilbert took the front passenger's seat with Allie on his lap. His dad revved the engine, backed out of the driveway, and headed up Dyer Road toward the day's adventures. Stewie rolled down his window, stuck out his head, and yelled, "Look out Roanoke; here we come!"

As they drove toward downtown, with Mill Mountain and its big, white star, Gil watched the neighborhoods change, the houses getting smaller and less well kept, finally blending into the business district. They passed the park along the Roanoke River until they reached the access road to the mountain and began their climb. The road swung back and forth in a series of horseshoes, each new turn offering a view out across the valley toward the Blue Ridge Mountains in the distance, glowing in the mid-morning sun

They neared the summit and Captain Jenkins pulled the car into a parking lot, already half full. The family piled out and came to a sort of platoon-like order. Gil stood next to his mother, holding Allie on his shoulders. Petie leaned against Katherine, taking in the new scene. Stewie made furtive jumps and starts away from the file.

"Okay, gang," John said. "Let's get rolling." He opened the trunk. "Think we should take the basket now?" he asked his wife.

"No, I don't think so. Probably better to get ourselves a table and stake our claim first. But we'll need the diaper bag. Allie's harness and leash are in it. Once we get out of the lot, we can let him walk a bit."

"Roger Wilco," the captain replied. He rummaged around, stood, and shut the trunk. "Success. And off we go." He led his little platoon across the lot and up a gravel path into the deep green of the park. "Stewie, you need to stay on the path until we get to the picnic area and the playground." Reluctantly his number two son complied, making do with jumping forward and backward on the tiers of log steps along the trail.

They walked into an opening which featured a dozen or so wooden tables and another great view of the valley below. Stewie ran over to three empty tables and jumped onto the board seats of each, checking whatever clues would inform his choice. "Perfect," he called. "This is the one for sure." His dad followed after him, carrying Petie, who had run out of gas halfway up the trail. Gil walked a bit ahead of his mother who was tending to Allie on his leash. She walked to Stewie's choice and attached the cord to one of the slats. Leaning down she ruffled her youngest's blond curls and said, "Okay, honey. You can have fun right here on the grass."

Gil felt as if some strange electrical charge had buzzed his consciousness. He looked at Allie, who crawled over to the table and managed to stand, holding onto the seat. Then Gil scanned the rest of his family, all of whom were seemingly settled into the morning. He shook his head and put the moment behind him.

"Okay, guys," John said. The playground's just over there. Let's head on over and give your mom and Allie a little together time. Could be that a diaper change is due." He took Petie by the hand, and the three brothers and their dad headed across the clearing.

The playground was just up the trail a bit. They passed a stream of fellow celebrants of a June Saturday: a young couple holding hands, a number of families, an older man and woman helping support one another in their descent. Suddenly from behind a voice called out, "Excuse us!" The Jenkins crew stepped to the side and a man, woman, and girl about Gil's age forged on past. The girl was holding a leash, trying with modest success to hold back a black-and-white English Setter.

"Cool, Dad," Stewie said. "I guess they allow dogs in the park." And then they continued on to the playground.

The brothers rotated through the playground's offerings. Three swing sets offered a variety of swings. Stewie immediately picked one that faced out toward the valley, climbed up, and, standing on the seat, began to pump and glide as if preparing to launch toward the Blue Ridge. The captain of the Jenkins platoon put Petie in a boxed-in wooden seat and began to slowly push his third son into a slowly elevating arc. "More higher," Petie cried. "More higher!"

Gil sat and swung with no real enthusiasm. After a few moments, he let go of the ropes, and the momentum of the swing gently launched him over the wood chip cushion of the play area. He walked away and leaned up against a big oak tree that partially hid him from the others on the playground. His mind jumped from Woods Street School to Margie's bedroom to the scrum of his Robert E. Lee classmates on the playground. Then a chorus of barking brought him back to the present. He watched as two dogs strained on their leashes, each trying to connect with the other.

The morning passed, and then Katherine came slowly up the path with Allie tottering from step to step. She walked over to her husband and said, "I think it's time for lunch. If you'll go back to the car and get the basket, I'll herd these guys back to the table."

"Can do," the captain said and headed back down the mountain.

"Okay, guys," their mother called. "Time for lunch. Gil, why don't you tend Allie? You can keep him under control with his leash. Come on, Petie. I'll give you a hand."

Stewie gave one last pump on his swing and flew out toward the others. "What do we have for lunch, Mom?"

"Sorry to say, all I could come up with were some tuna sandwiches. And," she paused a dramatic beat, "I had to use two of the cans of white tuna your dad gave you. Hope that was okay?"

"Oh yeah! Let's get going!" and the Jenkins's blond bomber headed down the path.

As lunch came to a close, the family planned the rest of the day.

"Guys, think you've had enough of the park for the day?" Katherine asked.

"Oh, no!" Petie cried. "Like swings, sandbox, too."

"And, don't forget, there's the zoo," his dad said. "There are lots of animals native to this area of Virginia. Some from farther away, too."

"Snakes?" Stewie asked. "They gotta have some cool snakes."

"I guess we'll just have to check it out. How's this for a plan: you guys can go back to the playground for another hour or so. Then we can all go to the zoo to end the day." He looked to his eldest son who was sitting at the table with his chin propped up in his hands. "Sound like a plan to you, Gil?"

"Yeah, I guess," Gil replied. "Whatever works for you guys is fine."

Katherine gave him a long look. "Are you feeling okay, sweetie?" she asked.

"Yeah, I'm fine," he replied. "Just a little tired. It feels like a long time since Petie jumped on my bed and shut down my dream."

His mother turned to John. "All this sounds like it will work. However, somehow we've got to work in a nap for Allie. And we probably shouldn't stay too late. I'll need time to cook supper when we get home."

"How about this: I'll take Allie and the basket back to the car and you can go with the guys to the playground. While he's napping, I can listen to the Senators game on the radio. They're playing the Yankees today.

"That sound good to you guys?" she asked.

"Maybe you can change Allie now? That'll make things easier back at the car. And," John paused, "what would you think if we ate an early supper at the little restaurant here at the park, after the zoo?"

"Yeah, yeah," Stewie chimed in. "A Virginia loaded burger would be great, on top of *my* white tuna fish!"

"That should be fine," his mother concurred. Then she picked up the bag of Allie's needs, stretched her youngest on the table and commenced his clean-up. "It's about two thirty. Let's meet at the playground in about an hour. Then we can head over to the zoo and later the restaurant."

"Sounds like a deal. If I'm a few minutes late, you can go on over to the zoo, and I'll catch up," her husband replied. Then he shouldered Allie and headed down the path toward the parking lot.

After another hour of swings, teeter-totter, and sand box, Mom and three sons took a trail that wound its way around the mountain, following the signs toward the zoo. Their trek took them past the base of the giant star that soared upward, seemingly higher than the peak of the mountain. When they reached the entrance to the zoo, they were surprised to find that there was an entrance fee. And Katherine had not brought her pocketbook from home. The boys stood staring at the gate while she tried to figure out their next step. "Okay, guys," she said, "here's the plan. Gil, you go back down to the parking lot and get your dad and Allie. Make sure that you bring up the diaper bag and that your father doesn't forget his wallet. Stewie, Petie, and I will wait here."

"Mom, Mom! I can go down," Stewie cried. "I know the way and I'm a faster runner than Gil!"

"I don't think so, sweetie. Your dad may need help carrying Allie and the diaper bag. You can keep Petie entertained for me. Gil, head out but don't run on the steep places."

Gil headed off down the path, encouraged by his mother's choice. When he reached the parking lot, he walked over to the Mercury. At first, he thought that both his dad and Allie were asleep, the toddler son curled up on his father's chest, Dad's head back over the top of the vinyl bench seat. He tapped on the hood and his father stretched and looked at him, seeming only a little surprised.

"Hey, Gil," he said. "What's up? I was just listening to the ballgame while Allie snoozed."

Gil explained the situation.

"Fine," his father said. "It's up and at 'em. You grab the diaper bag, and I'll carry your brother."

"Okay," Gil replied. "By the way, who's winning the game?"

"The Yankees are up five over the Senators. One more reason that I'm ready to climb back up to the zoo." Father and sons headed up the trail.

The zoo wasn't that large, but the boys were excited by each new display they reached. There were a series of cages containing a variety of cats: bobcats, Canada lynx, two spotted ocelots, and a rather sad looking mountain lion. Another section was dedicated to reptiles: turtles, two large tortoises, and a variety of snakes. Stewie was entranced by the rattlers, moccasins, and a huge, mottled boa constrictor. The birds held less attraction for the boys despite their mother's attempts to point out their varied markings and different bills. Finally it became clear that all six Jenkinses were running out of gas. As they reached the exit, they passed a solitary cage in which a pair of gray coyotes were curled in the corner taking a late afternoon nap.

"Okay, troops," Captain Jenkins said. "One more trek down the hill to the restaurant, a quick supper, and home. Forward, march."

They entered the take-out line of the restaurant and stood looking at the big menu posted over the counter. Several groups were in front of them. Gil scanned the offerings while his father read out choices to his brothers. "Remember the rule," he said. "You can order anything you want, but you have to finish it." He knelt down next to Petie. "What would you like for supper, little man?"

"Hot dog!"

"And what do you want on it?"

"Ketchup! And some french fries, too?"

"We can get a family size and share." He turned to his wife. "And what can I get for you, my dear?"

"A grilled cheese would be nice, maybe with a slice of tomato."

John turned to the young woman behind the counter. "For starters, we'll have a cheeseburger with fried onions, a grilled cheese with tomatoes, a dog with ketchup, a large french fry, and a small white milk." He turned to Stewie. "Your call, slugger?"

Stew looked up over the counter. "A burger with everything."

"Please," added his mother.

"Please. And a chocolate milk." He looked at his mother to see if his ploy had worked. She nodded.

"And you, young man?" the waitress asked Gil.

"I would like a cheeseburger with ketchup, mustard, relish, and fried onions, please. And," he rode Stewie's initiative, "a small Coca Cola." His mother flinched but seemed to decide that now was not the time to drop the "no soft drinks" gauntlet.

When their number was called, Gil and Stewie helped their dad carry their feast out to the picnic area. They all dove in while Katherine gave Allie sips of milk out of his travel cup. As Gil finished his meal, he turned away from the table and watched other groups. His attention was captured by a husband, wife, and young son. As they dined, each in turn took fries or little smidgens of rolls and used them to reward their little dog for obeying a variety of commands. Even though Gil knew it was bad training to feed pets from the table, he envied the boy.

Supper finished, the Jenkinses trooped down the hill to the parking lot. Only a few cars remained. As they reached the Mercury, clearly the only car with a Maine license plate, a young couple entered the lot from another direction. The woman held a leash that barely restrained a young, energetic, golden cocker spaniel pup. Gil watched as she lifted the pet, received rapt kisses, and climbed into the passenger's seat. Suddenly he felt as if the world was more than he could bear. Without saying a word, he climbed into the rear seat on the driver's side and slumped down against the door. The rest of the family took their places. and Dr. John drove off down the mountain curves into the valley, past the park and downtown, and out toward Dyer Road. At one point, Gil roused himself and looked out the rear window back to Mill Mountain. In the dusk, the white lights of the star were just blinking on.

By the time they reached their driveway, Petie had dozed off, leaning against Gilbert. John and Katherine had let any conversation wane. Even

Stewie was sliding toward bedtime. They parked, and John opened the trunk. Gil grabbed the picnic basket, and Stewie took the diaper bag. They followed their mother, Allie on her shoulder, up the front steps and into the front hall. Without a word, Gil dropped the basket inside the dining room and climbed the stairs. He went into the bedroom he shared with his brothers, rolled onto his bed, and curled up facing the wall. He could hear the family commotion downstairs but tried to push it and everything else out of his mind. One after another he took deep breaths until he began to doze.

Katherine brought Petie into the bedroom, followed by Stewie. "Okay, Stew," she said. "Go into the bathroom and brush your teeth. I'll bring Petie right along." She walked over and sat down next to Gilbert. "Gil, Gil. Sorry to bother you but your dad and I want you to come downstairs for a few minutes. We have a couple of things we want to talk about." She reached over and ruffled his head. Then she pulled Petie's pajamas on and carried him out of the room.

Stewie returned and plopped onto his bed. "Wake up, Gillie," he said. "Mom says to head downstairs."

Gil sat up, shrugged and trudged out of the room, down the stairs, and out through the kitchen to where his father sat in the sun-room. "Pull up a seat, son," his dad said. Your mom should be right along. Would you like something to drink?"

"No thanks, Dad. What's going on?"

"Well, your mother and I have a couple of things we need to check on with you." The two sat at either end of the table, looking out into the backyard. They heard Katherine coming downstairs and through the kitchen. She stopped for a glass of water and joined them at the table. Each sat for a moment as if unsure of who should speak first.

Finally, Dr. Jenkins took the lead. "Gil, your mom and I are a little concerned. You seem to have had a kind of rough day up at the park. Is everything okay?"

Gilbert took a deep breath and tried to steel himself. "Yeah, I guess so, Dad. I guess that I'm just a little tired…or something."

His mother stepped in. "Well, sweetie, both your dad and I really feel that there was something that happened during the afternoon that caused you to be upset. And during the ride home you seemed really far away. It's not like you just to rush upstairs like you did."

"Whatever it may be, son, you need to know that your mother and I are here for you. But, if there is something, well you've got to trust us."

Suddenly it seemed to Gilbert that a rolling sense of loss and loneliness that had washed over him for months couldn't be pushed aside. "Well," he said, a tremor in his voice. "Well, it's just that sometimes I miss Honey so much. And, like today, when I see other people loving their dogs, it makes me really sad."

"Oh, Gil," his mother said. "I know that it's been really hard for you. And I wish that there could have been some other solution for Honey when we had to come down here."

"Your mother and I talked it over many times while I was away at training. But you have to understand that she was all alone with four boys. And you were all going to have to travel down here to meet me. That was hard enough without trying to fit in a pet as well."

"And we felt really lucky that we were able to place her with the Verrills. They're a great family and were really glad to take her in."

"But you never asked any of us; never talked to me about what was going to happen…until the day when Mr. Verrill stopped at the house, loaded her food and bed into the car, and drove her off to the other side of the town, across the river."

"We thought that it would be the easiest, for you, your brothers, and Honey. Think how much harder it would have been if you'd known ahead of time. And understand: your mom and I, we're the grown-ups in the family, and sometimes grown-up people have to make hard choices."

As the three sat at the table, all the energy seemingly had been exhausted. Gilbert stood and without a word headed away from the table. He turned back, looked at his mother and said, "So it must have been even harder for you on both of the times she came back." Then he walked through the house that didn't feel like his home, climbed the stairs and plopped on the bed that wasn't really his, not bothering to change out of his soiled Mill Mountain clothes.

* * *

The stadium gates opened, and a riot of twelve-year-olds flooded toward their school buses. Teachers stood in front of their arks, directing their students toward their ride to school and home. The music festival had been a singing success.

The yellow arks pulled out of the parking lot and away. In the dust and roar, a solitary boy remained. Gilbert Jenkins was alone.

As he realized he'd missed the boat, he shrugged and went into strategy mode. Although Roanoke had been a reality for only seven weeks, his family's excursions had left him with a general sense of its layout. Mill Mountain, with its giant white star, rose behind the stadium. If he stood facing away from the civic landmark, home was off in the distance. How far? That detail was unclear, but he had a sense that he knew the way home. He shrugged and began his trek.

Gilbert walked through the adjoining park, by the little river that flowed along his path. On the bank he saw a fisherman, patient over his pole. The man was old and gray haired. A "Brownie" as Auntie back in Maine had instructed him to call the "them" he would surely see in "Ole Virginny." Not "Darkies" and especially not "Blackies." After all, they were "God's children too."

The boy walked down to the riverbank. "How are they biting today?" he asked.

The old man looked up with a start, took in this young man from across town. "Not much happening, young Suh. But one's got to be patient. You let your bait sit, and eventually you'll get some of what you come for."

"Well, I hope you all have good luck," Gilbert said. He hoped he sounded like a local, not a damn Yankee.

"Thank you, Suh. And you have a good day."

The boy walked back to the path, toward home. He passed a tennis court. A kid about his age stood on the far side of the nets, decked out in shocking white shorts and shirt blending into blond hair. He was slapping at balls lobbed over the net by an older man, also in whites. Gilbert wondered if the man was the boy's father or maybe a coach. The mystery of that scene carried him out of the park, onto a street on the southern edge of downtown.

Gilbert sort of recognized where he was; he'd ridden through the neighborhood with his father, going to or from the induction center. It was so different from Dyer Road, the place that he was trying to think of as home. Here were dirty curbstones with blooms of trash, unpainted concrete bungalows, and faded corner stores.

After a block, he turned left onto what seemed to be a main road leading west. The road flowed up and down, like waves cresting toward a future. For the first time, the boy felt unsure. What was the best direction? How many blocks were left before the Bijou Theater and his new school would direct him home?

He slowly became aware that his was the only white face, block after block. The boys and girls on a vacant lot, two women on a porch, a young man sitting in a '52 Mercury convertible, the same year as his dad's sedan. Each face looked at him as if a distant, separate species had swum into their pond.

Gilbert stopped and looked down two stairs through the open door of a clapboard storefront. The interior was a deep, dark black with a blaze of light. A green swatch was punctuated with dots of various colors, some solid, some striped. One after the other, sharp clicks punctuated the darkness, rearranging the dots. He thought that they resembled the cartoon version of atoms that his class had watched during science.

And up through the darkness, a spectral form approached, an indistinct human like a shadow in a dream. Bright white eyes and a rack of glowing white teeth gave a sense of depth, of substance to the looming being.

A young black man stepped out and up onto the sidewalk. "Looking for some action, young man?" he asked. "Not sure you've come to the right place, 'less you're some sort of miracle shark. Nine ball or straight pool your game?"

Gilbert pushed away a tide of anxiety. "Action? What's that mean?"

"Well, I didn't think you was really a shark. Anything else I can do for you?"

"I'm walking home. I live out in the west, near the Bijou Theater and the Kroger's store. Am I heading in the right direction?"

"Yes sir," the young man said. "My momma and a couple of her friends do cleaning out in that section. Maybe one of them does your house."

"Oh no," Gilbert replied. "My mom does all our housework. She always is asking me and Stewie to help her out. Mostly I don't mind."

"Well I guess that's not such a bad deal. You'll get older soon enough. You want to come in and watch the play?"

"No thanks. I've got to head on home. I need to be there before supper time." The young man nodded, and Gilbert turned and walked on.

As his trek unfolded, block after block, he became aware of the gradual change of the neighborhoods: the houses became better tended and a bit larger with grass on the lawns and occasionally a tree or a shrub. He crossed a major intersection and gradually became aware that the faces in the yards and the shops were all white, except for small groups of black women waiting at the intown bus stops.

Gilbert tried to get his mind around the new issue of race as he'd seen it since arriving in Roanoke. Back in Sutton, it was never an issue. In his whole life before last March, he'd seen maybe two or three Black people. "Different" in Maine meant the French Catholics who lived across the river in Frenchtown. But you couldn't see the difference. His dad took care of French patients. And, especially in the high school, all students from the different elementary schools would come together and mix and match. Some of the best athletes were French; Bunky Benoit and Toots LaChance were stars in basketball and baseball. Some of the cutest cheerleaders were right out of Frenchtown.

But here it was really different. His school was all white kids. That wasn't different from home, but it was clear that mixing wasn't going to happen. Gilbert thought back to the afternoon's music festival. Every one of the kids on the field had been white and every face in the stadium had been white too. Yet, only a couple of blocks away, every kid in the neighborhood was black. And it felt as if nobody was aware of it; like it was supposed to be that way. His mom and dad had never spoken about it, but they had to be aware. He'd have to ask them sometime, when the moment seemed right.

Gilbert walked out of his thoughts and back into his journey. It seemed that the street seemed more familiar. He looked down a side street and recognized Margie's house. He thought of the afternoon he had visited with her, the fluffy, pink covers on her bed and the dolls propped up against her pillows. And then the thoughts during his journey returned: all the dolls on her bed had white faces. The dolls had been chosen by whoever had bought them: Margie with her allowance, adults as birthday gifts. All white faces. At the same time, they all seemed like nice people. Her mom had been glad to see him, a stranger from Yankee country. And Margie really seemed glad to spend time with him, even, he thought, ready maybe to kiss and be close.

A few more blocks, and there was the Bijou. He crossed the road and, passing the Kroger's, headed down the last part of his unexpected journey. The clock in the steeple of the red brick Methodist Church read 5:35. Things at home would be in supper mode. He thought for a moment that maybe his dad would pass him, returning from his duties at the center. No matter. He'd managed to move along through his adventure; maybe that might be a sign of being kind of grown up?

Gilbert paused as he turned onto Dyer Road. He looked down the hill toward his house with recognition that it was where he lived; whether or not it was "home" seemed a very different issue. The neighborhood was very quiet as people settled into dinner and the evening. However, his memory called up the rush hour traffic on Sutton's Main Street and the bangs, groans, and whistles from the Nine Falls Paper Mill. His buds would be finishing up their afternoon of baseball. And Honey would be waiting for her supper, whining only a little. He took a deep breath and walked on the slope toward the white Dutch Cape where his family waited for him.

As he reached the vacant lot, he could look through the shrubs into his backyard. Stewie flashed in and out of sight, chasing whatever game or band of outlaws he had created. The green Mercury was parked in the driveway. His dad had beaten him home, and their paths had not crossed. He walked across the yard and up the steps and into the front hall.

Through the door into the living room, he saw Petie in front of the television. Gil instantly recognized that the moment had arrived in *Romper Room* where Miss Molly and her young guests cried out "Music, Mr. Music." And then attention focused on Mr. Do-Bee, a gigantic bumblebee who always had some suggestion of good behavior to share with kids. Today it was "Be brave. Always behave." Gil rolled his eyes at such a kiddie program and walked into the kitchen. His mother was at the stove; his dad was sitting in the dining nook reading the *Roanoke Times*.

"Hi, Mom," he said. "What's for supper?"

"Frikadeller and potatoes. It's Danish night in the old South."

"Super. Dad and I both love those special burgers." He turned to his father. "What's cooking in the news, Dad?"

His father put down his paper. "Not great news, I'm afraid. It seems that the US did a nuclear test the other day. And a town in Utah, St. George, got covered with fallout. Looks like everyone's going to be fine, but some sheep out in the fields got sick."

Gilbert felt a wash of fear. "Wow, that's awful. Was it an accident?"

"Of course," his father replied. "Our military takes every precaution when it shoots a test weapon. Sometimes things don't go just as planned."

"But we gotta do it, huh? I mean the Russians won't wait on us?"

"That's what the power people say," his mother interjected. "Millions for defense; pennies for peace." She paused. "You're pretty late getting home, Gil. I thought the buses would have had you back to school an hour ago."

The eleven-year-old felt he was on the edge of a cliff. His choices were to stop at the edge or step over into the truth. "Yeah, Mom. The festival lasted a lot longer than everybody thought. And then the traffic was pretty heavy coming out of the park." He waited a moment and shifted the focus. "Our performance went really good; the people in the stands gave us a big round of applause."

"Went really *well*," she said. "Well, go out and call Stewie in." And scrub up for dinner. The frikadeller are going in the skillet right now.

As the spring unfolded, it seemed to Gilbert as if he were more and more on his own. His parents still asked how his school day went, but it felt as if they took his positive responses for granted, not with the real concern they had shown as he and Stewie were starting off at Robert E. Lee. Of course, his mom had double kid duty with Petie and Allie. And when his dad returned from a day of physical exams at the induction center, he was really focused on just sitting and talking about his day with his wife over coffee, so much more relaxed than back in Sutton where the next phone call was almost guaranteed to pull him away for a house call or another baby delivery.

And so Gil was free to roam Roanoke as if it were his real home. After school he might play ball in the schoolyard, but that ran the risk of refighting the Civil War. It was clear from being last chosen and his bumps and bruises that he was still a damn Yankee. Often he would go into the Kroger's market and look through the magazines on the rack inside the door. If he had a dime he might buy a comic book, *Looney Tunes* or *Batman*, if he thought he could sneak it past his mom. For the most part, the staff in the market paid him no attention. He thought he could probably stuff a comic under his shirt but wasn't quite brave enough to take the chance. Once or twice, he moved down the rack to the adult section and took down a *Modern Photography*. He would take a quick peek inside where often there were pictures of nude women, all angles and curves with shadows and glowing patches of light. He sensed that there was something about those photos that drew him in, but he wasn't quite sure how he should feel. And the glances could only be brief because of the threat of discovery.

A couple of times, he went with Margie to her house after school. Usually, he had asked his mom for permission over breakfast. But once he just went off on his own and then called home to explain that he and "Marty" had been given a last-minute assignment in social studies and needed to work that afternoon. His mother was understanding and reminded him to thank Marty's mother for her hospitality. Mrs. Coleman was always welcoming, and he and Margie would just sit in her pink-and-blue bedroom and talk about school, classmates, and the world. Then, the bus ride back to his neighborhood gave him time to develop a story of the almost completed project.

One afternoon after his return, Katherine once again said, "Maybe you can bring Marty home someday. I'd like to meet him. It sounds like you've got a good friend there."

Gil barely skipped a beat. "Yeah, Mom. That's a great idea. Only thing is that his mother likes him to be home in the afternoons…to help keep an eye on his little brother and sister. But I'll check with him, for sure."

At home, dinner was more and more often timed around the nightly news on television. Gil and his dad would sit in front of their RCA while John Cameron Swasey reported on the events of the day. Once in a while, his mom would join them, but only if she wasn't needed in front of the stove and if Petie wasn't having a tough afternoon. Father and son followed the fighting in Korea, the Cold War, problems of the French in their Indo-Chinese colonies, and the tensions at home over issues of civil rights and Russian espionage.

One Thursday in May, the news led with a story that, at long last, Mt. Everest had finally been scaled. The screen filled with a photograph of two smiling men in mountain gear that Swasey identified as the intrepid mountaineer Edmund Hillary of New Zealand and his porter Tenzing Norgay, a Nepalese Sherpa. As Dr. Jenkins and his son watched, Gilbert was washed over with a sense of loss. For years he had dreamed that someday he would be the hero to brave the 29,000 feet to Everest's summit. When the broadcast finished, his father effused about the victory of man over mountain.

"Gil," he said. "It just goes to show that with enough strength and courage, humans can achieve what seems beyond belief."

His son, on the verge of tears, opened himself. "But I had dreamed that I would be the first to the top. The North Pole, the South Pole, Everest: they've all been done. There aren't any left for kids my age."

"There are always challenges, Gil. We humans can always grow and rise to the occasion. When I was your age, polio crippled thousands every year. But in time, Dr. Salk developed the vaccine that protects you and your brothers. And, just think, when he was a young man, Franklin Roosevelt was struck down by polio. But despite his crippled legs, he became one of our greatest presidents and perhaps made the difference between the America you and I know and what might have happened because of the Depression and World War Two."

"But that's different, Dad. Those things are important, but I hoped that I would be able to stand on top of the world."

"So keep on dreaming. Someday, probably while you're a young man, men will fly into space, even to the moon. Don't let others'wins stop you from becoming all that you want to be."

* * *

The last day of school finally arrived. When the final bell rang, the sixth graders at Robert E. Lee Elementary roared toward the door like the spring deluge on the Roanoke River. Gilbert was almost out of the classroom when Mrs. Starr called to him. "Gil, could you wait? I'd like to chat for a moment?"

Gil turned and walked back to his teacher's desk. "Yes'm?" he said, trying to sound as little like a boy from Maine as possible. He waited for whatever direction his school day would take.

"Gil, I just wanted to compliment you on the wonderful addition you've been in my class. I know it must have been a difficult adjustment, the new school, new classmates, the new city."

Gilbert could feel his cheeks flushing while, at the same time, his uncertainty vanished. "Thanks, Mrs. Starr," he said. "It really hasn't been that hard."

"Well you've done a great job, and I'm sure that your classmates have benefited from getting to know you. Now you have a great summer and make sure you stop in to say hello when you come back to seventh grade next September." It was clear the conversation was over. He headed out of the classroom and, at the door, turned and said, "Thanks again, Mrs. Starr, thanks for everything."

When Gil reached the top of the stairway, he found Margie sitting on a bench. "Hey, Margie," he said. "Forget how to get out of our jail?"

His best sixth-grade friend stood up. "No, Gil," she said, laughing. "I'd never forget that." She paused. "I just wanted to tell you that it's been special, getting to know you and all."

"Me too, Margie," Gil replied. "It's been special for me too. You've made it a lot easier." He felt there was more to be said but couldn't seem to find the words.

Margie walked over to him. "I really like you a lot, Gilbert Jenkins from Maine." She opened her arms and he stepped into a hug that felt like it went on and on. "You have a great summer, and maybe we can get together sometime. I'd really love to meet your family."

"Yeah, for sure. I'll give you a call, after we get settled in and all." Then the two of them walked down the stairs and out into the sunshine of June 19, 1953.

Scattered groups of students milled around on the sidewalk and over toward the playground. Margie reached out and squeezed his hand and then walked away toward a clutch of girls. Gil looked around for Stewie. Then, a group of about-to-be seventh-grade boys walked over to him. Walton, the alpha male, who had faced him down over their different versions of "Dixie," stepped up to him.

"Jenkins," he said. "The guys and I want to tell you that you're okay. I mean you seem like you are up for becoming a real Virginian."

Gil exhaled a breath that had felt like it might be his last. "Thanks, Walton." There didn't seem to be anything else he could say.

"Well, in August me and a bunch of the guys will be starting up football season. If you want to, you can join us."

Gilbert looked around at the group. If there was any lasting antagonism, he couldn't see it. "Cool, Walton," he said. "Let me know when you start up." He stepped away. "There's my brother Stewie. I've got to look after him for my folks. See you."

He walked over to his blond bomber brother, and the two Jenkins boys headed off toward Dyer Road. "Boy, Gil," Stew said. "That Walton is a big guy! Hate to face up to him in football."

The brothers were greeted at home with chocolate chip cookies and milk. "Well, boys," their mother said. "Summer vacation at last."

"Oh yeah, Mom!" Stewie said. "Two whole months without homework. We can do whatever we want to."

"Don't get too carried away. I can use some help around the house. For starters, one of you can take Petie outside. We've been cooped up all day. And Allie would love to have a walk. You guys decide how to split it up."

After a short negotiation, Stew took five-year-old Petie out into the backyard where they rolled a ball back and forth across the lawn. Petie jumped up and down with excitement. "Me catch it! Mommy, me catch it!"

Gilbert put Allie's harness on and attached the leash. Then he carried his little brother down the front steps and headed off up Dyer. The afternoon sun gleamed on Allie's curly blond hair, and suddenly, Gil was thrown back to Sutton and memories of taking Honey for walks. He tried to understand his mother's point of view: four boys to transport to Virginia, a new, rented house that might not allow dogs. The Verrills would take good care of their new addition. A lump pushed its way into his throat. His eyes stung like when soap got into them during a bath. He and Allie reached the top of the hill, paused, and headed back to this home that wasn't. He unsnapped and coiled the leash and carried Allie up the steps and into the front hall.

Their mother was sitting at the table in the eat-in sun-room watching Stew and Petie bounce around the yard. Allie toddled over to her. Katherine picked him up, mussed his hair, and gave him a hug. Gil sat down across from her. "Mom," he said, "can I ask you something?"

"Of course, sweetie," she replied. "What is it?"

Gil took a deep breath, pushing down the lump in his throat. "Well, I'm wondering." He paused. "Well, back home, after the Verrills took Honey away…well, she found her way home twice. And both times we sent her back. When that happened, how did you feel?"

His mother shifted Allie on her lap and turned to face her eldest son. "Oh, Gil. It was really hard…not as hard for me as for you, but I felt awful. But…well, sometimes grown-ups have to be strong, especially when there aren't any good choices."

He tried hard not to let anger take over his voice. "I guess you did what you thought you had to, huh?"

"That's right. And I'd talked it over with your dad when he called one night. He agreed that it had to be done. I felt bad that we didn't let you in on the decision, but at the time I felt that it was better to just do what had to be done. Talking it over wouldn't have solved the problem or made it any easier."

Gil stood up. "Okay, Mom. I guess I understand," he said, although he didn't. "You know what really bothers me most?"

"No, Gil. Please tell me."

"Well, sometime, when Dad's service is over, we'll move back to Sutton. And when I think of that, I don't know if I could stand seeing Honey over at the Verrills, over on the other side of the river. It's kind of like half my hometown would be sliced off. I'm going to go up and read for a while." He turned and walked away.

* * *

With school at an end, summer seemed like an open world, as the Old West must have been for the pioneers. Gil could ramble and discover on his own. Some days he took a bus downtown and roamed the streets, watching the parade of people, wondering what their stories might be. Across Dyer Road from his house stretched a huge open field. One day he walked across it and discovered that he had reached the highway that led away from Roanoke, north toward Lynchburg and beyond that Washington, DC. A bit farther, he came to a side road with a sign for the Old Monterey Golf Course.

Once in the spring, he and his dad had gone to the course; Dr. Jenkins had thought he might take up the game now that he had predictable free time. "You can be my caddy, Gil," he'd said. "And afterward you can buy our drinks with the caddy's fee you've earned." Then, on the way home, his father had explained the different clubs and the caddy's duties. However, it seemed that day never arrived. Golf had faded in his father's mind.

The day after his discovery, Gil retraced his steps and started walking the road toward the course. A car stopped, and two young men asked if he was going to Old Monterey. When he replied he was, they offered him a ride for the last mile.

In the parking lot, Gil screwed up his courage and asked, "Would either of you like a caddy?"

"Well," one of the golfers replied. "I do want one. You see the bunch of kids over there?" He pointed toward the club house. "They're all regular caddies. The caddy master decides who they'll carry for. But, if you want my bag, we'll skip the crowd. My name's Jerry; and that's my worthy opponent, Marshall"

"Sure thing," Gil replied. "I'll be happy to."

When their turn came, Jerry and Marshall teed off and, followed by Gil and the other caddy, set off down the fairway. The other boy, larger and seemingly older, kept pace behind his player. Gil hustled to keep up and watched his counterpart as he handed over a club and then held the flag when they reached the green.

For the first nine holes, Gil was able to keep up with the others. He helped his player search for a ball that had strayed into the rough and handed over the requested clubs. But on the back nine, the course became hillier and the late morning sun hotter. Bit by bit, Gil fell behind the pace of the other three. The bag seemed heavier; sweat kept running down into his eyes. He kept searching for a water fountain with no success. Once or twice, Jerry looked back at him with obvious impatience. Finally, on the sixteenth green he walked over to Gil. "Listen," he said. "I know that it's hot and it's clear that you haven't had much experience toting bags. But for the last two holes you've *got* to keep up!"

Gilbert took a deep breath and nodded. It took all his strength but he hustled after the others, managing to stay just a few steps behind. Then they were on the eighteenth green and Jerry was putting out a ten-footer that won him the match one up.

He came over to Gilbert. "I'll take my bag from here," he said. "I don't think you'll make it to the parking lot."

"I'm really sorry," Gil replied. "You could probably see that it was my first time carrying. I didn't mean to hold you up."

"Well, if it had been one of the regular caddies, I probably wouldn't have paid him, but...." He reached into his pocket. "Here's fifty cents." He walked away with his bag to the clubhouse.

Gilbert felt like he was drained, both from the four hours of toting and from his disappointment that he hadn't climbed this little mountain. He trudged through the parking lot and down the road toward home. After about a half mile, he heard a car approaching from behind. He stepped onto the gravel shoulder to let the car pass. However, as it reached him, it stopped, and the passenger rolled down the window. It was Marshall.

"Hey, young man," he said. "Why don't you climb in back, and we'll drive you home. We've all had a pretty good workout today."

Gil climbed in, and the car started off. Jerry looked back over his shoulder and winked. "All part of a day's work," he said. "You know, by the time you're our age, caddies will probably be as out-of-date as wooden-shafted clubs. They'll probably have Crosley sized cars just for the courses."

"Really?" Gil said. He sat back in the breeze and tried to imagine a course with little cars driving all over it. The picture seemed crazy.

They approached the side of the huge field. "You can drop me here," Gil said. "I live just across the field. Thanks for the ride."

"Just one more fairway to cross," said his chauffeur.

Gil walked across the field, the white Dutch colonial he tried to call home looming larger. The green Mercury was parked in the driveway; either he was very late, or his dad had gotten out of work early. He crossed Dyer Road, mounted the front steps, and walked in through the front hall to the kitchen.

His dad and mom were sitting at the table in the sunporch, cups of coffee at the ready. Allie was on a blanket, playing with his stuffed yellow elephant. Petie was off to the side stacking blocks and watching them tumble down.

"Hey, Mom, Dad," Gil said. "Where's Stewie?"

"We sold him to the gypsies," his mom replied.

"Get a good price?"

"Enough for all of us to go for ice cream this evening," his dad added.

"Good deal," number one son said. "Thing is, what are we going to do with all those cans of tuna fish you bought him?"

"Think of all the sandwiches you'll get to eat when school starts up," his mother said. "Where've you been off to all day? We missed you at lunch."

Gilbert opted for the truth. "I walked over to the golf course. Jimmy Smyth had told me that they were looking for caddies. I got to carry a bag for the first time."

"And how did that go?" his father asked.

"Pretty good. I kept up with my player and helped him find a lost ball.

Jerry, that was his name, won his match on the last hole. And he paid me fifty cents. Said I did a great job."

"Nice start. Think you'll like the game?

"Oh yeah! It was cool when one of the guys really hit a good one. The way the ball jumped off the club. And the putt my player hit to win made a huge curve across the green and dove into the hole."

"Two really interesting things about golf," his dad continued. "One, it's the only game I know where the lowest score wins, just the opposite of baseball or basketball. And the other thing is that it all depends on the players being honest. Everyone keeps his own score."

"I'd like to learn how to play," Gil said. "Do you think I could ever be good?"

"No guarantees but you sure could try. Who knows, maybe you'd be the next Sam Snead."

"Who's he?"

"One of the very best pro golfers in the world, right along with Ben Hogan. Slammin' Sammy, they call him. And he started in a place where you'd never have thought he'd have a chance to be great: a poor boy in the Blue Ridge Mountains of Virginia."

"What happened?" Gil asked.

"He started caddying when he was just a young kid at the ritzy golf resort in his hometown. And when he wasn't carrying, he was practicing. I understand he had to use borrowed clubs for many years. And it paid off. He won a couple of local tournaments and then became a full-time pro."

"Wow! Does he make a lot of money?"

Dr. Jenkins chuckled. "Oh yeah. He's won more tournaments than any other pro in history. But, you know, I'm sure the money is great, but even better must be the sense of success. A year ago, he won the Masters, one of the four biggest tournaments in golf. And it's played at the Augusta National Club in Georgia, maybe the most exclusive club in the country. Not bad for a hillbilly boy from Hot Springs."

"Great story, Dad. I'll remember it when I start to learn."

"Just remember to keep your head down and always count all your strokes."

* * *

June oozed over into July with heat and humidity that only confirmed to Gil that Roanoke wasn't Maine. To make things worse he caught a horrible case of poison ivy. As best he could tell, he'd gotten it while playing in the tangle of vines and shrubs on the edge of the big field across Dyer Road. He and Stewie had been pretending to be American soldiers sneaking up on the Red Chinese troops across the 38th Parallel in North Korea. The strange thing was that, while the rash spread across almost all of his body, Stewie didn't get so much as a blister. For over a week, all Gil could do was lie on the living room couch with a fan blowing in a futile attempt to cool him. His mom applied cold towels soaked in an aluminum acetate solution to dry the open sores. To pass the time, he read *Etuk the Eskimo Hunter* twice, wishing he could be in Greenland's chill, mushing his sled dogs across the ice, alone, in charge of his path. Finally, his dad pronounced him recovered but warned him against adventures that took him into unfamiliar territory.

More and more, Gil and his father shared the world of sports. On the twenty-one-inch RCA, they watched the Friday Night Fights and the Saturday Major League Baseball Game of the Week. His dad showed him how to keep score on special printed forms they got at the local Kroger's market.

One night the sports news reported that Ben Hogan had won the British Open by four strokes over three other professionals.

"Boy, Gil," his dad said. "That's a great win for Hogan, really special."

"How come, Dad?"

"Well, three years ago, just as his professional career was really taking off, he and his wife were in a horrible car accident. They survived, but Ben had multiple fractures. It wasn't even clear if he'd be able to walk again. And yet, six months later, he was back on the tour. A great story of a poor boy who made good through hard work and courage."

"Super, Dad," Gil replied. "Say, do you think we could go out and play sometime?"

"Could be, Gil. Could be. Of course we've got to think of your mom and brothers. They need our attention too."

Freed from the couch, Gilbert continued his solo exploration of Roanoke. A couple of times he spirited a bit of his allowance and went into a matinee at one of the huge, gaudy movie theaters downtown. Mostly he just wandered the streets, watching the parade of characters, black and white, young and old, for free. Often he gave them names and stories based on his outsider's understanding of southern culture.

His parents' awareness of him ebbed and flowed. With his dad doing his duties at the induction center, their connection revolved around the nightly news and dinner. Golf seemed to have slipped his father's mind, and Gil didn't feel he should push the promise. His mother stressed how his father needed his down time and space. Mostly she seemed very much in charge of the home front. If Gil or Stewie were derelict in their chores or complained about having to watch Petie or Allie, she made it clear that these were the price of being part of the family. Once when he grumped a bit about playing with Petie in the yard, she sat him down at the kitchen table.

"Gil," she said. "You're getting closer all the time to being a young man. And that means you've got to take responsibility for yourself. There will be a time when your dad and I aren't going to be in charge of you and your choices. And choices, you'll find, are the key to being a grown-up."

There didn't seem much that he felt he could say in response. They sat for a few long moments.

"I know it's hard, being the oldest," she continued. "But when it seems that you have a decision to make, you need to take the path that you know is the right one."

They sat for another charged, silent moment.

"Tell you what," Katherine said. "Why don't you load Petie into his stroller, and you and Stewie can take him down to Kroger's." She grabbed her pocketbook and took out fifty cents. "You can treat your brothers to popsicles. Just don't tell your dad; he'll think I'm spoiling you."

On the second Saturday of the month, the TV game of the week featured the Red Sox playing at the Philadelphia Athletics. Gilbert and his dad settled into their slots in the living room.

"This should be a good one, Gil," Dr. John said. "A real pitchers' duel. Bobby Schantz is starting for Philly. He's super, even though he's the shortest starter in the whole American League, just five food six. And Mel Parnell for the Sox is one great lefty."

As the game began, Stewie wandered into the living room and joined them.

"Hey, guys," their dad said. "Give a listen to the color commentator. That's Dizzy Dean. He was a great pitcher himself for the St. Louis Cardinals. A real country boy from the Midwest. He and his brother were the best pair of hurlers in the league for years."

"Why did they call him Dizzy?" Stewie asked.

"Because he was a real character. You'll hear his great hillbilly accent and sense of humor. And his brother, well they gave him the nickname 'Daffy.'"

"I've heard of them, Dad," Gil said. "And I guess there was one time when his brother was up to bat and a wild pitch went right at his head. Know what Dizzy yelled?" He paused a couple of beats, looking at his father for a response. Getting none, he yelled, "Daffy, Duck!"

Stewie screeched out a laugh. Their father looked at the two of them, wondering what was so funny about a dangerous pitch.

"See Dad," Stewie said. "Daffy Duck: he's one of Bugs Bunny and Porky Pig's buddies. He's a black duck with a squishy way of saying his words. Their cartoons are on TV."

"Oh, okay," their father said. "I guess you have to have been there."

At that, Stewie had had enough indoor time. He got up and headed for the backyard.

Gil and his dad settled in for the game. Everything went great for the Sox. Billy Goodman hit a long double into deep center field and scored on a single by the catcher, Sammy White.

"That's a real plus for the BoSox," Dr. John said. "White isn't one of their best hitters. Matter of fact, some fans call him 'Toaster.'" He looked over at Gil and waited a couple of beats. "Because he's always popping up."

As the game neared its end, Dizzy Dean reported that the Sox great left fielder, Ted Williams, was set to be discharged from the Air Force after serving a tour of duty as a fighter pilot in Korea.

"Great news," said the father. "The Sox will really be powerful when Ted's bat returns. He's an all-time great."

"How come he was in Korea?" Gil asked. "I mean he was signed to play for Boston, right?"

"Yes. But he had been a pilot during World War II, and Uncle Sam needed his skills for their fight against North Korea and Red China. When your Uncle calls, you answer the call."

"Sort of like you, huh?"

"Well, I don't want to seem as though I am as crucial to the war as Ted, but yes. We're down here, and my practice back in Sutton will have to wait until I have done my duty. Anyway, it'll be great for the Sox and all their fans to have Teddy Ballgame back."

"Maybe we could go to a game sometime," Gil asked.

"For sure. Probably not this season. But once we get home, we can make our plans. For now, we can follow the Sox and their schedule. Why don't you make a habit of checking the paper for any BoSox news?"

"Okay, Dad. Sounds like a plan."

The next day, Gil pored through the sports section of the *Roanoke Star News*. In the major league baseball segment, he found a schedule for the

Washington Senators. On August 10, they were to host the Red Sox, the only game matching the two teams in DC for the remainder of the schedule. He jumped up and rushed out into the sun-room where his parents were sharing the morning.

"Dad! I was just looking at the Senators' schedule, and they're going to play the Sox at home on August tenth; that's a Saturday. Do you think we could go up for the game?"

His father took in the information and his eldest son's excitement. Then he looked over at Katherine. "Well," he said. "That might work. We'd have to leave pretty early in the morning and..." He paused as if doing a complex math problem. "I think it's at least two hundred fifty miles. We'd have to be on the road early in the morning to make it by game time. And then another long haul home." He looked over at his wife. "What do you think, Kate? It might be a good father–son outing."

"Seems like a lot of road time to me; but then I'm not a baseball fan. It's up to you, I guess maybe you could get a motel somewhere along the road back."

"It would be great, Dad! Maybe Ted Williams will be back with the team. It would be super to see him."

"Well," his father replied. "Let me give it some thought, but it would be an adventure."

"And Stewie, too? I bet he'd really love to go with us."

Again, his father paused in thought. "I think it would be better for just the two of us. It would be a long time in the car for Stewie. And he could help your mother hold down the fort while we're away. You know, let's just you and me plan on it."

"Super, super, Dad. Thanks."

* * *

Gil walked out of the sun room into the backyard. There were two faded white, wooden lawn chairs that he'd found in the basement. He and Stewie had wrestled them up the stairs and outside leaving only a couple of minor dings in the woodwork of the white Dutch Cape on Dyer Road that, after all, wasn't really home.

The chairs were in the shade, facing across the lawn to the two-story brick house that faced away toward the next street over. After five months, he still had only a vague idea of who lived there: a flash through the shrubs of someone mowing the lawn, the yip-yip of a dog that sounded as though it was hardly worthy of the species.

He sat in one of the chairs, slouching, feet barely touching the lawn. He let the heat of the Virginia summer sun press itself on him. His eyelids slid down until the world was a mottled blur of yellows, greens, and browns. He let his mind take him where it would. Margie in her backyard in a blue bathing suit on a yellow beach towel. The cool dark of the pool hall downtown with young black men coming and going, the click and flash of the many-colored balls across the green felt under a man-made sun, the movement of splitting atoms. And then he could see Honey romping through the field next to the woods in Sutton, near his home, not the make-do house of strangers.

And the summer heat pulled Gil away from concrete, personal places toward a future created out of newspaper headlines and the solemn intonations of John Cameron Swasey on the Camel Cigarette Nightly News. Reports of Russian nuclear tests; film of a mushroom cloud over the Nevada desert as American servicemen climbed out of trenches and began a tentative march toward ground zero; a recaptured memory of talking about the H-bomb and the destruction of the whole world with Tommy, back in Sutton before Roanoke was even an idea of his future. He let the heat draw him deeper into an imagined world in which a new, truly super weapon was unleashed to save the world. Developed by a secret, international group of scientists, named "The Savior," it released a global wave of radiation that killed only and killed all humans, leaving the plants and trees, animals, fish, reptiles, and sea creatures to live beyond the impact and memory of the species to which God had granted sovereignty.

As if from a vast distance, his mother's voice rode down into his consciousness. "Gil, time to come in and get ready for supper. Your dad's home, and he'll want to watch the news."

* * *

Gilbert rolled over in bed onto his back. He lay there for a moment trying to hold onto a dream.

He was back in Sutton, down at the Nine Falls baseball park. He was sitting in the old wooden grandstand watching the Sutton High baseball team, the Blue Flames, play against their hated rivals, the Rams. There were a few old men in the stands with him, and a bunch of younger kids running around in foul territory near the right field fence and beyond that the Nine Falls. Suddenly, Coach O'Patrick sent up a pinch hitter: it was Ted Williams! But a much younger Ted, not yet ready for the Red Sox and Fenway Park. It seemed to Gil that he was the only one in the stands who thought anything so dramatic was about to happen. The old men smoked their cigarettes and pipes, passing around a brown paper bag that masked whatever bottle they had bought at the green front state liquor store downtown. The kids in right field ran and screeched as the Rams pitcher wound up and prepared to hurl his first pitch at "the Splendid Splinter."

And then the dream faded, and the young kids' shouts became Petie in the living room, on Dyer Road, in Roanoke. Gil stretched and let the morning light flood his awareness. And suddenly he realized that the light was much too bright for early morning. He and his father should have already been on the road to Washington and the Senators–Red Sox game. He jumped out of bed and ran downstairs, not bothering to change out of his pajama bottoms.

He glanced into the living room where Petie sat, alone, tossing blocks into the air and yelling in a language all his own. Gil walked through the kitchen and out into the sun-room where his dad and mom sat at the table over coffee. His father held Allie on his knee, bouncing his youngest up and down.

"Dad," Gil said. "What time is it? Aren't we supposed to be driving to Washington? What about the Red Sox?"

His father stood and put Allie into his high chair, sat, and looked over at his wife and back to his eldest son. "Well, Gil, after you went up to bed last night, your mother and I talked it over and we decided that the DC outing just wasn't going to work. Too many loose ends.'

"What do you mean? I thought it was all worked out."

"Sweetie," his mother said. "There was going to be so much road time to get to the game and back. And your dad has to go to the induction center early on Monday."

"But that's not fair. You promised that we'd go. It was all planned out."

Dr. Jenkins looked out to the backyard, took a deep breath, and turned back to his eldest. "Gil. You're getting to the age where you need to learn that things don't always work out just the way you think they should. That's a big part of growing up."

"But you didn't keep your promise."

"That's enough, Gilbert," his mother said. "Your dad explained why we decided against the trip, and that's all there is to it."

"When you're grown up," his dad continued, "you'll be able to make all your own choices. But for now, you need to accept ours."

Gil could feel his eyes starting to tear up. He turned away, walked back through the house that had never really been home, and climbed the stairs to his bedroom. He lay down on the bed, rested his head on his hands, and tried to deal with what seemed like a huge bump in the road that had led him to Roanoke. And suddenly he felt like he had to take charge of his life, to make decisions, like his father had said.

He stretched, and took a long, deep breath. Shucking his pajamas, he dressed and laid out a change of clothes on the bed. Then he walked to the upstairs hall closet and pulled out a military issue knapsack that his father had brought back from training. He went into the bathroom and grabbed his toothbrush and a half tube of Colgate. Then he returned to the bedroom and packed the backpack. From the top of the dresser, he emptied his summer savings out of a jelly jar. He counted it out: one dollar bill, a half dollar, three quarters, a dime and four nickels: $2.55. He pocketed the cash, looked around the bedroom that wasn't really his bedroom, and headed down the stairs.

Gil looked out through the dining room into the kitchen. He couldn't see his mother but could hear her talking baby talk with Allie. He walked out the front door and down the steps. His father was standing next to the green Mercury, chatting with Mr. Arsenault, another expatriate from the North—New York, in his case. His dad looked up with a momentary flicker of surprise. "Going somewhere, Gil?" he asked.

Gilbert looked him directly in the eyes. "Home; Sutton, that is. I'm sick of Virginia."

"It's a long way home, son. Are you sure?" Dr. Jenkins looked over at his neighbor with what seemed to be a roll of his eyes.

"I'm sure. I'll let you and Mom know when I get there. I can stay with Uncle Harry, Aunt Anita, and Grandpa—until you finish here and move the others back home."

"Well, be careful on the road. You know you're always welcome back here."

Gil turned and walked away, across Dyer Road and through the huge field that ran off toward the north. He had an urge to turn to see how his dad and Mr. Arsenault were reacting to his departure, but he shrugged and walked off, alone and in charge of his path.

When he reached the main road heading north from Roanoke, he stopped on a straight stretch, shrugged off his backpack, and waited for the occasional car to approach. When the first one headed toward him, he raised his right arm and stuck up his thumb, as he had seen other, older men do. The car slowed slightly, then the driver swerved out toward the other lane and continued on by. That happened with the next several cars, as well. In one, an older woman in the front passenger's seat looked at him as if he was some strange creature that had walked out of the tangle of vines across the roadside ditch. After a half hour, Gil was starting to wonder if his journey was going to end before it began. Then an old, gray Ford sedan pulled over and stopped.

Gil grabbed his knapsack and hurried up the shoulder of the highway. The driver, seemingly an older man, had leaned over and rolled down the passenger's window. Gil walked up and looked in.

"Where you headin', young fella?" the driver asked.

Gilbert hadn't really thought of how he would explain his travel plans. Maine seemed a very long way to explain to a stranger. "I'm going to Lynchburg," he said. There was a pause. "I'm going to visit my aunt and uncle who live up there."

"Well, I'm not going that far," the man replied. "But you all climb in. I can get you on your way."

Gil climbed into the front seat and put his knapsack on the middle of the seat. "Thanks very much," he said. "I was wondering if I'd ever get a ride."

"Well, lots of folks aren't willing to share. I'm always happy to give a young fella a lift. It's nice to have some company on the road." He accelerated off down the road. After about a mile they passed the turn-off to the Old Monterey Golf Course where he had pursued his short-lived career as a caddy only a few weeks earlier.

For the next few miles, they chatted; mostly Gil responded to the questions that the driver asked him about school, about his favorite sports, about whether he had a girlfriend yet. It seemed nice that the man really took an interest in him as a person, was open to listening to what he had to say.

They had passed through the rolling hills and small farms along the highway. As they came to a crossroad, the driver slowed and started to turn to his right and then stopped. He looked over at his passenger. "My place is about a mile on down this road," he said. "I need to stop and check a couple of things out. If you wouldn't mind the wait, I could bring you back out to the main drag and up toward the next town, Bedford." He paused and turned so that he was facing across toward Gil. "You know," he continued, "the chances aren't that good that you'll make it all the way to Lynchburg. It's almost noon. If you came down to my place, you could call your folks and tell them that you'll be there tomorrow. Wouldn't do for them to worry about you."

There was something about the man's gaze that made Gil uncomfortable. He was smiling and seemed to be concerned about his journey but there was a kind of nervous, excited air that helped the passenger make his decision. "No, no thank you," Gil said. "I wouldn't want to put you out. I'll just keep on my way." He reached over and grabbed one of the straps on his backpack. Then he opened the door and started to climb out. The man reached across and put his hand on the pack.

"You sure?" he said in a tone that almost sounded like he might cry.

"Yes, sir. I'm very sure." He climbed down from the car and pulled his pack after him. Without looking back, he walked off toward Bedford and the long road toward Maine. He heard the car drive down the gravel side road. Gil took a deep breath, relieved without being quite sure why. He headed away until he reached a straight stretch of the highway next to which there was a tall oak tree that offered some shade from the noonday sun.

After about a half hour, a lone car approached and pulled over next to Gil. A white-haired lady in a black dress and matching hat rolled down the window on the passenger's side of the two-toned Chevrolet. "Where you heading, young man," she asked.

Gil stuck with the Lynchburg version of his journey. "I'm heading up to Lynchburg," he said. "Goin' to visit with my Uncle Harry and Aunt Nita." He hoped his attempt at southern English would hold up.

"Well, we're only going as far as Bedford, but we'll be glad to give you a lift. Climb in."

She scooted forward in her seat and leaned over the dashboard. Gil was able to push the back of her seat forward just enough so that he could squeeze behind and into the rear seat. "My name is Mrs. Daily," she said, "and this is my husband Fred—Mr. Daily, that is."

"It's nice to meet you. And thank you very much for giving me a ride."

"It's our pleasure. How old would you be, Son?"

Gilbert opted to stretch the truth a bit. "I just had my thirteenth birthday." He hoped that the fib would make him seem more grown up, more road-worthy. "Just last week."

"Well belated best wishes." And then she launched into a monologue that ranged from her granddaughter's thirteenth to the hot stretch of weather they'd been having to President Eisenhower's role in getting the armistice with the Koreans to her hope that the Bedford Panthers would have a great football season.

Gil settled back into the vinyl-covered rear seat and let his mind roll over Mrs. Daily's chatter. It must be early afternoon by now. Would he make it to Lynchburg by evening? And, regardless of where he ended the first day's travels, where would he spend the night? He remembered his father talking about how sometimes during his medical school years he would stay at a YMCA while making the journey from Maine to Nebraska. Maybe there would be a Y in Lynchburg—and maybe it wouldn't use up too much of the $2.55 that was his nest egg for however long it took to get back to Maine.

The Chevy drove past the Entering Bedford sign and slowed as they passed along the main street. Mr. Daily pulled over at an intersection. "Well, Son," his wife said, "I guess we ought to drop you here. We'll be heading off the main highway at the next block." She opened her door and again squeezed toward the dashboard. "Don't forget your knapsack."

Gil squeezed out of the rear seat. Mrs. Daily closed the door and rolled down the window. "Thank you very much for the ride," Gil said.

"It was our pleasure. I hope you make it to Lynchburg without too much trouble. You take care now, honey."

He watched the car drive down the main street and take a left turn out of sight.

He sat down on a sidewalk bench in front of a small Woolworths. He closed his eyes and imagined his golden cocker spaniel sitting on a porch on the other side of the Nine Falls River. Maybe when he got to Maine, his aunt and uncle would let him reclaim Honey, and that would give him pride of ownership when the rest of his family returned to Sutton.

Gilbert snapped back from his reverie into the afternoon heat and the muted bustle of Bedford, Virginia. He looked up and down the main street and spied a United States post office. It seemed to him that perhaps he owed his parents information on how his homeward journey was unfolding. He walked into the lobby and up to the window. A graying man behind the grate looked up. "Yes, sir. How might we help you today?"

"I'd like one of your post cards. Not with a picture; just one of those plain ones that doesn't need a stamp."

"Yes, sir. Coming right up." He reached down and slid a tan card out to Gil. "That'll be two cents, if you please."

Gilbert reached into his pocket and pulled out one of his four nickels. "Here you are.:

"Thank you, sir. And here's your change." He pushed out three pennies. "I read once that the mother of one of America's richest men, maybe Andrew

Carnegie, told her boy when he was about your age: 'Take care of the pennies, and the pounds will take care of themselves.' Good advice for us all. You have a good day now. "

Gil turned and walked across the little lobby to a stand-up desk. He took the black, nibbed pen out of the inkwell and as carefully as he could, he wrote his father's name and the Dyer Road address on the front of the card. Then, after waiting for the ink to dry, he scratched a cursive message to his parents:

Dear Folks,
I'm not in Washington yet, just Bedford.
I will push on toward Lynchburg soon.
Love, Gil

He dropped the card into the out-of-town slot and walked back out into the sunlight. He thought that he should probably walk to the town limits before he continued his hitchhiking journey toward home. And suddenly he was aware that he was very hungry. With all the upheaval at home that morning, he'd not had any breakfast. He looked down the side street across from him and saw a sign for a drugstore. He walked down the little hill and looked into the store through the big plate glass window. As he had hoped, there was a soda fountain that promised a quick, and not too expensive, snack.

He walked into the store and climbed up on one of the swiveled seats. He took in several pies on the counter under glass domes. Across from him was an ice cream cooler backed by frappe mixers, plates and sundae cups, and soda water spigots. In the mirror behind the cooler, his reflection looked deeply into his eyes.

A man dressed in a druggist's white jacket walked over and behind the counter. "Good afternoon, young man. What can I get you today?"

"How much are your pies?" Gil asked. "And a scoop of ice cream too?"

"The pie would be ten cents—that would be for a slice. And a scoop of ice cream would be another nickel. That sound doable to you?'

"Yes, please. I'd like a piece of the custard pie and a scoop of strawberry if you have it."

"Sure can do." The druggist slid a slab of deep yellow pie onto a white plate, turned, and scooped a generous serving of pink ice cream next to it. He put the plate down in front of his customer. "Spoon or fork?" he asked.

"A spoon, please." Gil reached into his pocket and pulled out a dime and a nickel. He put the coins onto the counter.

"Perfect. There are napkins over in that container. Anything else I can do for you?"

"No, thank you. This looks great."

"Well, I'll be over behind the drug counter if you think of anything. Enjoy."

The first couple of bites of the pie and ice cream went down in a flash. Then, gradually, he slowed his pace, trying to make the flavors take the place of his hunger. As he approached the crust and dribbles of melted strawberry, he became aware that in the past half hour he had spent seventeen cents of his total stash of $2.55. Clearly, the remainder wasn't going to get him to Washington, let alone Sutton. He thought of the druggist's offer to help with anything else and that maybe he could include help with his nest egg. He sopped the last of the melted ice cream on the final bite of crust, wiped his mouth and fingers and walked over to the drug counter.

"Excuse me," he said. "I was wondering if you have any odd jobs that I might do for you. I'd like to earn a little money while I'm here in Bedford." In truth he had no idea of how long that might be but that even this afternoon might offer a start.

The druggist gave a long look at this young stranger with an accent that clearly wasn't grounded in western Virginia. "Well, there might be something. As a matter of fact, I'm waiting on Donny, my assistant and jack-of-all-trades, to come in after high school football practice lets out. You could go out with him when he does the deliveries. I'm sure he'd like the help."

"That would be great," Gil replied. "I really appreciate it."

"Well, do you have any questions?"

"I…I'm not sure what you mean. What kind of questions?"

"Well, for starters, you might want to know what I can pay you. And maybe what other types of chores you might have to take on."

"I see," Gil said. "I haven't had much experience looking for work. But I guess whatever you thought was fair for pay would be okay. And I'd be glad to do whatever else you needed help with."

"Well, we can work that out as you get more experience. For now, what do you say we start you off at fifteen cents an hour? We can bump it up after you've been with us for a spell. Sound fair."

"Yes sir. I really appreciate the job and I promise to do my very best."

"I'm sure that you will," said his new boss. "Now I'm going to have to take down your personal information: home address, phone number, parents' names…for the tax records I have to keep for all my employees." He pushed over a pad of prescription sheets. "Why don't you write it all down for me."

Gil took the pad, walked over to the soda fountain counter and in his best handwriting wrote:

> Gilbert Jenkins
> 284 Dyer Road
> Roanoke, Virginia
> Parents' names—Dr. John Jenkins and Mrs. Katherine
> Telephone: Roanoke exchange # 6725

He walked back to the drug counter and waited until his new employer turned away from his workstation. "Here you are, sir. I think that's all my information." He handed over the prescription folder and pencil.

The druggist looked it over. For just a moment he seemed a little surprised. "That should do it, Gilbert. Is that the name you go by?"

"My family and friends all call me Gil, but you can use Gilbert if you prefer. And, sir, if you don't mind me asking: what is your name?"

"Henry Goggins," came the reply. "I was named after my great-grandfather. He was one of General Lee's troops during the War Between The States."

"You must be proud of that," Gil said. "So, do you have any chores for me while we wait for your helper? What was his name again?"

"Donny. Donny Maxwell. Well, I guess you could grab the push broom that's out in the back hall and sweep down the sidewalk out front."

"I'll get right to it, sir. I mean Mr. Goggins." He turned and walked to the back of the store. As he carried the broom to the front door, he looked over at his boss. "I found it okay." Then he walked out and swept the sidewalk over and over until, he thought, "you could have eaten a piece of custard pie off it…if you needed to, that was."

When he returned to the store, Gil found a young man behind the soda counter wiping dishes including the service that had held the pie and ice cream. "You must be Gilbert," he said. "Henry told me that we had a new hire." He put down his dish towel and reached over the counter and held out his hand.

Gil couldn't remember the last time he had shaken hands but decided that it was important for him to return the greeting. "Are you Donny?" he asked. "Mr. Goggins said you'd be in soon."

"Just got out of practice. It was a long week there today. I'm always glad to be here and do things that actually are useful. And I gather that we're going out together on deliveries."

"I guess so. I hope I can be helpful; I mean you're going to drive and know all the addresses."

"But you can take some of the orders up to the door. I'll just cool my heels in the car. And so I guess that we ought to get a move on." He walked behind the drug counter, talked quietly with Mr. Goggins, and emerged carrying a cardboard container that held a number of white envelopes. "I'm parked out back, Gilbert. Let's be off."

Gil followed his young mentor out into a back lot. Donny walked over to a Model A Ford coupe. He pulled up the lid over the rumble seat and put the orders inside. He motioned Gil into the front seat and climbed in behind the wheel. "Tell you what," he said. "I've got the list of the houses we're heading to. If you'll read each address, I'll be able to drive there without having to check each time." He started the car. "Where to first?" Gil read him the top address and they headed off up to Bedford's main street, turned south toward Roanoke, and then took several turns until Donny pulled over. "There's number one. Let's go." He got out of the car, opened the rumble seat, reached in and handed Gil a white bag. "These are all paid for ahead or the customers have a charge account. All you need to do is hand over the goods." With that he climbed back into the car and Gil walked up to the front door for his first real moment in the working world.

He lost track of how long they had been out on deliveries. However, finally Donny announced that the next stop was their last. Gil handed the order over to a gray-haired older woman who gifted him with a smile and a thank-you. He returned to the car, and they headed back downtown and into the lot behind Goggins Drug. He followed Donny into the store. As they entered, a man sitting at the soda counter swiveled on his seat. It was his father!

"Dad! What are you doing…I mean, how did you get here?"

"Mr. Goggins was kind enough to phone and let us know where you were. Your mother stayed home with the boys and I used the afternoon of my day off driving up here." Dr. Jenkins turned to where the druggist had emerged from behind the counter. "Sir," his father said, "I want to thank you again for reaching out to us. And I hope that Gil's surprise arrival didn't complicate your Saturday."

"Not at all, Captain. It was my pleasure. I feel like somehow I've been able to repay you for the understanding you showed to our family. My brother will always be in your debt."

"Isn't it strange how fate seems to work that way. Well, thanks again." He turned to his son. "Gil, the car is parked out front. Let's head out and back to Roanoke. Your mother and I will have to sit down and thrash out this entire misadventure of yours. And don't forget my backpack."

Climbing into the Mercury, Gil tried to disappear into the front seat. His father started the car, backed into the entrance to the drugstore lot, and headed up to the main street and off into the countryside. Neither father nor son spoke for the first several miles. Finally Gil turned in his seat. "Dad," he said, "how did you find me? How did you know where to look?"

"You know, Gil, I'd just as soon not go over this whole story twice. We'll wait until we get home, and your mother can be part of the conversation." That put an end to any further discussion, and Gil slid into looking at landmarks that he remembered as part of his journey up to Bedford.

When they drove into 284 Dyer Road, Gil's dad parked and walked into the house without a word. Gil sat for a moment, looking at the Dutch Cape that he had turned his back on that morning. It seemed like days since he had walked down the driveway that morning. He took a long, deep breath and reached into the back seat for his knapsack. Then he got out of the car and walked up to and into the house, trying to prepare himself for whatever was going to bring this strange day to its end.

Stewie and Petie were in the living room. Stewie looked up at him as if he had seen a ghost. Then he turned back to cartoons on the RCA. Gil put his pack down in the hall and walked through the kitchen. His mother and father were sitting at the sun-room table. His mother looked up at him with a jumbled look of sadness and anger. His father looked at his coffee mug, then up at his son. Gil sat and the three of them kept the silence for what seemed to be an hour or a lifetime.

Finally, his mother broke the silence. "Gil, whatever were you thinking? When you disappeared…we had no idea where you had gone."

They sat in silence. "Gilbert," his father said in a tone of voice that was wholly new. "Your mother asked you a question, and she deserves an answer, right now."

Gil swallowed and then his response began to pour out. "But Dad, I told you where I was going this morning…I told you I was going home to Sutton. And you didn't say anything to stop me."

"Because I couldn't believe that you'd do anything so foolish. You're growing up, Gil. You have to learn to make choices that are good for you but also for those whose lives you're a part of."

"But this morning you decided we weren't going to the Red Sox game. That hit my life too, not just yours, not just your Saturday."

His mother intervened. "Gil, you have to realize that part of being grown up is learning how to deal with disappointments and to understand how others can't always see things your way."

Mother, father, and son sat in silence. Finally, his mom straightened up. "I've got to get Allie up from his nap and get supper started. Your father and I have talked over how we're going to deal with your bad decision. John, you explain the consequences to Gil." She got up and walked out of the room.

"Here's the deal, Gil," his father said. "You are to spend the next few days in your bedroom, except for mealtimes. We want you to be in a situation where you can think over how bad a choice you made…and how fortunate you were that this all ended safely. Now I want you to head upstairs and unpack your—that is my—knapsack. We'll call you down when it's time to eat."

Later, dinner seemed to drag on in a forever silence. He toyed with his food, even though the custard pie and ice cream, his only food of the day, seemed to be so long past that it was as if it had been a dream. From time to time, he looked up from his plate. A couple of times Stewie was staring at him as if trying to understand a distant relative. After dessert, Gil started to clear the table.

"That's okay, Gil," his mother said. "Stew will take care of the table tonight. You head on up to your room. I'll be up in a while when I put Petie to bed."

On his bed, Gil suddenly felt as if all the energy had been drained out of him. He stretched out and tried to recall moments of the day: his father and Mr. Arsenault exchanging grown-up looks, the strange man who had offered his home to his hitchhiker, pie and ice cream in Googins Drug, his astonishment as his father turned at the soda counter to face him.

He heard footsteps on the stairs. His mother and Petie came into the bedroom. Katherine tucked son #3 into his little bed. Then she came over and sat down on the end of Gil's bed. "Gil, we've told Stewie that he can sleep on the screened porch tonight. It's probably better for both of you to get a good night's sleep."

"Okay, Mom," he replied in a voice that seemed drained of all energy.

"Sweetie, I know that you're hurt and confused. It's been a long, hard day for us all. But I need you to know that your dad and I love you with all our hearts. We're proud of you and at the same time are sorry that you've had to adjust to this place where none of us had planned to be. But we're a family, and part of that is helping each other through hard times. Your father is confused and a bit hurt that you were so upset with our decision on the ball game. It's up to us all to help and support each other. That's family. Now try to get some rest." She stood to leave.

"Mom," Gil said, "can I ask you a question?"

"Of course you can."

"How did you, you and Dad, find out that I was in Bedford?"

She turned and sat down on his bed again. "The druggist called us after he got your contact information. For taxes, I guess he told you. Of course he knew that there must be a concern when a twelve-year-old boy with a knapsack walked into his store and asked for a job. That's something that doesn't happen every day."

"So he tricked me, you mean."

"Let's say he tried to help you when you maybe didn't even know you needed help. And there's more to the story, a twist that makes me think that God looks out for his children."

"Why?"

"Well, when the druggist, Mr. Goggins, saw your last name and that Captain Jenkins was your father, he couldn't believe his eyes. You see, his younger brother had been called by his draft board to report for his pre-induction physical at the Roanoke center. And this young man was very upset about being drafted; he didn't feel like he could deal with being in the army and perhaps being sent to the Korean War. And somehow, he came to believe that the army doctor, your father, would understand. And so he poured out his fears and your dad gave him a 4-F rating, which meant that he was medically unable to serve. And when he returned to Bedford, he told his family about the doctor from Maine who had saved him from a life path that he couldn't bear. So you see, oftentimes a good deed is rewarded in ways that we never fully understand."

"Wow, Mom. I thought that Mr. Goggins just thought I'd be a good worker, that that was the reason he gave me the job."

"And I'm sure he saw that in you, Gil. There are lots of people who will see that deep down you're a fine young man. Now, you need to settle in so that we don't disturb Petie. Sleep tight, my dear." She reached over and gave him a hug, stood, and walked out of the room, clicking off the lights on Gilbert's very long day.

Two days and nights passed in a blur. Gil could hear his brothers running around in the yard but didn't have the will to look out at them. At night, Stewie returned to his bed but didn't ask his elder brother for tales of the road.

Late in the afternoon of his third day of exile, Gil heard the Mercury pull into the driveway. The car door slammed, followed by his father's entrance into the house. Since their conversation after his adventure, he and his dad had hardly spoken. It felt as if Dr. Jenkins was waiting for him to say something, but Gil couldn't think of how to begin a conversation.

After a while, his mother called up the stairs, "Gil, please come down right now."

It seemed early for dinner. Gil got up off his bed, walked down the stairs and out to the sun-room. His parents and Stewie were gathered around the table. Petie sat on the floor clicking two blocks together. Gil sat down and looked from his father to his mother, trying to get a hint of what was to come.

"Boys," Katherine said, "your father has some news that he wants to share with all of us." She turned to her husband and waited for his response.

"Well, guys," their father said. "I got some big news at the center today, something your mom and I had been expecting for a bit but didn't know any details." He paused. "So, here's the story: When I got into work, the CO called me into his office. He'd just received orders that I'm to be reassigned to a different post. And that post is Fort Williams, back in Maine, just a few miles from Sutton. So the great news is that we'll be heading home soon."

Stewie jumped up and down. "Home! Home! We're going home!"

Petie looked up from the floor as if trying to figure out his brother's excitement.

Gil just sat. The news, on top of his aborted journey and banishment into his upstairs cell, seemed too twisted and bizarre to get his head around.

"When are we going? When do we leave?" Stewie asked.

"They haven't given me a date yet, Stew," his father said. "But my guess would be sometime in September."

"We think you'll probably start school here," Katherine added. "That should help pass the days, and you'll be up to speed when you get back to Woods Street and your old friends and teachers." She looked over at Gilbert. "What do you think, Gil? Isn't this just stranger than a fairy tale?"

"For sure, Mom," he replied. "It sure is." And then he couldn't think of anything else to say.

"Well, I've got to get dinner ready," she said. "What do you say if we have a tuna casserole and some green beans? We need to finish off those supplies that your dad bought for you all back in March." She looked down at Petie. "No Cheerios tonight though, sweet one. You'll have to wait until breakfast for those."

Gil followed his brothers out into the backyard. While Stewie and Petie ran around playing their own version of tag, he walked over and climbed up on the outdoor fireplace on the edge of the lawn. His parents hadn't banished him back upstairs and they were all moving on toward a new chapter. And whatever that brought, it would be back in Sutton a long way from the Star City of the South.

First Love In Three Acts

GILBERT COULD FEEL HIS EXCITEMENT rising as his father turned the '52 Mercury onto Glen Street and into the three-lane, cement driveway behind the gray Victorian house, his real home. He and Stewie, sprang out of the car, only to be stopped short by their mother's road-weary voice.

"Boys," Mrs. Jenkins called. "You've got to help unload the car. You can explore later. Gil, you take Allie into the kitchen and check to see if he needs a diaper change. Stewie, you can help your dad with the bags."

Gilbert reached into the rear seat of the car and released his brother from the car seat. As he raised the two-year-old, curly blond to his shoulder, he inhaled deeply and was glad to find no telltale odors after the four-hour final leg of the Jenkins's five-day road trip up from Virginia. He walked up the seven steep steps to the back porch, propped Allie against the wall, and opened the door to the kitchen. Inside was the same round, vinyl-covered table with five worn, matching chairs that he remembered from eight months ago. He laid the baby on the table, unsnapped the flap on the blue-and-red, one-piece outfit and, with deep relief, determined that the diaper was still pristine. As the others of the family entered, he turned to his mother. "Allie's all good, Mom."

"Thanks, Gil," his mother replied. "Now I know you're itching to go find your friends, but you need to help bring the rest of the luggage in. You can take your bag and Petie's right up to your bedrooms." She picked up the baby and began an inspection tour of the first-floor rooms.

After what seemed a never-ending stream of trips to and from the car, Gil approached his mother and father sitting at the kitchen table. "It's all done, Mom. Can I go out now? I really want to find Vince."

"Well, it's just about lunchtime," his mother said. Gilbert could feel his excitement deflate.

Dr. Jenkins stepped into the moment. "Why don't you go ahead, Gil, and find your friends. But try to come back in a half hour or so. I think we should all go down to Del's and have burgers and fries for lunch. I know I've missed those Sutton fried onions for way too long." He turned to his wife. "It's been a long road trip, honey. You and I can use just a bit of time to catch our breath."

"Thanks, Dad," Gilbert said as he hurried through the door into the outside world.

The neighborhood looked the same: a variety of houses with the woods at the end of the street. Vince's house was on the corner of Glen and Monroe Street. Gil took the stairs to the porch two at a time and rang the doorbell. After what seemed an endless wait, the door opened, and Mrs. MacAllen stepped out.

"Oh, Gil," she said. "It's wonderful that you're home. But Vince isn't here right now. I think he was going to play with Johnny over on the other side of Woods Street. You remember where the Rochleaus live, don't you?"

"Sure thing, Mrs. Mac," Gil replied. "I'll go right over."

He leapt off the porch and ran up Monroe to where it merged with Woods Street. There on the corner was the Woods Street Elementary School, two stories of brick substance. He paused at the intersection with Main Street and then ran across at the first gap in the traffic. Halfway up the next block, he could see several kids throwing a football back and forth.

One of the players recognized him and materialized into Vince. "Jenkins!" he shouted as he ran to meet his buddy. "You're finally back!"

Seamlessly, Gilbert merged into the group. Johnny threw the football to him. For a moment, Gil remembered a conversation with his father on the way north. He had explained that he really wanted to be a better baseball player and Dr. Jenkins had suggested that he recruit his buddies to play year-round. But standing in the early October sunshine, he realized that baseball was not an option. It was football season and there was no way he was going to make waves. "Go long, Vince," he called and lobbed a pass to his best friend forever.

Late in the afternoon, the two boys returned to the MacAllens's porch. Vince brought Gil up to date on the seventh-grade school year at Woods Elementary. "Mrs. MacGowen is pretty tough, but mostly she's okay. And there are lots of new kids in our class, the ones who've moved up from the other school down by the mill." He paused for a dramatic moment. "There are a couple of really cute new girls," he said. "I really like Sharon. But Beverly and Faith are pretty neat too." Gilbert caught the excitement in Vince's voice. Seventh grade sounded cool.

As he headed home, he realized he had not returned after the agreed to half hour with his buddies. He climbed the stairs and walked into the kitchen. His parents were at the table. "Mom, Dad, I'm sorry, I forgot all about lunch."

Dr. Jenkins smiled a patient parent's smile. "It's okay this time Gil. Your burger is on the counter…unloaded."

* * *

Monday felt like the start of the school year, even though the blazing maples testified to October. When school had opened in Virginia, his father's transfer to Fort Williams and their return to Maine had already been confirmed. And, except for Margie, he had no real friends there; for the past year he had been an outsider, a Yankee. Home was here in Sutton with the Nine Falls River and the great concrete chimney of the paper mill piercing the sky.

Gil and Vince walked up the three tiers of granite slab stairs to the colonnaded porch of Woods Street Elementary and squeezed through the tall doors among a throng of students. A half century of young feet had created a dry river system in the dark oak floors: a deep channel into and through the lobby with smaller streams branching off to the classrooms. Now, however, Gilbert's path led to the central stairway. For the first time, his classroom would be on the second floor, a distant region that he had visited only twice in his younger years when summoned to Principal Cleveland's office. Seventh grade now promised an elevated status in the kindergarten-through-eighth-grade hierarchy.

* * *

With an involuntary shudder, Gilbert wafted back to the start of his sixth-grade year and his first visit with Mr. Cleveland. His class had been reading "Ben and Me," the story of a tempestuous relationship between Benjamin Franklin and a highly capable mouse. In the climax to the story, Ben put his murine friend into a tiny basket attached to the kite that America's great experimenter flew into a thunderstorm. Gil had been spurred to creativity by the story, his inspiration resulting in a poorly drawn cartoon of the mouse looking down toward a tiny, long-haired scientist on the ground. In between bolts of lightning, a voice bubble expressed the mouse's resentment of his situation using every profane word and phrase that the artist's limited exposure had garnered.

In search of peer appreciation, he pushed the drawing across to his tablemate Bruce, losing contact with the classroom world around them. The literary conspirators were suddenly jolted back to reality by a shadow looming over them from behind, then taking on arguably human form in the person of Miss Franklin. The teacher snatched up the drawing and expressed her deep displeasure with such profanation of her classroom. Gil hurriedly claimed all responsibility and was dispatched to Mr. Cleveland's office. The principal, having digested the sad slide of creativity, called Mrs. Jenkins and requested that she return with her son after lunch. Until then, the artist was exiled to a seat in the hallway where all who passed could observe his disgrace.

Lunch at home was somber. Fortunately, Dr. Jenkins was making house calls, which deferred one layer of disapproval until dinner time. Stewie enthused about playground time with friends. Petie clung close to his mother, enervated by the separation from home that first grade required. Mother and eldest son chose silence. Finally, Gilbert cleared the table and waited until his mother made sure that the cleaning lady, Mrs. Burke, was comfortable watching Allie for an hour. Then the two walked in silence to the school and up the seemingly endless stairs into the arms of authority.

Mr. Cleveland apologized to Mrs. Jenkins for intruding into her busy day. However, he was disappointed and concerned by Gilbert's lapse of judgment. Boys would be boys, but in this world it was important that they understand the dangers of popular culture. Then he passed the cartoon across his desk to his fellow adult. Gil's mom scanned the offending art with no change of expression. Then she thanked the principal for his concern and promised that she and Dr. Jenkins would discuss this with their son that evening. Mr. Cleveland then suggested that Gilbert not return to his classroom. In the morning, he could have a fresh start and, of course, he would apologize to Miss Franklin. The principal stood, shook hands with Mrs. Jenkins, and mother and son descended into the world.

Back at the house, his mother finally spoke. "Gil, I want you to wait right here while I check on Allie. We need to talk." Clearly, this was not a request. She walked out to the front hall, and he could hear her climbing the stairs to the second floor. He sat and looked at the brick chimney on the opposite wall, too numb to even plan a defense.

His mother sat down across the table and drew him in with her eyes. "Gil," she said. "I have to tell you how really disappointed I am with this whole thing. Disappointed but, even more, very surprised at you."

"Mom, I'm disappointed too," Gil replied. "I really didn't mean anything bad by it; I was just trying to be funny. I'm sorry."

"Sorry for what you did or because you got caught?"

He tried to calm his voice. "Mostly because you had to be involved. I wasn't trying to be bad. I just made a stupid mistake. And I am sorry."

"I'm sure that's true," his mother replied. "But you need to understand that words really matter, that people judge you by what you say or put on paper. There were words on that page that I've never even heard before. Where did you learn such nasty language?"

He suddenly felt that he couldn't take the whole hit; he had to have a co-conspirator, someone else to take some of the blame. "Well, I learned a lot of those words from Freddy and some of the older kids on the other side of the river." As he offered up his excuse he could feel its unfairness, its untruth. Yes, they had been language coaches. but it was he who had been excited by the power of the words, who had chosen to add them to his vocabulary.

His mother commanded his eyes. "I'm sure that's true, too. But in the end, it was you who chose to make the drawing and to use those words. You have to be responsible for who you are, how you show yourself to others. And I think we'll keep this bump in the road between the two of us. Your father is so busy. He doesn't need another thing on his plate."

Gil felt one level of stress ebb away. "Okay, Mom. I think that's probably a good idea. And I do remember the second part of 'I'm sorry. I won't do it again."

* * *

Vince and Gil turned right at the principal's office and entered Mrs. MacGowen's classroom. Most of the student seats were already taken; the empty ones gave no clue if they were spoken for or free. Gil stopped at the left edge of the blackboard, ten feet short of the teacher's desk. He thought he couldn't remember a moment in which he had felt more solitary and more on display. Many of the student faces were familiar from the previous year, but other than Vince and Johnny, none seemed to have any connection for him.

Mrs. MacGowan stood and eyed the class into attention. Then she turned toward Gil and smiled. "Class," she said. "We have a new student today, Gilbert Jenkins. Of course, he isn't really new to many of you who shared Mrs. Franklin's room with him in sixth grade. Gilbert, why don't you tell us all of your travels over the last year. And you can choose whichever of the empty seats you wish."

Gil could feel the impact of his southern exile. In spite of himself, his voice took on the timbre of western Virginia. "Yes'm, Miz MacGowan. Mah family moved to Roanoke, Virginia when mah dad got drafted into the army. We all are back now 'cause he got reassigned to Fort Williams."

"Well, welcome home. If we can help you adjust back into Maine, we'll be happy to." She turned to the class. "Boys and girls, this is a great example of the power of language. In just a few months, Gilbert has taken on a real southern drawl, it shows that his experiences have become part of who he is. And now it's time for math. We'll be going over your percentages homework. Take a seat, Gilbert, and join in."

Gil chose a seat close to Vince and Johnny on the left side of the double horseshoe of student desks. Directly across from him were two girls who must have been newly arrived at Woods Street. It seemed as if they were whispering about something other than decimal points and fractions. And they kept looking over at him, dropping their eyes when they saw he was gazing back. He couldn't decide if he was embarrassed or excited. Whatever, it felt good. The morning oozed on, and then it was time for lunch. Mrs. MacGowen asked him to stay behind for a minute and sign for his textbooks.

Outside, Vince and Johnny were waiting for him. They agreed to join a bunch of other upper-level boys in the park for a touch football game after school. "Gil," Vince said. "You might want to change into some less dress-up clothes. There's gonna be lots of grass stains." Johnny set off toward Woods Street and home. Vince and Gil headed to their neighborhood. As he approached home, Gil could see the family Mercury parked in the driveway lane closest to the house. His dad was home. For a moment he was overcome by a fear that there might be bad news or big news from the army. His dad said there was always a need for doctors in Korea. He hurried up the stairs and into the kitchen.

His mother was bustling in the pantry. Stewie and Petie were at their places. Dr. Jenkins sat facing the outside door, making that chair the head of the circular table. He was still dressed in his captain's uniform; clearly his day at the fort was not over. Gil walked around the table and gave his dad a glancing hug. "Glad to see you, slugger," the Doctor said. "A good morning at school?"

"Not bad, Dad," said Gil. "It's good to see my buddies again. A bunch of us are going to play football after school."

"No baseball?"

"Nobody's interested," the boy continued. "Everybody's into football in the fall."

"Can't get better if you don't practice," said his father. "Your call. Have fun at it."

Mrs. Jenkins swept into the kitchen with a tray of pancakes. "Eat 'em while they're hot," she said. "I'll bring the syrup and sugar right in. Gil, help Petie put on his bib, please."

"Breakfast for lunch," said her husband. "Boys, this is why it's such an adventure to be married to your mother. Real Great Plains traditions."

"It wasn't part of my plan," his wife replied. But I didn't get a chance to use the car to go to the supermarket yesterday, and I haven't set up an account at Jensen's down the street so that Gil can go pick up things we need on our tab."

"No problem," said the captain. "Dig in, boys."

"So what did you study your first morning back, Gil?" his father asked as his wife returned to the table.

"We did math work on percentages for a *LONG* time. And then we started some projects using the Portland newspapers."

From off to the side, his mother asked, "Did you study political cartoons?" He could hear the hint of irony in her question and kept his eyes locked on his father. The question went unanswered.

Lunch hour passed, and the three boys left for school. Mrs. Jenkins reminded Gil to keep an eye on Petie so he didn't get confused about where to go. At the corner Vince was waiting. The four boys headed up the hill toward Woods Street.

"It's super you're home, Gil," said Vince. "Does it feel weird?"

"Not really. The new teacher, she seems okay. And a bunch of new faces." He paused. "I was wondering, who are the two new girls sitting across from us?"

"Beverly and Faith, the new class queens," his best friend replied. "Beverly is the one with the short haircut. She's kinda cute. Right now she and Bruce have got something going, sorta. Faith is really pretty *and* pretty smart. She's always answering questions. Sort of Mrs. MacGowen's pet. Along with Martha, of course."

* * *

On a January Saturday, Gilbert came home from a morning of basketball in the little, second floor gym in a building that had been gifted to Sutton by

Cornelia Stevens, the daughter of the Nine Falls Mill's owner. It felt like his head was still echoing with the shouts of the players, the clang of the balls off the metal backboards, and squeaking sneakers on the hardwood floors. He'd had a good day: fifteen points, a few rebounds, and defense in the key against Sammy, his larger and more aggressive opponent.

He walked up the back stairs, kicked the snow off his boots, and stripped off his outdoor gear. The rich smells from the kitchen gave promise of warm cookies and, perhaps, a hot chocolate—the perfect lunch after a morning in the gym. He could hear Stewie explaining to Petie the rules of whichever game they were playing in the TV room. Then the eldest Jenkins son turned, picked up his gym bag and headed to the basement to drop off his sweaty tee shirt, shorts, white wool socks, all wrapped in the towel he'd used after a full morning workout. As he started up to the kitchen, he heard his mother calling out something to Stewie. He walked in and said: "Hi, Mom."

Katherine jumped just a bit at the sound of her eldest's voice. "Oh, hi Gil. I didn't hear you come in. I was upstairs getting Allie ready for his nap."

"I hope I didn't scare you. And, I didn't help myself to the cookies. Maybe now…?"

" I guess that will work. Probably a little too late for a big lunch."

"Great," he replied. "And maybe…some hot chocolate?"

"Sure," she said, with a smile. "As long as you wash the pan afterward."

As he headed into the pantry, Gil asked. "So where's dad? Not another baby delivery?"

"Thankfully not. He had a couple of house calls but shouldn't be too long."

The cocoa brewed, the cookies plated, Gil went into the TV room. Stewie and Petie looked up at him, each reacting in their own way to his arrival.

"Cookies," Stewie shouted. "Did you leave any for me Gil?"

"Cocoa, cocoa," Petie added. "Want some too!" And with that they headed out to the kitchen for their share.

Gil walked over and turned on the TV. He flipped through the three local channels and settled for the NBC coverage of a national figure skating contest. A bite of cookie, a sip of hot chocolate, and the seeming effortless gliding of the young women across the ice. It seemed his life could not be smoother. To top it off, his brothers hadn't returned to challenge his concentration on the screen.

Around four o'clock, Katherine came into the den, carrying Allie, followed by Stewie and Petie. "Okay, guys," she said. "Your father just called to say he's on his way home. He should be here in just a bit." She paused for a moment. "And he's bringing a surprise home with him. So what I want you to do now is guess what the surprise will be. Who wants to go first?"

"I do, Mom," said Stewie. "Me first!"

"Okay, Stew, give us your best guess."

"I think he's bringing us pizza home for dinner."

Dr. Jenkins had made a discovery of this new family favorite while lunching in Portland one day with some of his colleagues at Fort Williams. Within minutes, the Jenkins brothers had moved pizza from unknown to high on the all time best list.

"Good guess, Stewie. It is Saturday. Petie, what do you think?"

"Cheerios, Mommy. Pizza is good but I still love Cheerios best. Any time."

"Maybe you're right Petie," said his mother. "We are almost out. Gil?"

Gil decided on another tack. "I think Dad's going to take us on a road trip tomorrow, up into the White Mountains so we can see all the sights. He's talked a lot about the scenery and he's just gone out to get house calls off his list. Yeah, I think that's it!"

"Pretty creative guess," his mother replied. "So pretty soon you'll see which guess is right or closest. So what I want is for you all to stay right here. I'll bring your dad in when he arrives. No peeking, now. Maybe you can play with Allie and some of his toys." With that she departed for the kitchen.

After only a few minutes, she returned. "He's here boys. Now, before I bring him in, I want you all to sit on the floor and cover your eyes. Your dad will tell you when it's ok to check out the surprise. No cheating." And then she retraced her steps to the kitchen.

Two pairs of adult footsteps announced the big moment.

"Okay, guys," their father said. "On my count of three, open your eyes to the surprise. One, two (No cheating!) and THREE!"

Gilbert's eyes came into focus and there, on the floor, was a bouncing black puppy.

"Oh, wow, wow!!" Stewie shouted. "It's a doggy! Is it ours? Is it really ours?"

"It sure is, Stew," said their father. "I learned from one of my patients that their beagle had just had a litter of pups and they were looking for folks to adopt them."

Katherine looked over at Gil. "Your dad and I agreed that now we were settled in enough to be able to take on a new pet." She picked up Allie, walked him over to the pup and helped him reach out and give a gentle pat.

Stewie looked like he was in dog heaven. "What's his name, dad?" he asked.

"Well, guys, he doesn't have one, not yet. They waited so that his adoptive family could make that choice. Any ideas?"

Petie jumped up and hopped over to the beagle. He reached down and stroked its back.

"Snuffie," he said. "I think he's Snuffie."

"Why's that honey?" his mother asked.

"'Cause his nose is snuffin' all the time. Snuffie!"

And the entire Jenkins family agreed; Snuffie it would be.

* * *

February snow was turning to slush as Gilbert and Vince walked down Monroe Place. They had spent two hours after school helping to decorate the small auditorium above the town library for the seventh-grade Valentine's Day dance that evening. By unspoken tradition, the dance held an aura of emergence into the world of teenagers, which would be solidified by the summer vacation and then their entrance into the new Sutton Junior High as its first eighth-grade class.

"So, have you decided what you're gonna wear tonight," Vince asked?

Gilbert scooped up a handful of snow and squished it into a ball. "I dunno," he replied. "I'd kinda like to wear this cool shirt I got back in Virginia. It's black with a pink collar, a pullover. Sort of like Elvis and other rock and roll singers wear." He coiled, turned, and threw his snowball at a squirrel that was skittering around the hedge in front of Dr. Morrison's house. "What do you think?"

"Well, I think it's supposed to be kind of dressy. Good slacks and sweaters for the guys. Nice dresses for the girls. You wouldn't want to be too different… even though 'you all' are a southern ray-ball!" Vince paused at the stairs leading up to his front porch. "I'm not sure that Mrs. MacGowan and Mr. Cleveland are ready for southern styles. Your call though."

"Vince, there's something I don't get. What's the deal with Beverly and Faith?"

His best friend turned back toward him. "What do you mean? What about them?"

"Well, ever since I came back from Virginia, it's kind of like they're having a flirting contest with me. I mean, one asking me how I like the other one's outfit, staring at me during class. Stuff like that. And then today after the class passed out Valentines, they came up and asked me which of their cards I liked best."

"Wow, that's a tricky question," Vince allowed.

"Well, I told them the truth. I liked them both, but I thought Faith's was a little more grown-up." Gilbert shook his head as if overwhelmed by the world of girls. "And then a little while later, Elaine came over to me and said she had a secret to share, but I had to promise not to tell anyone else. She told me that Beverly and Faith had switched cards; they wanted to see which one I would pick, and I guess that Beverly was kind of proud that I actually thought it was her card that was better."

"Girls!" Vince observed. "How do you figure out all their games? I mean, I'm never sure how I'm supposed to answer Sharon's questions—about us, I mean. And Beverly's supposed to be having a thing with Bruce, and here she is playing around with you." He walked up onto his porch and turned to his best buddy. "See you tonight. I think I'd pass on that shirt."

At the end of dinner, Mrs. Jenkins said, "Stewie and Gil, please clear the table and do the dishes. I've got to get Allie and Petie ready for bed.

"Mom," Gilbert said. "Can't I skip dishes tonight? I want to take a shower and get ready for the dance. I'm supposed to meet Vince in about forty minutes."

Dr. Jenkins saved the day. "Tell you what, Gil. You and Stewie clear and side up the dishes, and then he can wash and I'll wipe. Stewie, you and I can catch up on how the Sutton Blue Flames are shaping up. The Western Maine tournament's getting close."

"Wow! Thanks, Dad. That's great," Gil said. "And Mom, can you give me some help choosing what I should wear?"

"Sure, Gil," she replied. "I'll meet you up in your room after you've showered. Maybe you ought to use soap tonight, for the big dance and all." Gil just rolled his eyes, another mother joke.

Gilbert was laying out his Sunday best slacks and white dress shirt when his mother came into his room. "What do you think Mom? The dance is supposed to be sort of dressy and this is the best I can find."

"It's a good start, Gil," she replied. "But I think you need something to zip it up a little. Get into your clothes and wait here. I think I know just the right touch." She walked out of his third-floor room and down the flight of stairs. She returned with a sleeveless blue wool sweater with a cable knit design down the front. "Here, try this on, sweetie." I think it will work well with your gray slacks. And don't worry. There won't be anyone at the dance who will know that you're decked out in your mother's sweater."

Gilbert pulled the sweater on and looked in the mirror over the chest of drawers. For the first time in his life, he was impressed by the image that looked back at him. He felt suddenly grown-up. "Nice, Mom," he said. "I really like the sweater. And I won't tell if you won't."

Mrs. Jenkins gave her seventh grader a hug. "You're a handsome young gentleman, Gil. And I know you'll act like one at the dance."

Mother and son returned to the dining room. Dr. Jenkins was just emerging from the kitchen. "Pretty sharp, slugger," he said to his son. "Knock 'em dead, but remember your failings. Don't do anything that I wouldn't. "

"I'll be good, Dad," Gilbert replied as he headed for the back door. "And it's just a dance; no big deal, really."

At the library, Vince, Gilbert, and Johnny Rochleau mounted the flight of dark wooden stairs that led up to the community rooms. They stashed their winter coats on a rack outside the men's room and walked into the auditorium. Most of the seventh graders had already arrived and were standing around in pairs and clumps, boys, girls, and couples. The chaperones—Mrs. MacGowen, Miss Frasier, Principal Cleveland, and two women Gilbert assumed were parents—had established themselves just inside the entrance. At the far end was the disk jockey, a high school kid surrounded by speakers, a turntable, and a stack of 45s. He kicked things off with Carl Perkins's "Blue Suede Shoes." and the students oozed onto the floor and began to jitterbug. Vince spotted Sharon in a clutch of girlfriends. "Catch ya, Gil," he said and headed in her direction.

It was hard to believe that rock and roll songs could seem so endless. Gilbert stood near a group of boys he hardly knew, guys who weren't going to be asked during ladies' choice. He stared through a window across an expanse of dingy snow toward the Nine Falls River and Sutton's Paper Mill on the opposite bank. The smoke from the massive chimney was billowing upstream, a sure sign of stormy weather to follow. The DJ paused after Fats Domino's "Blue Monday." "Somebody asked for a slow one," he chirped. "Let's go with 'Young Love,' Sonny James." Gilbert scanned the girls standing and sitting across the floor. He spotted Martha, the classmate who always raised her hand. She seemed familiar, if not exciting, and he couldn't just stand alone all night. Taking a deep breath, he walked across the room and, in a voice that sounded much more formal than he would have liked, asked, "May I have this dance?" She nodded, and they took their place on the dance floor.

He could hardly remember the steps they had learned in Mrs. Johnson's dance classes on Thursday afternoons during the winter months of fifth and sixth grade. He was pretty sure the song was a fox trot and concentrated on the sequence of steps—*one*, two, three-four, *one*, two, three-four. He could feel the silky fabric of Martha's blouse under his right hand. He hoped his left palm locked onto her hand wasn't too sweaty.

"So, does it feel good to be back in Sutton?" Martha's voice seemed to come from far away.

He struggled to answer while continuing *one*, two, three-four, *one*, two, three-four. "It's nice," he managed. "Good to be with friends." *One*, two, three-four, *one*, two, three-four. Sonny James climaxed with "Young love, our love we share with true devotion." They stood, hands at their sides, unsure of how to continue or separate. Tommy Edwards eased their dilemma with "It's All in the Game." By default, Gilbert held out his arms, and together they picked up the new beat. "Many a tear has to fall, but it's all in the game." *One* two-three, *one* two-three."

Miss Frasier moved around the dance floor, checking to make sure that the dancers had sufficient separation in the thrall of "All in the wonderful game we know as love." "Twelve inches, please; Twelve inches please," she crooned, seemingly in sync with *one* two-three, *one* two-three. Suddenly, Gilbert wondered if there was any place in her life for the game of love. She wasn't young, wasn't pretty, and was here at a Valentine's Day dance checking up on kids who didn't know what they were doing. "Then he'll kiss her lips, and caress her waiting fingertips. And their hearts will fly away." *One* two-three, *one* two-three." And then, just at the song ended, Martha pulled away, just a little, and asked, "Don't you know anything to do but the box step?" Then she walked back to the sidelines, and after following her for a few steps, he gave up and returned to his place by the window. The evening unfolded in three-minute, top forty stutter steps.

Several times Gilbert started to cross the floor to ask for a dance, but each time he drew back, unsure of the song, the potential partner, himself. He made unnecessary visits to the men's room. Each time, Mrs. MacGowan smiled at him and asked if he was having a good time. And each time the adults smiled at him as if they were sure he really was.

And then, suddenly, Elaine was standing next to him. "Having a good time, Gil?" she asked him.

"I guess," he replied.

"Well, look," she said. "You need to ask Beverly to dance before the end of the night. She really wants you to. She told me so."

"But she and Bruce are together. They've got a thing. I can't break into that."

"Well Bev would be really happy if you did. And Bruce, she's pretty much over him…especially since you came back to town."

"Well, I guess…there isn't much time left, before the last slow dance I mean."

"Well, you're both good friends and I want you to know how she feels." Then Elaine slipped away, across the dance floor.

The DJ stepped into the breach. "Okay, girls, it's time for ladies' choice. Step right up and ask that special guy to dance. We got Gogi Grant's 'The Wayward Wind.'" Girls began to cross the floor. Boys stood stock still, trying to feign indifference. And then, Beverly was standing in front of him, and Gil, looking over her shoulder, saw Bruce leaving the auditorium, heading for the men's room.

She smiled up at him, seemingly calm and unhurried. "May I have this dance?" she. asked. And without waiting for an answer, she took his hand and led him to the middle of the dance floor. She settled into his arms as the first refrain flowed out of the speakers. "And the wayward wind, is a restless wind." He stopped worrying about fox trot or waltz, *one*, two, three-four or *one* two-three. She felt light and soft, as if she was supposed to be right there with him. And she looked up into his eyes and smiled her little smile. When the song ended, neither of them made a move to separate.

"I'm glad we could have this dance," she said. I've wanted to get to know you better."

"And thanks again for your Valentine," he said. "Like I said before, I liked Faith's card a lot, but the message on yours was special." They both smiled, armored in an extra layer of understanding.

"Okay, Woods Street seventh graders," the DJ crooned. "Coming down to the end of a great evening. How about a big thank you cheer for the chaperones for keeping you all on the straight and narrow?" A scattering of applause and ragged cheers bounced off the auditorium walls. The parent chaperones smiled and waved their appreciation. The teachers and Mr. Cleveland registered their appreciation of irony.

Then, Bruce was next to Beverly. "Let's get out on the floor, Bevie," he said, a bit too forcefully for the moment.

She turned toward him, establishing a barrier between the two boys. "Bruce," she said. "I'm going to spend a little time with Gil, here. I'll catch up with you later." She started to turn away from the one who had brought her.

"But there are only two dances left!"

"And Gil and I are going to share them. Please, Bruce. We can talk later." And she turned back to Gilbert, smiled, and took his hand. The Platters began "The Great Pretender," and she settled into his arms, a little closer than before. As they turned to the music, Gil saw Bruce. He stood for a moment as if frozen by anger or despair. Then he wheeled, strode across the floor and out the door.

"Still around." As the last strain of "The Great Pretender" faded, the auditorium lights dimmed for the last dance. Beverly moved even closer, and Gilbert felt his hand expand, fingers pushing into the soft space between her shoulder blades.

"I'm really happy, Gil. I've wanted us to get closer ever since you came home. I really like you."

"I like you too, Bev. A lot. But what about Bruce? I mean you've been together."

"He's a nice guy and I still like him, like a friend. That's if he can be okay with that. But people change, and new people come into our lives. And right now…you're the one that I want to be close to."

Johnny Mathis finished the evening. "And I say to myself, it's wonderful, wonderful/ Oh, so wonderful, my love."

As the song ended, just as the lights came up, she lifted herself onto tiptoes, her chest sliding up against his. And her lips brushed his as softly as a promise. "It's going to be wonderful, Gil! We've got the spring and summer ahead of us."

* * *

The school year oozed along like the old snow sliding into the Nine Falls. Gilbert survived math with Mr. Cleveland, lost himself in Chip Hilton sports novels during free reading, and dueled with Faith for top grade on social studies tests. Mrs. MacGowen wrote long comments on his papers, praising his insights and exhorting him to work hard on his spelling and sentence structure. "Lazy mistakes" she called them.

As the days warmed into spring, Mr. Overlock, the crew cut elementary phys ed teacher, took the seventh grade boys out to the playground to practice track and field. Gil suffered through the dashes and long jump sessions, events that required speed and coordination that his morphing body lacked. The shot put was more his speed, especially because his dad had been league champion in his senior year of high school. Dr. Jenkins had talked with his son about technique and told him that his Danish immigrant father, who could never fathom American baseball and basketball, had loved that his son could "trow de iron ball." "You've got a good start, Gil," his dad said. "But remember, just like baseball, just like school, it takes hard work to make the most out of your gifts. Have fun but work hard."

And there was Bev. Everyone knew that they were a couple, and when he looked at her across their classroom, he could feel his chest swell with how pretty she was and that she liked him. Weekends offered moments when they could be together: walking along the river, sitting on a limb of the big maple tree in her backyard surrounded by the first new leaves. One Saturday they met in the Star Theater, sitting through a double feature. They held hands during the western, and then, as the romantic comedy began, she leaned over, and he slid his arm around her shoulder. She looked up at him, smiled, and brushed her lips over his like an April breeze.

In May, one of their classmates, Bonnie, invited nine kids to a party at her house. Boys and girls arrived separately, melded into five couples. The evening started with charades directed by Mrs. Lombardo. Gil drew "wrestling with his conscience," and in trying to act out the phrase wrapped his arms around his shoulders and spun in circles. "Beverly," Vince cried out. "It's got to have something to do with Beverly." The group broke into laughter. Bev blushed and drew him into her eyes. Their hostess seized the moment and led the way to the dining room for ham and egg salad finger sandwiches, two varieties of potato chips, and tiny cupcakes and eclairs.

After dining, all returned to the living room. Bonnie shut the door, turned on her record player armed with a stack of 45s and turned off all but two dim lamps. The couples settled in on couches and easy chairs. Bev and Gil took a loveseat in a corner by tiers of bookshelves. It felt as if the other kids had disappeared into separate realms, that there were just themselves.

Bev put her hand on his cheek. "I really like you, Gil," she whispered

"Me too you, Bevie. So much," he replied. And he drew her to him, and they experienced their first full kiss.

How much time passed, he couldn't tell. There was just this girl who liked him and kisses that became deeper and longer. Suddenly, she opened her mouth, and her tongue traced his lips, unlocking new dark, soft moments when there was just her.

And then, as from far, far away, a girl's voice intruded into his dream. "No. No, Steve! You've got to stop it. Please, stop." He recognized the voice as Margie, a girl from the fringes of seventh-grade hierarchies. He felt Bev slide away from him just as the lights were turned up and Bonnie's mother came through the door. He looked across the room to where Margie, hair mussed, smoothed her white blouse.

"Well, kids," Mrs. Lombardo said with more enthusiasm than her posture suggested, "All good times must end. Bonnie and I want to thank you all for coming." Then she walked through the door into the front hall and waited as her guests gathered jackets, offered their thanks, and departed.

Out on the sidewalk, Gil and Bev stood as the others began their walks homeward. "Just a minute, Gil," his best girl said and she walked back to the front steps of the Lombardo home where Margie stood, very alone. Bev spoke to her and after a moment they walked together back to Gil.

"Margie and I are going to walk home together, Gil," she said, "She lives on the next street over from me."

Gil felt a wave of disappointment; his vision of the end of the evening was blurring. "I can walk along with you, Bevie," he said in as casual a tone as he could call up. "We three can go together."

"No, Gil," she said softly but with a firmness that he'd never heard before. "I think it's good that Margie and I have some girl time. We can catch up, remember old times in our neighborhood." The two girls started off down Main Street. Beverly turned back. "You can call me tomorrow, Gil."

Gil headed down the street, more alone than he had ever felt. Sometimes it seemed like no matter how good something was, it wasn't enough for the other people around him. Good ideas in school weren't as important as perfect sentences. Throwing the shot put wasn't just fun, it was an assignment. He and Beverly: it was great when it was just the two of them, but others—friends, parents, the world—couldn't let that be enough. Everyone had their own ideas of what roles each person should be playing. Why did people think they knew who he was better than he did?

The bell in the Sutton Congregational Church rang. Half consciously Gilbert counted the tolls: eleven. He was going to be home a little later than his mother expected. He picked up his pace down the slope of Main Street that led past Riverbank Park, away from downtown toward the mill and his neighborhood. He slid back into memories of Bev with him on the sofa, in the dark with songs of young love on the record player. How warm she was in his arms. Her lips. Her hand on his cheek. Her tongue, silently whispering that she liked him. Really liked him. He wondered if there was really more. Of course he knew all the medical details. Being a doctor's son meant early introduction to boys and girls, sperms and eggs, babies and responsibilities. He'd had "the talk" way before his friends, information that he'd passed on to Vince, John, and other boys on the playground about a half hour after promising his father that he would keep their conversation private. "Other parents would want to tell their kids when they thought it was time." And tonight and the thing with Steve and Margie. What had gone on? Why had things gotten out of hand and made her so scared? How did you know what was okay and when it was okay to try?

"Gil. Hey, Gil!" Vince's voice brought him out of the darkness of questioning into the streetlight of Main Street. His best buddy, coming downhill on Dover Street, caught up with him. Together they headed toward home.

"So Vince, did you get Sharon home in one piece?"

His friend took a deep, dramatic breath and exhaled like a blast from the mill boilers. "Oh yeah, in one piece and pretty happy, I guess." He paused, waiting for a cue for more details. None coming, he continued. "We stood out by her back porch and did some major kissing. It was like we were practicing for the mugging Olympics. I'd try to catch my breath, but she wouldn't let go. Not that I really minded, you know."

Gil tried a tone that he hoped would sound more experienced than he felt. "It's so weird, when you're making out, and it's like time disappears. It's all dark and quiet, and together."

"Well the dark and quiet ended pretty quickly," Vince said. "The light on the porch started flashing on and off. Then the back door opened, and Sharon's mom yelled that she needed to come in *right now*. It was late, and they were going to the early mass at St. Hyacinth's in the morning. That was that. Nice while it lasted."

"Better than Margie and Steve."

"Oh yeah! Stevie boy read that one wrong. He told me this afternoon that Margie had really come on to him outside school when everybody was coming back from lunch. Said she told him she was really excited about being at Bonnie's party with him. And she moved so that her boobies were right where he was looking. She poked them up just like she was Marilyn Monroe or somebody."

The two friends paused on the corner of Glen and Monroe. "Girls," Vince said.

"Yeah," Gilbert replied in a tone that he hoped expressed understanding. "You can't live without 'em; can't live with 'em." He turned and walked up Glen toward the big green Victorian that was home.

He walked into the dining room and found his father at the round table with a glass of water and a cigarette. "Good night, slugger? How'd you make out?" his dad said.

For a flash, Gil was taken aback by the choice of the phrase "make out." He decided that his father couldn't possibly understand the implications it carried for himself and his friends. "Yeah, Dad," he replied. "We all had a great time. Food was really good."

"But man does not live by bread alone. Hope you remembered your mother's teachings." The doctor's tone suggested that his words weren't quite as serious as their message implied, almost as if there had been a wink exchanged with his firstborn.

"It was all good, Dad. I know I'm pretty tired."

"Yep. Church in the morning. Sleep well and pleasant dreams."

* * *

The morning of Memorial Day, Gilbert walked his brothers down to the park for the parade. Stewie was in his Boy Scout uniform and Petie in his blue Cub Scout outfit. As he deposited each brother with his troop and pack, Gil felt like this year marked a change in his being. Scouts were a thing of the past; parades were for watching with friends. All except for the Halloween Parade, where the newly arrived adolescents strolled along at the end of the ranks of little kids, un-costumed and unruly.

His friends gathered in the shadow of the bronze statue of a Civil War soldier. Beverly stood with Faith, Elaine, and Margie, all dressed in their best casual spring outfits: slacks and white blouses with silky scarves at the throat. Bev separated herself from the girls, walked over to Gil, and took his hand. "What a beautiful day," she said

"Gorgeous," he replied. "Almost as beautiful as you." A pause. "Hey, would you like to go on the swings over there?" She smiled in assent, and they walked over to the gray metal swing sets underlaid with wood chipss from the mill. Bev climbed onto the only available swing, and he walked behind her and began to push her up and away. Higher and farther with each push, but each time she swung back to his hands. Her head tilted back, scanning the sky above the arc of her flight and her eyes returned to his at the moment of her return. She seemed weightless, like a dream. And then the drums of the high school band announced the start of the parade. Up, away, and back; three times she swung back to Earth, each time more gently, and as she stopped, he leaned down and kissed her forehead, barely touched by the sun with spring's promise of summer.

They followed their friends out of the park and along Main Street to where they could see the parade as it marched toward downtown Sutton. They stood apart as the Legion color guard led a row of city fathers, convertibles with high school girls smiling and waving, and the local National Guard company in tan uniforms, rifles on shoulders. Cub Scouts, Brownies, Boy Scouts, and Girl Scouts were herded into ranks by scoutmasters and mothers. And at the rear marched the high school band in baby blue-and-white uniforms with white tasseled helmets, driving all before them with John Phillip Souza.

Reluctantly, Gilbert said to Bev, "I've got to leave and get up to the end of the parade to get Stewie and Petie. I wish I didn't have to go now."

"It's okay," she replied. "I'm glad we could be together. Thanks for the swing. And we've got the whole summer ahead of us."

Her boyfriend started to leave and then turned back. "Bevie, I want to tell you how cute you look today. Your outfit is really sharp."

"Thanks, Gil. It's nice of you to notice. But I really like those plaid slacks that Faith's got on. They're the really cool style this spring." She sighed. "I asked my mom if I could use part of my school clothes money now rather than next fall, but she said we can't afford it. I told her they're not going to get cheaper, but she wouldn't budge."

"Well, you'll be beautiful whatever you wear. And now I've got to go for my brothers." He paused. "I like you Bevie. I mean I love you." And then he was gone.

His mother was in the kitchen when he herded his brothers up the back steps. "Good parade, guys?" she asked. "Anybody ready for lunch?"

"Mom," Gil said. "I'm going to skip lunch if that's okay. I've got an errand I want to run, and I'm supposed to meet the guys down at the ballpark. We've got a pickup game against a bunch from across the river."

"Okay. Have fun but make sure to be home for dinner. Now Stewie and Petie, how's about some luscious Campbell's chicken noodle."

Gilbert walked down Main Street as if he were on a mission, like the spy in the Cold War who alone could save the day against the Russians. Downtown Sutton was crowded with shoppers left over from the parade and from the surrounding towns making their weekly trip to the A&P and First

National grocery stores. A red brick, two-story commercial building on the corner of Church Street housed the Fournier's Clothing Store, the outlet of a larger store in downtown Portland. Most of the Jenkins' apparel was purchased locally, and Dr. and Mrs. Jenkins had occasional social connections with Mr. O'Donnell, the branch manager.

Gil entered the store and walked over to the side where the women's fashions were hung and shelved. Feeling out of his element, he tried to seem casual as he scanned the racks of dresses, coats, and slacks, searching for a flash of telltale plaid. After a few strategic moments, Mr. O'Donnell stepped into the boy's indecision. "Young Mr. Jenkins," he said. "Gilbert, if my memory serves me. How are your folks? Dad as busy as ever?"

"Yes sir," Gil replied. They're both fine." The two stood between the women's suits and the shelves of sweaters.

"So, how can I help you today?" the manager asked. "I don't usually see your family on this side of the store."

The novice took a deep breath. "Well, I'm looking for a present for a friend. A pair of plaid slacks."

"Well, we can help you with that, for sure," came the reply. "Just walk down this aisle, and we'll get you taken care of." They moved off toward the rear of the store and paused by a rack blazing with multicolored cloth. "First off, I need to know her size. Then we can pick the perfect pair for this special someone."

Gilbert might as well have been asked the precise diameter of Saturn. "Well, she's not very big, my age…and smaller than my mom."

"I'd guess that would make her 'teenage petit.' We've got a whole bunch of plaid slacks in that size right here. Just got a delivery yesterday. Any of them would be really nice. Take your time and pick what seems just right." He chuckled. "Or, I would guess, just what the doctor ordered."

Gil scanned the various color combinations, trying to connect one with how he could see Bevie in his imagination. A pair with dark red-and-blue patterns set on white seemed to be the best of the lot. Hoping he was following shopping decorum he picked them off the rack. "These, Mr. O'Donnell. These will be just what she'll like."

"A very good, grown-up choice, Gilbert," said the salesman. "I think they're the pick of the litter. Now let's get these packed up and get you on your way. Just follow me back to the counter." As Gil followed Mr. O'Donnell, he noticed the sharp crease of his trousers, the strip of white shirt above the roll of the suit coat, and the bald spot on the back of his head.

"Now let's get these boxed. Would you like gift wrapping? No extra charge for our special customers."

"No thank you. Just a box will be fine." The dark blue cardboard was embossed with FOURNIER in gold.

"There you go. And now the final question: how would you like to pay for this wonderful gift? Cash today? Or would you like me to put it on your parents' account."

In the excitement of his quest, Gilbert had almost forgotten the financial side of the purchase. "Oh, on my parents' account please. My mom told me to tell you that it was okay."

"And so it is." Mr. O'Donnell wrote out a slip and passed it to his new customer. "And please give my best to your parents. They must be tickled and proud to have such a grown-up young consumer." There was nothing left to say, so Gilbert took the box and headed out down Main Street and Bevie's house.

As he walked down Fitch Street toward her small yellow row house, his excitement grew just as his feelings for her had increased over the past nine months. He walked up the three wooden steps onto the back porch and knocked on the door. After a moment, Beverly's mother opened the door.

"Gilbert. What a nice surprise! Can you come in?"

"I don't think so, Mrs. Jackson. Is Bevie home? I'd like to see her just for a moment."

"You wait right here. I'll get her." She turned to go inside and turned back. "I heard the parade was great. Any parties on the horizon?"

And then Beverly was on the porch. "Gil, wow! Twice in one day!"

"I can't stay, Bevie. My mom's going to be wondering where I've gone. But…" He held out the blue box. "Well…well I bought you a little present. Just because I really like you. I hope you like it."

"Wow, Gil! What a surprise. Let me get a knife to slit the tape, and I'll open it. Just take a minute."

Gilbert suddenly felt that he couldn't stay to see her reaction. "No, Bev, I've got to leave right now. I'll see you in school tomorrow." He turned and walked up toward Main Street and home without looking back.

When he walked into the house, Stewie was on the dining room floor playing with his big model bulldozer, pushing pieces of Lincoln Logs into piles, making roaring diesel noises. Without looking up he said, "Mom's upstairs with Allie. He loaded his diaper big time."

Gil walked to the refrigerator, changed his mind, and reached into the cookie jar for three of Mrs. Jenkins's world-famous Toll House cookies. His mother came into the kitchen, Allie on her hip.

"Gil, you're home at last. Did you have a good baseball game?"

"It fell through, Mom. The kids from across the river didn't show and we didn't have enough guys for a real game."

"Well, I've got to think about starting dinner. Your dad has delivered two babies since last night. Some holiday for him! He's been out straight ever since he finished his army tour. He's going to be starving and tired when he gets here. Do me a favor and put your brother in the playpen. Hopefully he'll stay dry and clean for at least a half hour."

Gil took Allie into the den and put him in the playpen. Then he returned to the kitchen and climbed up on the counter. "Mom," he said. "I've got something to tell you."

His mother turned to him. "Nothing bad, I hope."

"No, Mom. Nothing bad. It's just that I…well I stopped into Fournier's today and bought a friend a present."

His mother's gaze hardened a bit. "Without asking, Gil? That doesn't sound like you. What did you buy? Who for?"

"Well, I got a pair of plaid slacks for Beverly. She was talking at the parade about how she didn't have any, and she really wanted them. So I wanted to surprise her, like a special friend would. I didn't have time to ask you. I didn't think you'd mind."

Mrs. Jenkins turned away. She pushed the mixing bowl across the counter. He could see her take a long, slow breath. Then she returned her gaze. "I'm really unhappy with this, Gil. It's wrong in a lot of different ways."

"I didn't mean to be bad, Mom! I just wanted to do something nice."

"Well, in the first place, you really shouldn't have made this purchase on our credit without getting my okay. Your father and I have made a good place for ourselves in Sutton, and we don't want people to get wrong impressions about our family."

"I didn't have time. I really wanted her to have the slacks today."

"And that's the next part. Clothing isn't an appropriate gift from a young man to a young woman. It's much too personal, especially because her parents didn't have any say."

"But I didn't mean…. "

"When you're a grown-up you'll be able to make choices on your own. But that's a lot of years and a lot of experiences off in your future. For now, you need help from the adults who care about you. And a big part of growing up is finding out how to tell who they are....Lots of times, the people who love you the most are those who will say no to you.... because we love you. The rest are just salesclerks, doing their job."

"So what should I do?"

"This is what we, you and I, will do. We'll go down to Beverly's together. I'll explain to her parents that you've made a mistake and understand why your choice wasn't a good one. And you will apologize to them, especially to Bev. Tomorrow I'll take the slacks back to Fournier's and explain to Charlie, Mr. O'Donnell, that we had a misconnection on getting the gift." It will all work out. But for now, we need your father to come home so we can make our visit."

Gilbert felt more tired than he could remember. "Okay, Mom. I'll just wait in the other room."

"Check in on your brothers, please."

He walked into the den. Stewie and Petie had gathered on the floor in front of the mahogany cabinet RCA television.

"Time for Mickey. Turn on," Petie said.

The black-and-white screen emerged into Disney World. "MIC...KEY... MOUSE." The Mousekcteers, white sweaters, black-eared beanies, and gleaming smiles welcomed the club members from afar to the afternoon's revels. Gil and Stewie had had major debates over whether Annette or Darleen was the cuter. Gil argued that Darleen was more grown up. Stewie, sneering as only an eleven-year-old, younger brother could, claimed that it was only Darleen's boobies that won Gil's loyalty.

Gilbert was brought back to the now by the front doorbell. Expecting one of his father's patients who occasionally appeared unannounced, he walked to the entryway and opened the door. There in the twilight stood Beverly, alone, dark blue box in hand. "Hi Gil," she said. "Can I come in? I need to speak to you and your mother."

Wiping her hands on a dish towel, Mrs. Jenkins asked Beverly in and led the two seventh graders into the living room. "I'm glad to see you Beverly," she said. "I'm glad that you could come."

"My mother said to tell you she was sorry that she couldn't come too. Anyway, I want to bring back the slacks that Gil gave me. I really love them but when I get them, I want it to be on my own."

"I understand," Gil's mother replied. "And I think it's a very grown-up decision that you've made. Gil understands that sometimes we make choices too quickly, even when we have the best of reasons."

And they walked, mother, son, and best friend, to the front porch where the glow from the Nine Falls Mill was just beginning to rise out of the river valley.

* * *

On the last day of school, Mr. Cleveland came into Gil's homeroom to give his end-of-the-year speech. The principal, gray haired and a little red in the face, perched himself on the corner of Mrs. McGowen's desk. The teacher wheeled her chair off to the side and fixed her eyes on the boss; a small smile spoke of collegial, of adult, connection. Mr. Cleveland took a noticeably deep breath and, as he exhaled, panned his gaze around the room, making eye contact with each of the twenty-two students.

"Boys and girls," he began. "Or as I should more properly say 'young men and women,' I've wanted to come in and share a few ideas with you as you leave us here at Woods Street and prepare to move into our town's new junior high school next fall." He paused. Mrs. McGowen scanned her charges and smiled. The twenty-two sat and returned his gaze, faces reflecting either respectful academic apprentices or zombies frozen in place waiting for twilight. "Junior high will be a new, exciting, and challenging world. Here at Woods, we're like a big, happy family. Sometimes a little too rambunctious but all together, from kindergarten all the way to eighth grade. We care for each other. This year you have been great role models for the little ones." He paused for effect. "At least, most of the time." Mrs. McGowen nodded her agreement.

It was the first really warm day in June. The afternoon sun poured in through the huge open windows of their second floor classroom. The hum of the school merged with the more distant but harder roar of the Nine Falls Mill. Fourth and fifth graders were out on the playground for their annual field day. Their shrieks and laughter sang soprano over the tenor of the old school and the bass of the paper industry. Summer seemed possible.

"Junior high will be your first real step into the grown-up world that education makes possible. Your job is to take the good habits and foundations of learning we have given you and use them to find your own path." The principal's gaze jumped from face to face, reinforcing his willingness to speak to each student as a real individual. "And before you've finished with Sutton schools, you can discover where you best fit into our new and exciting America. Some of you will prepare to move on to college." He made eye contact with Gil who then watched as the connection was offered to Faith, to Vince, and a couple of others who regularly got the highest grades and praise from Mrs. McGowen. His tone changed just imperceptibly. "But there are other wonderful paths that you can take: the business track, vocational, and homemaking for you girls who will become the young wives and mothers that make everything else possible. And that's what it's all about, being free to make your choices."

Gil rode Mr. Cleveland's words like a magic carpet into his own world. That was the best thing about grown-ups' speech: You could fly out beyond the message and imagine yourself as you wished. It was like Pastor Andreason's sermons on Sunday mornings. As he called out a world of sin and redemption, Gil could think about what it meant to be really a good person, how to try to understand all the lusts and temptations that God forbade. He looked across the room to where Bev and Faith sat. Faith's eyes were locked on the principal, a smile on her face that expressed her connection with his lessons. Bev's gaze slanted above the teacher's desk, seemingly focused on the neatly printed posters expressing grown-up values. Her smile was less formal, for herself alone. Gil wondered if maybe he was part of the future behind that smile.

The classroom bell rang Gil back into the real present. His classmates burst out of their chairs for the last time at Woods. Mrs. McGowen was a bit flustered but Mr. Cleveland stood, smiled, and over the din of scraping chairs and stomping feet said, "Thank you for your attention and for your eight great years at our school. You will be remembered." And then the exodus burst out the door and into the promised land of summer. As Gil followed them, Mrs. McGowen stepped into his path.

"Gil, I want to tell you how much I've enjoyed our time together this year."

Gil downshifted his excitement into second gear. "It's been great, Mrs. Mac. I'll miss you."

"You have great potential, as much as any student I've ever taught. But success depends on hard work as well as great gifts. Be yourself, explore, but do your homework."

* * *

Summer opened like a gift. Gilbert settled into a routine of no alarm clocks, helping his mother with his brothers, and basketball and softball at Nine Falls Park, which led to contacts with older boys. The bruises and teasing gradually ebbed into what passed for a sort of inclusion. And after the games there was time for a dash to the pool, cannonballing off the high board, and contests to see which of his crew could swim the longest underwater. AND, there was Bev. Even when they were hanging out with their separate friends, he was aware that she was near. Often, when he wasn't needed at home for lunch, they met on the slope below the pool that ran toward the fields, courts, and the river. They lay on the thick grass, close but rarely touching, and talked about the teenaged world that swirled around them, the approaching junior high year, and the clouds that floated down the river, over the smoke from the soaring concrete chimney at the mill and on to the sea

One day Gil spirited fifty cents out of his savings, and he and Bev walked to Morrisette's Variety Store. His windfall bought two Italian sandwiches, two bags of chips, an orange soda, and a carton of milk. They returned to the park and followed the path to a point at the river's bend. They sat down and ate to the background music of flowing water over the mill's hums and sighs.

When they finished their lunch, Gil suggested they go look at the bronze statue at the tip of the point. The romantic piece was of a young boy seated with a dog lying at his feet. An inscription at the base dedicated the work to the memory of the nephew of the mill's founder. Sutton lore had it that the boy had drowned while swimming in the Nine Falls and that the dog had also perished in its attempt to save his master. And the boy was nude! His childish penis was there for all to see. Gil, already aware of the statue's realism, had wondered how his best girl would react to such a graphic depiction. And, in the moment as they walked around boy and dog, he stood off to her side trying to get a sense of her response. But her face never changed, and they walked away from the moment, together and silent.

Their times together seemed like the heart of the summer. Mostly they hung out with friends, together but not touching. As they parted from the park or outside her house, if there was time for him to walk her home, there was a quick kiss or a hug. It felt as though they both knew that there was more, but that the time was not yet right.

One early July day, they teamed up with Vince and Sharon to ride up along the Nine Falls to a swimming hole upstream from an old covered bridge. Bev's bike had a flat tire, so she sat on the crossbar of his Colombia. At one point they coasted down a long, curving hill toward the river, and his best girl leaned back against his chest. The sun shone noontime bright, and the breeze from their descent flowed over them like a promise. Gil thought that this moment was perfect; nothing that the future would bring would ever surpass now.

They parked their bikes in a grove of pine trees and walked along the bank to the swimming hole. The Nine Falls had carved a small cove into the banking. Near the shore the water was shallow but quickly dropped off into the dark swirl of the current. They had all worn their bathing suits and now shucked their outer garments, leaving them with their towels. Then, like young otters, they slid down into the cool stream. A long rope was attached to an oak limb over the river, and Vince and Gil took turns swinging out and bombing down into the deep water. Sharon and Bev alternated swims with stretching out on a glacial boulder that marked the downstream side of the cove. As the river flowed toward the mill and the sea beyond, the afternoon flowed toward its end. Vince and Sharon exploded into a riot of splashing, retreating and charging together, only their heads and shoulders visible above the surface. The retreats grew shorter and then ended.

Gil sat near the shore, the water up to his chest. Across the cove, Bev stood up on the boulder and stretched. She was wearing her one-piece bathing suit, brown-and-yellow stripes with a little ruffled skirt. It was the only suit she had worn since the summer had unfolded. Then she slipped into the water and swam across to Gil. As if he knew what he was doing, he leaned back, and she floated into his arms. He hugged her close and could feel her chest against his, a strange and exciting mix of firm and soft.

She looked way deep into his eyes. "This is a wonderful day," she said. "And I think you're pretty wonderful, too."

"Me too you," Bevie," he replied. "And I don't think I've ever told you how cute you look in your swimming suit." He hoped his vanilla observation carried a hint of peppermint. "I'd be happy if this summer could go on forever."

"We've got today," she said, and leaned up and kissed him, a soft and gentle kiss.

"Well, I've got to get home. Mom has a meeting and I have to watch the brats." He stood and stepped up on shore. "Come on, you two," he yelled over to Vince and Sharon. "Get your bods out of the drink, and we'll hit the road."

* * *

August brought changes to the summer. For four days, Gilbert went to his grandfather's farm to help his uncles with the haying. His chief task was to ride on the old dump rake, laying rows that could then be forked loose onto a trailer and hauled into the barn, fodder for the farm's remaining cow. His uncles, giving up half of their vacations, sweated, joked, cursed and teased their nephew about being a city kid, living on the right side of the tracks. On breaks they drank deep glasses of home brewed beer. Gil drank root beer that his uncle crafted. In reality, he much preferred it to the sips of "the real thing" that powered the men.

A couple of days when they were still in the field at lunch time, he stayed behind and walked down to the little river that marked the farm's western boundary. Back from the dirt road and out of sight of the Nelsons' farm on the other side, he stripped bare and jumped into the shallow stream. Barely two feet deep in the summer, the water felt cool but couldn't support him over the deep layer of gray marine clay that formed the riverbed. He thought what it would be like if Bevie were there with him, away from all eyes but their own, like the Indians who had once roamed the countryside, or Adam and Eve. Across the field, he heard his uncles' voices and the start-up roar of the old steel-wheeled John Deere tractor. He stood up at the edge of the river and, as best he could, washed the river mud off his body. Then he scrambled up the bank and stood for a couple of long minutes in the sunshine, drying off a little before dressing and rejoining the grown-up world of work.

Gil returned from the farm to find the household in a furor of preparation for the family vacation that was to begin the next day. Dr. Jenkins had committed to nine days away from his practice, although he had made it clear that if there were any babies to be delivered, he would fulfill his responsibilities. They had rented a cabin on Big Loon, the lake which fed the Nine Falls. The eldest son had hoped to find time to see his best girl but soon saw that he would have to be satisfied with a quick phone call.

"Hi, Bevie," he said. "I'm really sorry that I can't get away to see you."

"Me too, Gil," she replied. "It would have been nice, but families come first. I'll be thinking of you while you're off at the lake."

"I wish I could call you while we're up there. There is a phone; my dad has to have one for medical stuff. But it's a toll call down to Sutton, and my mom's death on phone charges."

"Don't worry, sweets," she said with a laugh. "You go off and have your fun and know that I'll be thinking of you every minute. Ten days isn't a lifetime, you know. My mom's calling me. Love you." And the phone clicked off in his ear.

The Jenkinses returned from the lake in a bit of disarray. Petie had been afraid of the ducks along the shore and had to be carried into the water by

Gil or his mother. Stewie had claimed that he had caught the biggest fish, a lot bigger than Gil's, but that it had flopped back into the water just as he was taking out the hook. And hardest of all, Dr. Jenkins had delivered seven babies over the ten days. Twice he'd spent the night at the hospital while a second happy mother-to-be completed her labor. But now the car had been unloaded, Allie's diaper changed, and the youngest three boys bedded down. Even though it was after eight thirty, Gil picked up the phone and gave the operator Bev's number.

"Bevie, I'm home," he announced to his favorite voice. "Hope it's not too late."

She sounded a little surprised. "I'm glad you called. I can't really talk now, though. My mom is expecting a call from her mother up in The County."

"Okay, I understand. I'm free tomorrow after my chores. Can we meet down at the pool, maybe about ten thirty?" He could feel a rush in his voice. "I can buy us some Italians. There wasn't anything to spend money on at the lake."

There was the hint of a pause, like the hiss of a tire as you tried to check the pressure. "I'm sorry, Gil. I'm going to be tied down all day tomorrow. I've got errands to run with Mom. We went clothes shopping last week, and I've got a couple of things to return. How about Tuesday, say later in the afternoon? I really do want to see you."

He tried to mask his disappointment. "Okay, Bev. Sure, that will be fine. Have fun with your mother. And I'll see you later."

The phone clicked off.

Tuesday morning passed with a halfhearted softball game at the pool. Returning home, he finished his lunch and then retreated into his third-floor bedroom. He figured that picking up his stuff would help pass the time and earn him credits with his mother. At three thirty, he walked into the kitchen where she was sterilizing some of his father's syringes in a special pan on the electric stove.

"Mom, if it's okay, I'm going down to the pool for a while."

"Another ball game?"

He paused and decided to be open. "No. I'm going to meet Bev and we're going to catch up with everything that's gone on while we were up to the lake. This afternoon was the first time she could get free."

"Well, I'm sure you two missed each other. Please say hello from me. And don't stay too long. It would be great if you can take Allie out for a ride around the neighborhood. I haven't had a minute to get out all day. Your dad should be home for dinner sometime after six." She walked over to him and ruffled his crewcut. "You're getting to be all grown up. Have fun."

Gil's spirits rose as he walked down Main Street toward the mill, the river, and the park beyond. He stood at the edge of the parking lot above the pool and searched for a glimpse of his best girl with no success. After a few static moments he walked down the slope and around the fence that set off the pool. The last of the young swimmers were straggling out of the water and through the dressing rooms to the outside. The lifeguards were picking up after the horde in preparation for the adult swim that would begin at seven o'clock. Bev was nowhere to be seen. Unable to think of any other strategy, he sat down with his back against the chain links and stared across the softball field to the point in the Nine Falls where the little bronze boy and his dog rested in their innocence.

And then Bev was next to him. He jumped to his feet and, holding out his open arms, received a glancing hug.

"Bevie," he said. "It's so great to see you. I really missed you these past two weeks."

"And I'm glad to see you too, Gil," she replied.

"Let's take a walk down to the river where we can be a little bit alone."

She took a step back, away from the fence. "I can't stay, Gil. My mom wants me home soon." She looked at him with an expression he'd never seen before. "Gil, I need to tell you something. I've been changing while you've been away. And I need you to understand that I feel like I've moved away from what we've had since the dance. I'm sorry, but I just don't feel close like I used to. I hope you can understand."

He felt like he might fall and slide down the hill. "Bev," he said in a voice one hair from crying. "I don't understand. I thought we had a wonderful summer together. What happened that…?"

"It's not you; you're a great kid, kind and generous. No, it's me. What I felt before has gone, like it floated downstream over the last falls and out to sea. It's me, and I need to be honest with you." She took another step away and turned to leave. "And now I really have to go. I'm sorry."

He had to try once more. "Bev, maybe you just need some time to think. But maybe after some time you could like me again."

Her voice signaled finality. "I do like you Gil, like a very good friend. But that's all I feel now, and that's not going to change. Goodbye." And she turned and walked away, never offering any hope that she would stop and turn.

Two weeks later, Gil was mowing the front lawn. Elaine came walking down Main, away from her neighborhood on the hill above the river. He stopped as she approached.

"Hi Elaine. Where are you off to?"

She stopped and gave him a little smile. "Actually, I was hoping to find you, Gil. Thought it might be good if we had a talk…about you and Bev and what's happened. Can we sit down on your porch steps?"

Wordlessly he led her over to the old curving concrete stairs and sat down, back against the house. Elaine settled onto the next stair higher so that their eyes were on the same level. "Well, I don't know what Bev told you about why she broke up with you. But I'm sure that you're really hurt. You're my friend and I want you to know what's really going on."

"Okay…okay, Elaine. I'm glad you want to help. You've always been a good friend."

"Thanks, Gil. Your friendship is really important to me, too."

"And…Bev?

"Well, what happened was that while you were away, Johnny O'Connor—he's a sophomore, lives over across the river—well, anyway, he swooped down at the pool and put some moves on Bev."

"Moves?" he said. "What kind of moves do you mean?"

"He played up to her like she was a high school kid. Like, she had just bought a new bathing suit, a lime green two-piece suit. He started calling her 'Limey Bean' and telling her how great she looked in it, how grown-up. And she bought into it like he was Tab Hunter or something. I think he's just out for what he thinks he can get, and I'm afraid she'll end up getting hurt, just like she hurt you. And I'll feel bad for both of you. You're both my good friends."

"Well, what should I do? I really miss her so much. Do you think we could…be together again?"

"Who knows about love, Gil? But I sure can't see anything like that happening while Bev's floating on her big-girl cloud. Just be yourself; it's a wonderful, lovable self. And you never can tell what will happen. Maybe someone else will show up who will love you like you deserve."

Elaine stood and Gil followed. They reached out to each other and shared a long hug. Then she stepped back and patted his cheek. "I love you like a brother, Gil. I want you to know that."

It seemed to him that his response would be important, whatever he chose to say. "And you're as great a friend as any guy could want, Elaine. I'm glad you wanted to tell me the truth. It helps."

After a long moment, she smiled at him. "Thanks, Gil. That means a lot. Happy mowing." And she turned and walked back toward the Nine Falls and home.

Across The Aisle

Gilbert Jenkins let his attention slide away from the sentence diagram that Miss Weeks had chalked onto the blackboard. He looked out the second-floor classroom of the Sutton Junior High School. Over the wood-framed houses, he could see the smoke from the paper mill's tall chimney streaming upstream over the Nine Falls River. As any resident over the age of five in the town knew well, the east wind promised rain or, on this late November Friday, the first snow of the season. As if from inside a cloud, he became aware of Faith's perky voice tracing the path of the subordinate clause sliding southeast from the verb. Then, as if confirming hope in the future, the passing bell rang, jangling over Miss "Endless" Weeks' assignment.

Like the Children of Israel fleeing the Pharaoh's indenture, students flowed through locker-lined channels and into the Promised Land of the weekend. Gilbert and his crew—Vince, Ollie, Johnny, and BJ—gathered in the lobby that led from the gym to School Street. And, as was recently often the case, a clutch of girls, the self-styled Hi Teeners, settled in across the room. At lunch, a plan had somehow evolved that the place to be that evening would be the Star Theater, two blocks away downtown. Sharon had checked the newspaper during her period as a library aide and reported that the twin features for the weekend were *The Kentuckian*, starring Burt Lancaster and *The Man With The Golden Arm*. Now, the space between the groups ebbed and flowed with bantering about possible pairings, suggestions of necking, and passionate denials by those so named.

As the groups began to dissolve toward basketball practice, cheerleading tryouts, or home, Elaine fluttered up to Gilbert.

"So, Gil," she said. "Are you gonna be there tonight?"

"Yeah...yeah," he replied. "I want to be, and I think my mom will say okay."

Elaine leaned in closer and breathed, "Well, Judy said she's going for sure, and I think she'd like to sit across the aisle...that is, if you're there."

Gilbert looked across Elaine's shoulder to the few remaining girls. Judy was there, busily engaged in chatting with Rachael. She wore the regulation Teeners' outfit: white blouse and plaid skirt over a ruffled petticoat. Her light brown hair was done in a page boy and seemed to highlight the skin of her neck, which still revealed hints of summer's tan. Involuntarily, he took a deep breath, as if preparing to explode into a play on the football field. "Yeah!" he said. "I'll be there for sure."

Elaine nodded knowingly and returned to the Teeners' fold. Gilbert, Ollie, and Ron, almost late for basketball practice, agreed to meet with Vince and BJ at Vachon's Drugstore at six and walk over to the Star together.

After practice, the eighth- and ninth-grade teams toweled off and dressed. Teenage banter banged off the gray metal lockers. Wayne, the tallest of the ninth graders, held court, recounting his latest conquest.

"Her parents were right out in the kitchen. Her old man was carrying on so loud I'm surprised he didn't spill his beer. Anyway, we had the TV sound turned up real loud; *Wyatt Earp* was on, and they couldn't have heard us anyway. At first she pretended that she didn't want to really make out. But then her mouth opened up, and we French kissed like we was from Paris. I didn't go for bare tit, with her parents right there. But we did some pretty good rubbing together and I know for sure that she knew I liked her!"

"Come on, you scrubs! Get yourself dressed and out of there so I can get home for dinner," shouted Coach Marlon. "And don't forget to take your homework for the weekend." He was rewarded by groans and an exodus as the custodian began to turn off the lights.

Snuffie, the beagle, greeted Gilbert as he walked into the back hall. She luxuriated in his ear skritchies and followed him into the kitchen with the eternal canine hope for a snack.

Mrs. Jenkins was peeling potatoes to accompany the pot roast that Gil could smell in the oven.

"Oh, Gil," his mother said, "I'm glad you're home at last. I've had a crazy day with Petie sick and your dad's laundry. Be a good boy and set the table for me."

"Okay, Mom," Gil replied and walked to the cupboard. He took down five plates, counted out place settings of silverware, and walked them over to the dinner table. Then he moved Allie's high chair next to his mother's seat. "So, Mom, when are we gonna eat?"

"I'm afraid it's going to be late tonight, sweetie. Your dad had an emergency house call up in Buxford. He won't be home until probably seven o'clock. Can you hold out that long?"

"Well, here's the thing. A bunch of the guys are planning to go to the movies at the Star tonight and they really want me to go. The first movie starts about six thirty. Do you think I could just have some leftovers? Can I go? I haven't used up my movie for November, you know."

His mother ran water over the potatoes in the pan and set them on a back burner of the new General Electric range. "What movies are showing?"

Gilbert tried to use a reassuring tone. *The Kentuckian*, and *The Man With The Golden Arm*. Burt Lancaster is starring in *The Kentuckian*. It's supposed to be a really good Western."

"What about the other one," said his mother. "What's the 'golden arm' thing about?"

Her son tried to be smooth as he concocted a response he thought would pass inspection. "Well, I'm not really sure. But BJ told me that it's a baseball story, a movie about a young pitcher who has to come through in the World Series. He's like a kid from the country and all." He hoped that his mother hadn't heard the real scoop on that film, about a jazz musician strung out on drugs, very much a forbidden topic in her book. Movies and comic books were said to threaten young kids, and she wasn't going to shirk her motherly duties. But, also, she wasn't really a movie fan, and his white lie seemed to work.

"Well, I guess it's okay, Gil," she said. "But isn't tomorrow the day you're going deer hunting with your dad? You know you'll have to get up really early. I think maybe—"

Gil interrupted, trying to hide his growing concern. "It won't be that late, Mom. I'll get plenty of sleep. Please?"

"But you know how important this is to your father. He gets so little time off, and he really wants to be with you in the woods. And you've got the new gun he gave you for your birthday. Tell you what: how about you go to the first movie and then come right home. That way you can spend time with friends and still get the sleep you need."

"Okay, Mom." Half a loaf was better than none. "Can I have my allowance? I need to go right away. I'm meeting the guys at Vachon's Drug. I don't need to eat right now. I'll get some popcorn at the movies and eat when I get home."

Mrs. Jenkins went to her purse and removed two quarters. "Here's your allowance, sweetie. And the second twenty-five cents is a bonus for the help you gave me with Allie all week. Now be careful and behave yourself."

Gilbert started on his walk downtown. The late autumn night had fallen with a darkness that seemed to frame the lighted windows of the mill townhouses and the just-closing shops. Down Oxford Street, the glow of the mill pushed against the low clouds, and the great gray chimney thrust upward as if piercing the sky itself. The wind was still bearing in from the east and chilled him despite his hunting coat.

He tried to get his head around the evening to come. He hoped his buddies wouldn't give him too much grief about having to leave after the first movie. But the hunting trip should make sense to them. They might even be a little jealous that he would be out in the woods with grown-ups. But they would all be together in the Star and the Hi Teeners would be there too. And Judy...what would happen with her? How would he make it happen? He closed his eyes and could see her, her soft hair and long smooth neck. Her body just beginning to change, showing curves, especially in her cheerleading outfit. When she spun, and the blue skirt flared up above her knees, her face looked excited and free. But how would he know...how to start...what to try? Would he be the one to cross the aisle?

And then, as if from out of the clouds above the mill, he thought of an afternoon last summer. He had gone over to Terry's house to play. Terry was not one of his regular gang. Really, he couldn't remember why he had gone. But as they were hitting badminton shots back and forth, Terry's sister had come out of the house. She was two grades ahead and seemed very grown up to Gilbert. She told Terry that their mother wanted to speak to him. When her brother left, she came up to Gil and looked directly into his eyes. He had been frozen, unsure of what her attention meant.

"I wonder," she said, "if you know what the difference is between boys and girls—down there, I mean?"

He was shocked into a direct answer. "Well, a boy's is long and a girl's isn't."

She laughed. "How do you know? Have you ever seen?" She took his silence as confirmation of innocence. "Come into the garage with me and we'll look. Quick, before Terry comes back."

He followed her into the empty garage. She gave him a fierce smile and pulled down her plaid shorts and then white cotton underwear. The curve of her stomach drew his eyes down to her crotch. There was just a fluff of dark hair. "And now you," she crooned. And he undid his jeans and showed her, half afraid she would laugh. But instead, she reached over and gave him a quick caress just as they heard the back porch door open and slam. They had just enough time to cover themselves, and she grabbed the croquet game as Terry came into the garage and told them that their mother had cookies if they were hungry.

Gilbert was so lost in memory that he walked across the intersection of Church and Main just as a car was making a turn. The driver hit the brakes and then accelerated up the hill toward the cemetery. One of the passengers, a high school kid, shoved his head out the window and hollered back, "Asshole!" But then he was at Crosby Square and entered Vachon's Drug. His crew was at the soda fountain.

"Jeekers, Gil," Ollie said. We thought you weren't coming. We're gonna miss the cartoons if we don't get there quick." The boys finished their ice cream and headed for the door. "Don't get 'em in an uproar, Ollie," Vince said. "They always show the news first."

Outside the Star, only a couple of adults stood at the ticket booth. The crew handed over their fifteen cent admissions, walked through the outer lobby decorated with posters of coming attractions, and handed their tickets over to a pimple-faced high school boy decked out in a shabby red uniform. Then it was on to the concession stand. Suddenly, Gil was starving. He sprang for a large popcorn with butter, wiping out his allowance but leaving in reserve the bonus quarter his mother had given him. The others ordered in turn, and they walked across the lobby and entered the theater through the doors on the right side.

The RKO *News of the World* was just finishing with soaring closing music enhancing the deep, dramatic narration of tensions along the Iron Curtain. The black-and-white images faded into a moment of deep darkness in the theater. The crew stopped their descent along the aisle, trying to make out groups already seated in the middle section. The theater was lit by the technicolor glow as the Looney Tunes cartoon—Sylvester the Cat and Tweety Bird—spilled over the screen. Ollie spotted seven Hi Teeners clustered in two rows in the center of the seats. Other patrons were scattered throughout the theater: adult couples and quartets toward the rear, younger kids way up front where the black-and-white cat was constantly befuddled by the little yellow bird. "I taut I taw a putty tat! I did! I did see a putty tat." Ollie and Vince took seats next to Rachael and Sharon. Ron and BJ sat right behind Elaine, Faye, and BettyJane. Gil could see that Judy was sitting just on the other side of Sharon. He took a deep breath and passed through an empty row to the rear, went down the aisle, walked into her row, and took the seat next to her.

She smiled at him, at once shy and direct. "Hey, Gil," she said, "I'm really glad you made it. I was starting to wonder."

He tried to be more in control than he felt. "Oh yeah, Jude. My mom wasn't sure if I could come, but I told her that she shouldn't worry. I can take care of myself." There was a long silence as if both had temporarily forgotten how to breathe. The moment passed as Porky Pig emerged from the giant screen calling, "Thee and a thee and a thee…that's all, folks."

Gil offered Judy some of his popcorn. She demurred; she'd had supper with her folks; her dad was working the night shift at the mill, and they had to eat early. "What did you have for supper? Anything good?"

Judy made a face of dramatic distaste. "Fried fish, what else? Fishy Fridays for us Catholics. Bad for me; good for Mr. Trapp the fishman."

Gilbert laughed. "The funny thing is he delivers in our neighborhood on Thursday so all us Lutherans get to eat fish a day sooner and a day fresher. It's still fish, though."

The theater began to dim, and from behind the drawn curtains of the big screen, heroic music served as prelude for the first feature film, *The Kentuckian*.

"This should be good," Judy whispered. "I love Burt Lancaster. He's such a hunk." Gil responded to her observation by taking an extra-large handful of popcorn. Throughout the theater, the audience quieted down in anticipation of action. Gil scanned the rows to his right. Vince and Sharon were leaning toward each other with no contact while staring straight ahead at the screen. BJ had his arm resting on the back of Faye's seat and leaned forward until his head was almost next to hers.

Gilbert tried to concentrate on the movie. Burt Lancaster was leaving old Kentucky, striking out for Texas territory. But Judy's nearness kept pulling him away from the screen. He could just catch the scent of whatever perfume she was wearing. He took a careful glance toward her; she was looking straight ahead at the screen. He tried to lean across the seat between them, and suddenly his box of popcorn slid off his lap and cascaded down the sloped floor. There was a momentary flurry of attention from the kids around him. Quietly, Judy slipped her hand across the arm of their seats and took his hand. "It's okay," she whispered. "I really wasn't hungry at all." And then she looked back toward the screen, but left her hand in his amazed grasp.

He thought the movie must be more than half over. Burt and his kid had somehow bought a pretty young woman, but she wasn't a slave. They were in a Texas town and were having problems with the sheriff. Judy's hand was cool and still in his. He hoped his palm wouldn't start sweating. And then, of all things, he had to go to the bathroom, bad enough that he knew he couldn't wait for Old Bert to save the day. Trying to be smooth, he whispered to Judy that he'd be right back. And then he had to climb past a man and woman sitting on the aisle in his row.

Out in the lobby, he saw that the skinny usher was trying to chat up the girl behind the concession counter. He hurried into the men's room and was relieved to find it empty. As he began his return to the theater, he suddenly had an idea to cover his embarrassing exit. He walked over to the concession stand. The girl seemed almost glad to have her conversation interrupted. "I'd like a Snickers bar, please,'" he said.

"Ja want the one- or two-piece one," she replied.

"I'll take the double."

"Twenny cents." He handed over his bonus quarter and almost forgot to get his change. He could hear the rousing music of the soundtrack through the walls. He hurried through the doors, not wanting to miss the climax.

He made his way down the aisle, his eyes adjusting to the darkness away from the screen. He could make out the clutch of his friends and the Teeners and the couple sitting on the aisle of his row. But Judy wasn't there. For a moment he was almost dizzy, caught between the swirl of color and sound from the front of the theater and the empty spot where, until five minutes ago, his evening had been all that he had hoped for. Had he blown it? Had she dumped him before he had even begun to try? He looked up and down the rows of the center section but she was nowhere to be seen. And then suddenly from behind him he heard her in a loud whisper, "Gil! I'm right here, across the aisle." He turned and saw her sitting low in the fourth seat in the row. He slid into the third seat and faced her. "I couldn't see well where we were," she explained, leaning so close to his ear that he felt her breath on his face. And then she didn't move to sit up, and his arm slid over and around her shoulder, and their lips brushed softly.

After that he lost all sense of time and place. There were just the two of them. Her breath drowned out the soundtrack. The changing scenes on the screen were just flashes on his eyelids. The Snickers bar fell onto the floor but didn't seem important.

And then suddenly, as if from far away, he heard someone calling his name. "Gil! Gil! I'm here. Pay attention to me. It's late." And he emerged from the grotto of passion and looked up into the face of his mother, leaning down over the seats of his row from the aisle.

"Mom! What are…why are you here?" Judy scurried straight up into her seat and puffed her hair while trying to shift her focus onto the screen.

"It's almost nine o'clock, Gil. You were supposed to leave for home after the first feature. When you didn't show up, I got concerned. Now come on; we're leaving right now!"

Gil stood up and started out of the row of seats. He turned back to Judy, but she was wholly engrossed by the image of a young man sitting at a set of drums and talking to a beautiful woman. There was nothing to say. He followed his mother up the aisle as the crew and the Hi Teeners watched him depart. A flourishing drum roll chased him through the door into the lobby.

Outside the Star, the streetlights on Main Street lit up a swirl of blowing snow. Mother and son walked half a block to the family Pontiac. Gil slid into the shotgun seat while his mother dusted the snow off the rear window. He sat looking straight ahead as she climbed in and hit the ignition. The car moved slowly down the empty street toward home. He felt as if the universe had suddenly become a silent movie.

His mother pulled into the driveway, and Gil started to get out and open the door to the garage. In a quiet, measured voice Mrs. Jenkins said, "Gil, wait a minute. I want to talk with you before we go in." He sank back into the seat and waited. He could almost feel his mother breathing up composure. He stared out the car's windshield. The snow clung to the twine net hanging from his basketball backboard. Finally, she reached over and softly but with determination turned his face to hers.

"I'm really disappointed with the way this evening turned out. I trusted you to do what we'd agreed was going to happen. What happened, Gil? Did you plan to deceive me? Did you think I wouldn't be concerned when you didn't arrive home as you'd promised?"

The boy sat silent for a moment, holding his mother's gaze. "Mom, believe me, I didn't go to the show planning anything like this. My friends and I got there, and then one thing just led to another. I just sort of lost track of time at the end of the first movie. I never planned to stay for the second. And Judy—one thing led to another, and we crossed the aisle. She really started it."

"And it looked to me like you were trying to finish it! With all those others in the audience. Didn't you think how it would look to them: your friends, the adults, some who are probably patients of your dad?"

"No, Mom," he said, a little more forcefully than he felt. "It just happened. And we didn't go too far, neither of us."

"But sweetie, you're growing up fast and you have to be in control of yourself. It's really a man's responsibility to not force himself on a woman, no matter how much they think they like, or even love, each other. That's a big part of what being a real man is all about."

Gil thought back to his getting together with Judy. He sort of wished it had been his moves that had brought them together. He had just wanted to be with her. The making out had been exciting, but he'd really liked just being with her and knowing that she felt the same way. Maybe they had crossed the line a bit, but nothing big had really happened. But that's not what his mother had seen, or thought she'd seen

"I'm sorry Mom," he said. "Sorry that you're disappointed; sorry that I made you come out in this bad weather." He took a deep breath to override a sob that he could feel swelling in his throat. "She's really nice, and she likes me a lot."

"I'm sure Judy's nice, and it's nice to get attention. But you're really just kids, even if your bodies are changing. And those hormones can get racing, and one thing can lead to another." She reached over and put her hand on his arm. "Oh, Gil! One moment, one step too far can change a young person's life forever—especially for girls. Please, please, when moments like those come up again, stop and think of all the places you have to go and the new, exciting people who are waiting out there to meet the real Gilbert. And they will, because you're a handsome, smart, and kind boy." She squeezed his arm. "And always remember, your mother and father love you more than anything. We have faith in you and know that your goodness will always guide you if you take the time to listen to that little voice inside. Now, please open the garage door and brush the snow off the car. You don't want it all frozen on when you and your dad start off to the woods…in six hours!"

When Gil walked into the kitchen, his father was sitting at the table, still in his starched white shirt and suit pants, finishing a plate of leftover pot roast and gravy. Dr. Jenkins looked up at his son. "Long first feature, slugger?" Although his voice and face were serious, Gil thought he could detect an amused gleam in his eye. "Your mother was pretty concerned, you know. And I have to agree that privileges are earned. A deal's a deal, and a good man never goes back on his word."

"I told her I was sorry, Dad," Gil explained. "And the girl I was sitting with and I didn't really do anything much."

"Well, we can talk it through in the car tomorrow morning. And now it's almost ten o'clock and that means you've got about six hours to get some rest and prepare for the woods. Are your hunting clothes all ready? Better take extra socks and wear an extra shirt. The snow is supposed to stop, but it will be windy. Is your shotgun clean? Got extra shells in the ammo pouch your uncle Bill gave you?

"It's all set, Dad. See you in the morning. And thanks for letting me go out with you and your friends." Gil walked over to the table and gave his father a glancing hug. "I love you, Dad."

His father slapped him on the shoulder. "Me too you, Valentino. Sleep well. I'll call you about four. No rolling over."

Gil went to the second-floor bathroom and brushed his teeth. Stewie, Petie, and Baby Allie were in the bedroom they shared down the hall across from their parents' room. Gil had moved out and up to a third-floor bedroom that had been maids' quarters in the decades before his parents bought the Victorian-style home from a couple, Mr. and Mrs. Fredericks, who had long been part of Sutton's elite. The only remnant of that affluent age was the bell on the wall that had been wired to summon the servant at the call of the lady of the house. Now it was only a bedroom for a thirteen-year-old boy.

He pulled on his pajama bottoms and climbed into the four posted double bed. He switched off the bed table lamp and lay back into the stiff, cool sheets. He thought that he should pray—for wisdom, for social understanding. The words wouldn't form in his mind and, with a sigh, he lay back against his pillow and began to take long, deep breaths to lead himself closer to sleep, to relief from the jumble of pictures, feelings, questions, and fears that bounced round his head like bright steel balls bouncing around a pinball machine all at the same time.

There was a gentle knock on his door. His mother let herself in and stood for a moment letting her eyes adjust to the dim light that flowed in from a streetlight across Main. She sat down on the edge of his bed by the footboard. "Gil?"

"Yes, Mom?"

"I just want you to know, to tell you again, that I'm not angry with you. And I want my disappointment to pass, to really believe that this evening was just a misstep. I don't want to lose my trust in you."

Gilbert fought off a growing frustration. This was going on much too long. But he looked at his mother with what he hoped would pass for sincerity. "I promise, Mom. It just happened, but now I understand why I need to be careful. It won't happen again." His mother stood and for a moment seemed to be considering her next step.

"I do believe you, sweetie. Pleasant dreams."

In the dark, Gilbert lay still, trying to settle his mind. Flashes of the evening, of the past few weeks thrust themselves into his consciousness:

Judy swirling her cheerleader skirt up and away from her thighs, the feel of her little breast as his arm moved to encircle her opposite shoulder, the scent of her perfume rising from her soft neck. He could feel the excitement rising throughout his body. And then he heard the voice of his father: "C'mon Gil. We have to leave in a half hour to meet the guys."

Gilbert hunkered down in the Pontiac, his red-and-black hunting coat, red wool pants, and boots with two pairs of heavy socks barely keeping his teeth from chattering while he waited for the car's heater to kick in. They crossed the Nine Falls by the mill and soon were beyond the streetlights. There was an inch or so of snow coating the blacktop, insufficient to call out Sutton's road crews but enough to slow their pace. Neither father nor son spoke, as if any break in the silence would require a review of the previous night. For Gil, the night at the Star came back as a flow of sensory memories: the flickering lights, the smell of Judy's perfume mingled with popcorn, his confusion while he searched for her as he returned with the Snickers bar, and his elation when he saw she had crossed the aisle. And he could feel the flow of her hair over his cheek. He closed his eyes and tried not to think of what his return to school on Monday would bring from his friends, from the Hi Teeners, or from Judy.

And then the car turned off blacktop and bumped down a single-lane dirt road. His father stopped the car, and Gil jumped out to swing open the gate that separated a bare farm field from the beginnings of deep forest. As he climbed back into the car, his father said, "Keep yourself braced, Son. The snow on this downgrade may make for slippery going, especially because another car has packed it down on the gravel." He put the Pontiac into first gear and let the transmission slow their descent. A half a mile father, the road leveled, and they drove into the open space next to his uncle's camp.

Past the pine trees and across the open water of the lake, the sun promised to rise behind the low hills. As father and son climbed out of the car, Uncle Harry and three other men came out of the cabin. Dr. Jenkins handed his son the car keys. "Get our guns out of the trunk. And our ammo pouches. Make sure to keep the actions open until we go into the woods." Then the men started discussing their plans for deployment. Gil opened the trunk and took out the two shotguns, his father's vintage Winchester and his brand-new Ithaca pump. He grabbed the ammunition pouches by their straps, crooked a gun inside each elbow, and walked back to the men.

"Okay," said Uncle Harry. "Gil, Doc, and Peter will set up along the bottom of the ridge, just in front of the brook. Willis, Freddie, and I will head back up the hill and then drive down toward the lake. Make sure before you shoot. Good hunting."

Gil and his father followed Peter into the woods. After about a quarter mile, they stopped by a small clearing. Peter forged onward and was soon out of sight. "Okay, Gil," his father said. "Here's your spot. You can sit on this windfall tree and use a limb to brace your gun if you get a shot. Come with me." They walked across the open space to where it began to rise into the ridge. His father pointed at tracks in the crust of snow. "See here. This is where they tracked uphill last night, heading for the feeding ground in the beech trees. Once they get moving, they may pass right back this way." They walked back to Gil's spot. "I'll be about a hundred yards down the brook line. Be careful."

"Dad," Gil asked. "Don't you think it would be okay if I loaded extra shells, not just the one in the chamber, like usual?"

"Not yet, son. You need to get used to the excitement of a shot with other people around. And at this range, if you shoot well, one buckshot round will be plenty." His father turned and disappeared along the trail that Peter had left.

At first, Gil was grooved into the moment. He could hear the wind through the bare branches. He carefully practiced resting his shotgun on a branch of the downed tree and imagined the smooth pressure on the trigger as his target appeared. It would be just as he had practiced out on the farm with Uncle Harry. The coming sunrise began to light the treetops around the clearing. A crow called as it flew from up the ridge toward the lake. His mind seemed to follow the flight of the unseen bird, back away from the hunt and into the Star. He couldn't remember the look on Judy's face when his mother loomed over their seats. What would he say to her in school? Would she think he was just a mama's boy? Would she be sorry that she had let him follow her across the aisle?

A sudden sound brought him back to the woods and the morning. Across the clearing, a small deer had descended the ridge and was halfway to where the track led down to the brook and out of sight. Gil spent crucial seconds refocusing on the moment and deciding how to make his shot. He raised the Ithaca and swung it on an arc away from the supportive branch. Just as the yearling was about to disappear, he jerked the trigger. The roar of the shot seemed to overwhelm the forest. The deer stopped and looked back at the boy. Then, with no sense of hurry, it trotted down the path and out of sight. Gil jacked the spent shell out of the chamber and sat back against the downed tree. There seemed to be no hurry to reload. It seemed as if life was just an endless path past missed chances.

After an hour, the three drivers, Peter, and Dr. Jenkins emerged into the little clearing. The snow was spitting again, the wind coming up the brook from the dark water of the lake. All agreed that the best hunting for the day was past; the next stop would be Andy's Diner down the road. The six hunters broke the actions on their guns and walked back out to Harry's cabin. No mention was made of the single shotgun blast that had marked the morning. Guns were stowed, cigarettes snubbed, and then the cars climbed the hill, passed through the gate, and headed out on blacktop toward civilization.

Gil sat in the passenger's seat staring out into the morning. He wished that he knew the rules of the game. Were you supposed to tell about getting a chance, even if you missed? After a mile of silence, his father said, "Was it a good shot, son?"

"I was a little bit late, Dad. I tried to be real careful, and it was just a second too late, I could have had it if I'd had another shell in the gun; I'm sure I could have." He hoped his father couldn't catch the tremble in his voice.

"It's all experience, Gil. It took me more years than I want to remember to make the right shot. You're just starting out, and every missed shot helps you grow up. Mostly I'm just real glad that you and I can have this time together." The Pontiac slowed down, and his father pulled into a parking space at Andy's. "You call the shots for breakfast, son," his father said. "Go for the steak and eggs if you think you can manage it."

The six hunters squeezed into a booth across from the swinging door into the kitchen. Their waitress hurried up, handed out menus and took orders for five coffees and a hot chocolate. Gil watched her as she disappeared into the kitchen and then returned with orders for the red-coated men sitting at the counter. He thought that it must be hard to be the only woman in the diner, always running to make truckers and hunters happy. Wisps of her blond hair swirled around her face, and her cheeks were rosy from the warmth of the kitchen. Her blue-and-white-striped uniform blouse clung to her as she had worn it over the years since a younger, slimmer version of herself had taken the job. She approached their table with a tray with six plastic cups. She placed coffees before the men and last, with a flourish, set his cup of hot chocolate at his place. "Saving the best for last, sir!" she trilled. Then she reached into the pocket of her apron and dropped a handful of individual cream cups. "And now, what can I get you gentlemen," she asked with just a hint of irony. One after another the hunters placed their orders. Gil decided against the steak and eggs and ordered a western omelet. "Back in a flash with the hash," she said and spun away toward the kitchen.

At the end of the counter, a hunter stood up and turned to go, knocking his cup onto the floor. Barely slowing her pace, the waitress leaned down and scooped it up. As she did, the hem of her skirt hiked up, exposing a flash of white thighs.

Gil's tablemates reacted as if scripted.

"Almost to the Promised Land!"

"She should be playing second base for the Red Sox."

"Be still, my beating heart."

Gil's father sat back in his chair. He looked at his son and then his brother. Rolling his eyes he crooned, "Just once and die!"

A wave of confusion ran over the boy. It felt exciting to be part of this little grown-up moment. And his father had invited him in somehow. But his mother's admonition and his father's concurrence, only the night before, slammed into the moment and left him alone and confused about when and how to cross the aisle.

The Stuffed Shirt

THE CAST OF *THE STUFFED SHIRT* ROILED around the makeshift dressing room on the second floor above the stage in the Sutton Junior High auditorium. Each cast member played a second role, that of cast member on opening night. David emoted his nervousness that everyone could tell he didn't really feel. Faith practiced pirouettes around the room, making sure that her full skirt swirled just so. Gilbert sat off to the side watching the performance and realized that the prop people, the prompters, and the other kids backstage were all as much a part of this production as the cast. Out of the corner of his eye, he could see Beverly starting to dust Bruce's hair with the magic powder that would touch his auburn shock with the gray highlights of middle age. She seemed so relaxed and matter-of-fact, as if her first betrayal, now two years in the past, had never happened, or at least hadn't really mattered. A little rhyme popped into Gil's head:

Bruce and Gil were the first two
Johnny, next she will dump you.

Miss Dexter brought him back to now. "Time for me to do your makeup, Gil. Just a touch to help people believe that it's summer on the stage."

Gilbert tilted his head back and focused on the glaring eye of the ceiling light. "Okay, Miss D. You're the boss."

She smoothed her hand down over his cheek. "Director, not boss, Gil. My job is to help you be that character on the stage. It's hard for most students to understand that, but I think you get it. Close your eyes, please." Her makeup pad flowed over his brow. Her fingers traced his eyelids.

He wondered what it must be like for Miss Dexter to be plain. She wasn't homely, but nothing about her would catch your eye. His mind ran with that thought: How many of the girls at Sutton Junior High would never be seen, never thought of except for maybe in a snotty joke in the boys' locker room. Never be like Faith: beautiful and smart and so comfortable, who knew her role and was playing it like the school was Broadway. Or Beverly: more real and prettier, with those eyes that had pulled him in at a seventh-grade dance and held him long after she had started liking him "as a friend.'" And then his mind spun out another circle, and he could see the boys at the school: the fat ones, the slow ones, Franklin who rumor had it was queer. They would never have a starring role, would never have the cheerleaders singing their praises along the sidelines of the field on the banks of the Nine Falls River.

Miss Dexter patted his cheek. "All, set, Gil. I know you're ready, so get out there and break a leg." She turned to the cast: "Places everybody."

The players moved onto the stage. Faith, in her white blouse and frilly skirt, reclined on a couch, center stage. Bruce, playing her father, stood to her left, angled so that he was facing both her and the audience. Martha, the mother, feather duster in hand, was to the rear near the door to the kitchen. Gil's entrance would be from stage right. He took the pebble that Elaine had given him for good luck and rubbed its smooth contour. Then he placed it on the prop table where it would transmit energy for his make-believe. Across in the opposite wing, he could see Beverly holding a tennis racket that David would carry on his entrance. He wished that their eyes would meet so she could see how honest his feelings for her were. He wasn't at all a faker. That was just the role he had been given to play. Instead, both her eyes and his were drawn to the thin line at the center of the curtains as it slowly widened. Gil took a deep breath and tried to erase everything about himself, tried to become "The Stuffed Shirt."

Bruce had the opening line. Facing "Margie," his daughter, he asked, "So who is this Tim who's asked you out tonight?"

"He's the district sales manager in the office, Daddy. I'm one of the secretaries in the pool who support the men who work out in the field. He's just been promoted from our offices in the Midwest district."

"So we don't really know much about him, do we?"

Martha, the mother, moved upstage. "Now, Dad," she said, "I'm sure he is a fine young man. After all, we've raised our children to be good judges of character. Margie is nineteen; she's ready to be out in the world."

Enter David, kid brother, stage left. "Hey, there's a really cool car that just pulled up outside. It's a Caddy Eldorado. Never seen one of them before in our neighborhood."

Sammy, the prop guy in the right wing, rang the doorbell. Gil took a deep breath, took in the scene, and as Martha approached to open the door, stepped out into the lights.

All flowed smoothly until the last few lines of the first act. Gil, supposedly standing aside while Faith reassured her parents that all would be well, looked out over the audience. He spotted his mother and Stewie sitting in the third row. His dad wasn't there; probably had an emergency call. Mrs. Burke was babysitting Petie and Allie.

Suddenly, Gil was drawn back to the action on stage. Something wasn't right. The other four actors seemed to have lost focus. He listened to their lines and realized that they had veered off script and couldn't find their way back. Off stage left, he caught a glimpse of Miss Dexter, trying to catch any of the cast's eyes to give a prompt. Gil stepped into the breach. The key was to bring the act to a close. Walking over to Faith, he took her hand. "We need to leave now if we're going to be at the dance on time." Then, turning to Bruce he said, "Mr. Fowler, I want you to know that your daughter's in good hands. I promise that she'll be safe." With a steady pressure, he guided Faye toward the stage right exit. The curtain swung shut behind them. The crisis had passed.

Backstage, Miss Dexter leaped into damage control. They had let their focus slip, but she doubted that any of the audience had caught the glitch. "Part of the actor's job is to work on two levels: to be the character while simultaneously concentrating on the stage and the actions. Gil figured that out when you all hit the bump in the road." She looked directly at him. "That was a very grown-up reaction, Gil. I think you've had one of those moments where you discover something about yourself that you didn't know before. I'm proud."

Act II flowed smoothly. The cast seemed to have come together, almost as if they were beyond acting. As story unfolded: the fact that Gil's character was a phony slowly emerged. His confidence and abilities were all a sham; he was the stuffed shirt. Margie lost her faith in him and, as the last scene approached, was preparing to push him aside.

They were alone on the stage. Gil's character was to see the light and promise to mend his ways. When his climactic speech arrived Gil suddenly was caught up in the fictional moment, moved past the blocking of the stage directions. He turned away from Margie and walked downstage to the curtain line, to the invisible fourth wall that Miss Dexter had drilled them on. He looked out over the audience. "Margie," he said. "I know that you're right. I haven't been straight with you. I'm sorry." Then he moved beyond the script: "Our world is always telling us that we have to sell, to sell our products, our company, but really it's all about selling ourselves. But it doesn't work; I know that now. And you've helped me see that. You're real." He turned his back to the audience, one of Miss Dexter's cardinal sins, and walked back to Faith. The script called for a kiss at the curtain. Through every rehearsal, the two principals had stopped short of that climax. No one had spoken of it. Now he reached out to her, and she stepped into his arms. They kissed and again it was as if the stage disappeared and they were two real people, taking a step into life. He could feel a surge flow from Faith and through him like a spring swell on the Nine Falls. As if from a different world, he heard the swish of the closing curtains and then, only slightly muffled, the applause from the audience. Without a word or a glance, he and Faith separated and walked off stage left.

The curtain call brought the audience to its feet. Martha and Bruce, holding hands, walked to the fourth wall and bowed together. David bounced on stage and down as if he were warming up for another tennis match. Then Faith entered from stage right, took two steps downstage, pirouetted to her family, and made a low, graceful curtsy. Finally, Gil joined the "family." He and Faith twice bowed into the applause. Then he took her hand and led her three steps beyond the invisible boundary and again they bowed, stepping back just as the curtain began to swirl closed.

Backstage was a whirl of energy and relief. Miss Dexter came up to Gilbert. "Oh, Gil," she said, "that was amazing. You really grabbed the role and made it yours." She reached out and grasped his shoulders. "You made everyone believe that you were really a young man." They stood for what seemed a long time. Slowly, the director removed her hands but kept her intense eye contact. "Don't give up on the stage; it's a gift you're lucky to have. Most of us don't, you know." She turned back to the room: "Okay, everybody. Great job. Now let's all pick up after ourselves. Props back to the storeroom. We'll meet for the cast party in my room in fifteen minutes."

Gilbert suddenly remembered that he'd left his good-luck pebble on the prop table stage right. He walked across and was relieved to find it there. It seemed that it actually had worked that evening. The bullet dodged at the end of the first act, his connection with the audience, and the kiss, how he and Faith had come together: Maybe Miss Dexter was right. Maybe he did have a talent, even though it was hard to believe. Suddenly, high school seemed a lot less threatening.

He turned and began to walk across the darkened stage, the invisible wall shrouded behind the curtains: Exit stage left. In the dim glow of the lighting panel, he saw Beverly. She was straightening the prompters' table. She looked up as he approached, met his eyes with no surprise or hint of the nervousness that he could feel swell in his chest.

"Oh, hi, Gil," she said. "I thought I was the last one out."

"I forgot something across the stage," he replied. "It's my good-luck piece." He took the pebble from his pocket and showed it to her, trying to keep his outstretched palm steady.

She smiled. "Cool. It must have been helpful at the end of the first act."

"Oh," he said. "You noticed."

"I think Miss Dexter and I were the only two backstage who caught it when it happened. She looked pretty relieved when the curtains closed. You really pulled it off. Good going."

"Thanks, Bev," he said, trying to control the quiver in his voice. "I'm glad that you think so." Almost without intent he took a half step toward her. The glow from the dimmed ceiling light fell across the sweep of her short brown hair and her cheek. She stood her ground, held his nervous eyes. "I mean, it's special that you think so."

She crossed the half step between them. "Well, you're special too, Gil. I've always thought that."

She tilted her head to the side, never losing eye contact. His mouth moved down to hers, and their kiss was long and soft. There was no script, only their being together. And then, too soon, it ended, and she retreated the half step.

"Oh, Bevie," he began. "I've wanted to...."

Her fingers floated up in front of his lips, gently silencing him. "Gil, like I told you once before, I really like you as a friend. And I think you're going to have a great time up at high school, and as you grow up, there will be a super future for you. But I'm writing my own play, and it's got a different cast. I'm sure we'll see each other, but I need you to know that this was a very loving goodbye kiss." She turned and walked toward the door lit by a red exit sign. The door opened outward and then sighed closed, leaving Gil behind the curtain, wondering about the next act.

Sutton Tales—Coda

Je m'appelle Hélène Honoré & Growing Up Gilbert

GILBERT PULLED INTO THE MIDDLE of the Jenkins' three-lane, concrete driveway. He took a deep breath, as if searching for the scent of Marie's perfume. Finding not a whiff, he climbed out of the Chevrolet sedan, walked over to and up the stairs onto the back porch. As he went through the entryway and into the eating kitchen, he looked at the antique clock on the far wall: 11:45. He pulled out a chair and sat, facing his father. "Beat the clock again, Dad," he said.

Dr. Jenkins smiled. "You're off the hook, slugger. Did you have a good night? Hope you remembered your failings." He took a sip of a brown beverage from a small glass.

Gil returned his father's grin. "For sure, Dad. Marie and I spent most of the time talking about getting ready for college."

"Well, it's a big night for both of us. You had a good time and I'll never have to wait up for you again. Once you graduate, it's all up to you. No more curfews; nobody checking to see if you've done your homework."

Gilbert thought that sounded just about perfect.

"Gil," his father continued, "I know I've said this before, but your mother and I are tickled pink that you got into Dartmouth. Your first choice. All that good work paid off." The doctor took another sip of his pre-slumber dose. "Ivy League, it's an awfully different world from when I got into Dana, in the heart of the Depression. I was given a chance to prove myself and discovered that I could come up to the test. Not bad for the youngest son of Danish immigrants."

Gil had heard the story many times before. Still, he was moved by his father's sincerity and pride in his eldest son's step up the ladder. "It's going to be great, Dad. I owe you and Mom a lot."

His father finished off his beverage. "I'm ready for some shut-eye. You'd better get to bed soon." He stood and walked out of the kitchen toward the front stairway.

Gil picked up the past week's edition of *The Sutton Journal.* The lead article featured the upcoming graduation ceremonies for the Sutton High School Class of 1961. Saturday, June 8, at 2:00. One hundred twenty-seven graduates, the largest class to date. Honoring Miss Selah Franks for her four decades of devotion to generations of Sutton English Students. The featured speaker: Miss Hélène Honoré Lévesque, Sutton class of 1942. He picked up his father's empty glass, sniffed, walked over to the kitchen sink, and put it on the sideboard. Then he climbed the stairs to his room on the third floor. Changing into his pajama bottoms, he sat on the edge of his old double bed. He shut off the lamp and lay down on his back, arms folded, head resting on his hands. A bit of a breeze blew in through the screened window. Off in the distance, the Nine Falls Paper Mill groaned through the night shift. Gilbert Jenkins, Sutton High School Class of 1961, took a series of deep breaths, urging himself down into sleep.

* * *

After dropping Dorcas off at her parents' red brick home, I drove the long way back through Sutton, turned left onto Oxford Street, past the Congregational Church where my dearest friend and I had suffered the grief of loss, of war, and love, now a quarter century in our past. She had traveled up from her home in Wellesley Hills to be with me, as she had always been. Over Italian standards at the Village Café in Portland, we caught up. Her daughter was now the same age that we had been when we entered our senior year at Sutton High, the year that had brought me exile and loss. I was about to begin my second year as a fully tenured professor of French Studies at Pembroke, the women's college now integrated into Brown University in Providence, Rhode Island. For the five years after graduating from Wellesley, Dorcas had taught biology and math in the nearby town of Natick. Then, marriage to Bill, and now, living the life of wife and mother in a split level near the Charles River. I explained that teaching both Pembroke and Brown students, women and men, was a different experience from our days at Smith and Wellesley, but in general I found the process was positive. Mostly we shared our memories of coming of age in a somehow more innocent era, in Sutton, in America.

I crossed the Nine Falls and drove up and away from the Sutton I had known, toward *la maison DuBois et Lévesque*, the home shared by my grandmother and my parents; for me, always, their house but not my home. I had bypassed Frenchtown; tomorrow I could drive through that neighborhood of the younger Hélène Honoré. I turned onto Brook Street and then left onto Maple Drive, up to number 18. The side door light of the white garrison house welcomed me back. I parked and walked in through the breezeway. Bénédicte, my "little sister," was sitting at the kitchen table. She got up and gave me a long, long hug.

"It's so good to see you," she said. "Seems like forever."

"I'm really glad to be home," I replied.

"Your drive up was not too bad?"

"Well, getting around Boston is always a challenge. But after that, pretty much smooth sailing. The new extension of the turnpike makes the last leg a lot easier. How about you?"

"Driving down Route One isn't bad this time of year. The tourists are all heading north."

"And school? Are you pretty much on vacation?"

"One week to go. And I've got some Sutton schools news. Turns out that you're not the only Lévesque educator in their sights."

"What do you mean?"

"This past week I got a letter from the new principal at the high school, Mr. Kimball. It seems Mr. DiRenzo is moving on. You remember we both had him as a social studies teacher. He was wondering if I might consider joining the department."

"Oh, Béné! That's great! Are you interested?"

"At least enough to check it out, to interview. I really like my little town on the coast, but…well Sutton's still home, and the salary scale is a pretty good chunk better. We'll see."

"Cream rises to the top," I said. "And if you're ready, let's head to bed. It's been a long day."

We stood, hugged, and went upstairs into our shared bedroom, sisters together once again. Just before we turned off the light, Béné turned and looked over at me. "Hélène," she said. "I'm sure this won't be a surprise but Mémère, Maman, and Papa are so, so proud of you and so happy that you're getting the respect that you've always deserved." All I could do was smile as I reached over and shut down our day.

I awoke later that morning to the familiar clanking and conversations from the kitchen, now downstairs rather than on the same floor as my childhood home. I got up, pulled on my robe, and walked down to the living room. There sat Papa in his chair, his coffee on the end table to his right. He looked up and gave me a great smile. "Ah, Hélène," he said. "It's wonderful to have you home. *Bienvenue*."

"*Merci, Papa*," I replied. "I'm glad to be here with you all."

"Well, of course, all but your brothers. Paul, he has the morning shift at the mill. He should be able to come to the ceremonies."

"I hope so. And what do you hear from Geno and Erland?"

"It seems like all is going well. Geno is working around DC; he's got a good job doing technology for some new government agency. And Erland, he's still on the battleship somewhere in the South Pacific, not too close to Indochina, I hope."

"Amazing that he's got almost twenty years of service under his belt."

Just then Béné came in through the dining room. "*Maman dit à table.* There's a big pile of ployes waiting for us." We followed her to the table where the warm scent of Québecois buckwheat pancakes greeted us.

Mémère and Maman joined us. Mémère said a brief prayer. Coffee was poured and ployes passed around, followed by a choice of maple syrup, brown sugar, or my grandmother's wonderful wild blueberry jam. The first round of cakes quieted us all. Around seconds, we traced the plans for the day. I needed to be at the high school by about one o'clock. The ceremonies would begin at two. Uncle Marcel, Aunt Jacqueline, and Cousin Eugénie would stop by, and the whole family would go over together. Maman and Béné started to get up to clear the table.

"*Un moment,*" said my father. "Hélène, we want you to know how very proud we are of you." The three women murmured assent. "Of course," he continued. "I can only imagine how successful you would have been if you had stayed with that good job as a welder at the shipyard. Ah well, c'est la vie." We all laughed, and I headed upstairs for a shower to brace myself for my approaching day at Sutton High.

* * *

"Gil!" Stewie's voice rattled up the stairwell and into Gilbert's third floor bedroom. "Mom says to get your butt down here for breakfast." His brother's voice erased whatever dream his sleep had been floating on.

"Okay, okay! I'm up!" He rolled over, set his feet on the hardwood floor, and stretched. The morning June sun flooded through the double windowed dormer, reflected off the oval mirror over his old, dark dresser, and glanced over to his bed. After a couple of deep breaths, then he shucked his pajama bottoms and pulled on sweatpants and a T-shirt. Breakfast, a shower, and then get ready for what everyone saw as a major point in the ongoing saga of Gilbert Jenkins.

He walked down the two flights of stairs and into the dining kitchen. Stew, Petie, and Allie were already at the table. Snuffie, the family beagle since their return from Virginia, now six years ago, was at Stewie's feet, hoping for whatever treats might come his way. Gil sat and poured a glass of orange juice from the pitcher. He heard his mother bustling in the cooking kitchen and, before he could offer to help, she walked in carrying a plate piled with pancakes.

"Here you go, guys," she said. "There'll be more where these came from."

"I don't think we'll need more, Mom," Stew said. "Petie said he wasn't hungry. He doesn't really like pancakes anyway."

Petie took his next older brother's bait. "No, no! I love pancakes! You know I love 'em, Stewie. I want two right now!"

"Okay, Petie," Gil said. "There'll be plenty for all of us." He reached over, took his thirteen-year-old brother's plate and plopped on two pancakes. "This will get you started. Do you want syrup or sugar?

"Syrup, Gil. I always like syrup." The cakes properly anointed, he grabbed his fork and dug in.

The Jenkins brothers attacked breakfast, and their mother joined them with another plateful. Then, Katherine sat and took a long sip of her coffee.

"Where's Dad, Mom?" Gilbert asked.

"He had to go into the hospital to check on a couple of patients. He got an early start and should be back any minute. Wouldn't do for him to be late on his son's big day." She put a pancake on Allie's plate. "Petie," she asked, "have you had enough? I wouldn't want you to get too full."

"No, no, Mommy. Me…I can eat more, for sure."

"Well, help yourself, sweetie." Then she turned her attention to her eldest, "Gil, are you all set for graduation?"

"Oh yeah, Mom." He looked up at the wall clock. "I just need to take a shower and then get dressed. My suit and shirt are all ready to go up in my bedroom. We're supposed to get to school around one o'clock. Dad said I could take the Chevy, and you all could come later in the Pontiac."

"Sounds like a plan," said his mother. She looked over at son number three. "Don't you think you've had enough breakfast, Petie?"

"Oh no! I got plenty of room for that nice big one there!"

Gil pushed the plate over to him. "Enjoy them, Petie. Mom's pancakes are the best." He stood up. "Okay, I'm going to jump in the shower, shave, and get dressed. Feels kind of strange getting on my Sunday best on a Saturday."

Just before one o'clock, Gil pulled into the big parking lot in front of Sutton High School, a mass of brick and glass rectangles on top of a knoll facing toward the Nine Falls River and the looming concrete chimney of the paper mill. Now, after three school years, he was going to be one of 127

Sutton students, the Class of 1961, the largest graduating class ever and the first to have spent three years in the new building. He sat there for a moment, trying to get a grasp of what this day really meant and what the next four years as a college student would be like. His father, his teachers, and Sutton alumni all seemed to have very different takes on the journey he was about to take. He hoped he'd be ready.

He climbed out of the car, grabbed his cap and gown, and joined a cohort of classmates making their way up the walkway and into the school. Sutton '61 students were gathering in the cafeteria. Over in one corner were Gil's best buddies—Vince, Ollie, BJ, and Ronnie—guys who had shared Little League, playground basketball, touch football on a neighbor's lawn, and games of hide-and-seek and war against commie hordes in the tall pines behind Gil's and Vince's homes.

"Hey, Jenkins," Ollie said. You're looking pretty sharp! Your mom tie your necktie for you?"

"No, no," Vince said. "Look closer. I'm pretty sure it's one of those clip-on numbers. I mean, Gil couldn't even learn knot tying in Scouts."

"Be careful you don't drool on your shirt, Ollie," Gil said. "I saw you staring over at Peachie."

While the buddies continued their ad-libbed script, Gil looked across the room to where a clutch of his soon-to-be Sutton alumnae were gathered. Martha and Faith, valedictorian and salutatorian, were chatting up a storm. He thought for a moment that that picture fit with his entire Sutton school days: the two girls in his class who were always waving their hands in class and who had edged him out for '61 honors, Faith by less than one grade point. *Damn, trigonometry*, he thought. Then he saw Bevie, deep in conversation with some of her friends. Gil let himself fade back into his seventh-grade year, when he and Bevie had shared his first love, and then, when she moved on to older guys and new social pathways. And that one night in ninth grade when, on the darkened stage, following his performance in *The Stuffed Shirt,* she had kissed him, long and soft, and then told him that she loved him as a friend, but only as a friend.

Gilbert snapped back into the present as Principal Kimball called for Sutton's seniors' attention. "Ladies and gentlemen. It's finally time for our school and our community to honor you, the Class of 1961. In about ten minutes we will be lining up in the hallway leading to the auditorium. Please pair up with your processional partner and be ready to join the queue when Mr. Monroe calls your names. All our best wishes."

Gil walked over to Jillian, his marching partner. The class began to flow toward the door where Mr. Monroe, the guidance director, stood up on a chair. "Okay, ladies and gentlemen," he said. "I'll begin to call off the order in a moment. But before I start, for the faculty and staff of Sutton High, and, I know, for your parents and families: please, please remember to be safe and smart as you celebrate your big day over the weekend. Remember that cars, excitement, and moments of bad judgment can have horrible results. And maybe, for a moment, remember your classmate Billy Moran and his brother Dickie, who in a flash and a crash were taken from us."

Gil took a deep breath. The Moran brothers had been on the very low edge of the Sutton High student body. And then, last September, Principal Kimball announced with a catch in his voice, that early that morning, at the intersection of two roads, two towns away, their car had slid through a stop sign into the path of a logging truck heading toward the Nine Falls Mill.

"Next: Jillian Jacobs and Gilbert Jenkins," called Mr. Monroe. The pairs moved on into the corridor and out into the lobby. Inside the auditorium, the high school concert band struck up "Pomp and Circumstance." Gilbert took a deep breath. Jillian reached over, patted his arm and said, "Well, here we go."

* * *

After my shower, I dressed and sat on the edge of the bed reviewing my notes for the Sutton graduation ceremony. Just before noon, I walked into the living room. Paul, my eldest brother, was there with his wife, Jeanie, and his two sons. We shared hugs.

"It's super to see you, Hélène. It's been too long. You look great."

"Thanks," I replied. "I really appreciate you coming after the night tower."

"I wouldn't have missed this for the world. I got a couple of hours in the sack."

"Well, I'm off to the high school. I'll see you all after the festivities."

"*Bonne chance*," Mémère said.

"We are all so very proud," Maman added.

I grabbed my purse and keys, blew a kiss to *toute la famille Lévesque*, and walked out to my car. Then, as I retraced my route out of the suburbs toward the Sutton, Maine of my youth, I detoured and drove toward Frenchtown. I parked for a moment next to the playing fields, St. Hyacinth School, and le couvent. To my right was the gray, two-family house that had been my home. To the left, down the hill, the golden spire of the church, the winding course of the Nine Falls, and then downtown Sutton. Memories of my younger life flowed like a documentary film shown at triple speed. I restarted the car and drove down and away from my roots.

I parked in the huge lot next to the high school, the new school, a quarter century away from my years in the old, brick structure back on Main Street. A young teacher, looking about the same age as my French II students at Brown, smiled and directed me down the corridor to the principal's office, where Mr. Kimball introduced himself and welcomed me to the day's celebration. On entering his inner office, I found three of the formative adults of my teenaged self: Principal Sampson, Mr. DiRenzo, my social studies teacher, and Miss Franks, one of the women who had supported me in every way—the young Hélène Honoré Lévesque. I shook hands with the men and congratulated Mr. DiRenzo on this, his last day as a member of the Sutton faculty. Then I turned to my mentor, now retired.

"Miss Franks," I said. "It's so wonderful to see you. Thank you for being here. Congratulations on being recognized today for all your years of sharing the worlds of language and creativity."

She smiled. "And kudos to you, my dear. Your life's course is a wonderful story in itself."

"It seems so long since you shared Miss Dickenson and *All Quiet on the Western Front* with me."

"Great writing never ages," she replied. "Only the reader's understanding is polished and expanded."

"And now," Principal Kimball said. "If you'll all please follow me. The festivities are about to begin." We walked down a corridor past empty classrooms and into the cafeteria where the last of the enrobed senior class were lined up. Entering the backstage of the auditorium, to the boom of "Pomp and Circumstance," we walked out onto the stage, facing an ocean of faces and a long train of Sutton's seniors marching down the center aisle and taking their places.

The ceremony began with a short prayer from Martha Miller, the 1961 valedictorian. Then the assembled stood and recited the pledge to the flag. Mr. Kimball welcomed the parents and guests to this proud day. Then he introduced three educators who had touched the lives of so many Sutton students over decades of service. In turn, Mr. Sampson, Mr. DiRenzo, and Miss Franks stood to the applause of the audience. "And now," he said, "it is my privilege to introduce our Sutton Alumna of the year, a member of the celebrated Class of 1942, Miss Hélène Honoré Lévesque."

I stood and walked to the podium. As I adjusted the microphone on the lectern, I looked out at the audience. There, in the first row behind the women graduates, I saw my family. I felt a momentary catch in my throat, not unlike at my first presentation in my Smith senior seminar on the writers' world of seventeenth century France, *le monde des écrivains du dix-septième siècle.* I took a deep breath.

"Good afternoon," I said. "To the faculty and staff of Sutton High, parents, family, and friends, and especially the graduating Class of 1961, I want to express my deep gratitude for the honor and privilege of this opportunity to share some thoughts today. As always when I return to our town, memories of my younger life flow like the Nine Falls: sometimes smooth and comforting, other times rough and powerful."

"Clearly the high school, our community, the nation, and the world have evolved and are very different from three decades past. Then we were in the first months of war, a global catastrophe like no other. While we united in that common cause, other factors—race, gender, genealogy, and class—strove to undo our sense of union. As I look back to June 1942, I am moved by the many, many people who helped Hélène Honoré Lévesque move through a tumultuous year and to emerge as a Sutton High School graduate, a young woman with opportunities that would have been unthinkable to most women in Sutton, in Maine, and in the United States only a generation or two earlier.

"This afternoon you have been called to recognize three of those formative educators, Principal Sampson, Mr. DiRenzo, and, especially, Miss Selah Franks, who challenged me, believed in me, and cared for me. I only hope that I can bring that same sense of rigorous compassion to my students, regardless of, but not unaware of gender, race, and class."

"Today, you, the Class of 1961, are about to step into an adult world where issues of social justice, war, and peace loom over future horizons. Regardless of what directions your lives may take—academics, military service, good jobs in an ever-evolving economy, in Sutton or away—I have faith that the foundations of family, faith, and the practical and cultural skills your school years have bestowed will help guide you as students, proud workers, husbands, wives, and parents."

"It is in that ever-changing world that you will live out your lives as citizens, as laid out in your civics classes and the writings of as diverse an American group as Whitman and Dickenson, Steinbeck and Baldwin. To all your teachers, all our teachers, friends, parents, let us offer up our thanks together."

"Finally, once again, thanks to all of our Sutton community for bestowing this great honor on me. *Mémère, Maman, Papa, chère Bénédicte, Paul, mes amis et les profs de Sutton, encore merci, merci, merci.*"

As I turned toward my seat, Mr. Kimball rose and shook my hand. The applause from the audience seemed warm and sincere. Once again, Hélène Honoré Lévesque had managed to rise to the occasion.

Then, one by one, from Susan Adams to Stephane Zaharias, the Class of '61 rose, crossed the stage and received their diplomas. One young woman, my cousin Eugénie's daughter, Catherine, walked over to me, bent down, and kissed my cheek. Finally, Principal Kimball announced that he wished all present to join him in recognition of three of the class for academic achievement. First, he called Martha Miller, valedictorian. Next, Faith Hansen, salutatorian. And finally, he was pleased to announce the recipient of the James Stuart Fredericks Award, as established by his parents in loving memory of their son who gave his life as part of his nation's crusade for freedom in 1942 in the skies over England. The 1961 award was being given to Gilbert Jenkins. A young man rose from among his classmates, walked onto the stage, and shook hands with the principal. Having received a leather-bound document, he made a quick bow toward the audience, left the stage, and returned to his seat.

James Stuart Fredericks! My Jim, my love. It was as if he had reached out to me once again since our parting. "There comes a time, Hélène; there comes a time." And, as the lights began to dim, I wondered if *Bébé, notre bébé*, the baby that neither he nor I had ever held or even seen, was somewhere in Québec on this very day graduating from *le lycée*, from high school?